THE RAINMAN

Ike Hamill

THE RAINMAN

www.ikehamill.com

ISBN: 9798407620471

For everyone trying to make sense of the senseless.

CHAPTER ONE

Group

Pasadena

"Rainy days always remind me," Jessica said with a sad smile. "That's the great part about living here. Fewer rainy days."

She glanced around and saw some of the others shifting in their seats. Jessica knew the feeling. The circle was an uncomfortable place for small talk. Unless someone was in the meat of their story, the chairs were too hard and sitting still was like torture.

Jessica swallowed and got to the meat.

"Dad died on a rainy day. Murdered, I should say. I'm going to put fewer weasel words around it. I need to confront it. He was murdered."

One person nodded. Another looked down at his shoes. They were dealing with different kinds of grief, but all of them harbored guilt. That was a big part of it. That was the part that was difficult to really let go.

"We had a deep porch on the southwest side of the house. Dad called it a summer porch. Because the porch was so deep, you could sit out there on the hottest day and be wrapped in those shadows right until sunset. Those weren't the days I liked to sit out there though. I liked to go out there when we had thunder and lightning. Sitting on the bench against the side of the house you would never get wet. You could watch the pounding rain making the creek rise but you would be cozy as a pair of socks right out of the dryer. That's what he took away from me when he killed my father. I would never feel cozy like that again, and I would never be able to enjoy a good thunderstorm again."

Jessica looked down at her own hands. One thumb pressed against the other palm, trying to rub a hole right through it. Self-soothing always turned into self-harm, at least in Jessica's experience.

They were waiting for her to finish and she hadn't even really said anything yet.

"Anyway," she said. "Sorry. I guess I'm not going to be able to share anything after all. I just wanted to say that I miss being able to enjoy the rain. I have my memories of family and I get to enjoy those any time I want. But when it rains, I just want to be able to relax and enjoy it again like I used to. That's the reminder that bothers me right now."

The woman across the circle folded her arms.

The man looking down at his shoes glanced up.

Some were hoping that it would be their turn next. Others were dreading it.

The man on Jessica's left was the Larry—the guy who organized the grief circle. Larry asked, "Who else wants to share something?"

That was the cue for everyone to go silent. Even the ones desperate to get something off their chest were not eager to break the silence.

"How about you? Are you ready to share?"

All eyes turned to the man who was sitting across from Jessica. She had never seen him before—she guessed that it was his first visit to their little circle of grief. That wasn't unusual. Desperate for solace, people would show up once or twice and then disappear forever. Instinct would drive them to comfort's door, but it couldn't make them open it. Jessica figured that this guy would shake his head and they would never see him again.

The man looked up at Jessica, staring right at her.

He cleared his throat.

"I lost my wife and son ten years ago," he said.

"We usually start with a first name—doesn't have to be real—and a quick thought about why you came tonight," Larry said.

"I'm Joe," the man said. His eyes never left Jessica's. "I came to talk."

Larry opened his mouth to greet Joe, but he didn't get the chance. Joe was already spilling his story.

"I lost my wife and son ten years ago when a stranger came to the door. He wore a dark green hat that was so weathered it looked like maybe it was covered with moss."

Jessica shrunk into her uncomfortable chair. The others were sitting up tall. Even Larry already seemed captivated by what Joe was saying.

"He asked if he could dry off. My wife went to get some towels. When he took the cigarette out from his pocket, I could see how wet it was I knew there was no chance that it would ever light. I couldn't even believe that the paper didn't fall apart as he put the thing between his cracked lips. His lighter was one of those heavy metal ones. You could hear how solid the thing was just from the way the metal sang when he flipped open the top of it."

Jessica wanted to throw her metal chair to the side and sprint out of the room, but her body was frozen in fear. She could picture every atom of the scene that Joe was panting with his words. She could smell the man's mossy green coat and she could hear the scratch of the metal against the flint and the tiny crackle as the cigarette somehow caught fire.

"I've never smoked," Joe continued, "but I could understand the deep satisfaction of the habit in the way he inhaled. My son told the man that he wasn't allowed to smoke in our house, and I was conflicted. My son was right, of course, but he was also wrong. The rules of our house clearly didn't apply to this man. Trying to impose them would be..."

"A sin," Jessica whispered. The words just slipped out of her mouth before she had formed the intention to say them.

"Precisely," Joe said.

"Maybe this is a good time to discuss how we like to share in this circle," Larry interjected into the tiny gap in the narrative.

Joe blinked like he was coming out of a trance. He glanced over at Larry.

"Sorry. I'm done," Joe said. "I guess I don't have anything to share after all."

Jessica didn't really hear another word that was spoken in the circle. She spent the rest of the evening trying not to look across the circle at Joe.

Parking Lot

Normally, she would have stuck around and helped Larry fold up the chairs and dump the leftover donuts and coffee. Tonight, she ran to catch up with Joe before he could slip away. She followed him down the hall and out into the parking lot. They were alone. When he passed under a streetlight, she called his name—or at least the name he had given in the circle.

"Joe?"

He stopped and turned.

"How did you know that?" she asked.

"It's not your story."

His stupid arrogance made her clench her jaw and brace herself for an argument.

"Don't you dare say that to me. I know what you're trying to do. I've already been over this dozens of times. I've gone over every pertinent detail. I just need to know how you knew about the wet cigarette and the lighter. Did they find more evidence? Is there something I need to know?" Jessica asked.

"You never told the police or the FBI," Joe said.

Jessica straightened up and narrowed her eyes.

"You're not FBI?"

"Did you ever ask *why* you didn't tell anyone those details?" Joe asked.

"I have reasons," she said.

"What did you tell yourself? You were holding back because you wanted some positive confirmation when they found the guy?"

Jessica folded her arms across her body. She felt completely exposed under his gaze. He could see right into her brain.

"The police hold back details all the time," Jessica said. "They leave out some fact that their investigation revealed so that they can rule out false confessions, right? I just did the same thing. I knew that eventually they would come to me and say they had the guy. Maybe they would pick up some random homeless person and try to pin the crimes on him. They need to clear crimes in order to meet their goals—it's like any business. But until they came and told me that their suspect was a smoker and had a particular lighter, I knew that they didn't really have the right guy."

"What about his face?" Joe asked.

"What does that mean?"

"Surely, you would recognize him. When the cops showed you the mugshot of their suspect, you would know from that, right?"

Jessica didn't say anything for a moment. She was lost in the memory of the night when she had lost her family. She could see the man's tattered hat, soaked with rain. She could see and smell the coat that he wore. It might as well have been made out of an old army blanket that had been left out in the woods for a few years. The thing was practically made of decomposing leaves and dense moss.

"I didn't get a look at his face," Jessica said. Her voice sounded small and apologetic. She hated the way it sounded like she was almost pleading.

Shaking her head and taking a deep breath, she composed herself.

"Answer my question," she said. "How did *you* know about the cigarette and the lighter."

Joe frowned. He looked so tired—she wondered why she hadn't seen that before.

"I knew because it's not your story," he said. "That was *my* story. I didn't see his face either."

Jessica was too stunned to say anything. She stood there, mouth hanging open as Joe turned and walked away. The sight of his brake lights coming on and the sound of his engine starting were what finally got her moving.

Coffee

Jessica didn't know why she was following him.

The only explanation that she could come up with was that he was like another lonely lighthouse in the darkness. It wasn't hope that made her turn into the parking lot when she saw his signal. Maybe it was just the glow of his knowledge. He parked in front of a strip mall. Only one business was awake in the line of stores. Through the window, she saw a mostly-empty counter and a couple of occupied booths. Joe parked right in front of the door and went inside.

Jessica's car was stopped right in the middle of the parking lot as she watched.

He sat down at a booth near the window.

She shrank down behind her steering wheel when he turned to look directly towards her. Out in the night, beyond the glow of her headlights, she told herself that there was no way he could see her. That's when he raised a hand and motioned towards her. She knew what he was gesturing.

"Come on in," his wave said. "Find out the rest of what I have to say."

Jessica pulled into a spot a few down from his car. She locked her doors and maneuvered one of the keys between her fingers, so it would gouge if she needed to punch.

After taking a deep breath she opened the the glass door of the diner and jumped when the bell tinkled above her. The waitress behind the counter waved. Jessica walked by the, "Please seat yourself," sign and went to Joe's booth.

Right on her heels, the waitress arrived and set down coffee in front of Joe.

"One for me as well," Jessica said.

"I'll give you a minute to look at the menu."

Jessica nodded and looked to Joe. He was still turned to look through the window.

She saw what he was looking at. With the city lights, the only feature visible in the sky was the setting moon. It was clear—no clouds.

She said as much.

"Vegas is technically a desert," he said. "Less than an inch of rainfall per year."

"I didn't follow you to talk about the weather."

Joe turned to her. He nodded.

"Why did you come?"

"Tell me what happened to your wife and kid. Tell me about the man who murdered them," she said.

Joe shook his head. "I won't. Not alone. Not without witnesses and rules."

Jessica frowned.

"But..."

He interrupted the question before she could form it.

"I'll tell you about *you* instead," he said. "You live alone. You're friendly but don't have close friends that you still talk to. You have trouble keeping a job."

"Stop," Jessica said, putting up her hands. "How long have you been following me?"

"I haven't," Joe said after a sip of his coffee. "I don't have close friends either, but I have people I associate with. One of those associates, Laura, is a computer expert. She keeps two completely anonymous databases. One side logs who looks at what stories on a particular server, the other cross-references to an unsolved crime database. If you match Column A and Column B, we start visiting grief counseling group sessions. On my third try, I found you."

"Why?"

"I've been in your position," Joe said. "I was looking for someone like me, but I didn't know how to even form that idea into a first step. That's when Laura found me. Just like I found you."

"I'm not looking for someone like you," Jessica said.

"Then why did you follow me here?"

"Great point," Jessica said.

She started to stand up and saw that the waitress was already approaching with coffee. Jessica dropped a bill on the table—enough to cover the coffee, she figured—and left.

Home

After locking her door and checking the weather, Jessica went to the kitchen counter and cycled through the stack of bills until she found the unopened letter. Even without a return address, she would have recognized Frida's handwriting.

Jessica sighed before opening it. It had been sitting in that stack for days.

"Months," she whispered, correcting herself.

She scanned the letter. It was the normal stuff. Talk about Frida's family and, of course, how they missed hearing from her. Frida had stopped calling a while ago. When she bothered to answer, Jessica never gave more than one or two words for answers to the inevitable questions.

"I can never understand what you went through," Frida said one time. "But I will never stop trying, and I will never stop being your friend."

Jessica had answered that with a grunt. She almost wished that tragedy would befall Frida so that they would finally have equal footing and something to talk about. But, of course, shame flooded through Jessica at that thought. She had hung up seconds later.

In one written response, the best way that Jessica could phrase it was, "The heaviness that has settled on me feels contagious. I can't risk spreading it to you. Give me time to heal and then I'll be a better friend again."

Jessica put the letter down and moved to the window.

Keeping her grief to herself was a form of selfishness. It was okay to talk about it with strangers. They would never try to take the burden away from her. But if she talked about it with Frida, and her oldest friend somehow managed to lighten the load, that would just be one more aspect of her father that Jessica would lose. She couldn't afford that.

The moon was dipping out of sight.

The sky was still clear.

Pasadena wasn't technically a desert.

"Does Joe live in Las Vegas? Is that why he brought it up?" she wondered aloud.

Her desk was in her bedroom. Jessica went to it and opened her laptop. The chair creaked as she sat down. There were tabs open on her browser. She closed them quickly, wondering if someone really had been monitoring her online activity. The idea made her blush—not because she visited any scandalous sites, but just because of the idea of eyes staring over her shoulder. For a moment, her fingers hovered over the keys. Instead of typing out her question, trying to dig up information on Joe, Jessica closed the laptop and sighed.

He had gotten into her head.

CHAPTER TWO

Arrival

Interview

"There are a number of things that I'm not allowed to ask you," Ms. Millan said.

"Okay," Jessica said.

With a wink that wasn't even slightly friendly, Ms. Millan said, "So I'm not going to ask you those questions, got it?"

"Yes," Jessica said. She kept her face perfectly serious. This person didn't appear to understand nuance, and that suited Jessica just fine.

"You pregnant?"

"No."

"Drugs?"

"No."

"Age?"

"Pardon? Oh, I'm twenty-eight."

"I'll get that from your ID anyway, and don't think I can't spot a fake one."

"Twenty-eight."

"Running away from someone?"

"No," Jessica said.

"It's okay if you are. I'm okay with a little drama, I just want to know if I should expect drama."

"No drama," Jessica said. She got the sense that Ms. Millan was lying—she was definitely *not* okay with drama.

"Running from the police?" Ms. Millan asked. She narrowed her eyes at Jessica.

"No."

Ms. Millan looked unconvinced. She put Jessica's application in a folder and then pointed to a board.

"I won't call before your shift. It's your responsibility to check the board and see what you have coming up. Be here Monday at nine for uniform fitting and paperwork with Jackie. That's your first test. One minute late and you're out. Miss a shift and you're out."

"Thank you, Ms. Millan," Jessica said standing up. She put out her hand automatically. The woman took it and shook Jessica's hand quickly while she scrutinized her again.

Jessica maintained her composure until she was through the door and out into the hot afternoon. Then, out on the street, Jessica smiled and laughed out loud at the mini dictator she had just encountered. The idea of working for the tiny despot didn't bother her. Jessica got along with bosses who ruled with an iron fist.

With a job secured, Jessica could relax a little. It wasn't the money—she had enough saved to coast for a while. Having a job was what really grounded her in a new town. Without that, she would feel like a tourist, and this was a town *full* of tourists. They were everywhere.

Jessica checked the time on her phone and picked up her pace.

There was a meeting starting in thirty minutes. That gave her just enough time to get home, change her clothes, and then find the community center that used to be a middle school. It was over near the beltway, according to her neighbor, but everything was near the beltway. That hardly narrowed things down.

Jessica took a different route back to her apartment.

Before she could settle on an appropriate outfit, she changed twice. The key was to look presentable and yet informal. To a first meeting, she wouldn't wear anything too cheerful, and definitely nothing morose.

The community center turned out to be easy to find. Jessica arrived while the guy—this meeting's version of Larry—was still setting up the coffee machine. He didn't accept her offer to begin putting up the folding chairs.

"I have a particular way," he said.

Jessica nodded.

"New to town?"

"I am," she said. "Pasadena, most recently."

"That's a good spot."

"It was," she said.

"Vegas can be a challenging place for some people," he said. "They come here because everything is turned up to eleven and then they can't understand why there's no peace."

"Oh?"

"I don't know," he said. "I'm Will, by the way."

"Jessica."

They shook on it.

"If you grab a couple of chairs, I'll show you how I like it done."

Other people began to drift in while Will and Jessica were still setting up the chairs. They stayed back, hovering near the door until the chairs were set. Apparently, they already knew better than to get between Will and his chair arrangement.

In the circle, one of the women introduced herself as Laura. Jessica stole glances, trying to figure out if it was possible that the woman was a computer expert. She didn't look like one. She was older—maybe old enough to be retired—and had long fingernails. They didn't look like the nails of someone who did a lot of typing.

Laura only gave a quick sketch of her story. Jessica glanced around and figured that everyone else had already heard it before. Laura's grief was centered around the guilt that she hadn't said the right thing to her sister. The suicide had happened more than ten years before and Laura was still lamenting her choice of words.

"I know," Laura said, "that she was going to do it regardless of what I said. Her mind was made up long before that night. But I also know that sometimes it only takes one burst of insight to make everything look different. Maybe if I could have said something..."

Laura sighed and looked towards the door. This was an argument with herself, and she would always lose.

"How about you, Jess? Are you ready to share?" Will asked.

"Jessica," she said.

Will nodded and she saw his lips move as he corrected himself silently. He wouldn't make that mistake again.

She looked down at her hands. Her right thumb was already in place in the center of her left palm. It was ready to start trying to rub its way through the skin and bone.

"My father, my dog, my little sister, and brother were all murdered," she said in one big exhale. "We were all together in the house when a man knocked on the door. I saw him kill Dad and I thought I could keep my brother and sister safe by hiding them in the attic while I went for help. He got them too. I lived because I ran. If I had stayed to fight, we all would have died. If I had tried to take them with me, we all would have died. It's easy to argue that the best possible outcome was for just one of us to live, and that's what happened. Of course, even though I lived, it's impossible to live *with*. I guess a lot of you also feel that way."

"This is just about you," Will said.

"I'm not comparing," Jessica said. "Just relating."

Laura nodded and then a couple of the others did too.

"I come to meetings like this because everyone here can relate. No judgement. No pity."

"If you could talk to yourself from yesterday," Will said. "What would you say to that version of Jessica?"

"I would remind myself the same thing that I try to remember every day—there's more than one type of tragic loss."

"How so?" Will asked.

"There's the kind where something is ripped from you, and there's the kind where you're not paying attention and you let it slip away. You can't control the first one, but the second one is completely your own fault."

Contact

Jessica stripped off her uniform and separated out the parts that needed cleaning from the ones that could survive another shift. After a week, when the hem was already starting to fray on her skirt, Gail had warned her not to wash it every time.

"These things fall apart. You're washing too much. You're either going to be mending or buying every week if you keep that up," Gail said.

Since then, Jessica had switched to hand washing and only focusing on the stains that might show. The next day, she could powder the dry uniform with baking soda to freshen it up. When she had cleaned up, Jessica powered on her laptop.

Before bed she had a ritual.

She had a list of websites and message boards that talked about cryptids, urban legends, ghosts, and UFOs. Before bed, she visited each one, ticking them off her list as she went. When she saw anything about the man with the wet cigarettes, she replied to the post. Somewhere, Joe's friend Laura had to be watching those sites. Jessica wanted to make sure that she was noticed.

When she turned off the lights and slipped into bed, she froze at the sound of distant thunder. On her phone, the local weather was only one swipe away. It couldn't be thunder–there was nothing in the forecast or on the radar. Still, Jessica had to get up and throw open the curtains. There was no moon, but she could see the brighter stars up there, even through the light pollution and haze.

Jessica sat down on the edge of the bed and hung her head.

After splashing some water on her face, she cleaned herself up a little in the sink and then put on some casual clothes before heading back out. A few blocks away, there was a diner that claimed to be open all night. When Jessica pulled up, she didn't see a single person inside. She paused with her hand on the car door before she gave in and committed to going inside.

The bell over the door startled her. She was reminded of Pasadena.

Walking to the counter, she was still pretty sure that they weren't open. Someone must have accidentally left the door open and the lights on.

A young man pushed through the doors from the kitchen just as she was sitting down at the counter. He slid a menu towards her.

"Coffee?"

"Please."

"Everything's available, but you'll have to wait a few minutes for anything from the grill. Trent will have to warm it up first."

"Gotcha," she said. She scanned the menu, looking for what might take the longest to make. Hunger wasn't the issue—killing time was.

Her shoulders jerked up towards her ears at another rumble of thunder.

"What is that—it can't be thunder, right?" she asked.

The waiter turned his head and shouted over his shoulder. "Trent? Construction?"

"Construction," a call came from the kitchen.

The waiter turned back to her. "They're demolishing something. You visiting?"

"Just moved here from Pasadena. Is it obvious?"

"Locals don't flinch about loud noises at night. We don't flinch at anything."

"Oh," Jessica said. She filed that away for further review. Communities prided themselves on different traits. Maybe this was the predominant trait of Las Vegas-ites. Jessica cocked her head.

"What do locals call themselves?" she asked her waiter.

"Las Vegans, or just Vegans," he said. "That's our demonym."

Before she could ask, he added, "Demonym is a name that a group of people give themselves. My favorite is people from Maine. Officially, they're Mainers, but they like to call themselves Maine-iacs."

"Clever," Jessica said with a smile.

"Figure out what you want?"

Jessica looked back to the menu and tried to find the fastest thing that didn't seem like a waste of time. Tonight, the sound had only been construction, but she might have to come back if there was actual rain.

"Does Trent have to warm up the grill for a BLT?"

The waiter turned his head again. "Trent? You have bacon you can nuke?"

"No."

"Yeah, he would have..."

His answer was interrupted by the sound of the bell over the door. They both turned. Jessica recognized the man, but not the woman who followed him in.

Jessica kept her eyes on Joe—if that was his name—but gave her answer the waiter.

"If it's not too much trouble, I'll take the BLT with fries. I think I'm moving to a booth."

"Enjoy," the waiter said.

She picked up her coffee and started to head towards the booth where Joe and the woman were starting to settle.

The waiter yelled, "Usual?"

Joe gave him a thumbs-up and the waiter disappeared through the swinging doors.

"May I?" Jessica asked.

Joe and the woman were both sitting on one bench. He gestured towards the other and said, "Of course. Are you going to drink your coffee this time?"

Jessica gave him a cold smile as she sat down.

"Still stalking me?" she asked as a rebuttal. She should have guessed his answer before he gave it.

"Yes, we've been coming here for years on the chance that you would move to our city. It's quite the devious plan."

"Sorry. I'm just on edge." She turned to the woman. "I'm Jessica."

"Vivian."

The woman didn't extend her hand to shake so Jessica kept her own wrapped around her mug. The waiter brought tea for Vivian and a soda for Joe.

"Pretty amazing coincidence then, I guess," Jessica said. "Seeing you here."

Vivian looked to Joe.

"It is and it isn't," he said. "I actually did know that you moved to town. Laura gave me that information a week ago. This is one of the places we come when there's thunder."

"I thought it..."

"It's explosives, but it sounds like thunder," Joe said.

"It's me," Vivian said. "I can't be alone in my house when I hear sounds like that. Joe is kind enough to come out with me."

"I don't sleep at night anyway," Joe said. "Superstitious."

Jessica nodded. She understood both of their points of view.

"So, with the thunder and your proximity, we took a chance and came here."

"Trent makes a wonderful omelet," Vivian said.

Ranch Story

"So, you recently moved here?" Vivian asked.

Jessica glanced over at Joe. He fished his straw from the plastic cup and set it on his napkin so he could drink the soda directly.

"Oh, he's the snoop. I always tell him not to gossip about other people with me," Vivian said.

Jessica nodded. She wasn't sure that she believed Vivian, but she nodded anyway.

"Yeah, a few weeks ago."

"How do you like it so far?" Vivian asked as she poured half of a packet of sugar into her tea.

"Hot. Good," Jessica said. "Have you lived here long?"

"Eight years. I moved here after I was attacked. Figured I could move here or Death Valley. Better airport service here."

"You were attacked?"

Vivian sighed.

"Joe doesn't like people to talk about their stories outside of the circle, but his rules are not mine," Vivian said. Joe frowned. "Yes, I lived in Tennessee—that's where the man attacked me. He showed up one evening during a thunderstorm. The road ran along the ridge and it wasn't safe to walk up there when there was lightning. I told him as much. He asked if he could stay dry in the barn until the storm passed. I said yes but immediately called my boyfriend and asked him to come over. By the time Ed showed up, it was too late."

"You survived," Joe said. The way he said it, and the way she reacted, it appeared that he had said the same thing to Vivian at least a thousand times.

"Not too late for me, but for all my loved ones," Vivian said. "My two horses, my cow, the cats, the chickens, and my dog—he got them all. Some people want to say that I was lucky because he didn't kill Ed and he didn't manage to maim me too badly, but that really makes me angry. Just because they don't have a close relationship with their animals doesn't give them the right to call me lucky. I lost my best friends that night."

"I would never..." Jessica started to say.

"No, I'm sure," Vivian said. "Forgive me, I'm defensive."

Vivian turned her attention to her tea again. She moved the tea bag from the spoon and then stirred.

"May I ask a question?"

Vivian looked up at Jessica to study her eyes for a moment before she nodded consent.

"What do you know about him—the man who attacked you?"

Vivian sighed. "Speculation, mostly. Joe doesn't like it when I engage with speculation, so I offer that as a disclaimer. He came with the storm. The first drops fell and he came just as the heavy stuff really started to fall. He was soaked through, so I believe that he had been traveling with the storm. My barn doors were wide open, so he could have just gone in there on his own, but he came to ask permission first. People will tell you that he *needs* permission, but I don't think that's true. I believe that he asks just so you'll blame yourself when it's over."

"He meant to kill you," Joe said.

Vivian dismissed the interruption with a wave.

"I heard the commotion when he entered the barn and it sent a cold dagger into my heart. I was already on the phone with Ed at that point and I explained it away. The animals, especially the horses, could spot a stranger invading their territory. Of course they would bang and yell at the sight and smell of someone wandering in out of the darkness."

Vivian took a sip of her tea. She was squeezing the mug between her fingers. Jessica looked down and saw that she had the same grip on her own coffee mug.

"We debate theories about why he does it. Is he harvesting souls or is he nourished by pain and suffering? I think he kills just because he enjoys it. There are some who delight in building things. They explore their creativity by putting order to chaos. It stands to reason that the opposite must exist too. There must be people whose only passion is to dismantle and ruin."

"We can't know his motivations," Joe said. "Some would argue that it doesn't matter."

Vivian nodded. "I tried to wait for Ed, but I could hear the ruckus out in the barn even over the sound of the rain and thunder. I put on my coat and boots and armed myself with a rifle that I had shot a few times. The sounds died down as I approached and I had a flash of false hope that everything was okay. Then I saw the blood flowing out from the open door, mingling with the puddles of rainwater. I raised the rifle to my shoulder and made sure that it was ready to fire."

She shook her head.

"In a hard rain," Vivian said after a moment, "there are no shadows to warn you of someone coming up behind you. You can't hear footsteps or breathing. It's the perfect cover for a surprise attack. The gun went off when his blade hit my shoulder."

Vivian took a breath at the memory and then looked through the window out at the night.

"Sorry, you asked about him."

"No, it's fine. It's your story," Jessica said.

"What I know about him is very little. As I said, he came with the rain. I didn't see any weapons on him, so I suppose that long blade he cut me with was hidden in a pocket in his coat. He had a raw, earthy smell to him. At the time, I figured that he smelled that way because his coat and clothes were soaked through, but now I'm not so sure. I have this feeling that you could dry him completely out and he would still smell the same way."

Jessica wrinkled her nose. From Vivian's description, she could smell the man too.

"I know that he can be surprised too. Lots of people want to talk about him like he's some kind of unstoppable, omniscient force, but I saw the surprise when Ed's headlights lit him up."

"Wait," Jessica said, "lots of people?" She looked between Joe and Vivian. "What do you mean, lots of people? When you found me, I figured maybe someone else had been attacked by the same guy. You mentioned Laura, so that made three. You're four."

Jessica pointed to Vivian. A chill ran down her spine when she saw the worried glance that passed between Joe and Vivian.

"How many people have been murdered by this guy?" Jessica asked.

"We don't know for sure," Joe said.

"A guess then. How many do you know about?"

"It's hard to say for sure," Joe said. He was pushed so far back in his seat that the back of the booth was creaking under the pressure.

"Just give me a number," Jessica said. She didn't like the way her own voice was rising. She was losing control.

"It's disturbing," Vivian said. "That's why we're hesitant to say. Mel's research suggests that, over the years, more than a hundred households have been visited."

Jessica pushed back from the table and eyed Vivian carefully. There were so many places to hide information in the sentence that she had just uttered. Facts were being carefully disguised.

"I'm going to ask you one more time," Jessica said. "Tell me your best guess of how many people have been murdered."

"Three hundred and forty-eight," Joe said.

Jessica nodded slowly and tried to keep breathing as she attempted to process the magnitude of that number.

"In the United States," Vivian said. After a moment, she added, "In the past thirty years."

Sandwich

The waiter brought out food while Jessica sat in silence.

She didn't feel particularly hungry, but something drove her to pick up the sandwich and start working her way through it. Eating helped put things in perspective. Right there, in that little diner, she was safe. There was no thunderstorm and she had people around her. For the first time in a long time, she didn't feel so alone. The two people sharing the booth had been through a similar experience. That fact alone brought her an enormous amount of comfort. They were proof that people could continue to survive.

All those nights that she stared up at the ceiling, afraid to fall asleep, might be behind her. If Joe and Vivian could keep functioning, then what was her excuse?

She slowed down and took her time with the food.

It appeared that they were too polite to continue the conversation while she was eating, so she methodically worked on the sandwich and considered the real message behind the information they had given her. If Joe and Vivian were right, the man had killed over three hundred people while invading a hundred households. That alone had to be keeping him more than busy, so there was little chance that he would have the time to try to go back and eliminate survivors. Further, Joe and

Vivian didn't look particularly fast on their feet. If they hadn't been hunted down, then surely Jessica had every chance in the world.

But, if she was honest with herself, survival was never what kept her awake at night. She could call it grief, but it was guilt. If the man came back and tried to attack her again, it might actually be a relief. Maybe that confrontation was exactly what she needed to close the book on what happened in the past.

Across the table, Joe and Vivian put their forks down and touched their mouths with their napkins. She had eaten part of an omelet and Joe had gone to work on some waffles. The waiter appeared just as Jessica was putting her own napkin on her plate.

"What's your goal?" Jessica asked.

"With?" Vivian asked back.

"Why do you get together? Why does this Laura person cyber-stalk victims? Why does Mel or whoever keep statistics. What's your point?"

"To stop him," Joe said.

"Revenge, then?"

"Don't you want to make him pay for what he did to your family?" Joe asked.

Jessica rubbed her neck and spun her coffee mug while she thought about that.

"If a bridge collapsed and killed your family, would you blame the concrete, the builders, or the engineers? You want him to pay —you think that's possible?" she asked.

"Of course it is," Joe said, raising his voice. "What kind of question is that?"

"Hold on, Joe," Vivian said. "I think I understand what Jessica means. You're asking if we should be thinking of him as a man, who has a moral obligation to not harm others, or if he's more like a force of nature."

"Yes. Like if a tree limb falls on your house do you try to take revenge on the trunk?" Jessica asked.

"If there's enough of it still standing that it might hurt

someone else, you're damn right I'm going to take my revenge on that tree," Joe said.

Jessica thought about that for a second. She could see past the anger in his eyes and understand what he was saying. Then, she felt a wave of shame that it hadn't occurred to her before. Ever since the attack, she had been trying to make peace with the knowledge that the world could be such a randomly cruel and violent place. Looking beyond that, she should have been thinking about how to prevent anyone else from suffering the same fate. That goal hadn't even been on the table—even now it seemed like an impossibility.

"What's your approach?" Jessica asked.

Neither of them said anything.

"Come on, you guys have to have a plan formulated, right? You're so fired up about doing something, Joe, where's your plan? I won't tell anyone, if that's what you're worried about."

After a few more seconds, Vivian looked over to Joe and then back to Jessica.

"We had a plan. It didn't go well. We're back to square one right now."

"Not square one," Joe said, looking down at the table. "We just haven't reintegrated all the new information yet."

Vivian raised her eyebrows and then nodded.

CHAPTER THREE

Christopher

Dorm

Jessica glanced around the circle and reminded herself of the names she could remember. On the couch, Joe sat next to a man named Wahid. In a big chair across the coffee table, Jessica recognized Vivian, even though she looked very different when she was put together. The three people at the bar were a mystery. They had mumbled their names and didn't seem to care to make Jessica's acquaintance. The woman directly on Jessica's right was Hilda or Hildie.

Christopher cleared his throat, putting a stop to all the side conversations.

"We're starting from the top," Christopher said. Jessica tried to guess his age. His skin was so smooth, he could have been twenty-five, but the weariness in his eyes made her think that he was twice that old.

She got her answer quickly enough.

"In eighty-nine, I was the resident advisor of Four West of my dorm," Christopher said. "It was the Monday after Thanksgiving. The bulk of the students wouldn't arrive until Wednesday, so we just had a few other RAs and a couple of students in the building. Grant was the senior RA, down in One East. He made it very clear—anyone who wanted to sleep in the building had to be in by midnight, or they would sleeping on the stairs out front. We were the last all male dorm on campus, so if people had a girlfriend, they would usually try to find more comfortable accommodations. Nobody with a better option stuck around."

Jessica heard a glass clunk down on the bar. She couldn't remember the name of the woman who raised her hand. Christopher nodded permission for the question.

"Do you really have to start all the way from the beginning?" the woman asked with a sneer.

Vivian was the one who answered. "Yes, Billie, we do. We'll go over everything again in case we missed something. And, if you hadn't noticed, we do have a newcomer."

Jessica blushed when all eyes turned to her.

A couple of seconds later, Christopher took back the focus with his story.

"It was eleven and I was down in Grant's room. Normally, Grant was a very solitary person, but that night he was trying to finish up his essay on some play. He was hopeless at symbolism, so I was trying to give him context for something."

"For what?" Joe asked. "Be specific."

"The play was Glengarry Glen Ross," Christopher said. "This was before the play was made into a movie. The professor was in love with Mamet, and I had a pretty good handle on that course. I knew it killed Grant to ask for help, so I kinda bent over backwards to give it. Grant was the type of guy who would never hesitate to help someone else but he seemed incapable of relying on anyone else."

Christopher rubbed his forehead and hunched over. The deeper he got into his story, the more it seemed to weigh on him. He was settling towards the floor as he spoke.

"Grant kept throwing out these crazy ideas. Maybe the jobs equated to purgatory and the salespeople were unborn souls trying to find their way back to existence. I kept trying to nudge him in the right direction. I knew the professor considered the play to be an allegory for how we invest our energy in someone else's vision of what life should mean. I couldn't come right out and tell Grant that though. The way he worked, I knew that if I was too direct, he wouldn't listen and would just want to argue with me. He had to reach the conclusion on his own."

Christopher paused to drink some water. Jessica glanced around the room again. Despite their objections, even the people at the bar seemed to be really paying attention. Nobody said a word while they waited for Christopher to continue.

"I figured out the perfect question to ask Grant when we heard the bell. All I needed to do was probe him on why he was even taking that class. In his major, it had to be an elective. Through one of the other kids, I already knew that Grant was trying to break out of the major that his father had prescribed for him. If I could make Grant see himself as one of the salesmen, he would get it. But, like I said, that's when we heard the bell."

"What kind of bell?" Joe asked.

"What do you mean?"

"Like, a doorbell? Was it one of those ringers that's mechanical and you turn it in a circle?"

"It was actually neither of those. Our dorm was old. They had plans to tear it down in a couple of years. Anyway, the bell was a literal bell on the inside. It just had a chain that went over a pulley or something and you could pull the chain from the outside to ring it. Usually, there was a pair of socks stuffed up in it so people wouldn't jerk the chain all night and wake Grant up. I guess someone had grabbed the socks before vacation though because we heard the bell loud and clear that night."

"Thank you," Joe said. Jessica spotted him scribble something down in a notebook and tuck it away in his pocket as Christopher started talking again.

"Grant was angry as he headed for the door. I followed just to move around a bit. I was starting to get tired and didn't want to start yawning while Grant was trying to work. That's the worst when you're trying to get something done and people are just yawning and yawning."

The suggestion made Jessica want to yawn. She swallowed it

back and her ears clicked.

"Grant yelled that everyone knew the door was going to be locked at midnight. He yelled that whoever was out there better have a damn good reason for waking everyone up. I was certain that it wasn't one of the residents. Before going to Grant's, I had done an informal walk through of all the floors. I knew all the guys staying there that night, and I knew they were all accounted for. A few of them were having a movie night in one of the lounges and all the other guys were already in their rooms for the night."

"Was there any other way in?" Wahid asked. "Any other doors that someone had a key to?"

"I guess," Christopher said. "I mean, there must have been a janitor or maintenance guy who could get in through one of the other doors. There was a stairwell that let out near the cafeteria. That door was chained though, as I found out later. Down in the basement, there was a door connecting us to the service tunnel, where they piped in heat, power, water, and all that. All the windows on the ground floor had bars."

Christopher sighed and blinked as he looked up at the ceiling.

"We could see the back door from where we were standing. You could almost see it from Grant's room. The lobby connecting the front and back doors passed through the whole building, you know? Anyway, Grant was marching towards the door, about to yank it open, when I told him to wait. I was looking at the puddle of water near the wall. I don't know why it sent a bolt of fear through me right then, but it did. I looked up and saw where the water was coming from. It was dripping from the bell that had rung. Somehow, the water must have made its way through the chain hole and run all the way down to the bell. He asked me what my problem was. I told him to look first."

Jessica was reminded that the rest of them had already heard this story. A couple of people sank into their chairs or folded their arms across their chests. They knew what was coming.

"Grant had to drag the bench over to the door so he could get a look through the transom window. I helped him move it and he climbed up as the bell rang again. A moment later, I joined him. The two of us looked down on the man standing in the rain. We saw his weathered hat and soaked coat. Grant mumbled something about how it had to be a joke, and I understood what he meant. The guy was right out of a slasher movie, you know? We would have to be crazy to open the door. Grant yelled through the glass, asking what the guy wanted. When he looked up at us, the rain made the guy squint."

"As much as you remember, can you describe his clothes?"

Christopher swallowed and nodded.

"I'm going to tell you, and it's going to sound like a contradiction later. Here's the thing—I know what I saw through the window, but it wasn't the same as what I saw later."

"It's okay," Vivian said. "We're here to listen, not to judge."

He nodded again.

"His hat was like a western hat, but it had a flat brim. The front dipped down from the weight of the rain landing on it. There was a hole or a dark spot near the top. The lights shining on him outside were those really orange lights that buzzed when they were on. Maybe because of that, his coat looked strange. It was soaked through, but I suppose it was really worn leather. It almost looked like old, worn rock. I don't know how to describe it. Overall, except for his face and hands, he almost looked like a statue or something. He was like mossy rocks and sticks, piled up in the shape of a man. Only when he moved did he look like an actual person."

Jessica realized that her hand had drifted up to cover her mouth. She tried to sit up straight and reminded herself that it was just a story. Picturing herself looking through the window was her own imagination running wild.

"Grant told him to go away. He said that we had no choice but to report to campus security, so the guy better get moving or else. The guy turned and left. He walked straight away from the doorway and we lost sight of him in the rain. His shadow blended in with all the other shadows out there. I almost fell off the bench when Grant asked me if I was ready to get back to work. I asked, 'You're going to call campus security, right?' and I was pleasantly surprised when Grant said, 'You bet your ass we're reporting that guy. Nobody walking around like that in a storm is up to any good.' That's just what Grant did. He immediately got on the phone. I could hear the guy on the other end asking perfunctory questions. They said they would send someone over. While we waited, I pretty much just told Grant what the play meant—or at least what the professor would think it meant. When we heard the knock, we were confused. Security should have just let themselves in."

"Wait," Wahid said. "What did you tell him the play was about?"

"I thought I mentioned," Christopher said, "I pretty much knew what the professor thought it was about. When I was in his class the spring before, he talked about the play and how it was about bending to society's expectations of what it means to be a man. There's a pressure to bend to historically masculine roles. I'm sure it's viewed differently now, but back then it seemed like everything was a struggle to redefine our understanding of gender roles and how they push people into a type of servitude."

"I'm just curious if... Keep going. We'll come back to it," Wahid said.

Christopher evaluated him with a long look and then shut his eyes to find his place.

"There was a knock. We were confused, because security had the key. Looking through the transom window, we saw the guy. Grant even made him take off his hat for a moment so we could be sure. When we opened the door for him, he complained that someone had shoved gum in the keyhole. It wasn't gum, but there was definitely something in there. At first I thought it was resin or epoxy or something. My uncle was a locksmith, and I've been with him on plenty of service calls, so I knew that whoever tried to replace that lock was going to have a hard time. But while Grant was talking to the guy, I pushed my thumbnail into the goop in the lock. It wasn't all that hard."

"*What* is the *point*?" Billie said after an exasperated grunt.

Jessica's anger flared at the interruption. "I'm sorry, but could you either shut up or get out of here? This is the first time I'm hearing this and I want to know all the details."

Billie stared at Jessica with narrowed eyes. Slowly, Billie started to get up from her chair. Panic and anger flooded through Jessica's veins. She started to get up too.

"Let's take a break," Vivian said. "Ten minutes. I'll remind everyone that interruptions are unwelcome. Probing questions should be short and rare."

Everyone stood at once, defusing the heat between Jessica and Billie.

Still, Jessica didn't take her eyes off of Billie until a friendlier face stepped between them.

"Hi, Jessica? Do you prefer Jessica, or Jess? I'm Hilda—I know it can be daunting to try to remember everyone's name on the first night. Would you like to go get some air?"

Over Hilda's shoulder, Jessica could see that Bill and some of the other bar people were headed towards the glass doors at the back of the room.

"The non-smokers usually head for the east balconies if you want to go," Hilda said, pointing. She was pointing in the opposite direction from where Billie was headed, so Jessica decided to follow.

Balcony

"It's actually pretty common for us to have little arguments and altercations," Hilda said.

"Why do you invite her back?" Jessica asked. She leaned against the stone railing and glanced down at the velvet green below them, wondering how much effort it must take to keep grass like that in such an arid climate.

"We're all equals here. There's nobody saying who can and can't come. And Billie is usually pretty agreeable. I think that Christopher's story is difficult for her because it's so much like her own."

"Oh. Right," Jessica said. She had forgotten that they were all there for the same reason.

"Also, Billie was hit particularly hard by Simon's death," Hilda said as she leaned on the railing.

"Simon?"

"Another story for another time," Hilda said. She looked over to Jessica. "Just know, Jessica, it's perfectly within your rights to ask someone to cease their interruption, but it's not okay for you to suggest they leave."

Jessica was stunned into silence for a moment. "I..."

"Probably just a poor choice of words," Hilda said. "Next time, just tell her to shut up and leave out the ultimatum."

Jessica wanted to argue that she had said nothing of the sort, but when she thought about what she had said, she understood. Apparently, "shut up or get out of here," was an ultimatum.

"Fine, but I can't promise to not throw the first punch if she looks at me like that again," Jessica said.

"Punching is fine. Leave it in the meeting though. Don't follow her to her room or anything."

Jessica didn't know if Hilda was joking, so she simply nodded.

For a few moments, they stayed silent, looking out over the grass in the waning light. It was a beautiful garden with tall bushes at the far end. Jessica wondered what she would find if she pushed through those bushes. There was probably a wall and then nothing but desert.

"What is this place?" Jessica asked.

"A private home," Hilda said. "At least it was. It's held in a trust now."

"For what?" Jessica asked, turning around. She couldn't even guess at how many rooms the building must have. She had see the front hall and the lounge with the bar. But the hallway that Hilda led her down suggested that there was much more to see.

"I'm not sure what the future holds for this place," Hilda said. "We're allowed to continue to use it as much as we need for meetings and respite. Nobody can stay on the premises more than one week each month, but I suppose that rule is bent on occasion. It's a lonely place. There are too many bad memories floating around for anyone to seek refuge here for long."

Jessica shook her head. "I don't get it."

"Get what?"

"The only thing we have in common is that we've been attacked by some random guy, right? Why is this building going to waste and why are we allowed to meet here?"

Hilda didn't answer. She let Jessica supply the answer herself.

"Because the owner lost someone or was attacked," Jessica said. "Seems like a lot to do for a support group. Which was is he?"

"That's not my story to tell," Hilda said. "And we always cover that kind of thing when we're all together."

"So everyone knows everything?" Jessica asked.

Hilda shook her head. "Superstition. One or two people thinking the same thing at the same time—that can be dangerous. We should head back."

Alarm

"My best guess is that it was sap," Christopher said. "In the lock, I mean. The color, hardness, and slight stickiness, it was like really thick tree sap that had hardened. Grant shut the door behind the guard and I locked it while Grant described what we had seen. The guard asked me if I had anything to add and I said no. Just passing along the information made us both feel better. We laughed with the guard about how maybe John Carpenter was trying out a new character or something. He said that security would do extra rounds every thirty minutes or so and they would keep an eye out. We let him out and locked the door again."

Christopher took another drink of water.

"Everything snapped into place with Grant's analysis. He got the bulk of his outline done and we decided that the two of us would do one last sweep through the building before we called it a night. I almost told him we shouldn't bother. There was an idea in the back of my head that maybe the more we probed into the mysterious guy, the worse things would get. There wasn't any logic behind the idea."

Christopher shook his head.

"Can you explore that more?" Vivian asked. "What do you think your instincts were trying to tell you?"

He looked up at the ceiling. "Maybe it's like when you get a cut and you're dying to take off the bandage to see how it's healing? If you do, maybe the bandage will pull off the scab and you'll be worse off than you were before. I don't know—this is a terrible analogy."

"No, keep going," Vivian said.

"We had a choice. We could just forget the guy and go on with our lives, or we could try to take control of the situation by trying to make sure that everyone was okay and everything was shored up. Maybe if we had just forgotten everything, that would have been it. Instead, by trying to guarantee our own safety, we were just beating the hornets' nest until they swarmed."

Jessica glanced around. A couple of people were nodding.

"We started at the top floor and worked our way down. Grant was still talking through the outline of his paper, so he was barely paying attention. I kept telling him not to overwork it. There's a fine line between considering opposing viewpoints and integrating them so much that you undermine your own confidence. But I really just wanted him to pay attention. The more we searched, the more I kept thinking that there was something wrong. We tried every doorknob as we went. We used his key to look in the supply closets. All the resident's doors were shut and locked. We made sure not to rattle the occupied ones. My friend, Nathan, had his door open and candles lit, but he was pretty much asleep. Grant wanted to confiscate his candles, but I said no and closed Nathan's door. We made it down to the second floor when we heard the bell again."

Christopher shuddered at the memory. His voice was quieter when he started again.

"Grant headed for the stairs, but I froze. I suggested we find the nearest phone and call security. He kept saying that it probably *was* security down there. It had been about thirty minutes. They were probably doing their rounds, as promised. I went along with that until we were halfway down the stairs. That's when it really hit me. It was the bell. Security knocked. In fact, most everyone knocked because ringing the bell would be fruitless. Everyone knew the bell would always have a pair of socks stuffed in it—why bother trying? Grant said there was no harm in looking through the transom window and I still balked. He had a good reason though. He said, 'We might need security before this night is out. We can't afford to call them until we know we have a reason to call. One false alarm, and they won't take us seriously.' I understood that. Credibility was a scarce commodity. If we squandered it, we would be hard-pressed to earn it back.

"We went through the same drill again. Grant yelled and didn't get an answer, so we pushed the bench up against the door so we could look through the transom window. He was back. The rain was coming down even harder. A river of rain was coming off of the front of the brim of his hat. He said he just wanted a place where he could get in from the storm and dry off. Grant said something that I thought was really smart. He said, 'The security building is only a couple hundred yards east of here. We told them that you were looking for somewhere to get out of the rain.' The man didn't move and didn't say anything for a minute. Grant and I looked at each other, wondering what we should do. I was about to say that it was time to go call when the man said, 'Just let me in to get dry.' I don't know what it was about the way he said that, but it didn't sound at all like a request. It was a command, and it took everything I could do to not obey. If I had been alone, I probably would have let him in. Together, Grant and I supported each other.

"One more time, he said, 'Let me in to get dry.' It was too difficult not to respond. Grant said, 'Listen, man, we would but we have rules. If it were just us making the decisions, then fine, but security would have our butts if we did that.' The man didn't say a word. He just turned and walked in the direction of the security office."

"Did you feel compelled to answer him?" Joe asked.

"I definitely felt the urge to let him in," Christopher said. "He was like an authority figure or whatever. It was like your dad telling you to do something in his dad voice."

"But you said that it was too difficult not to respond. You contained your urge to let him in, but did you also feel the urge to speak or to answer?"

"I think so," Christopher said.

Jessica automatically glanced over at Billie to see if she was going to object to people wasting time again. She didn't. In fact, Billie was nodding along with Christopher's answer.

"Grant and I had been about to head back to our rooms for the night, but after that second visit from the man, it seemed like sleep was going to be impossible. We left the bench there and went back to Grant's room so he could call security again and let them know the man was on his way. There was no answer, of course. We joked about it. John Carpenter might as well have been the director of that whole night. Everything was playing out like a horror movie. That's when we heard the sound from below. A big clank rang through the building's pipes and we both knew where it was coming from."

Christopher rubbed his eyes with his right hand.

"He didn't want to go. He tried to call security again. It just rang. Besides me and Grant, there were seven other guys asleep upstairs. I mean... Self-preservation told me to just run. I could sprint all the way to the south lot, get in my car, and drive. We both knew exactly what was going to happen. After taking a breath, I knew we couldn't leave those guys upstairs without warning them."

"You were convinced," Billie said. "Right from the start, you had no doubt that you were about to be hunted by a killer."

Christopher nodded slowly. "If I had been a little older, I'm sure I would have second-guessed everything, you know? It's confirmation bias for most people. The longer a person lives, the less likely they are to believe in outlandish circumstances because they've never encountered them. But Grant and I were young, naive, and a lot of our ideas of the world had been formed by watching scary movies and stuff. It all seemed possible, and it was.

"I said I would go up to the top floor and start banging on doors. The resident advisor in Four East was up there and he was a good friend. I knew I could enlist his help and we would work our way down. Grant had a different idea, and it sounded great. He went to the hall and pointed to the fire alarm lever on the wall. 'How about we pull that, get everyone down to the lobby, and get ready to defend ourselves.' A chill ran down my spine when he said that. Just the confident way that he put it, I thought he was right. We needed to be proactive and ready to fight. The moment I nodded, he pulled that lever and the alarm was louder than I could have imagined. I knew it was ringing on every floor and it would summon the fire department too. That's when I had second thoughts. It wasn't a movie, and we had just committed a crime by essentially reporting a false emergency. I mean, we hadn't even called the police first, we had just acted. Technically, Grant had acted, but we were in it together. Grant handed me a lacrosse stick and he had a baseball bat. We paced in the lobby, trying to keep our eyes on both doors and both halls at the same time. Guys began to appear from the stairwell. One or two had thought to put on coats, but most just had on t-shirts and underwear. The alarm stopped. Before we could say anything, a couple of guys turned back for the stairs. They thought the emergency was over. Grant yelled at everyone to stay put."

Christopher took a break for a moment and then drank more water.

"Explaining everything, it felt impossible to convey the terror that had driven us to act. One guy, I think it was Terrence but I could be remembering wrong, thought we were pulling a prank. Another guy said we were on drugs. Grant held his ground. He yelled something like, 'Go back upstairs and I will keep pulling the fire alarm all night. This is *serious* and we need your help.' If he hadn't been the head RA for the building, they never would have listened. Someone demanded to know what we intended to do and Grant and I looked at each other. Without talking about it, we knew we couldn't tell them that we wanted everyone to just hang out in the lobby. Going outside wasn't an option either—only a couple of people were dressed for the rain. Grant said, 'We'll go downstairs and check it out. If we don't see anything, you can go to bed.' I knew he was lying—just trying to buy some time—but I thought it was a decent plan. There were eight of us, together, and on high alert."

"I thought you said nine," Wahid said.

"Seven," Vivian said. "No, wait, you said seven besides yourself and Grant."

"Ten dead, one injured," Billie said. "That's what I read."

"Let him tell it the way he remembers," Joe said.

People nodded and Christopher took a deep breath.

Massacre

"Eight of us, armed with whatever we could grab from Grant's room, headed for the stairs. Kyle had a really heavy chemistry book in his hands. Dave had a fire extinguisher that he had ripped down from the wall. Terrence wasn't carrying anything. I gave Aaron the lacrosse stick because Grant let me take the giant flashlight he had. The thing had, like, seven D batteries in it, so it was super bright and weighed a ton. Grant still had his bat. Paul and Henry had screwdrivers. I can picture everything really clearly. We started down the stairs. We must have been halfway down to the basement when the lights went out. That's when everything got confusing."

"Did you hear any sounds when the lights went out?" Vivian asked.

"Not that I remember. We were trying to be quiet, but eight boys going down those echoey stairs—we wouldn't have heard much. When the lights went out, everyone started talking and shushing each other. Grant elbowed me and I remembered that I was carrying his flashlight to use as a weapon. I turned it on right when the people in the back were already starting to climb. Dave yelled that Terrence was missing. We heard a muffled shout from below. I immediately assumed that the guy had gotten Terrence. Kyle and Grant both argued that Terrence was probably just pranking us. They said, rightly so, that Terrence already thought he was being pranked and it would be just like him to try to turn the prank back around."

Christopher swallowed and exhaled.

"We were just about fifty-fifty on turning back or going forward. Four wanted to climb, three wanted to go find Terrence. I didn't listen to the others. I just kept descending. I think they followed me because I had the only light. With the doors shut upstairs, there was nothing but blackness above. We didn't have access to most of the basement. I don't even know what was beyond the locked doors on the corridor under the lobby. We were going the other direction—following the pipes and conduits that stretched down towards the big metal doors. There was another shout, and it clearly came from down that tunnel. Grant said, 'That's the tunnel that leads to the facilities room. I have the key.' We were about halfway there when Aaron stopped me. He tapped me on the shoulder with the lacrosse stick. Without saying a word, he pointed the stick towards the floor. I followed with the flashlight and the blood lit up in the glare of the flashlight beam. Nothing could have made us keep going at that point.

"We turned as a group and hands pushed me towards the front so I could lead the way with the light. The stairs seemed so far away. Everyone stood back to back, forming a tight circle with weapons out. When one of the guys in back—it must have been Paul or Henry—screamed, I didn't even turn to see why. The group just kept moving forward. Halfway up the stairs, the blood trail started again. Sitting right in the middle of one of the treads, in a small pool, was Terrence's right hand. Nobody had any doubt that it was his. Obviously, the idea that it was a prank had evaporated.

"We just ran. Everyone pounded up the stairs and they slammed into me when I couldn't get through the door. I thought it had to be locked somehow. One of my feet slipped out from under me and I went down on one knee. A hand reached over me and pulled on the handle. As soon as there was a crack, we all bolted through, pushing the door aside. Grant ran back and pulled the door shut again, pulling on the handle like he thought we were being chased and the guy was going to try to get through.

"I pointed the light down at myself. My pants had a big splotch of blood on the knee and I had blood on one hand. I thought it was my own and I patted around to find the wound before I realized that I had knelt in it. Someone asked where Paul was. I swept the beam around, counting. There were only five of us, including myself. Terrence, Paul, and Henry were all gone. Kyle had lost the book that he was carrying and had one of the screwdrivers in his hand. The end was wet with blood."

"He got past you?" Joe asked.

Christopher shrugged. "He must have. The best I can figure is that he dragged Terrence to the place under the lobby. When we headed for the facilities tunnel, he must have taken Terrence's hand up the stairs. Maybe the sounds bounced around. We thought we heard them from one direction, but they must have come from the other. I smeared blood all around the door when I came through, so I couldn't tell if the prints there were from us or from him. Grant ran for the door and jumped up on the bench. He kept asking 'Where are they?' and I figured he meant the fire department or security. Dave pushed him out of the way so he could move the bench. It didn't do any good. Even when he shoved the bench out of the way, the door wouldn't budge. Dave ran to the back door while Grant and Aaron tried to get the main doors open. They got the latch to turn, but the doors wouldn't open more than an inch or two. Something had been shoved through the handles to block them from pulling open. Later, I found out that the 'something' was the arm of one of the guards.

Dave got the back doors to open an inch as well. The thing holding those shut was a pair of handcuffs. He screamed that if we could get leverage, we could break the chain.

"Grant said that he had the key. Of course we all thought he meant for the handcuffs, but that didn't make sense. The cuffs were on the outside. There would be no way to unlock them from inside. He kept waving and yelling about a key and finally Kyle figured out that he meant the double doors closest to the cafeteria. It was chained on the inside and Grant had the key. We ran fast, pounding down the hall. The other guys passed me and I had time to count—still five of us at that point. I could feel him behind us, chasing. In the movies back then the bad guy never ran or rushed. He would just stalk at a slow pace and somehow keep up with the fleeing teenagers. That's what the guy was doing. I knew that if we stopped we would hear his slow, inevitable footsteps behind us. Ahead of me, Grant and the others were shouting at each other as they worked on unlocking the chain and getting through the door.

"I slowed down as I approached them. In all those horror movies I would watch with my friends, there would always be a really tense build when the group thought they were going to escape. You would always know it wouldn't work because there were still too many people alive. A movie like that doesn't end until there's one last survivor."

Christopher swallowed again. Telling the story was making his body tighten up. In her grief groups, Jessica had seen it dozens of times—people had to work to get to the point where their trauma would fall out of them easily. Until they did that, they had to relive the pain over and over.

"The flashlight flickered and I hit the side of it against my palm until it was steady again. I turned and pointed it down the hall behind us. It was empty. If he wasn't coming from that direction, then he had to be coming to get us from another angle. I swung the light up the west staircase. Someone shouted at me to point the light at the lock. There was some light from outside filtering through the windows, but it was barely enough to see. I told them we should slow down and think about this. They told me I was crazy. Kyle grabbed the flashlight from my hands. I watched as the four of them focused on trying to get the lock open. It shouldn't have been so difficult—just a padlock through some chains that were looped between the handles of the double doors. I guessed what Dave was going to say as he peered at the padlock."

"There was pitch in the lock," Jessica said. She blushed when angry eyes turned towards her. It had just slipped out. Jessica put her hand over her mouth.

"Exactly," Christopher said. "I knew he would say that and he did. It confirmed my suspicion—the man had already been there. I started to move towards the stairs. I know it's stupid to climb in an emergency, but my room was at the top of that staircase and it felt like I was going towards safety. Kyle said, 'Forget the lock. The handle isn't as strong as the chain.' It was a good point. Two guys moved to each door and they yanked. Something snapped and the door popped open a few inches. Grant looked through the gap and said, 'Hold on—there's...' The blade came through the gap and cut directly through his throat, exploding from the back of his neck. The shaky flashlight beam stayed pointed at the fountain of blood for a moment and then slipped out of Kyle's hand. The only noises were the pounding rain and Grant gagging on his own blood until the flashlight clattered to the floor. That's when everyone ran.

"Dave and Aaron ran back down the hall towards the lobby. Kyle ran by me, pounding up the stairs, screaming. Grant was on his knees with one hand holding onto the chain. The blade pulled back and Grant sagged to the floor. His hand went to his neck. That one hand seemed to be all he could use. I guess the rest of his nerves in his spine had been severed. I knew it was too late for him. The flashlight cast Grant's writhing shadow against the wall. Then, the blade slipped back through the gap between the double doors. It moved up and down, like it was looking to taste more blood. It clanked against the chains and twisted as much as it could. When the blade twisted and was facing me, it felt like it was watching me—like the blade was his eyes."

"What kind of blade? It had to be long, right? Was it a machete?" Billie asked.

Christopher shook his head. "I don't think so. I think it was too shiny and thick to be a machete, but I really don't know."

"What shape was it?" Billie asked.

Christopher held up his hand and shook his head. She got the message—that memory was lost.

"I watched the blade explore the gap between the doors. It slid up and rattled the chain and then went back to the door. I was frozen. In a way, it felt safe as long as I didn't turn my back on him. Everyone had been killed in a surprise attack. I felt like if I just watched him he wouldn't be able to get me. As the blade withdrew from the gap, I realized that I wasn't safe anymore. Still frozen, I wanted to simply stay put. I figured I would press my back against the wall and wait. At least when he came for me, I would see him. He wouldn't get me by surprise. That's when I remembered Nathan.

"You guys were asking earlier about the numbers. There were nine of us in the building but only eight went into the basement. That's because Nathan never came down for the fire alarm. He could sleep through everything. People used to call him Bear because he would pretty much hibernate through the winter. Also, he was enormous and had a beard. He was on the second floor, just a few rooms down from the stairs. I knew I could get to his room in seconds. All the other guys were panicked and running in fear. If I got to Nathan's room, he would probably be calm and I could explain to him what happened. That's what I wanted—someone calm.

"I didn't waste any more time. I figured I had a good shot of making it to Nathan's room because I had just seen the blade seconds before. As I got to the top of the stairs and ran for Nathan's door, I realized there was a good chance that the man had already gotten to him. The man had always been one or two steps ahead. I didn't knock, just slipped inside and shut the door behind me. I heard him snoring and realized that there was light in his room. Candles were forbidden in the dorm, but he had some on his desk. The window was open a few inches and the air in there was heavy with humidity. I heard Nathan snoring and I locked the door behind me.

"I had to shake him to wake him up. For a moment, I thought he was going to punch me, and then he recognized me and asked what the hell I was doing in his room. He sat up and rubbed his eyes as I explained. I didn't think he was going to believe me. Maybe he did—who knows. While I talked, he pulled on his pants and shoes. He asked one question. He wanted to know where Terrence's body was. I said I didn't know. Then he told me to write down my parents' phone number. I had no idea why, but he insisted, pointing to the notebook near his candles."

"Did you ever figure it out?" Wahid asked.

"He said that he thought it was a dream. He read the phone number while I told it to him aloud and he compared. He said that if it was a dream, the numbers would be different. Later, I thought maybe he wanted the number so he could call my parents and tell them I had gone crazy."

"Both might be true," Joe said. "Some people use written and oral tests like that to see if they can turn a regular dream into a lucid dream. But that doesn't mean he wasn't also getting a contact number for your next of kin. Smart, if you think about it."

Christopher sighed. "Well, it didn't matter. He tried the lights and was confused when they didn't come on. It was like he had only half heard what I had told him. He said that we had to go find Kyle, Dave, and Aaron. He said it was our duty, and that there was safety in numbers. In theory, I agree with all of that. In the moment, I kept telling him that this was what the killer wanted. The killer wanted it to happen just like a horror movie. But when Nathan demanded to know why I thought that, I realized that it wasn't anything more than a hunch. What are you supposed to say in that situation?"

"There's nothing to say," Vivian said.

"Exactly," Christopher said. "So I didn't say anything. I went along with Nathan's fresh confidence. We went back to the western stairwell and he stood on the stairs for what felt like forever, looking down at Grant's body in the puddle of blood. I realized that he probably thought I had done it. It was the way Nathan was standing. He refused to completely turn his back on me. Because he was fresh to the chaos, he said things that I wouldn't have thought of. He said we had to find the nearest phone and call the cops. That was right, of course, but the payphone at the end of the hall was dead. The phone in Nathan's room was dead too. At that point, he took my word for it that the doors were locked. We climbed the center stairwell to look for the others. We found Kyle's torso, missing his head on the third floor."

Christopher's voice remained steady but then his breath hitched in his chest when he tried to take a sip of water.

"Aaron was hanging halfway out of one of the fourth floor windows. We pulled him back in, but his intestines were dangling down the side of the building. As soon as we saw that, we both backed away. I said, 'This is crazy, right? Barely any lights, finding dead bodies.' Nathan put a finger to his lips to tell me to be quiet and then he waved for me to follow. I don't know how he heard the sound of Dave crying in the bathroom. I didn't hear it until Nathan pushed open the door. I wouldn't go in. It was too dark, and the sound of crying was echoing around in there. It was awful. I stared into the blackness as Nathan disappeared into that nightmare. I didn't even blink until Nathan led Dave out a few seconds later. He kept telling Dave that it was okay—everything was going to be okay. When Dave saw me, he tried to get out of Nathan's grip to run away. I don't know why. Maybe my presence reminded him of what was going on. Nathan eyed me again. I know that he thought that I was somehow connected to the murders.

"Nathan took charge again and told Dave that he had to be quiet. He led the way to the eastern stairwell—the only one without a body in it—and we went down the stairs. Descending again, back towards the first floor, I snapped. I demanded to know why we were going back down. Why couldn't we just find one spot, put a wall at our backs, and wait. If we were going to be killed anyway, why couldn't we just once see what was coming?

"Nathan managed me the same way that he managed Dave. He said that I was right, and we were going to do that, but we were going to do it back in his room. The idea really resonated with me. Since everything had started, Nathan's room with his candles and fresh air had seemed actually sane and cozy. I wanted to get back to that place too, so I went along. Dave was like a zombie by then. He was completely gutted emotionally. Then we got to the second floor landing and Dave started to twitch. I understood why. In the stormy glow coming through the windows, we could see that the floor and walls were white. There were smeared footprints in the white dust—Dave had shot off his fire extinguisher. Nathan pointed at the wall near the window and I saw it. There was the outline of the man in white dust. When Dave saw that, he really lost it. He started screaming and we practically had to drag him down the dark hall while he fought us. It was awful, but I just wanted to leave him. We couldn't afford to have Dave draw attention to us. Nathan picked Dave up, slung him over his shoulder, and just carried him. Like I said, his ability to sleep through anything wasn't the only reason that people called him Bear.

"I opened the door and Nathan carried Dave inside and put him on the bed. After closing and locking the door, I grabbed a candle and make a quick tour of the room—looking in the closet and under the desk and bed. I had to make sure that we were alone in there. Nathan closed the window, cutting off the sound of the falling rain. He went to press his ear against the door and I warned him to be careful. It wasn't rational, but I could just picture that blade slicing right through the wood.

"I didn't know where to stand. I went and looked through the window, seeing nothing but the bushes down below. Nathan was only on the second floor, but it still seemed like a long way down. I lowered myself to the floor and pressed my back against the wall under the window. I stared at the gap under the door, wishing we had put a candle in the hallway before we shut the door. It would have been nice to see the light under the door so I could watch for changing shadows. Instead, the gap was nothing but black. Anything could have been out there. Nathan went to his phone, trying it again. He said, 'No dial tone,' and put it back in its cradle. I think Dave was in shock. He had pulled his knees up to his chest and he was staring at nothing and rocking a little.

"Nathan must have spotted the lights outside. I flinched away when he ran towards me, but he was just looking through the window. 'Cops are here,' he said. I stood to join him. 'We can make a run for it...' he started to say. I stopped him. Even if we managed to get down to the lobby, we wouldn't get through the door before he got us. This was the kind of false ending that I was expecting, I told him. He didn't know that I was equating the whole night to a horror movie. It didn't give him much confidence in me when I explained that."

Christopher swallowed the last gulp of his water and glanced around.

"You guys mind if I take another break? I haven't talked about that night in this kind of detail in years."

"Of course," Vivian said. "I'm sure we could all use a moment."

Library

Jessica remembered where the bathroom was. When she returned to the meeting room, it was still empty. Through the glass she could see the orange dots and shuffling shapes of the smokers. She headed the other direction, trying to find the balcony that Hilda had led her to earlier. After a wrong turn, she wandered into a small library that had the dry, sweet smell of old tobacco. Half the walls were bookshelves and the others were paneled in dark wood. Jessica touched the back of one of the leather arm chairs. It was supple and warm.

Vivian startled her from the door.

"If you stay here, explore this library," Vivian said. "The books look like they would be boring, but there are some real gems in here."

Jessica glanced at the old, fragile spines of the books near her.

"I wouldn't dare," she said. "They look valuable. I tend to crease pages and fold over corners."

Vivian smiled and sank into one of the leather chairs. Jessica sat across from her.

"Well, I wouldn't do that, but I also wouldn't hesitate to read them. Simon always insisted that these books didn't do anyone any good unless they were enjoyed. A lot of self-made people are very tight, but Simon always tried to get the most out of life."

"This was his house?"

Vivian nodded.

"What do you think of the group?"

Jessica let out a slow breath, trying to find the right words.

"It's different. I wasn't prepared for the length and depth of Christopher's sharing. He remembers so much."

"We had a hypnotist at one point helping us explore our memories. Some people said it was just an excuse for us to invent elaborate fantasies and then convince ourselves that they were true. I believe that the memories we recovered were genuine. One of the details that I recalled during hypnosis was in the police report when I eventually saw a copy. I hadn't remembered it at all before."

From the way she spoke, Jessica got the sense that Vivian didn't want to reveal exactly what that detail had been.

"You think you'll come back, or has Christopher's story soured you on the group."

Jessica nodded slowly. "I think I will."

"But?"

"Honestly? His tragedy happened in eighty-nine? If he's still holding all that pain thirty years later, it doesn't speak well of the process," Jessica said.

"If this were a successful group, you're saying he would have moved on by now."

"It sounds cruel, but don't you owe it to yourself to recover at some point?"

Vivian shrugged. “I think you’d be surprised to see how well Christopher functions when he’s not thrusting himself back into that memory. You’re getting a glimpse of him at his most vulnerable, and he’s putting forth a lot of effort to dredge up all that pain, but I don’t think that means that he’s dealing with it on a consistent basis.”

“I wasn’t trying to criticize him or the...”

“No, I didn’t think you were,” Vivian said. “We are carrying some unfinished business, but I think that would be true if he was coming to this group or any other. Some wounds are too deep to heal completely. The good news here is that you can be guaranteed that everyone else understands your pain. We’re careful not to compare scars. This isn’t a competition of who was hurt the most, and that happens a lot at run-of-the-mill grief groups. I’ve learned that lesson well.”

“The other way is difficult too,” Jessica said. “When some people found out what happened to me, they shut down at the horror of my story and figured that they had nothing to say that could possibly comfort me. It felt so isolating and lonely.”

“And infuriating,” Vivian added.

“Yes. I would get so mad at their stupid pity. I’m very careful not to do that myself, but Christopher’s story is a lot to take in.”

“Speaking of which,” Vivan said, ”we should probably head back.“

They stood together. As they walked, Jessica asked, “So, you’ve spent time here?”

“Yes. It’s not exactly homey, but it’s comfortable in its own way.”

They were the first back to the meeting room, but others began to return quickly.

Escape

“I convinced Nathan that it would be stupid to try to run. We had made it that long—what was another few minutes? He opened the window and stuck his head out. He tried yelling to the police, but I guess they were too far away to hear. They were parked farther down, almost between our building and the security office. He kept trying the phone. I guess that was smart, but I just wanted everyone to hold perfectly still. I knew there would be one last attack and I wanted everyone to be waiting and ready for it. I wish I knew why I was so convinced that it was going to play out like a horror movie."

Christopher paused and looked to Billie.

"What's that thing you used to say about horror movies?"

She looked off to find the memory. "We enjoy them because they let us rehearse for the worst moments."

"Yeah," Christopher said. "I think that's true, but the opposite is true too. When you finally find yourself in the worst possible situation, you can't help but make the analogy that it's like a horror movie. The last time you witnessed anything so horrible, it was over in a couple of hours and there was no real blood on your hands. That's the bad part. I went to Nathan and took the receiver out of his hands. I made Dave sit up. The three of us sat on the bed, looking at the door. Nathan wanted to yell for the police, and I said we should wait until they yell out first. There was no sense in drawing attention to ourselves until we knew that they were actually coming. As far as we knew, they had headed the other direction to check in with the security office."

Christopher looked down at his hands and spoke slowly.

"The fire department lights came next. The flashes of red and white joined the blue flashes of the police. The engine was loud—I could hear it over the rain. Nathan wanted to yell. I implored him to wait until we heard the firemen make their entry. I figured they would have to use their axes in order to get inside. 'Can we at least look?' Nathan asked me. I don't know how I got to be in charge. Honestly, he looked a little frightened of me. It was weird how the power shifted. I told him to go ahead, but I stayed with Dave on the bed so I could watch the door.

"He told us that the fire department was much closer. They had pulled up in front of the door. Nathan waited until they started banging. We could hear them slamming something into the door to break it down. Nathan began yelling for help and then cursed me because I made him wait. He said that if he had yelled earlier they would have heard. A moment after that, there was banging on the door to the hall. The whole thing shook with each slow hit. 'Maybe it's them,' Nathan said. I shook my head. It was too soon. That's when the lights came on. Nathan dropped to his hands and knees so he could look under the door. He said, 'I think I see multiple people. It has to be the police or the firemen, right?' I told him no. If it was someone coming to help, they would be yelling to us. Nathan accepted that answer and pressed his face to the floor again so he could watch under the door. I started to tell him to be careful, but the words had just left my mouth when the blade shot through the gap. He was at least a foot away, but the blade crossed the distance instantly and found his flesh. Dave pressed back against the wall and I jumped down from the bed to pull Nathan back. The blade must have stuck into the bone of his cheek or something because even though I was pulling his arm as hard as I could, Nathan was slowly sliding towards the door.

"I yelled for Dave to help me, but he was frozen. My feet slid across Nathan's floor and we were both being dragged. I jerked so hard that I felt something in Nathan's arm popped. That did it. Nathan scrambled back into me as the blade disappeared under the door again. In his panic, Nathan had one hand clamped to the side of his face and the other was grabbing handfuls of my clothes and flesh as he tried to climb his way back to his feet. Finally, I managed to push him off of me and I threw myself up onto his desk so he couldn't grab me anymore.

"I saw his face. It wasn't a clean knife wound. There was a star-shaped gash on his cheek that looked like something had exploded out of his skull. Through the skin and muscle, I could see white bone. I was sitting up on his desk and I cowered away from the horror of his injury. The phone rang and in my panic I kicked it away from myself. Nathan was screaming. The knife was sliding under the door again, like it was a tongue, tasting the smears of blood that had spilled from Nathan. I yelled for him to calm down and he went for the window. I figured he was going to hang out and yell to the firemen again. I couldn't hear them banging anymore, so it was possible they had made it through the door at that point.

"The blade withdrew from its probing. Nathan was hanging out the window, shouting and pleading for help. I kept my eyes on the door, waiting for the blade to come back. I should have known—if he disappeared, it could only mean one thing. I guessed what the man was doing a moment too late. I yelled at Nathan to get back inside, but then he screamed incoherently with fresh pain in his voice. I pulled him back inside. He was screaming, but he looked fine until he slumped to the floor. That's when Dave and I saw that part of Nathan's skull had been sliced right off. There was barely any blood. We could see a perfect cross-section of part of his brain."

Christopher covered his face with his hands. While he took a moment to compose himself, the others shifted in their seats. Jessica took a deep breath and tried to shake the image from her head.

"Dave freaked out, of course. He ran for the door and threw it open. I could have told him what would happen. The man was standing right in the doorway. I saw the whole thing—every detail—like it was frozen in time. The lights in the hallway were on now, so the outline of his shape was, like, highlighted with light. Smoke curled up from the hand-rolled cigarette in his left hand. The rim of his hat was drooping in places and water dripped from it. There were patches of moss on his coat. All of his clothes were the exact same shade of brownish-gray. The top half of his face was lost in shadow, but the bottom half had deep grooves in the skin. Until he moved, he could have been a stone carving. He looked like a statue that nature is trying to reclaim. The knife shot out with his right arm, driving into Dave before he could move. I just spilled backwards, my legs churning as I tried to get away. I like to tell myself that it was just panic that sent me back through the window, but I knew what I was doing. I had a very keen sense of where that window was and I ducked my head as I rolled backwards through it. I know it only took a fraction of a second, but I had time to think as I spun towards the ground.

"I was screaming even before I hit, and I started running before I realized that I had broken bones. I didn't even feel those injuries until later. I just knew that my body wasn't moving right. The firemen who were milling around in the rain all froze and turned to look at me. My leg finally gave out for good when I was a few feet away. Running on a broken leg, one of my bones had chewed right through the skin. One of the firemen told me to take it easy. All I could do was scream."

Christopher seemed to deflate now that his story was over. Joe reached over and put a hand on Christopher's shoulder. The room was silent except for the sound of Christopher's breathing. When he straightened back up, Christopher used both hands to smooth his hair and he blinked to clear his eyes.

"Thank you, Christopher," Vivian said. There were other mumbled thanks from the group. Jessica added hers late. It seemed like a strange response to Jessica, but she went along with the others.

"I should add that they found plenty of evidence to support my claims. They found the bodies, and Terrence's hand right where I said it would be. From the man, they found footprints, moss, and a bit of cloth. They also had video of him when he killed the two security guards. He did that before he came to the dorm the second time. I thought I was going to be a suspect. I guess that's another horror movie thing where in the end nobody will believe the victim. It didn't happen with me. There was a search. They referred to him as an 'unknown assailant'. That sounds diminishing to me. It's like calling a tornado a brief period of wind. My overwhelming impression was that he was acting precisely as I expected him to. There's that movie, Poltergeist, where that psychic says, 'It knows what scares you. Don't give it any help.' It was like that. I was imagining the worst thing that could happen and it was coming true."

"It doesn't work both ways," Jessica said. "You can't describe him as a force of nature, like a tornado, and also blame yourself for bringing about the horror."

For her interruption, Jessica received a stern look from Billie. She looked to Vivian for support and saw that Vivian had a disapproving look on her face as well. Jessica crossed her legs and promised herself she would keep silent until she understood how this group worked.

"Thank you," Christopher said, "but that's unnecessary. I've made peace with my actions. I'm just trying to shed some light on what I consider to be the important part of how he operated, at least in my encounter. I've played around with different theories. It's interesting to think of the things he left behind. Terrence was a big, strong guy and wasn't afraid to fight. He didn't take any weapons when we went downstairs—nothing but his fists. That's what the man took from Terrence, aside from his life. He took Terrence's fist. From Nathan—the one who used his brain more than the rest of us—he took part of his skull, exposing the brain. Grant called the security guards and fire department. The man stabbed him through the voice box. It doesn't fit everyone, but I think there's some reasoning behind the way he dispatched each of us that night. I don't know why he let me live. That's the way I think about it—he *let* me live. There are ways he could have wrapped everything up. That case we talked about up in New Hampshire had similarities to mine, except there were no survivors. He made a choice to let me escape. I wish I knew why."

CHAPTER FOUR

Sleep

Work

"It's illegal, what Millan does, you know," Wendy whispered.

The woman was glancing over Jessica's shoulder as she counted out her tips to figure out what she had to contribute.

"I read that tip pooling was allowed in Nevada," Jessica said.

"Yeah, but not when Millan takes half of what we put in. Look at the numbers sometime. You'll see what everyone puts in and then do the math. She doesn't give back what we put in."

Jessica shrugged.

"Sometimes she barely covers minimum wage."

"Are other places better?" Jessica asked.

"Barely."

Wendy navigated through the maze of tables and then disappeared down the back hall.

Jessica didn't have a problem with her paycheck. It was enough to cover what she needed to cover. She wasn't trying to get rich or live in some kind of luxury.

"What *am* I trying to do," she asked herself and then glanced around to make sure nobody heard her. Christopher had been on her mind for days. Regardless of what Vivian said, Christopher was carrying all that around with him all the time. Even if he didn't think it was affecting him, that pain and tragedy lived in his head. After decades of time, he should have been able to hold all of it at arm's length and tell it like a story that had happened to someone else. At least that's what she hoped for herself.

"Everything okay?" a voice asked.

Jessica realized that she had been standing there with her tip money in her hand, just staring off at nothing.

"Fine, Ms. Millan."

The tiny despot narrowed her eyes. "The past couple of days, you don't look so good. Drugs?"

"No, nothing like that. I had a bad night's sleep I guess. There are some noisy neighbors at my place."

Her boss didn't believe the story.

"They don't know about earplugs where you're from?"

Jessica didn't want to be having this conversation. From watching her with other employees, she knew that Millan was a bulldog. The interrogation wouldn't stop until she got some sort of confession from Jessica. There had to be a way to derail her. Nothing came to mind until Jessica looked down at the money in her hands.

"Actually, I do have a question about tips and the tip pooling? Do you have a moment to talk about it?"

Ms. Millan turned and walked away as she answered.

"Make an appointment. I have a very busy schedule."

Jessica smiled. She had accidentally discovered a quick way to get out of an interrogation. Her boss was right though, she didn't look good. Ever since Christopher's story, deep sleep had been impossible. Every little sound woke her up. She needed to break the cycle of sleepless nights. There was only one idea that kept popping into her head.

Jessica double-checked the schedule. With Wednesday off, it was actually the perfect time.

Library

Jessica stared at the doorbell, wondering if she should press it again. Her finger was almost touching the metal when the door clicked and swung inwards. When she had come to the mansion for the meeting—Christopher's story—she had seen the man in the gray suit a few times, milling around and keeping everything tidy. Jessica hadn't gotten a chance to speak with him.

She had no idea if he recognized her.

"Hi. I'm Jessica. I was here a few nights ago and Vivian... or was it Hilda? Someone said that people can stay here if we... I just... I'm having problems getting a good night's sleep at my apartment and I thought..."

He pulled the door inwards and stood to the side with a sweeping hand gesture. She followed the track of his arm and saw a guest registry on a table under a big mirror.

"Oh. Okay. Let me just get my things."

He remained motionless. Jessica jogged back to her car and got the overnight bag from the passenger's seat. Still standing next to the door, he had his arms behind his back. Jessica forced herself to hold her questions inside—if he wasn't going to be polite enough to say anything, then she would remain silent as well.

Flipping open the guest book, she saw recent entries with names she recognized. Vivian, Joe, Wahid, and Hilda were all in there. Wahid had stayed four nights in a row a week before. Vivian had only stayed one night. Jessica filled her name in and wrote down the date. She glanced back to see if the butler would assign her a room. He was already gone. In the back of the registry, she found a handout that had guidelines for guests.

"Huh," she said, tucking the paper under her arm. She lifted her bag and headed for the meeting room. Putting her bag on top of the bar, she opened the refrigerator and helped herself to a sparkling water while she started to read the guidelines.

"Kitchen is open until 10," she said, glancing around as she talked to herself. "Wonder where it is?"

Jessica sat on one of the tall stools.

"Bedrooms with open doors are unoccupied. Close your door when you're not inside."

She was starting to regret not asking the butler a few questions. A map would have been nice.

"I guess I get to explore."

Jessica was about to get up when she thought of a better idea. It was possible that the butler or someone else would come and give her the official greeting. Just because he had been silent at the door didn't mean that she was on her own. There could be a whole process.

"Who just lets people come stay anyway?" she whispered into her sparkling water.

Glancing down at her bag, she wondered if the whole idea had been a mistake. She didn't have a ton of money, but there were a million hotels around. Surely she could find one cheap and clean enough to serve as a destination for a mini-vacation. For that matter, she could just go back to her apartment and try taking a long bath. It might be best to learn how to live with the mental images implanted by Christopher's story instead of running away from them.

"Thrashing. I'm thrashing," she said.

Jessica picked up her bag and walked back towards the entrance. There was a light on in the library. Instead of leaving, she headed that direction. In the doorway, she regretted her decision. Billie was sitting in one of the leather arm chairs with her legs folded under her and a book in her lap. She shook her head when she saw Jessica standing there.

"You making yourself at home?" Billie asked.

Jessica wasn't sure how to take that.

Her first impulse was to match the bristly tone that she thought was implied by Billie's flat delivery. Jessica preferred to meet a bully head on.

"Are you?"

"What's that supposed to mean?"

"I was told we could stay here one week out of the month. How long have you been here?"

Jessica was only guessing at the transgression based on the guest book.

Billie's response was something between a smile and a sneer.

Jessica strode into the room and set her bag next to one of the chairs. She turned and started scanning the spines of the books. Most didn't have any writing. Pulling one at random, she scanned the first couple of pages as she stood with her back to Billie, waiting for another confrontation. It didn't come. The book started with a long description of a dirt driveway and the boy and dog who lived at the end of it. Before the end of the second page, Jessica got the impression that the boy and dog were alone in the world. Everyone they knew had been taken away from them and it was up to them to survive or perish. The world wouldn't care one way or another. Those facts weren't presented directly in the text, but implied by the wording of the descriptions. It was exactly the kind of book that Jessica liked. It gave her room to spread out in the imagination of the author.

She found her way to her chair and kept reading as the boy and dog tried to catch something to cook for lunch. It was a beautiful relationship between the boy and dog. The kid caught a fish and the dog got a rabbit. They shared their meal around a small fire by the edge of the river. They ran and hid when a boat went by.

"Nobody wants your advice," Billie said.

Jessica looked up. In just a few short pages, she had become legitimately engrossed in the book and had almost forgotten that Billie was there.

"Pardon me?"

"Everyone came down on you in the meeting because you tried to give Chris advice. He doesn't want it or need it."

"Everyone? You gave me a nasty look. I think everyone else was fine. And, by the way, Christopher seemed perfectly able to tell me that he was fine. I don't think he needs you trying to meddle in his interactions either."

Billie shook her head. "You're here for one meeting and you already stepped in it. I'm just trying to help you fit in a little better. Some people can't be helped."

"Thanks for that," Jessica said. "Thanks for trying to give me advice. I don't want it or need it."

Billie got up, returned her book to a shelf, and left.

Jessica returned to the book. It was still good, but she found it difficult to fully lose herself in the world of the boy and dog again. The exchange with Billie kept playing over and over in her head.

Room

Jessica found the kitchen, eventually. The house seemed designed to keep company cordoned off into a a few public areas. The meeting room, bathrooms, library, and a couple of other sitting rooms were easily accessible. Getting to the kitchen meant going all the way to the end of a corridor that appeared to be a dead end. At the end, she realized that the hall jutted off to the side. The walls and lighting hid that fact until she turned and accidentally discovered it.

The kitchen and dining room felt cozy compared to the other spaces. The ceilings weren't as high and the decor was less formal. She found a refrigerator with packaged meals. The sign said, "Please serve yourself," so she did. With her book about the boy and the dog, she sat at the counter and picked at a salad with her fingers.

The feeling that she was an interloper wouldn't leave. It had been a mistake to come alone—she should have asked Vivian to show her the ropes. It had been an impulse, and she regretted the decision. That wasn't enough to make her leave though. As awkward as she felt, it would be even more embarrassing to be chased off by Billie's sour attitude.

After eating, Jessica decided that she would go to bed early and get out of there first thing in the morning. For the hundredth time, she read the handout. There was no map, or any indication where the bedrooms might be. If she managed to find an unoccupied bedroom, the door would be open—that was the only clue she had.

When she finished eating, Jessica tucked the handout into her book, grabbed her bag, and began the search for stairs. Based on what she had seen, the bedrooms had to be upstairs. In the main lobby, the stairs led up to an open space with another balcony. It looked over the back lawn. She figured that she had to be standing directly above the patio where the smokers congregated.

"Okay," she said to herself, looking at the big open room. There were no doors to lead to the rest of the second floor. It was just another public space—a dead end.

Defeated, she descended to the lobby again. Flipping through the guest book, she figured that she had to have missed something. There had to be a map or instructions or something. It was getting late to ring the doorbell again to summon the butler. She could handle being confused, but wouldn't resort to being rude. With that in mind, she came to a decision. The chairs in the library were comfortable enough. She could just camp out in one of those and read her book until she fell asleep.

Tucking her bag under the chair, she found a blanket on a bench and curled up with her book. It was clear that the boy and the dog were going to go on an adventure. It almost would have been better if they just stayed put. They had the river for water and fish. The dog seemed capable of catching rabbits whenever he wanted. They could just live there and grow up in peace. That wasn't the kind of story that made a good book though. Jessica had to admit that an adventure would be more interesting to read about. Still, she hoped that it would be an adventure of their choosing instead of having to flee from some ill-intentioned adults or something.

The more she read, the more she began to wonder if there were any other people in the fictional world of the book. It seemed like the boy and dog wandered around without worry of being discovered.

"No, wait, there was a boat," she whispered to herself. Jessica flipped back to confirm that it was true. Lately, it seemed like when she read a book she would really just skim over the words while she made up her own story. It was often more interesting and gave her less anxiety than trusting where the author would take her.

Jessica returned to the words, promising herself that she would pay attention and not let her imagination wander. The dog and the boy had found an abandoned house and were looting the pantry, trying to find any cans that hadn't exploded with rot. Jessica realized that her eyes were drifting shut, but she didn't fight it. Even cramped into a chair, sleep would be a blessing.

"Come on," a voice said.

Jessica almost dropped her book when she straightened up. Her heart was pounding as she blinked and recognized Billie standing in the doorway.

"Come on, you don't have to sleep in here. I'll show you the best room."

"Oh. That's okay."

"Would you rather be completely independent, or comfortable?"

Jessica thought about that. "Comfortable."

"Then follow me."

Billie moved fast. Grabbing her bag and leaving the blanket bunched up in the chair, Jessica shuffled after Billie as she rounded the corner at the end of the hall. Jessica recognized it from a few nights before. It was the same passage that Hilda had used to get to the east balcony. Billie didn't go through the drawing room though. Instead, she pressed on a panel that gave no indication that it was a door. There were stairs on the other side.

"Ullman is supposed to show you to the residence hall, but more often than not he skips the tour now. He has a bad tooth and the pain makes him angry at the whole world."

"Ullman is the butler?"

"Don't call him a butler. He'll strangle you. He's the caretaker. According to him, a butler manages staff and he doesn't have any direct staff, only service providers. I think he would like to be a butler."

"Oh. I guess I never knew what the title meant."

They were at the top of the stairs. In both directions down the hall, Jessica saw open doors of rooms.

"The best one is down here," Billie said, pointing.

"I'll take anything."

"Just take this one. It has a private bath and remote control shades on the windows. You'll need them. Otherwise the sun will chase you out early."

Billie stopped at the door. Jessica stepped into the room and flipped on the lights. It was a beautiful bedroom and she could see the attached bath through a door on the far side.

"You're on this hall too?"

"No. I'm a permanent resident. My room is next to Ullman's."

"Oh. Thank you."

Billie's answer was a wave as she walked away. Jessica closed the door and clicked the lock as quietly as she could.

Breakfast

In the soft black silence of the bed, Jessica stayed until a rumble of hunger drove her to reach for the remote control. Fumbling with it, her finger found the correct button and the blinds began to rise, letting in daylight. Her body was completely rested, but her brain was already firing with questions. Getting up and getting ready, she wished that she had brought better clothes. She left the door to her room open—she wasn't intending to come back.

In the light of day, the house didn't make any more sense to her. She found the stairs back to the first floor. After some fumbling and wrong turns, she reached the library. The book slipped into its spot, and disappeared into the collection of books on the shelf. Jessica didn't pretend that she would come back and read the rest of their adventure. The dog had been taken away from the boy and the adventure turned into a rescue mission. Jessica couldn't trust an author who would make such a naked play on her feelings like that. Regardless of how things turned out, the boy and the dog would have to live the rest of their lives knowing that they were destined to wind up alone. It was too harsh a lesson for a character so young and innocent.

The meeting room was empty. She glanced through the windows to the terrace to see if anyone was smoking outside. There were gardeners in the distance, taking advantage of the cooler morning temperatures to get some trimming done.

Jessica glanced at the front door, wondering if she should simply make a clean getaway. Her stomach clenched with a painful cramp and she decided on helping herself to another free meal before she hit the road. It was no easier to find the kitchen.

"They ought to paint arrows on the floor," she said to herself as she rounded the last corner.

Billie was at the table. She waved a piece of toast in what might have been a friendly gesture. Jessica walked over to her and set her bag down next to one of the chairs.

"Thank you," Jessica said. "I realized that I never thanked you last night."

"No, you did," Billie said. Crumbs blew out of her mouth when she spoke. She chewed for a moment before she finished. "You didn't sound like you meant it, but you did thank me."

Jessica shrugged and looked towards the stove. "What's good here?"

"Most days, Glen. He's the chef and he makes a killer grilled cheese. He's off today though. Everything's in the fridge."

Jessica headed that direction, stopping to pick a banana from the bowl. She found a bagel and orange juice. After glancing around for a toaster, she decided to eat the bagel cold. Her chair squeaked on the tile when she sat back down.

"This is so weird," Jessica said as she peeled her banana.

"Which part?"

"The part where there's this mansion and I've never met the owner but I'm allowed to stay and eat their food."

"You get used to it," Billie said. "And there's a price for everything."

"Oh?"

"Not, like, literally. I mean you've already paid the price for everything, you just didn't know it. If you could give up the free bed and food, and go back to the time before you were nearly murdered, would you do it."

"Of course."

"Then the price wasn't worth it."

"How did you know I was nearly murdered?" Jessica asked.

"It's the reason you're here. Remember Christopher's story?"

Jessica nodded. That story was pretty much invading all of her waking thoughts.

"He mentioned that there was video of the man. None of those people who witnessed the video are guests here. Christopher comes here because he was the one nearly murdered."

Jessica chewed on part of the bagel as she thought about that.

"If I were rich enough to have a house like this, I don't think I would invite other victims here. I would spend my money trying to forget my troubles, not remind myself of them."

"Misery loves company," Billie said. "Maybe you would set this place up like this to remind yourself that you're not the only person in pain."

Jessica picked up her banana peel. "One of these cabinets has a trash can. I found it last night."

Billie pointed over her shoulder.

Jessica found the trash and jumped when someone with a deep voice cleared their throat. She turned to find the butler glaring at her. She closed the cabinet.

"Yes?"

"We compost, miss," the butler said. Jessica reminded herself that he was *not* the butler, but she couldn't remember what Billie had said his job actually was. She also couldn't remember his name.

"Oh?"

He slowly extended his arm, pointing to a different cabinet.

"Thank you. I'll remember that next time."

Over at the table, Billie barked out a laugh. Jessica looked over, but Billie seemed engaged in staring down at the crumbs on her plate.

"We didn't formally meet last night," she said, extending a hand. "My name is Jessica."

He glanced down at her hand before he turned and walked off.

"Nice to meet you," she called after him. She went back to the table and found Billie smiling at her. "What?"

"He's doing his best to intimidate you."

"I don't understand—why would he be so gruff with the guests?"

"Fewer guests means less work, I imagine. And he's not gruff with everyone, just people he doesn't like."

"That makes me feel great."

"Don't worry about it. He absolutely *despises* me sometimes."

"Great."

Jessica chewed her way through more of the bagel, washing it down with juice when it became too gummy. Billie was looking at her.

"What?"

"There's a toaster over there, next to the oven."

"Good to know. You live here permanently?"

Billie nodded. "Yup."

Jessica nodded. "Is it tough to hear stories like Christopher's and then pass through that room where he spilled his guts to us?"

"I'm used to it."

"Every time I've walked through that room, I remember his descriptions of that night. He has such clear pictures in his head, and then he painted that room with his horrible memories. This place feels haunted by his trauma."

"I've heard worse," Billie said. Her voice was cold and low—the statement was nothing more than fact. "You will too if you keep coming back."

Jessica shuddered.

CHAPTER FIVE

Wahid

Office

Jessica was sitting at the bar next to Billie when the first of the group began to arrive. She had meant to move to one of the chairs so she wouldn't be looking down at the circle, but once the others filed into the room it seemed like it was too late. Leaving her spot would be like distancing herself from Billie in front of the group.

She introduced herself to the other guy who came to sit at the bar. He mumbled his name and she didn't quite catch it. He eyed her like she was an interloper. Jessica thought she might offer him her seat, but that's when Wahid started talking.

"Jessica, I'll offer you the chance to share tonight, but I would assume that you're not quite ready."

She rejected the idea with a tiny shake of her head. Between Billie and the mumbling man, she felt trapped at the bar and wished she could sit anywhere else. She was an interloper. The discomfort distracted her so she barely heard what Wahid said next.

A few seconds later, she forced herself to pay attention because it was clear that he was telling his story.

"The office occupied a space above a few shops. My

receptionist and technical person had gone home for the day. The only people left were the creatives. I never was able to predict when they would find inspiration, so I stopped trying. For myself, I made no plans as a deadline approached, knowing that on any given evening something might spark. As soon as I saw the clouds rolling in, I had the sense that the brainstorm might be coming. Foul weather was not always a good predictor of creative outbursts, but the opposite was usually true. On a good day, I couldn't keep them inside for anything."

Billie leaned back and pulled a can from the refrigerator. Jessica thought that it was for her until Billie stretched to hand it to the mumbling man on the other side.

Wahid continued his story.

"The rain came in an instant. By then, the staff were all collected around one desk. They were all working on the same big sheet of paper, drawing out their ideas as they explained them. Innovations were piling one on top of the other. They would work like that for minutes or hours and then, as if a bell had sounded, they would split up and go to their individual desks in order to execute their group vision.

"I had enough experience to know that they would stall out if they didn't eat. I waited for a lull in order to collect dinner orders and then I quietly moved to my office so I could call the order in. I was feeling proud of myself. When I started working there, my authority had been rejected by the group. I was an outsider and I didn't understand anything about the type of work that they did. They expected, I suppose, that someone should have been elevated from their ranks in order to manage the office. That would have been so silly. To take someone with their skill and put them in charge would have not only failed, but it would have also wasted their talents. I, on the other hand, knew only how to recognize patterns in behavior and facilitate smooth interactions. Those were my skills. It had taken me a few weeks to truly grasp how to keep things moving at a good pace, but I was happy that night because they were all happy. I grabbed my coat and umbrella and left them to go get the food."

Jessica felt the temperature of the room change at this part of the story. They all knew what was coming.

"As I exited, he was standing at the door. I told him that the shops were closed for the evening and pointed up the street to where the central market had shops open all night. He asked to come in to get dry. I told him that I couldn't and I closed and locked the door behind me. Normally, for such a short trip, I wouldn't have bothered to lock the door, but something told me that the man would try to gain entry after I left. I was correct, of course. I don't know who let him in, but I can guess that he knocked after I left. When I returned with the food, I found the door unlocked and puddles of wet footprints leading to the elevator.

"If my hands hadn't been full of bags, I probably would have called the police right then. I could picture the whole thing so clearly in my head. The man had no doubt knocked loud enough that they heard him upstairs. One of my staff would have broken away from the group to go resolve the distraction. I was irritated —not because of the man who was now loose in the building, but because he had disturbed their concentration. I pressed the button and stepped around the wet spot in the middle of the elevator when it came.

"I returned to the office, and distributed the food around to the different desks. The group was still huddled. Most of them had fallen silent by then, so I knew that they were about to break off and return to their individual desks. There, they would begin to burn through the assignment while they absentmindedly ate the meals that I had left. I put the last carton on Scott's desk and noticed that he wasn't in the huddle. Thinking that he might have gone to the bathroom, I went that direction. I suppose it was just the herding instinct in me. I wanted to know the whereabouts of my entire flock. There were three bathrooms off of the break room. One of the doors was closed, so I figured that must be where Scott had disappeared. That would have been the end of my search except I spotted a puddle just outside the closed door. It could have been water spilled from the sink, or a leak, but I knew precisely what it was."

Jessica put a hand over her mouth to stop herself from saying anything. She had a tendency to fill in silences with her own narrative. This group wouldn't tolerate that.

"I stepped carefully around the puddle so I could knock on the door. There was no answer. I called Scott's name. At that point in the creative process, everyone's attention could be broken by the slightest interruption. A few of the workers appeared in the doorway as I yelled for Scott through the bathroom door. I caught a glimpse of my audience and knew that the night was ruined. They would never get back on track. I had nothing to lose. I yelled one more time and then tried the handle. It was locked, but I had the key. I said something like, 'I hate to do this, but I'm coming in.'"

Wahid wiped his brow with the back of his hand.

"With me awkwardly straddling the puddle and opening the door, the others saw him first and gasped. He was blocking the door. I had to put my shoulder against it to gently push it aside. The door sweep was pushing streaks of blood and water across the vinyl floor. I barked for one of the others to call for an ambulance. These bathrooms were small–single occupancy–so it was easy for me to glance in the mirror and see that Scott was alone in there. I reached around the door, found his wrist and discovered a weak pulse.

"I called for one of the others to help me. I was too big to squeeze through the gap in the door, and Scott needed to be moved in order to get to him. I suppose I should have left him, since I guessed it was a crime scene, but I also thought that we should be putting pressure on whatever wound had left that blood on the floor. We couldn't let him bleed out just because it might be tampering with evidence. A tiny woman named Ophelia stepped up and said she could fit. She moved so carefully, stepping around the fluids and threading herself through the gap. I knew she would be too delicate to actually help, but I was wrong, She said that he had a laceration in his side and was unconscious. Then, she asked me for the hammer and screwdriver. I thought she was insane. I asked what she intended to do, but someone else was already handing them through the gap. A moment later, I heard her tapping and I understood. I suppose I had a communication deficit in my panic. I couldn't understand why she kept saying, 'Hinges. Hinges,' until I heard that tapping. I grabbed the door handle and then the other side of the door when it came loose. It was heavy. Two of us managed to pull it through and set it against the wall.

"Scott was splayed on the floor. His pants were still on. Ophelia's hands were dark with his blood. She had them pressed to his side. I took that as a good sign. He still had enough blood to flow, so I thought he might be okay. That's when Evan crashed through the doorway from the office. He was frantic and screaming about something. Again, I was having a hard time understanding what he was saying. I followed him because he was pointing and gesturing. Harlin was splayed on the floor between the desks. The phone cord was wrapped around his neck and he wasn't moving. I tried to go to him, but Evan held me back. April spoke to Evan very slowly and asked what happened. He told us that a man had appeared from the shadows and attacked Harlin as soon as he tried to use the phone to call for help. There was another phone on the wall in the break room. I reached for that so I could call for help, but Evan grabbed my arm. He was convinced that if I tried I would be killed too.

"April grabbed Evan's arms and told him to run down to the street and flag someone for help. The door to the stairwell was right there off of the break room. I'm sure she thought the same thing that I thought—the killer had to be on the opposite end of the building. Evan should have been safe running down to the street. Of course I don't have to tell you that we heard his scream as he ran down the stairs. We rushed to help him but found only a smeared trail of blood that led towards the basement. April said, 'There's more than one of them. We should barricade ourselves in here.' I liked the idea, but it was going to be tough.

We could shut the door to the office and move the table with the coffee machine in front of it. There was no way to block the stairwell though. I said that and April took charge.

"While Ophelia continued to tend to Scott, April and I moved the table in front of one door. Then, she helped me drag the bathroom door and we found a way to wedge it in front of the stairwell door. It wasn't perfect, but it was something. The two of us put our weight against the desk, just in case someone tried to muscle it aside. While we did that, April reached the phone and called. We were all so silent that I could hear the rain on the roof and the sound of the operator's voice from the phone. They told her to stay on the line—help was on the way. On the floor, Scott began to convulse."

Wahid took a deep breath and covered his face with his hands for a moment.

"It's difficult to watch someone die slowly. I'm sure a lot of you understand perfectly what I'm saying. His body, starved for circulation, was thrashing with the last of its energy. Ophelia tried to do CPR, but I think she knew it was a lost cause. I was pushing back on the table so hard that the edge cut into my hands. Holding the phone to her ear, April was clinging to the receiver. It was her lifeline to sanity. The rest of us didn't have that."

Billie reached over and handed Wahid a bottle of water. He drank half of it in two long swallows and then stared at the liquid sloshing in the bottle for a moment.

"He began to pound on the door from the stairwell, trying to dislodge the bathroom door that was wedged there. For a moment, I thought we should move the desk and flee through the office, but then I remembered what April said. There was more than one attacker. Driving us into the arms of another assailant was probably the whole point of slamming on the door. Ophelia gave up on Scott and looked up at me. 'What do they want? Why are they doing this?' she asked. I was one who facilitated everything. I brought them fresh supplies and fetched their dinner. I made sure that paychecks were mailed on time. It was natural that she looked to me for an answer, but in that moment, I took her questions as accusations. I yelled that it wasn't my fault. I turned the man away when I saw him. How was I to know that he would break in and start murdering?"

Jessica wanted to tell him that it wasn't his fault, but she kept her mouth shut.

"May I have a moment?" Wahid asked.

Introduction

She turned to her right.

"Hi, I'm Jessica," she said, putting out her hand.

"We met last week," the man said.

"I remember. I'm not great with names when they come at me all at once," she said, trying to smile. "So I thought I would re-introduce myself and hope that you might tell me your name again?"

"Keith," he said as he stood up.

She withdrew her hand as Keith walked away. Jessica took a deep breath and turned back to Billie, who had also stood up. Together, Keith and Billie were walking towards the doors to the terrace.

Jessica looked over at the couch, where Vivian was staring down at her cellphone. When Vivian looked up, Jessica said, "Too many names. I can't keep track."

"Oh. Yeah. We've all heard these stories a hundred times, so I guess the names are burned into our brains. I can almost picture little Ophelia. I suspected she resembled my girlfriend in college from the way that Wahid has described her. I think he cared for her a lot, although I don't know if it was romantic or like a little sister."

Jessica nodded. She had been talking about the names of the people in their support group, but she didn't correct Vivian. The names would come soon enough, she was sure. Either that or she would decide that staying with the group and hearing the terrible stories wasn't worth the nightmares. At the moment, she was still on the fence.

"I heard you stayed the night?" Vivian asked.

"Yes. It was interesting. I don't think that the butler—I know he's not a butler—I don't think he likes me much."

"That puts you in good company. I was going to invite you to join me here some weekend so I could show you the ropes, but I guess you beat me to it."

"I work on weekends," Jessica said.

Vivian nodded.

"Do you work?"

"As seldom as possible," Vivian said with a smile.

They heard laughter from the terrace.

Some of the smokers were filing back in. Jessica looked at one of the soft chairs and considered moving. She abandoned the thought as Billie and Keith approached. It would be rude to move.

Wahid was one of the last to take his seat. His face was shiny. He dabbed his forehead with a paper towel.

After a sigh, he said, "April was yelling into the phone for them to hurry. She said that the killer was trying to break down the door. I wondered how we would tell the difference when the police arrived, so I told her to ask when they would be here. She didn't seem to hear me. Ophelia found the screwdriver and hammer from earlier. I didn't know what she meant to do until I saw her trying to hammer the screwdriver between the door and the frame. I suppose she meant to wedge it shut, but I yelled at her to back away. I was afraid that she would accidentally make it easer for the man to get in."

Wahid paused and wiped his lips.

"This next part, I cannot explain. I suppose that's obvious, since none of us can explain any of these events, but this part..."

He shook his head.

"Scott sat up. I hadn't touched him since I felt his pulse, but I was sure that he was dead. He sat up and opened his eyes. April stopped yelling into the phone. Ophelia stopped hammering, and even the man stopped pounding on the stairwell door. The only sounds were the rain and the chattering of the operator coming through the phone. With open, but unseeing eyes, he turned towards me. Scott's voice came out like a croak. He said, 'When this is done, consume my flesh. I don't want to go to waste.' My vision swam and my body went weak. The animation washed out of Scott's body again and he collapsed to the floor. Everything resumed. April yelled into the phone, the man pounded, and Ophelia pounded at the screwdriver in response. I've thought about that moment quite a bit in the years since it happened. I want to say that it was just a dream or a random misfire of my brain due to the stress. I wish I could go back and understand what happened just then. It was a few seconds later that chaos invaded our break room."

Wahid shifted forward, leaning over his feet.

He spoke quickly.

"The door began to splinter and Ophelia gave up her attempt to bolster it. She yelled for me to do something. April yelled at me to stay put, holding the desk. She said that the others would get us if we didn't hold the office door shut. I was frozen. None of what they said mattered because the stairwell door was being split in two. He hacked at it. I assumed that he had an axe.

"Ophelia backed up when the door cracked. It fell from the frame and took the bathroom door down as well. He stood there in the doorway. His coat and hat were still dripping. His arms hung at his sides and I didn't see a knife or an axe anywhere. That's when he reached inside his coat. It didn't move like fabric —it was very still. His hand came out with a pouch and while we stared at him he dropped tabacco onto a limp piece of paper. The operator's voice sounded thin through the receiver. They were asking if we were still on the line. The man lifted a soggy cigarette to his lips and flipped open a metal lighter. When I was a child, I had perfect pitch. When he opened his lighter, the cover rang with a musical note. It was a an F."

Wahid whistled a single note. The sound of it, and the memory it evoked, made Jessica want to run screaming from the room. Her legs were solid rock though. If she had tried to run, she would have collapsed to the floor.

"When he pulled air through his cigarette, it crackled at the flame. I couldn't believe that it was dry enough to burn, but he exhaled a blue smoke proving me wrong. In the distance, I could hear sirens approaching. If I had been closer, I would have tried to stop Ophelia. She ran at him with the screwdriver aimed up at his heart. She was so small that it looked like a child was trying to attack the man. He didn't do anything except raise his hand. I suppose the hand held a knife because when she ran to him I saw it emerge from her back when she was impaled.

"I put a hand out and grabbed April's arm. At that moment, I thought that as long as we didn't run forward and throw ourselves at him, like Ophelia had just done, that we would be okay. I was wrong. Ophelia fell to the side, already dead before she slipped off of his knife. As he came towards us, we huddled together. It never occurred to try to move the desk and flee through the office or to try to bolt for one of the bathrooms and lock myself inside. I know why a deer freezes in headlights. There are some fates that are so terrifying to contemplate that the brain rejects the notion of dealing with them. My mind and body shut down. I simply watched."

Wahid looked down at the floor.

"April didn't say a word as he slit her throat. I stared at the burning orange end of his cigarette and heard the gurgling and splashing of her blood. The call to the operator had been disconnected and the phone clicked and, buzzed, and then complained with a loud alarm. I was arm's length, staring at the man's face. His skin was so thick and wrinkled that I thought it might be a mask. He was wet but also appeared to be caked in a layer of dirt. The cracked skin drank in the rain water, but was never sated. His eyes were cold stones. They turned to me. I remember thinking that he didn't even need to spill my blood. My life ended when I looked at his eyes. I assumed that any second my heart would stop beating.

"Through the door, over the sound of the rain, I heard the police shouting as they entered the office. I opened my mouth but no sound would come out. The man backed away from me and stepped over the broken door. A moment later, he was disappearing down the stairs and the police were pounding on the door behind me. I found my voice and yelled for help. They pushed against the door and the desk that I was leaning against. It took me several seconds to realize that I had to move so they could get to me. They burst through and one tackled me. I pointed at the stairs. A policeman leapt over the door, hit the puddle that had gathered at the top of the stairs, and his legs went out from under him. I believe he died at the bottom of that flight of stairs. His head smashed against the railing. I was forgotten for a moment while they ran to help him.

"Despite April being killed while she was right next to me, I barely had any blood on me. They photographed me numerous times as they undressed me. That evidence is probably what saved me from being accused. April aslo helped me a lot. While she was on the phone with the operator, I think she gave them our names and said we were being attacked by unknown assailants. The police knew they were looking for an intruder even though the only evidence they had of him were random puddles of rainwater. There was a camera in the lobby near the shops, but apparently it was malfunctioning. It held no evidence of me returning with the food or the man breaking in.

"I found Simon after reading about his story and I reached out to him. That's when I discovered that he had already joined this group of fellow victims. I'm happy to have met you. It doesn't ease my guilt, but it helps to know that others are surviving with the same feelings. I find it easy to forgive each of you for your actions in the face of this monstrosity. It's funny that I can hear someone else's tale and say, 'Nobody should be expected to handle that kind of event.' There's no possible way I could excuse what I did. I was a coward. Worse than being a coward is knowing that you would do everything precisely the same way if it occurred again."

The room was silent after Wahid finished speaking. Jessica looked down at her hands as she held back the platitudes and comforts that sprang to her lips.

They waited in silence for what felt like an eternity.

Hilda finally said, “Another break, or shall we be dismissed?”

“Let’s take a break and come back,” Bille said.

The majority of the group voiced agreement. Some, like Jessica, remained silent.

Business

Joe didn’t sit down when everyone arrived back in their meeting area. Instead, he stood near the head of the table that sat between the chairs and the couch.

“I’ve spoken with a few of you individually. I thought it was the right time to begin talking about business again, but opinions vary on this. I thought maybe we should put the matter to a vote. If anyone has thoughts they would like to share with the group before we vote are we all okay with doing that now?”

Jessica glanced around, wondering if anyone was going to explain what was going on.

People were turning to their neighbors and more than a few of them turned to look at Billie specifically. After most shook their heads, it appeared that Joe’s question had been answered.

“I’ll open with my thoughts—if we had any advantage at all, it is rapidly disappearing. I think a perfect plan a year from now has less chance of working than a good plan today. Simply because he might be on his heels, I would like to start planning immediately. Anyone else?”

Jessica started to raise her hand. She wanted to get context for whatever came next. When Hilda began speaking, Jessica folded her hands together in her lap.

“I’ll say what I think a number of us are thinking,” Hilda said. “He’s a planner. I think many of us can agree that he plans and plots carefully. If we give him time to do that now, we might not have another chance. He might seek to eliminate the threat before it can rise again. I agree with Joe that we should act fast.”

The group seemed to consider Hilda’s thoughts. A couple of

people nodded along, but Jessica could read most of them. Vivian was staring at a spot on the floor. Wahid appeared to be still lost in the story that he had told. Christopher seemed detached. Joe paced.

Next to Jessica, Billie's whole body was tensed. Nearly-visible lines of anger rose from her. Glancing to her other side, Jessica thought that the mumbling man seemed disinterested in the whole conversation.

"Billie?" Joe asked. His tone, always businesslike and to the point, was softer when he addressed her. "Care to offer counterpoint?"

"You know how I feel. All of you do. As far as we know, just getting together like this is a terrible idea, and we don't have to sit around and guess at the consequences."

"So, for the record, you don't want to plan our next steps. Does that mean you'll excuse yourself?" Joe asked.

"No, that's not what that means," Billie said. She slid from her stool and stood. Joe shrank to one of the chairs when Billie began to speak. Her presence commanded their attention.

"I understand perfectly well why you all are so fired up. I am too," Billie said. "But I'll remind you of what I said six months ago—you have to understand what you *have* and then you must be prepared to lose it all. Many of you sat right here and told me that you had *nothing left* to lose. Do you still feel the same way? Have you forgotten so soon, or do you still think that it won't happen to you? Look at me. Ironic, isn't it? I was the one sounding the alarm. When I shouted on and on about the barking dog, I was the one who was bitten."

"We all lost..." Vivian began to say.

Billie cut her off with a glance.

"I won't object to your plots and plans. In fact, I will help to the best of my ability. But you all better pray that you're not the one to catch it in the face next time. Pray that you don't find out how right I am."

Nobody spoke as Billie sat down again.

Jessica couldn't hold her tongue any longer. She couldn't

stand the tension.

"Can someone fill me in?" Jessica asked.

The mumbler was the first to get up and walk away. He went towards the smoking terrace. His movement seemed to be their cue. They all stood and headed off in different directions, leaving Jessica sitting there alone.

CHAPTER SIX

Vacation

Room

"You moving in?" Billie asked.

Jessica nearly dropped her book. After placing her bookmark, she put her hand to her heart and said, "You just scared the hell out of me."

"Sorry," Billie said from the doorway. Jessica waved her in. Billie sat on the edge of one of the chairs near the door. "I saw your car outside and just thought I would say hi."

Jessica nodded.

"Yeah, I have the day off tomorrow, so I thought it would be a like a mini-vacation to come stay. My apartment is fine, but they're replacing the sidewalks. They start a little early for me. I prefer to sleep in on my day off."

"You want to come downstairs and have a drink?"

Jessica looked down at herself. She was already in her pajamas, but they were her "formal" pajamas. She decided they were good enough for light social activity.

With a shrug, she said, "Yeah, okay."

"Don't forget to close the door," Billie said as they exited to the hallway. "Ullman will have your room cleaned if you leave it for five minutes with the door open."

Jessica laughed and said, "I just don't get that guy."

"He's going through his own things."

They turned the corner to the stairs.

"Oh yeah?"

"That's his story. I don't want to gossip."

"Of course," Jessica said.

"But suffice to say that he has every right to join our little meetings, if you know what I mean."

"Oh?" Jessica said. It took her a second to understand the implication. "Oh!"

"Dylan is joining us for drinks. Hope that's okay with you."

"Dylan?"

"You've met."

Jessica slowed for a second and then rushed to catch up with Billie again. Until they rounded the corner to the meeting room and she saw him, she had no idea who Dylan could be. It was the mumbler. Since moving to Las Vegas, Jessica was pretty sure that there were only three people who didn't like her. The first was her boss—the tiny tyrant. The second was the butler—or *not* the butler—Mr. Ullman. The third was the man at the bar who had only sneered at her attempts at conversation.

"Dylan, Jessica. Jessica, Dylan," Billie said as they approached. "You guys met."

Jessica waved. Dylan raised a glass in response.

She sat down on the couch nearest the bar, feeling self-conscious about her pajamas.

"Seven and seven?" Billie asked.

"Light pour," Jessica said with a nod. "Too much before bed gives me nightmares."

"Fair enough," Billie said. When she poured the alcohol, she went slow and stopped when Jessica nodded. It was barely enough to call it a cocktail. Jessica didn't have any intention of losing any inhibitions.

"You must have been confused as hell the other night," Billie said. "I thought about it later, and how you reacted. You were all like, 'Can anyone explain what's going on?' and we all just left."

"Guilty," Dylan said, raising his hand.

"But, believe me, that tension was completely real. You'll catch on eventually."

"Yeah, that was weird," Jessica said. She thanked Billie as she took her drink and sipped it. "What exactly was that all about?"

Dylan was taking a sip of his own drink when she asked. He waved a hand and shook his head as he swallowed.

"He's right—we shouldn't talk about it. I know this is weird, but people freak out about conversations outside the group. One thing that the whole group claims to hold sacred is no side chatter."

"Preach," Dylan said.

"I guess I'll just be in the dark then."

"Don't take offense," Billie said. "They have their reasons. You'll get the story eventually, but it will go easier at the beginning of a talk instead of after a big long story like we had last time."

"Thank you," Jessica said.

There was a brief silence. Billie clinked another ice cube into her glass, sipped, and then smiled for a moment. It was a sad smile.

"You work?" Dylan asked.

"Me? Yeah. I work as a hostess over at Rosie's."

"The meat grinder," Dylan said.

"Yes, that's what a lot of people there call it," Jessica said. "It's not too bad."

"There are better places," Dylan said. "If you can survive the meat grinder for six months, you'll be able to get a job in any number of places. Rosie's will take anyone—it pulls in all the fresh meat and grinds them up. But if you survive there, you've proven yourself."

"They do have a lot of turnover," Jessica said. "Even since I've been there, it feels like some of the best people have already moved on."

Dylan nodded. "I did eighteen months there while I was on probation. They were the only place that would take me."

Billie reached over and smacked his arm with a smile. “You never told me that. *I* worked there when I was on probation—until Simon got me out of it.”

“Oh, I know,” Dylan said. “I kept it to myself. You needed the job and you didn’t need me whispering about what a hole that place is. I let you do your time in misery on your own.”

“Huh,” Billie said. “Well, fair enough. So, Jessica, are you on probation?”

“Me? No,” Jessica said, immediately regretting her tone. “No. I just... I have to find a job when I move to a new place. It’s the only way that I really feel settled. I had a little money in savings when I moved to Sacramento and I always felt like I was an imposter there. It was just like the world’s worst vacation. After that, I decided that my first priority had to be employment, regardless of how good or bad the job.”

“That’s smart,” Dylan said.

Billie shook her head. “I’m too lazy for all that. I only work when I absolutely have to.”

Dylan laughed.

“I’m serious,” Billie said. “I’ll have to get a job soon. I’m about to lose my cellphone.”

“Ullman will cover it,” Dylan said. “He won’t let his precious get her hands dirty.”

Billie sneered at him. “You’re a jerk.”

“Wouldn’t offend you if it weren’t true,” he said.

“Where do you work now?” Jessica asked, hoping to steer the conversation back to a more civil place.

“I work in free enterprise,” he said.

“Sorry?”

“He works for Enterprise car rentals,” Billie said.

“Yes, where everyone feels *free* to vomit in the car before they return it. Free Enterprise,” he said, raising his glass. “On a good day, the vomit hasn’t dried into the carpet and the tips flow like... vomit that hasn’t dried into the carpet, I guess.”

Jessica frowned at the mental image his words conjured.

“The worst part is how quickly you get used to cleaning

people's fluids, you know?"

Jessica nodded. "Actually, I *do* know."

"Oh, of course, hostess at the meat grinder. Yes, I forgot who I was talking to for a second," he said. "You probably see as much puke as I do."

"That's a competition I'm proud to no longer be a part of," Billie said.

"You know what bothers me?" Jessica asked. "I mean, I'm okay with cleaning up accidents. People come here to really cut loose and sometimes they go too far. I get all that. What bothers me is that I can't turn on the TV or go to the movies anymore without seeing someone puke. In horror movies, romantic comedies, you name it—when they want to show someone having a strong reaction to something, they always make them puke. Why is that an acceptable thing to put on the screen?"

Dylan nodded. "Totally. I'm with you."

"I would assume you guys were desensitized," Billie said.

"Nope," Jessica said.

"Well, what about slasher films. That's what I don't like. Why is it okay to show *that* on screen? All that stabbing and blood," Billie said.

"Didn't you say something about that the other night? We like horror movies because they allow us to rehearse for the worst moments?" Jessica asked.

"Great memory on this one," Dylan said, nodding.

"Yes," Billie said. "I believe that watching scary movies is like a rehearsal for dealing with trauma, but that doesn't mean I condone recreating scenes with stabbing and blood flowing everywhere. There are some things that people might not be equipped to see. It's possible to stare at the sun so long that you damage your eyes permanently. Maybe blood and gore has the same effect on your soul."

"Maybe," Dylan said. "But this also might be the most sanitized time in history. In the past, people were constantly confronted with war and butchering animals and all that. As a generation, we've probably seen less real blood than any generation to walk this planet."

"Did you just try to slip into my generation?" Billie asked. "Do you even realize how old you are?"

"Very funny," Dylan said. "At least I still look good for my age."

"Can I ask you guys something?" Jessica asked.

"As long as we don't have to promise to answer," Billie said.

Jessica nodded. "Have you guys been coming here long. I keep thinking about Christopher reliving his pain, year after year, for the last three decades. I don't know if I can deal with the idea that this will consume my life that long."

"Thirty years is nothing," Dylan said. "You wouldn't believe how long that Hilda..."

He stopped talking when Billie reached over and swatted his arm.

"Jessica, you're looking at this wrong, I think," Billie said. "Maybe when you lost whatever you lost you were young enough that you thought that life was owed to you. Some kids get hit by a truck when they're riding their bikes home from seventh grade. They didn't get to complain about hauling baggage around for thirty years. They might have jumped at the opportunity. You have to understand that you could have been killed in the rain, just like everyone you knew and loved. Count yourself lucky and shoulder the guilt and pain with pride. That's your price of admission. And if you don't like the show, you can always walk out. That's been your choice all along. If you're still here, that's on you."

Jessica fought to keep control of herself as she set down her drink and stood up.

They didn't call after her as she walked towards the hall. She managed to keep her composure until she shut the door, closing herself into her room.

Lunch

Hunger finally drove her into the kitchen just before noon. She hoped that nobody would be there. When she saw Dylan sitting at the counter, she nearly turned around and left.

"I guess you got a good night's sleep," he said when he spotted her.

Jessica nodded. She hadn't. All night long, she had turned over Billie's words in her head.

"Glen made some amazing sandwiches—there's one in the fridge for you."

Jessica opened the refrigerator and saw a white paper package with her name written in grease pencil. She still hadn't met the chef, but he had left her a gift. The thoughtfulness of that brought her to the edge of losing control again.

"Thanks," she said, taking the sandwich and a can of soda.

"Don't thank me—it was all Glen."

Jessica clutched her sandwich and soda to her chest and fled. She didn't want to hide up in her room again, but she found herself heading that direction. Before the hall turned, she dodged through an open door and walked into a lounge. On the far side, she found the door to the balcony and slipped through. There was a small table tucked into the shade of an overhang. Jessica hid there in a corner of the exterior wall. She had her own private nook.

The day was so bright that she had to squint to look across the garden. An older woman stood at the far end, spraying a hose in the direction of some flowering bushes. It looked like the water was evaporating before it ever hit the ground. Jessica frowned at the sandwich once she opened the paper. The bread looked stiff and crusty—the kind that would cut the corners of her mouth when she tried to bite into it. Hunger forced her to give it a try anyway.

"Holy... What the..." she said through a full mouth. The bread was tender and amazingly tart. The flavors were layered and the textures combined to form an amazing experience. She resolved to find Glen and learn his secrets.

While she ate, Jessica looked out over the garden and watched the woman with the hose. She was very selective in choosing which bushes and plants would get water. In between, she would stop and bend to inspect a plant, sometimes straightening back up and waggling her finger at one. Jessica could hear the scolding tone, but not the words.

As the woman approached the house, coiling the hose as she walked, she continued to talk to herself. Jessica smiled.

When the sandwich was finished, even the crumbs, Jessica slumped back in her chair and sighed. There were tiny wisps of clouds high up in the sky. If she stared at any of them long enough, she saw them dissipate, burned off by the harsh sun. New ones would form, not lasting long. They were no match for the sun.

Her eyes drifted shut and sleep came finally.

There were no visions of herself walking out of the show, as Billie had suggested. It seemed so arrogant that Billie had assumed the this was new information for Jessica. Of course she knew that sticking around to live with the pain was a choice. It hurt to have it thrown in her face like that.

Sleep took away the pressure of that idea.

Company

Jessica was falling.

Her legs stiffened and she caught herself, only to realize that she hadn't been falling at all. It was a silly trick her mind had played on her body as she woke up. Working her tongue around her mouth, she sat up and straightened her back. There was still a sip of warm soda in the can. Reaching out to put the empty can back on the table, Jessica realized that she wasn't alone.

"Oh!"

"Sorry," the woman said. "I didn't mean to frighten you."

"No, just startled," Jessica said, clearing her throat. She recognized the hat and shirt the older woman was wearing. "I fell asleep after I ate. Did you get all your watering done?"

"For now, I suppose. Some of those plants will never acclimate. I apologize for invading your space. This is the only spot of shade this time of day."

"No problem. I was just about to head inside anyway."

Jessica was gathering her lunch trash when the woman said, "I wish you wouldn't. I could use some company for a few minutes."

Jessica felt obliged to remain in her chair. She felt like this was the woman's secret hideaway, and even though she had gotten there first, she was clearly the interloper.

"I'm Jessica," she said.

The woman nodded. "I'm Riley. We met briefly a couple of weeks ago, but you were probably overwhelmed with new faces and names."

Jessica peered at the eyes under the brim of the hat. "Of course—yes, you sat in the chair behind the couch. I didn't see you last week."

"No, I was busy last week. Honestly, I never go a whole month with perfect attendance. I don't have that kind of stamina."

Jessica nodded.

"Yeah. I've only been to two meetings and I'm starting to wonder how many more I can survive myself."

Riley nodded.

"You're from St. Louis?" Riley asked.

"No," Jessica said with a smile. "My father was though."

"I can hear it in the way you say 'wonder.' Very distinctive."

"Oh. Huh," Jessica said.

"Nothing to be self-conscious of," Riley said. "Sorry, I shouldn't have mentioned it."

"No, that's fine. I guess I don't... I mean..." Jessica could seem to form a full sentence. She covered her face with her hands.

She heard Riley sigh.

In the silence after, Jessica managed to compose herself and sit up straight again.

Quietly, just above a whisper, Riley said, "I sometimes feel like one of those plants. I will never acclimate to this world. They take the water I spray on them, and they don't seem to realize that it's not going to come forever. I tell them over and over that this is all artificial. They weren't meant for this place, and they're going to have to fundamentally change if they want to really take hold here. They don't listen to me at all. Shame on me for assuming that they would want to fundamentally change even if they could. Shame on them for not even giving it a try, right?"

Jessica glanced at Riley, who was just staring out at the garden.

"I have no idea," Jessica said.

"Don't listen to me. I'm just talking nonsense."

"I should get going," Jessica said.

"Please don't leave on my account. We can sit in silence."

Again, Jessica felt obligated to stay, at least for a few minutes. She wiped her hands on her shorts, wishing she hadn't balled up her napkin with the rest of the trash. Riley simply sat there, unmoving, looking out over the garden.

The clouds were all gone. The last of them had been burned away by the sun. Jessica watched a tiny dot of an airplane traversing the sky. It didn't even leave a contrail behind itself.

"Were you friends with Simon?" Jessica asked when she couldn't bear the silence any longer.

Riley laughed. "I suppose—as much as any of us were friends with Simon. He and Billie were close. The rest of us were just people he tolerated in order to get what he wanted."

Jessica was intrigued by the way she said that, but she didn't really want to go down that path.

"Have you lived in Vegas long?"

"Too long," Riley said. "You?"

"Just a few months."

"Months turn into years before you know it."

Jessica nodded.

"How are your teeth?" Riley asked.

"My teeth?"

"I always wanted to go work in Antartica, but my teeth were lousy. They won't take anyone who is prone to needing emergency dental care. I don't know why. It seems like it should be easy enough for them to employ a dentist down there. Maybe the equipment is difficult to ship? I don't know. If I were your age and I had good teeth, that's where I would go."

"I don't really like freezing cold temperatures."

"You can always wear more. It gets to a point where it's difficult to wear less."

"True," Jessica said. She was itching to leave. It still felt like the wrong time.

"Snow is a funny thing," Riley said. "It's impossible to move through it or over it without changing it forever. You wake up and there's a fresh blanket covering the landscape, but the second that someone invades that space they've left a mark that can't be erased. And when it comes inside with you it changes even more. That's when it leaves its own wet mark on you."

"I guess."

"I think I just figured something out," Riley said.

"What's that?"

"You're getting sick and tired of people giving you advice."

Jessica laughed.

"I hope you'll forgive me. Sometimes I fall into the bad habit of assuming that younger people don't have the same insight that I do. We're all living through the same things, making our own mistakes, and every revelation feels so important that we're just dying to share it."

Jessica sighed, leaned back, and closed her eyes.

"Seen any good movies lately?" Riley asked.

"No, not really."

"It turns out that I'm a complete sucker for found footage movies. Have you ever seen one of those?"

"I'm not sure," Jessica said.

"They're so compelling because it's like you're seeing a direct window into someone else's life. In the best ones, you really can't tell if the people are acting or not. It's just raw. I don't know why someone doesn't make a found footage movie about a couple who fall in love, or a perfect summer day. For whatever reason, they're almost always horror. I don't mind that, but I would appreciate a little variety."

"I don't really do movies, honestly."

"Oh? Why is that?"

"I guess it's the same reason I'm terrible at finishing books. I don't trust the storyteller."

"You have trouble suspending disbelief?" Riley asked.

"No, it's not that. Maybe even the opposite. I get so invested in the fiction that I get nervous it's not going to land. It doesn't have to be a happy ending for me, but it has to be a satisfying ending. I think I saw enough disappointing movies that I decided not to invest in them anymore."

"Forgive me for saying so, but that's sad, Jessica. Good fiction is a wonderful escape and a beautiful way to learn about the world and yourself."

Jessica shrugged.

"I should get going. I have things to do at home," Jessica said.

"See you soon," Riley said.

CHAPTER SEVEN

Jessica

Preparing

It was too soon.

Joe had come to her as soon as she arrived at the mansion. He had been kind, but unyielding. They needed to hear her story before it became adulterated by the other accounts she was hearing.

"Some stories just align and converge. You hear other descriptions of him and it twists your own memories. We want you to feel comfortable, but we want to hear *your* memories," he had said.

Jessica had just nodded. In the back of her head, she had suspected that today was the day. While at work, she had silently rehearsed the way she would say certain things. There were emotions that had distinct colors and forms in her head that she could never reproduce with words. Tonight, it was important that she got everything right. Stepping into the mansion, she was acutely aware of the air conditioning as the sweat evaporated from her. Talking to Joe, she had shivered.

He reached out to put a hand on her arm and then pulled it back. They didn't have that kind of relationship.

She and Joe were the first ones there. Jessica went to the

library to compose herself and try to settle her nerves. After scanning the shelves, she finally found the story about the boy and his dog. She flipped to the middle to discover that boy and dog had been reunited and were on an adventure to find strawberries. According to what the boy told the dog, it was the right time of year, but the usual patches weren't producing. Then, the boy almost lost his mind when the dog lifted his leg and peed on the one strawberry in the whole patch. The boy sat down and cried with his hands covering his face and the dog pushed through his arms to lay his furry face against the boy's.

"You ready?" a voice asked.

Jessica jumped and nearly dropped the book. Billie was standing in the doorway.

"Me? Yes," Jessica said.

"Just so you know, I'm not a very outwardly emotional or empathetic person."

Jessica nodded. This wasn't something she needed to be explained to her.

"But the first time I had to tell my story," Billie said, "I cried so much that I couldn't talk. It took hours to get through it. This is a difficult thing, but nobody will judge you if you have difficulty."

"I've told my story before."

Billie nodded.

"It might feel different this time. You won't have to spend any time convincing us that you're not crazy. There's not a person in the group that you'll shock with any details. This is just about you and him. None of the other blockades will exist when you tell your story tonight. I promise you, it's not going to be like before."

"Is this a pep talk? Are you trying to ease my concerns or make me even more nervous?"

Billie smiled and looked down at her own feet for a moment. When she looked back up, she seemed to be a different person. None of the normal sneering contempt was in her eyes.

"I'm telling you that it doesn't matter if you're nervous or not. We're all going to take you at your word, and we're here for you.

Nervous, stuttering, sweating, crying—we've seen it all. Take your time. Be honest with yourself. Don't worry about being honest with us, just be honest with yourself. When you're finally heard, you'll feel better."

Jessica took a deep breath.

"Thank you."

She followed Billie back out to the meeting room. They were all assembled. There were some faces that Jessica didn't recognize. They went around the circle, introducing themselves. The names of the new people flew right by Jessica. As far as she could tell, the only person missing was Keith. She had overheard that he wouldn't be coming back, but not the reason why. She looked down and noticed that she was still carrying the book. When she started to speak, she held the book in her lap.

Beginning

Mom died when I was little. She had cancer and they went to do surgery. They said that the surgery had an eighty-percent success rate. I didn't know what that meant and I have no idea why my father chose to tell me that. I think he was trying to comfort himself.

When I asked him to explain, he said, "That means that eight out of time times, the person is just fine after the surgery."

I couldn't get my brain around the numbers. My little kid brain kept thinking that they were going to do the surgery ten times on Mom and that she would be fine eight of the times.

"Why don't they just do it once?" I asked.

Dad couldn't understand. He was busy with my brother, who was just an infant. My sister was old enough to walk around, but she wasn't out of diapers yet. They never could remember Mom later. At least I got to carry around a picture in my head of what she looked like—how bright and beautiful she was.

After she died, I had balance problems for years. I would be walking along and I would just tip to the side and then fall over. Dad took me to doctors and they diagnosed me with an inner ear problem that eventually corrected itself. They were all wrong though. My balance problem came because Mom was half of what was keeping me upright and she was gone. That hole she left behind would pull at me. Later, when I was in high school, our family doctor said that my hips were tilted and my left leg was an inch longer than the right. He suggested that maybe that had been at the root of my balance issue. I would say the opposite is true. The pull, due to the absence of my mother, had compressed my entire right side over time.

Anyway, the reason I bring up all of that is because my balance was totally screwed up on the day when the clouds started rolling in. I was crashing into walls and falling out of chairs. Dad laughed it off. By then, he was pretty well convinced that my balance problem was psychosomatic. He thought that if he paid too much attention to it, I would only get worse.

I was upstairs, lying flat on my back when the rain started. I wanted to move down to the porch, but the bed was still swaying under me because of my inner ear issue. I had to settle for listening to fat drops of rain thumping on the metal roof above me. My little sister, Julia, came into my room and shut my window over my objections. She hated humid air up in the bedrooms.

She asked me where Nigel was. I told her that I didn't know. Nigel was our dog. He could sleep through anything, and I guess she was afraid that he was still out in the rain. She went to go look for him. I tried to close my eyes, but that made the bed spin and do flip-flops, so I was forced to just stare up at the ceiling. Over the sound of the rain and wind, I heard my sister scream. I sat up and got to my feet, only to stumble and sit back down hard on the bed. My father pounded up the stairs and stood in my doorway.

"Jess, I have to take Nigel to the vet. I think he got hit by a car."

"No," I said. I just couldn't take that news at that moment.

"I know," he said. "Make dinner for your brother and sister. I'll be back when I can."

"Hurry," I told him.

Later, I wished that I had rushed down the stairs behind him to help put Nigel in the car and say goodbye. Of course I couldn't have known that it was the last time I would see Nigel, but I knew. In my heart, I knew. Some surgeon would tell Dad that Nigel had an eighty-percent chance of making it through the...

Anyway, I knew.

We had a pretty somber dinner. Peter wanted macaroni and cheese. Julia wanted hotdogs. I made both, and a grilled cheese for myself. It was comfort food. We were all comforting ourselves, but not each other. That just wasn't something we did.

Dad came back and he seemed pretty optimistic. He said they were going to fix Nigel up and keep him overnight for observation. I guess I let myself believe him, even though I knew he was lying. It's hard to know now what I really believed. I mean, like I said, I was sure that he would never come home, but... My father's story was so much more pleasant.

Dad's comfort food was chili, sprinkled with diced onions, and with a dollop of sour cream in the middle. I made it for him while he got cleaned up and changed. I went out to tell him that it was ready and I found him at the front door. Before I could move to the side and see who he was talking to, he shut the door.

"Who was that?"

"A homeless person, I guess," Dad said. He was whispering, maybe thinking that the guy could overhear us from the porch. "He's looking for a dry place to spend the night. I told him about the shelter in town. He's going to try that."

"What's he doing out here?"

We lived about three miles from town and there was really nothing around us. There were a couple of big farms—one with beef and the other with corn, soy, and whatever. Our chunk of property had been split off from those farms because of the creek that ran right through it. There was a setback from the creek where you couldn't farm or spray pesticides and fertilizers. Instead of letting that go to waste, one of the farms had just split it off as a building lot. The people before us had built the house, stayed for ten or twenty years, and then sold it to Dad when he moved us there. After Mom died, I suppose he needed a change of scenery. Secretly, I think Mom would have hated our house. It was too far away from everything. She liked to walk to the grocery store.

"I don't know," Dad said, about my question as to why the man was out on our road. "Maybe he was at Bisson's trying to get work?"

Bisson's was the beef farm. They turned away job seekers because everyone who worked there was part of the family. Dad's story made just as much sense as anything else, so I shrugged and went along with it.

"Why don't you go lie down, Jess. You look exhausted."

I nodded but I didn't head for the stairs. Instead, I got the wool blanket from the cedar chest and I went to the side porch. That porch had a deep roof and a bench right along the wall. The overhang of the roof was so deep that even when it was pouring down rain you wouldn't get splashed if you sat on the bench. I went there to listen to the rain and watch the flashes of lightning in the clouds. Every now and then I heard the roll of distant thunder. Even with the rain, it was getting warmer and warmer outside. I heard a door slam upstairs and smiled. It was funny the way that Julia would get so mad at the humidity. I was just the opposite. There was nothing better than sitting out on that porch and watching the rain come down.

Some of the flashes of lightning cast strange shadows out in the field. Peter had put up a scarecrow years before, but it had tipped to the side and Dad made him dismantle it. He was a kid, but he was always building stuff. Anyway, the way that the lighting flashed and cast shadows from the trees around the creek, it almost looked like the scarecrow was back. I heard the screen door and my father came out with a cup of tea and sat next to me. I extended my wool blanket to cover his legs.

"We messed up," he said.

"Huh?"

"We should have gotten more bread from the store. We're

almost out."

That was the way he was with me. He would say "we" as if I wasn't just a kid and he wasn't the only parent. It put some of the responsibility and blame on me when things were forgotten. I resented that Mom had taken a chunk of my childhood with her to the grave. They say you can't take it with you, but she had. I didn't always hate it. There were times when I felt like an adult and I enjoyed it. Not that night though—that night I was sick of it.

"Why didn't you get some when you were out?" I asked. "I made dinner. Everything was fine here. You had plenty of time."

I knew the answer as soon as I finished my outburst. He hadn't known that I was going to burn my first grilled cheese and have to start over. He hadn't known that because we were out of hotdog rolls, I would wrap Julia's hotdog in bread. When he left the house, bread hadn't been a crisis.

Dad pushed the blanket off of his legs.

"I'll go get some," he said.

"You don't have to."

"We'll need it to pack sandwiches for lunch."

"Oh."

He was right.

"Could you make sure Peter gets to bed on time?"

"I always do."

He touched my head before he left me on the porch. Obviously, he meant it to be an endearing, affectionate gesture, but I chose to take it as a condescending dismissal of my anger. That was just the mood I was in that night. Around the corner, I heard him run through the rain across the gravel to get to his car, and then I heard the engine. I should have told him... it doesn't matter.

The headlights swept across the yard and I saw the scarecrow again, but it wasn't a scarecrow.

My brain immediately jumped to the worst conclusion, but I forced myself to stay calm. There was someone watching the house, waiting for an opportunity to attack. I thought it likely that he was waiting for me to be alone, and now I was. I cocked my head and called, "Okay, Uncle Jack. I'll be right in."

This was something my father taught me years before. If someone came to the door when he was out, I should pretend my Uncle Jack was home with us. After going inside, I turned out the kitchen lights so I could press my face to the window and look out into the darkness. I thought I saw him moving out there. After locking that door, I ran to the front and locked that one too. It was lucky that Julia hated humidity—she had already closed all the windows.

I sprinted up the stairs.

All the lights went off just as I got to the top.

I snatched the phone from the cradle and grabbed Julia's hand as she emerged from her room.

She asked, "Why are the lights..."

I shushed her and dragged her to Peter's room. We slipped inside and I closed and locked the door behind me. Peter had a nightlight that had a battery for when the power went out. Where we lived, it went out pretty often.

"What?" Peter asked.

I shushed him. My brother and sister must have heard my fear because they both shut up without complaint. That *never* happened.

"There's a man outside," I said. I had my back pressed to the door and I punched the buttons on the phone.

"It won't work," Julia said.

"What are you..." I started to ask as I pressed the phone to my ear. I realized what she meant—the phone was cordless. It wouldn't work without power. The only phone with a cord was down in Dad's room, next to his bed. Us kids didn't have cellphones. Dad said they were a distraction.

"You guys stay here. I'll go call."

"Who?" Peter asked.

"The police and then Dad."

"Don't," Peter said.

"Yeah, don't do it," Julia said.

"I have to. What else are we going to do?"

"Hide here," Peter said. "We can sneak up into the attic. Where's Dad?"

"Store," I said. "Just left."

They both knew what that meant. The only store open at night was the Walmart and that was nearly fifteen minutes away. Dad would walk around, whistling, trying to make sure he didn't forget anything. We would be lucky if he got back in an hour. Our attic was a pretty terrible place if you had to be up there for ten minutes, getting down the Christmas decorations. An hour up there would be torture.

"I'll call. Dad literally just left. He'll turn around and get here before the police."

In the light of Peter's nightlight, I saw them both nod.

"You lock this and get under the bed. Don't make a sound."

Julia nodded. I made sure that Peter nodded too. They had to both buy-in or else they would just bicker after I left. I pressed my ear to the door before I unlocked it.

There was no sound except the rain.

I slipped through and heard it click behind me, followed by Peter and Julia whisper-fighting.

Alone

I stayed to the shadows and moved pretty slowly. In the worst-case scenario, the guy was already in the house and I wanted to make it to Dad's room without being caught. It wasn't difficult for me to move silently. I had plenty of practice. On Mondays, Dad slept in. It was up to me to get breakfast ready without making too much noise. The only part of the house that I wasn't good at sneaking through was my father's room.

I paused in his doorway, trying to sense if the guy was already inside.

For one tiny moment, I thought maybe I was being ridiculous. It was possible that the shape I saw outside was just a scarecrow. The power going out during a thunderstorm wasn't unusual.

Maybe I was spooked because Nigel was at the vet. He was a big dog and his presence in the house was even bigger. Without him, of course I felt vulnerable and frightened.

"No," I whispered to myself. I wouldn't be that person who underestimated danger and then got bitten by it.

I slipped into my father's room, pushed the door most of the way closed and avoided the windows as I found his phone on his bedside table. The dial tone was crackly and wavering as I lifted the phone to my ear. It still sounded beautiful.

I dialed my father's cell first.

This was the exact opposite of what I had planned to do. I can't explain why I mixed the two things up, but I did. Listening to Wahid's story, it occurred to me that I actually made the calls in the correct order. If I had called the police first, they never would have let me hang up so I wouldn't have called Dad at all. Anyway, the line was full of static and I could barely hear my father when he answered.

I whispered slowly—putting space between each word, "Dad, there's someone here. The power is out."

Through the phone, I could hear his brakes squeal on the wet pavement and the engine roar.

He must have heard me perfectly. He said, "Hide. I'll be right there."

I don't know if he hung up or if the line simply disconnected. It didn't matter. I was about to hang up anyway. It was a huge relief and validation when my father reacted so quickly. Instantly, I knew I had done the right thing because I heard the urgency in his voice. Usually, when I was overreacting, Dad was the first one to downplay my panic and tell me that it would be okay.

The satisfaction of being right only lasted a fraction of a second. The real ramification hit—if Dad was freaking out by what I told him in two quick sentences, then the situation was serious. My fingers felt numb as I dialed 9-1-1. They had questions, and I tried to answer them. Maybe it was the static, or maybe my whispering wasn't clear, but they kept asking the same things. I wanted to scream. I was convinced that they should be able to pull my address from the phone line somehow. I couldn't imagine why they kept asking.

"What is the emergency?" the man kept asking.

I boiled it down to one word. "Intruder."

When he finally repeated the address back to me, I felt like I won the lottery. He listed my address and asked me to confirm that there was an intruder.

"Yes!" I said. "Yes."

The line was dead. I had no idea if he heard me. Based on his skeptical, dismissive tone, I had no idea if they were going to send anyone. I tried to call back, but the buttons on the phone didn't do anything. The buttons weren't even lit up anymore. The line had been cut—I was sure of it.

I set the phone back in the cradle and froze, staring at the window. I couldn't see anything at all out there. The rain was coming in waves. It swelled and faded, but it was never less than a drenching downpour.

I opened my father's door slowly, cringing at the creaking sound that the hinges made. At that moment I knew that the guy was inside the house. I scanned the darkness, looking for the shape of him. Of course I couldn't see a thing.

A tiny sound escaped me when I heard the pounding on the back door. For a moment, I thought there must be two of them. On one hand, I was certain that someone was already in the house. On the other, I heard his voice from outside.

"I just want to get dry," he yelled. "You promised."

My brain raced. I said something that I thought was intelligent at the time, but as soon as it came out of my mouth I regretted it.

"I'm alone here, but my father will be back any second. I called him and he's on my way."

Before you judge me, you should know that my first thought was for my brother and sister. I kept thinking that the guy might not know about them. I wanted him to think that I was the only person around so if he did break in he would just come after me. And, I really thought that telling him that my father was coming home might scare him off. Then I realized that I had just given him a deadline for whatever he planned to do to me. I had told him that he better be quick and that whatever he did would have no witness.

Just before I ran up the stairs, I heard him say, "I know," and he rattled the doorknob, trying to turn it.

Maybe my adrenaline rush cured the dizziness, or maybe it just went away on its own, but I absolutely flew up the stairs in the darkness. I pushed off the wall and got to Peter's room in a flash. Julia unlocked the door and I only let her open it an inch.

I told her to get herself and Peter in the attic. The panel to get up there was in Peter's closet. You could open the drawers of his dresser and climb them like stairs to get up there. Even Dad could do that—it was a sturdy dresser. Julia, did as she was told and I heard the door lock as soon as I pulled it shut again. I ran back for the stairs, hoping that he wasn't there yet.

The window at the top of the stairs opened to the porch roof. Like I said, it was a deep porch roof, so it wasn't very steep. The only problem was that it was a metal roof and I knew it would be slippery as hell. It wouldn't be good enough to escape, I needed him to follow me, so I opened the window and waited, looking down the stairs into the darkness. The shadows were so deep I was afraid that he would get close enough to grab me before I saw him. I put my legs through the window and sat on the sill, waiting for him.

The rain soaked through my pants in a matter of seconds. My body was shivering from the cold and anticipation. In the distance, through the rain, I could see headlights coming down the road. My intention had been to wait there in the window until the intruder saw me. I figured I could lure him away from the house to keep my sister and brother safe. It was a long way to the next house. But when I saw that car, I gave up on trying to lure him and I decided I had to go flag the car down.

I pulled myself through the window and flopped down onto the metal roof. It was wet, and I thought I could slide right down it and get some speed so I would clear the sharp edge. It didn't work that way. Instead of sliding, I simply tumbled.

The edge caught me in the side and I flipped in the air before I landed on the wooden stairs. My head swam and I heard a window smash.

Pain burned in my side and something grabbed my pants. Kicking and thrashing, I managed to get free by clawing at the lawn. When my leg pulled free I ran straight for the creek. Hopping the creek and running through the tall grass was the fastest way to the road. I tripped again and got up a little more slowly the next time. My dizziness was threatening to come back and I knew if I really lost my balance I would be dead. That's when I realized that I didn't know where the car headlights were.

Through the pounding rain, I heard Dad whistle.

Break

"Pardon me for a second," Jessica said.

"Of course," Vivian said.

The rest of the group was silent. Nobody moved. After dabbing her eyes with balled up tissues, Jessica looked down and saw the pile of them at her feet. She hadn't even realized that she had been crying. Her hands had automatically sopped up her tears. Telling the story had consumed her completely. Reality had disappeared.

When she stood, Jessica expected vertigo and tried to brace herself against the chair. Hilda moved quickly to stabilize her and stood next to her until Jessica felt solid on her feet again. She went to the bar and Dylan handed her a glass of water before she could ask. She drank it with both hands and saw that Billie was holding an unlit cigarette in her hand.

"I'll be a minute if you want to go smoke that," Jessica said.

Almost everyone got up at once. Some headed towards the bathrooms and others went towards the terrace to smoke. Jessica sat on the warm stool that Dylan had vacated. She reached over the bar and refilled her glass.

"You don't have to do this all in one go," Joe said.

Jessica looked over and almost laughed.

"You saying that for me or for yourself?" she asked.

"Sorry?"

"You look like you're in more pain from the story than I am."

He looked down at his feet for a moment before meeting her eyes once more.

"I have to admit, your story is difficult for me to listen to. There are similarities."

"There are similarities for all of us, right?" she asked before she finished her second glass of water.

"Maybe it's the way you tell it. Anyway, my point is that you can take your time. It's not crucial that we hear everything tonight if you want to break it up and wait until next week."

Jessica smiled. "It's painful to remember, but I'll survive. If I survived the real thing, I can make it through my own memory of it."

He nodded but looked unsure.

Vivian returned from the hallway and went to the refrigerator. She found a can of something fizzy and smiled when some of the bubbles overflowed.

"You're okay, right?" Vivian asked.

Jessica nodded. "It's tough, but I have the feeling that getting it out without editing myself is going to be..."

"... a relief," Vivian said, finishing thc sentence with her.

"Exactly," Jessica said.

"It probably will be, to some extent. But, don't be surprised if things change more than they get better."

"How so?" Jessica asked.

There was a noise from the terrace and Vivian turned to see what was going on.

Dylan stumbled his way through the door, laughing. This caused Billie to laugh as well. A man followed them through, quietly scolding them. He was one of the newcomers that Jessica didn't recognize.

"What's happening?" Jessica asked.

"Ignore them," Vivian said.

Jessica glanced towards the couch when she heard someone giggle. She saw Hilda whispering something to Wahid and then he flashed a quick smile at her. Jessica was surprised to find that she wasn't offended by their high spirits. She felt it too. The catharsis of releasing her story was already raising her spirits.

The group gathered quickly and the mood settled. They sat, politely glancing at Jessica or looking down at their hands as she filled her glass one more time and then took her seat. With a deep breath, she tried to put herself back in the yard when she heard her father whistle.

Return

The police asked me over and over why I ran away and then returned. I kept telling them that I didn't know it was my father's car on the road. I really didn't. I saw the headlights, escaped through the second-floor window, crashed to the ground, and simply kept running for the road. It didn't occur to me that the car would have already pulled into the driveway. I wasn't exactly running a stopwatch, predicting how far the car would have gotten while I fled.

But when I heard his whistle, I knew I couldn't just run away.

Some people can put two fingers in their mouth and make a shrill whistle that cuts through noise and carries for a mile. Dad never learned to do that. He would put his fingers in the right place, but the only thing that would come out was a breathy low tone. It was very distinctive. In a way, it was better that he never learned to do it correctly because the way he whistled we always knew it was him. He would call us with that whistle when we were scattered in the grocery store and it was time to checkout. Even at the fair we could hear his whistle under the sounds of the calliope.

In this case, I knew what he was trying to communicate.

He was telling us that he was home and it was going to be okay.

I screamed, but my voice was drowned out by a crash of

thunder. I started running towards the house, yelling. I was panting so hard it felt like I couldn't get a deep enough breath to make any noise. I tripped and fell in the creek trying to leap across it a second time. When I got back to my feet I could see my father going inside the house. His flashlight lit up the living room windows. I ran past the car and started up the stairs towards the open door.

The flashlight was right in my eyes for a moment. I raised my hands to shield my face—I thought something was attacking me —and then the light was gone. It hit the floor and flickered for a moment but then returned to full strength. It lit up the blood that was flowing across the floor. Stumbling into the house, I dropped to my knees and reached past the blood to grab the flashlight. My hands were trembling as I turned the beam towards the floor and tracked the blood back to its source.

In the time it took me to run across the yard, he had decapitated my father. His heart gushed out one more burst of blood through the neck and then his body was still. I didn't have time to think about that. I heard the man's lighter clink and then saw the blue flame. Behind me, rain fell. In front of me, I heard water dripping from him to the floor as he touched the flame to the end of his cigarette and inhaled. For a moment, his face was lit up in blue.

I turned the flashlight on the man as he exhaled.

The vapor that came from his mouth didn't look like smoke, really. It sank quickly, like the fog from dry ice does. It was heavier than the air. The smoke dropped and rolled across the floor away from him.

My breathing was so heavy that it ripped in and out of my throat, making a pained, hoarse sound.

I asked him something. My face was numb and my brain was descending into survival mode, I guess. I couldn't even make sense of the words coming out of my mouth, but it was something like, "What did you do?" or "How could you do that?"

The end of the cigarette flared orange when he took another drag. His eyes were just dark holes in his face.

In the back of my brain, it occurred to me that he still might not know about my brother and sister. It was a long shot, but it was all I had. I couldn't fight the man, but if I ran he might follow, and they might be safe. There wasn't much time though. Julia and Peter could only stay quiet for a short time. They were both impatient and impulsive. Besides, they had probably heard my father's whistle. They might already be climbing down from the attic.

I stood up slowly and took a careful step backwards, towards the door. The guy took a tentative step forward. He was taking the bait, but I didn't know how to set the hook.

I said something like, "I'm going to get the police, and they're going to arrest you."

When I took a second step, the guy took an even bigger step towards me. I thought I had him on the line. The flashlight on his features revealed nothing. There was no emotion there that I could read. His face might as well have been carved from stone.

I backed all the way through the door until I was sure that I was at the top of the porch steps. He was just farther than swinging distance. If I tried to back down the stairs, I was sure I would fall, so that's when I turned and ran. While I sprinted, I refused to look back. The moment I looked back, I was sure that the knife would be driven through me. Or, worse, I imagined that the last thing I would see was a spiraling descent, ending with me looking at my own headless body.

At the driveway, I hit my stride. There were wounds on my side and my leg, but the dizziness was gone. Nothing could have caught me. For a moment, as I accelerated even more, I forgot the purpose of running. I was supposed to be luring him away from my brother and sister. If I outpaced him by too much, he might turn around and discover them. In the rain and darkness, I told myself that it was better to keep running. Returning home wouldn't do anybody any good. There was no way I could fight him off. Julia and Peter would stay hidden and I would get to the neighbors' in a couple of minutes and I would get help.

Maybe Mrs. Bisson would call the police while Mr. Bisson

would return to the house with me to make sure everything was okay. With that in mind, I kept running, telling myself that lie over and over again until I almost believed it. Once I saw the lights of their house, I pushed myself even harder even though a creeping realization began to take form in my thoughts.

Reaching their house, my body simply gave out. All the injuries and fatigue hit me all at once and I was barely able to pound on their door. The porch light came on and I was lying there, sobbing on their doormat. Mrs. Bisson was normally the nicest person in the whole world, but there was something about my appearance that turned her voice cold.

"What do you want?" she asked.

"Call the police. Send them to my house. Please."

I dragged myself to my feet and began limping away. I knew they would be no help. My father told me one time, "Help, around here, comes when you need it, but not often when you ask for it."

He was convinced that our neighbors would always lend a hand, but only when it was their idea. If they saw you struggling to dig a hole for a fencepost, they would drive a tractor down and take over. But if you went to them, hat in hand, and asked to borrow the tractor to move a rock, you would be turned away.

With that in mind, I called back over my shoulder, "He cut our phones before he killed Dad." I said that so she would know that I wasn't asking for no reason. It must have been the stress or the shock or something. I don't know why I didn't lead with the fact that my father was dead.

I *do know* why I didn't stick around and demand help. The kids were my responsibility and it had been my decision to attempt to lure him by running away. That effort had failed, and it was my responsibility to deal with the aftermath.

The more I walked, the greater the pain. I knew my side was split, there was a bleeding wound on my leg, and I had hit my head at some point. The pain also told me that there was nothing really *wrong* with me. It was constant. I didn't *have to* limp. As long as the pain stayed constant, I could adjust to it. By the time

I saw the dark shape of my house again, I was walking tall.

I didn't let myself think about my brother and sister. Maybe part of me was afraid that if I even thought about them, he would know that they were hiding in the attic. All my thoughts were focused on my father. When I pictured his head and the terrible look of surprise and pain on his face, it made me want to curl up into a ball and fold into myself, so instead I tried to imagine that Dad was injured and needed my help.

Lightning lit up the sky as I started up the driveway. I could see that the door to the house was hanging wide open. Before I climbed the porch stairs, I bent over and grabbed one of the rocks that lined our walkway. My father hated those rocks. Every summer one of us kids would clip one of those rocks with the lawnmower and then he would have to sharpen and rebalance the blade. I intended to smash the guy's head in with that rock. It would be a gift from our whole family.

But as soon as I stood on the porch and thought about stepping into the darkness, I couldn't help but think about my father again, and how his blood was pooled on the living room floor. Unless I wanted to step in it, I would have to go around to the other entrance, and that was locked. The strength and conviction ran out of me. The rock fell from my hands.

That's when headlights swept across the porch.

I turned to see Mr. Bisson's truck pulling to a stop behind Dad's car and I lost my nerve entirely. I tried to run to him, but stumbled down the stairs and landed in the mud and grass, sobbing. Mr. Bisson shuffled over to me with a rifle in his hand. He was wearing a crinkly rain jacket that made a rubbery sound when he leaned over me.

"Where's your father, sweetie? Who did he hurt?" Mr. Bisson asked.

I tried to tell him that he was all wrong, but only mumbling gibberish would come out of my mouth. Mr. Bisson dismissed me and stood. I think maybe he heard something from the house. If so, he didn't mention it. Clicking on a flashlight, he started forward. I rolled over so I could watch. He got about as far as I did before his flashlight found something that made him freeze. I suppose he was looking at my father's head. That was enough to dissuade him from entering. Mr. Bisson backed down the stairs, whipping his head around as he moved to make sure that nothing was creeping up on him. He got to the other side of me and knelt again, keeping an eye on both me and the house.

"Did you do that, sweetie?" he asked.

I mangled to tell him, "No. There's a guy."

"We better just wait here for the sheriff."

My fear overrode my superstition and I had to tell him.

"No, you have to help my brother and sister!"

"Sweetie, we better wait out here for the sheriff."

I tried to get up then—I really did. It was clear to me that I couldn't rely on anyone else. The police were going to come and they were going to say the same thing in a different way. If I didn't go help, then nobody would. When I tried to get up, Mr. Bisson grabbed a handful of my shirt and pulled me back down.

"Wait here, sweetie," he kept saying.

I fought him, but I didn't want to hurt him. Then, I got so frustrated that I didn't care if I hurt him or not. He lost his grip on my shirt and grabbed my leg instead. His thumb pressed right into the wound on my calf. I felt his thumbnail dig down into the muscle, and I screamed, but he didn't let go. We were still struggling when the next set of headlights came into the driveway. After that, I was restrained and wrangled by many hands.

I was wrapped in a scratchy blanket and transported against my will. They wouldn't tell me what happened to my brother and sister. They wouldn't tell me if they caught the guy. Every time a new person came to talk to me, I wondered if it was really the guy in disguise. I had the idea that he had changed his clothes and put on a uniform to blend in with the police. When they had a doctor look me over, it felt like I was being attacked all over again. Their first priority seemed to be collecting evidence rather than fixing me up. My health and well-being took a back seat to their investigation. Maybe they thought I was the killer. Maybe they just thought that I was being too cold about the whole thing. One of the policemen actually asked me, "You're not crying enough. Why is that?"

I guess it was his way of accusing me to see how I would react.

I was in shock.

Hindsight

They never let me see my family again in person.

Finally, after asking so much that I was convinced that they couldn't hear me, one of the policemen came and took my hand. He said, "Your brother and sister have passed on."

The words didn't make sense to me. Who says that? Passed on?

I demanded to know if they were dead or not.

He said, "I'm afraid so."

Again, I had no idea what he was saying. It seemed like he meant that he was scared that the answer might be yes, but he wasn't sure. I had this image in my head of Julia and Peter being so injured that they were being "passed on" to a special hospital, and this officer was "afraid" that they might be dead, but wasn't sure.

Finally, when I wouldn't shut up about it, they sent someone else over with pictures and asked me to identify Peter and Julia. Who could be so cruel to show a kid pictures of their mutilated siblings? Later, a lawyer somehow heard about me being forced to identify them with pictures of the crime scene. The lawyer wanted me to sue for emotional distress or something. By that point, I wanted everything to stop.

When it seemed like they wanted to blame me for the deaths, I pretty much had to agree. Everything I did that night was wrong. If there was a bad decision to make, I made it. When I finally got back to the house and had a rock in my hand, I couldn't go back in that house even though I'm certain that Peter and Julia were still alive then. When they carried the stretcher to the ambulance, I think I saw that the sheets weren't pulled up over their heads. They wouldn't have moved them like that if there wasn't a chance to save them, so that meant that I was probably cowering in the lawn when they were murdered.

They searched for the guy. They collected evidence and put up sketches based on my descriptions. I had to learn to be circumspect when I talked about him. Nobody wanted to know that he was carved from living stone and covered with mold and moss. They wouldn't believe that his eyes were two dark holes that held no spark of life. The cigarette was the one detail that they latched onto. At one point, they took me out of a picnic bench and made me close my eyes while they wafted smoke from different types of cigarette under my nose. The closest they found was something they called a Dutch Shag. They never reproduced the sound of his cigarette though. It had a particular popping sound when he inhaled, almost like the paper was infused with gun powder or something. It crackled, almost like seltzer water or something. I've never been able to describe it, and they always seemed mystified by that detail.

I never told them that the cigarette was wet, and I never told them about the lighter. I remember one of the officers asking me how he lit it, and I just said that I didn't know. The police were holding back on the details that they told the public, and I was holding back from the police. Our motives were the same. The police wanted to eliminate false confessions and copycats. I wanted to make sure that I had some identifying features that only I knew about. At some point, I knew they were going to point the finger at the wrong guy, and I wanted to have an attribute or two that I could use to refute their accusation. Of course, it never happened that way. As far as I know, they never even settled on a person of interest, aside from me. I was eliminated quickly as a suspect, but I was still the closest thing they ever had.

The sheriff and most of the department lost their jobs over the handling of the case. It was national news for a moment. The public was outraged that the investigation had been so botched and the killer never brought to justice. Everyone blamed it on their ineptitude. I'm not suggesting that they did everything perfectly, but there are some murders that can never be solved. It took more than a year for me to come to that conclusion. All those details that I had learned to hold back, they were the ones pointing to the... I hate to say this, but they pointed to a *supernatural* element to the crime.

The power was only out at our house. Later, the power company said that they believed lightning had damaged the transformer. In a report from the technician, it was stated that there was no external damage visible. Somehow, the lightning had fried the circuit without leaving any charring or evidence on the transformer or pole. The idea, I guess, is that a line was struck and the surge traveled down the line until it burned up just our transformer. But that same surge didn't take out anyone else's power at all.

Somehow, they blamed that same surge on the phone outage. Over and over, I told them that the lights were out when I called my father. Gently, at first, they said that the phones would have been disabled at the same time as the power outage. I couldn't convince them otherwise.

The other thing that really stood out to me was the picture of Julia. Before moving her, someone had taken a photo of her in the attic. I don't think it was a real crime scene photographer because they moved both my brother and sister so fast. It seems impossible that they had the real photographer out there in time for that. Anyway, in the background of the photo, I saw a broken piece of wood and I knew what it was immediately. Peter had found it up there one time and used it to brace the trap door shut. The kids must have thought of that when they hid—they had essentially locked themselves into the attic. I asked one of the detectives about it, and he said that the first people on the scene had spotted footprints in the dust on the top of the dresser and guessed that someone was in the attic. To get up there, they had to break through the hatch.

"How did the guy get up there then?" I asked.

The guy worked to hide his smile—they thought that they were so clever to figure it out.

"It wasn't blocked when the killer went up. Then, as the killer was leaving, they propped the board up at an angle so it would fall into place as the hatch was lowered."

I shook my head, telling them it didn't work that way. Everything I said made them either dismissive or suspicious.

Group

Jessica looked up from her hands and around the eyes of the group members. She realized that her story had ended a while ago. Now she was simply listing out her grievances about the investigation and the way that she had been treated.

"Anyway, I guess that's all."

"Thank you," Vivian said, leaning forward and touching her hand.

Jessica nodded and looked down.

"Are you ready for some questions?" someone asked.

When she looked at him, he must have read the confusion in her eyes.

"I'm Mel," he said. "I keep a database of everything. I know it's difficult, but can you clarify a couple of points?"

"Okay," Jessica said.

"First, you mentioned a dog named Nigel. May I ask what became of him?"

Jessica felt her throat close with grief. She had expressed all her pain about her human family, but he had found a wound that she had forgotten about. With focused concentration, she managed to hold her voice steady as she answered.

"Yes. Nigel died overnight at the veterinarian. They tried to reach us at home, but the phones were still out. I got in touch with them a couple of days later and learned..."

A sobbing cough burst from her chest before she could finish.

"Cause of death?" Mel asked.

"Lacerations," she managed to say.

When she finally was able to take a deep breath, she was able to stuff the grief back down again.

"Your brother and sister..."

"Decapitated, like Dad."

"And their ages?"

"Ten and twelve," she said.

"Thank you. I have the rest from my research, I believe. I'll ask you to review it when you have a chance."

Mel handed a sealed envelope and it passed through several hands on its way to her. She retrieved the book from beside her chair and tucked the envelope inside.

"May I?" Wahid asked with his hand halfway raised.

She nodded to him.

"You sounded very sure when you mentioned that the man was supernatural. Aside from the phone line, power, and the attic door being closed, what else made you so sure?"

"Are you kidding?" Jessica asked. "The man appeared out of nowhere and started chopping off the heads of my family without leaving a clue."

Wahid held up his hands and shook his head quickly.

"Forgive me, please. I haven't been clear. I have no reason to doubt you. Sometimes we simply know something is unnatural or *supernatural* without even requiring evidence, but I have the sense that in this circumstance you do actually have particular things that have pointed you in that direction."

"Sorry," she said with a big exhale. "I forgot who I was talking to."

Jessica found it difficult to set aside her own defensiveness, but she worked hard at it, seeing her memories with fresh eyes and exploring the roots of her convictions.

"The dizziness was my first clue. I mentioned that it started when Mom died. I've come to realize that when death is close to me, it pulls me off balance. Maybe I wouldn't have said that at the time, but I know now that it's a warning sign for me. Second, after Dad left the guy appeared in the same spot as Peter's scarecrow. That thing always creeped me out and I had the distinct impression that the guy had chosen that spot to watch the house because he knew that it would inspire fear in me."

Jessica saw that Wahid was taking notes on a little pad. She sat up a little straighter and tried to organize her thoughts.

"Third, the power went out when I was climbing the stairs. He couldn't have had time to get to the house and cut the line. Besides, they said the lines were damaged at the pole. Fourth, the phone went out when I tried to contact an outsider. He wanted us in the house and nobody else. I think he intended to leave me as a witness, and he wanted Dad at home, but not the police."

"Pardon," Vivian said. "It's your impression that the sheriff came in response to your neighbor's call and not yours?"

Jessica nodded. "They told me that they hadn't gotten a 9-1-1 call from my house. I *know* I talked to someone. Next, he managed to pound on our back door while he was already in the house. You might assume that he wasn't working alone, but..."

She shook her head.

"There was only one person. His spirit was in the house, but his physical presence was still out on the porch. I could feel the fact that he was able to disconnect himself like that. Then, the biggest thing of all was his appearance. I swear that his clothing was made of stone and moss, but it moved like fabric. His eyes were just holes in a deeply-lined face that didn't appear to be skin. His cigarette should have been soaked through. The smoke didn't move like smoke. The flame didn't look like flame. There was nothing about his appearance to suggest that he was a normal human being. The physics were, like, all backwards or something. That's the best I can explain it. Then, you have the attic door problem, and the fact that he disappeared without a trace. They found puddles of water inside, but no fingerprints, broken windows or locks, or any sign that someone had broken in to attack. I don't know how someone could look at the evidence and think that it wasn't supernatural. None of it makes sense."

"Of course," Wahid said. "That's a very thorough list. Thank you."

Joe nodded too. "A lot of us have had the same notion that something was just *off* or *wrong* about him, but you picked out several really precise details that led you to that conclusion. Well done."

"Thanks?" Jessica said. She wasn't sure if he was being patronizing or not.

"Other questions?" Joe asked the group.

Billie raised her chin in response. "Yeah. You said your mom's death made you dizzy, and you were dizzy before your family was killed. Any other times?"

"Yeah," Jessica said. "The vertigo came back very strong right before I got in touch with the vet and heard about Nigel. I was finishing high school and living with my aunt and the dizziness hit me again before her stroke. The stroke wasn't a surprise. She was a heavy smoker and it was her third or something. I was dizzy right until she died. A couple years later, I kept having dizzy spells walking to work when I would pass by a shop that was closed. I saw on the news later that the owner had died in there and it took a week to find his body."

"So, sometimes it's before, and sometimes after?" Billie asked.

"I guess so, yes. I hadn't though about it."

Billie nodded and seemed satisfied by the answer.

"More questions?" Joe asked. "If you think of more, hold them for the meeting after next."

CHAPTER EIGHT

Retreat

Work

"It's a two-minute walk from your place. What's the harm?" Sadie asked.

Jessica looked down at her wrinkled uniform. It would have to be cleaned and ironed before she came in tomorrow.

"I just don't have the energy. Between shifts, I barely have enough time to sleep and get ready for my next shift."

"You know what your problem is?" Sadie asked.

Jessica sighed and rolled her eyes. "Please—give to me the gift of your wisdom."

Sadie was looking at her like she was crazy.

Jessica tried to smile and said, "Go ahead."

"Your problem is that you don't know how to have fun. When you don't know how to have fun, everything is a slog. You should be tap dancing through these last twenty minutes because you know that it's all that's left between you and a good time."

"I have to go home, change, clean my uniform, hang it up, get something to eat... There are a million things between me and a good time."

"Or... you could grab one of those fresh uniforms off the rack. The troll won't notice them gone until next month. If your conscience gets the better of you by then, put it back. Meanwhile, you can go directly from here to the bar without any of that other nonsense."

"Why do you need me to go so badly?" Jessica asked.

"I told you, Steve won't go for someone he thinks he can get. If I show up alone, I'm going to strike out. I need a girlfriend to dance with. Then, he sees me, thinks he can't get me, and, bam!"

Jessica smiled. She loved Sadie's enthusiasm and determination, even if her predatory approach to dating was a little disturbing.

"Okay, fine, but there better be at least one more of us."

"How come?"

"So I'm not alone when you go off with Steve."

Sadie tapped the side of her head with a finger. "Smart. Very smart. Let's go work on Travis. He's always up for a good time."

Dancing

After ten minutes, swimming in the loud music, Jessica lost herself in the collective trance. She, Sadie, and Travis formed a triangle at first, unconsciously mirroring each other's moves, smiling, and laughing. Someone tried to hand her a drink and she waved it off. With work still looming the next day, she had no intention of drinking any alchohol, let alone whatever might be slipped into some random drink.

They had been dancing for ten or fifteen minutes when the beat increased and she didn't think she could keep it up anymore. Jessica opened her eyes and looked for Sadie to ask for a break.

"Where did Travis go?" she yelled in Sadie's ear.

Sadie smiled and pointed to the corner, over near the bar. Travis had split off and was slow dancing with someone.

"How does he do that?" Jessica asked.

Sadie turned up her hands with a shrug and a broad smile. She waved for Jessica and they headed for the bar. Sadie ordered something tall and fancy. Jessica asked for a seltzer water and said that she was the designated driver.

"Driver?" Sadie asked.

"They don't charge designated drivers. Otherwise, they want five bucks for a water."

"You're kidding!"

Jessica pointed to a small sign. Throwing her head back, Sadie laughed.

"You're always paying attention, Jess. If we could get you to break the rules more often, you'd be unstoppable."

"I'm already unstoppable," Jessica said. Sadie laughed, throwing her head back again and then smiling as she tilted her head and took a sip from her cocktail.

It took a moment for Jessica to figure out why Sadie was being so animated.

Jessica nodded and then leaned forward. "He's here, right?"

"Yeah," Sadie said, smiling like Jessica had said something else funny. "Over by the speakers."

"Is he looking?"

"Yes," Sadie said. Then, a moment later, "Okay, now look."

Jessica stole a glance. He was handsome, but not what Jessica would have imagined to be Sadie's type.

"Huh."

"What? You don't think he's good looking?"

"Oh, he's definitely good looking. I just figured from the way you were playing it that he would be one of those guys who *knew* he was good looking. He looks almost... I don't know, shy? Can't you just go talk to him without all these games?"

"I've tried that. This isn't my first conquest, Jess. I know what I'm doing. If I'm not otherwise engaged, he's not interested. Let's go dance again. You watch—he'll follow us like a magnet if we don't appear interested."

Jessica shrugged. She had to admit that she didn't have that much experience with pursuit. Most of what she thought she knew about flirtation came from a few movies she had seen when she was still a teenager. Movies never matched real life.

They finished their drinks and Sadie led the way back to the dance floor. The music wasn't as loud—it seemed to move through a progression of moods, perhaps so it wouldn't be overwhelming. At the moment, it was a little softer and the beat a little slower. Jessica found it more difficult to drop back into her trance, but that was okay. She didn't want to lose herself in the music again because it would mean that she couldn't pay full attention to the drama unfolding between Sadie and Steve.

When the beat sped back up, Sadie grabbed her hands and the two of them twirled, carving out a circular space on the floor. Jessica laughed at first and then she grew a little dizzy from the spinning. She shook her head and had to let go of Sadie's hands.

"You okay?" Sadie asked into Jessica's ear.

"Just dizzy. I'm okay."

They resumed dancing, but slower and more subdued. The display that Sadie was putting on was working on Steve. Every time Jessica's eyes passed over him, she could see that he was stealing glances at Sadie. The next time that Jessica had a chance, she leaned in again and said, "You should just go over to him."

Sadie smiled and held up a single finger. She began to waggle it with the beat. Jessica laughed. It was just about to happen—Steve put down his drink and seemed to be getting ready to make a move. Jessica turned her body so she could keep track of him out of the corner of her eye. Normally, Jessica wasn't a fan of games like these. They seemed so childish and insincere. But she had to admit that it was interesting to see Sadie exercising her will over Steve from a distance. Her understanding of the situation was masterful. With the roles reversed, Jessica imagined she would have chased Steve away a dozen times already—at least if she accepted Sadie's narrative.

He approached. Pretending to not see him. Sadie jumped when he reached out an touched her arm. She smiled and laughed before greeting him. The music was too loud for Jessica to hear the conversation. Sadie looked completely at ease. Gesturing towards Jessica, Sadie introduced them and Steve waved. Finally, Sadie leaned closer to Jessica and said, "We're going to get another drink. Come along?"

Jessica suspected that the invitation wasn't real. She probably wanted Jessica to make an excuse and bow out.

"Sure," Jessica said. She followed the couple around the corner to the quieter end of the bar. They weren't far from where Travis was still engaged in an embrace.

"This is Steve," Sadie said. "I might have mentioned him at some point. He's a friend of Caroline's?"

"Friend of a friend," Steve said. "I think we met at her place though?"

Sadie shrugged. They ordered more drinks and Steve offered to pay. Sadie was too quick—she had already put down money for the three.

"You guys both work at the meat grinder?"

"Yeah," Sadie said.

Jessica laughed. "That's the second time I've heard it called that. Does everyone call it that? How come I didn't know?"

"Because if you get caught saying it on the premises, you'll get the boot before the end of your shift."

"Oh," Jessica said. She understood the unspoken part of that sentence—this was the first time Jessica had ever interacted with any of her co-workers outside of work.

"Jessica just moved here from LA, like, a month ago," Sadie said.

"Two months," Jessica corrected. "And I'm from Pasadena."

"She's already living with a rich guy up in Highlands."

"I'm not living there, I just stay there sometimes. Wait—how did you know that?"

"People talk, Jess. You should be aware of what they're saying."

"What are they saying?" Jessica asked.

Sadie just smiled, laughed, and patted her arm as she took another sip of her drink. She couldn't help but think that this was another facet of Sadie's plan. Jessica wasn't dismissing herself, so Sadie was driving her away. Just when she thought that Sadie might become a friend, Jessica was finding out that people were gossiping about her and Sadie knew about it all along.

Jessica turned to Steve.

"Are you seeing anyone? Sadie is single, you know."

For a fraction of a second, Sadie's forehead wrinkled and then her eyes narrowed in anger.

Jessica didn't have the stomach to be really cruel to Sadie. It would be too simple to sabotage all her careful plans.

"Don't listen to me," Jessica said. "I'm exhausted. I think I need to get going so I can get some rest before work tomorrow. Sadie, are you staying?"

She smiled. "Yeah, I think I'll stick around for a bit. I want to dance a little more. See you at work."

"Bye," Jessica said to Steve. Jessica backed away before she could do any more damage.

Pushing out through the door of the bar, Jessica let the night air wash over her. For once, it was cool and nice outside. She closed her eyes and drank it in. There was a little humidity to the air and it smelled almost like...

"Rain?" Jessica said. Her eyes flew open. The city lights were too bright—it was impossible to see the night sky. She pulled out her phone and frantically scrolled to the weather app. "Scattered showers," she read.

The idea seemed impossible.

Jessica sprinted for her car. She made it to the door and ripped it open by the time the first drops began to fall. The inside of her car was hot and stuffy. The smell of the upholstery somehow reminded her of an attic. After locking the doors, she spun around to look in the back seat. It was empty. Starting the car, she stomped on the gas pedal after dragging it into gear. Fat drops of rain pelted the windshield and the world began to tilt as vertigo set in.

"No," she whispered between panting breaths. "Stop."

She was headed the wrong direction. As she passed under a streetlight, a shadow moved through the car and she jerked the wheel before she could get control of her muscles.

"Calm down. Calm down," she told herself, trying to regulate her breathing. There was no traffic coming the other direction, but she refused to slow down and double back. If someone was following her, she would be headed right back into their arms.

Jessica barely slowed as she took a left at the next intersection. She didn't know the roads in that part of town well, but she knew that there had to be a major artery she could enter. At that moment, she wanted to be driving fast on a well-lit highway. Up ahead, someone on the sidewalk was standing with one foot in the road and their thumb out. They were wearing a long coat. Jessica nearly swerved into the oncoming lane as she moved as far away from the hitchhiker as she could.

Still accelerating, she took the onramp a bit too fast and her tires lost traction on the wet pavement. She regained control when the car skidded onto the shoulder. Jessica forced herself to slow down a little. At the next interchange, she got on the road towards Simon's mansion.

Safety

Skidding to a stop, Jessica threw open her car door and ran for the house. Before she could ring the bell, the front door opened. Ullman waved her inside. Jessica spotted people in the lounge and didn't slow until she was standing next to the bar.

Billie handed her a towel. Jessica used it to dry her hair and then draped it over her shoulders as she shivered.

"You're okay," Hilda said. "You're safe here."

"How can you be sure? I saw a guy on the road. I think it..."

"Shhh!" Billie said. "You're safe. Trust us. Don't say another word about it."

With a deep breath and a slow exhale, Jessica dabbed her face. It wasn't just the rain. Fat tears were leaking from her eyes as she shook her head.

"I was careless. I didn't even look at the weather before I went out. I never expected..."

"It's okay," Hilda said.

"Come on," Billie said. "I have some warm clothes upstairs you can borrow."

"Okay," Jessica said. She let Billie lead her towards the hall. Jessica stayed very close to Billie as they navigated to the stairs next to the kitchen, up to the second floor, and down to Billie's door.

"Where do those stairs go?"

"Third floor."

"I didn't even realize there was a third floor," Jessica said.

"The facade of the house kinda hides it from the driveway. You can only really see it from above."

She stopped Billie before she could enter the room.

"Are you sure it's safe here?"

"I am."

"How?"

"We've ridden out storms here before, Jessica. Rain is rare, but not unheard of. You're right to be frightened out there, but not here. Here, you're safe."

"Why isn't everyone here then? All the others?"

"Most of them are," Bille said with a smile. "More are coming, I'm sure. The ones who never come aren't the type of people who want to avoid confrontation."

"Really?" Jessica asked.

Billie nodded again. Her room didn't fit the rest of the house. The decor looked almost like it belonged to a midwest teenager, longing for life in the city. There were posters and drawings. Blankets hung alongside the curtains. A bandana had been pinned over the ceiling light. Billie went to a purple dresser and turned around with a pink sweatshirt and yellow sweatpants. Jessica took them and headed to the bathroom after Billie pointed the way. As soon as she took off her damp clothes and put on Billie's sweats, she felt more at ease. Sitting on the edge of the sink, looking through the window, the rain seemed like it had stopped. Billie was sitting on her windowsill, blowing smoke out into the night when Jessica emerged.

"You tell Ullman about this, and I'll kill you," Billie said, gesturing with her cigarette.

"Of course not."

"Don't look at me like that."

"Like what?"

"I can tell that you're nervous about me sitting in the windowsill. Listen, I've been here for years. If he was coming after me here, he would have taken me out years ago."

"I just don't understand why you're so complacent about your own safety."

Billie reached down and stubbed out her cigarette on the outside wall before shutting the window. Jessica went to the door of the bathroom while Billie washed her hands and then gargled with mouthwash.

"I'm not complacent. Let me ask you something—do you think it's a mistake that you're alive?"

"A mistake?"

"Do you think that he really couldn't have killed you if he wanted to?"

"I don't pretend to know," Jessica said.

"Talk to Mel when you get a chance. He has statistics on his attacks and how often he leaves survivors. Mel can't predict the future, but he's really good at analyzing the past. His data shows that none of the survivors have ever been chased down later in life."

"Never?"

"Not at random. Not when it wasn't... Anyway, my point is, you're safe. People get together here—myself included—when it rains because we like to feel safe. We like the support of each other. It's not because we fear for our lives. It's because we're remembering the past. When it rains, you can't push the memories away. Any other time, you might be able to find a way to distract yourself."

Jessica nodded.

"Your'e not convinced."

"No," Jessica said.

"Well, maybe you're right. I mean, who knows, right? It would be kinda arrogant of me to say that I have anything except anecdotal evidence to support my claim. But I do have that anecdotal evidence, so I'm going to be calm, okay?"

Jessica thought about it. "Yeah. Okay."

Billie regarded her carefully for a moment.

"You're not comforted at all, are you."

Jessica smiled sadly and shook her head.

"Let's go see who else is here."

They stopped in the kitchen and Jessica realized that she was hungry while Billie dug through the refrigerator. Normally, Jessica would be at home with a full stomach by now, trying to find an interesting documentary to fall asleep to. All the stress of the evening had delayed her appetite, but it had chased her down.

"Hand me that, would you?" Jessica asked as Billie pushed something to the side.

"Leftover sushi? Are you crazy?"

"It looks good. Did Glen make it?"

"No, it's some prepackaged thing that shows up on delivery day. That's the stuff that nobody wanted. This is a desert, by the way. Any raw fish in this refrigerator had to travel at least a couple-hundred miles to get here."

"People eat sushi."

"You're crazy. Here—knock yourself out."

She handed a plastic container over her shoulder and Jessica opened it on the counter. She sniffed one of the pieces before she put it in her mouth.

"Oh! So good!"

"You're crazy."

Billie came out of the refrigerator with a sandwich, carrots, and some dip. She pushed the door shut with her knee and led the way while Jessica picked through the pickled ginger from her plastic container. They stopped at a drawer that held napkins and Jessica found a paper sleeve of chopsticks to go with her food before they continued towards the hall.

"I hope you weren't offended," Billie said over her shoulder.

"By what?"

"Nothing, I guess."

As they rounded the corner to the lounge, Billie picked up her pace.

"Laura's here," Billie said, sitting down on the couch next to an older woman. She set her food down on the coffee table and waved for Jessica to sit with them. There were other people in the room. Jessica had a difficult time deciding what was more rude—sitting apart from the main contingent, or ignoring Billie's invitation. She decided she would accept Billie's invitation and she sat own on the floor on the other side of the coffee table.

"Laura, you've met Jessica, right?"

"Not one-on-one," Laura said, extending her hand.

The long fingernails reminded Jessica where she had first seen Laura.

"Wait, you were at a grief meeting at the middle school, right?"

Laura nodded and they shook.

"I wondered if you were the Laura that Joe told me about, but I dismissed the idea when you talked about your sister. I just now made the connection."

Laura nodded. "People can have more than one thing they're grieving about."

"Of course," Jessica said. "Sorry, I didn't mean to say the wrong thing."

She wasn't actually sure why what she had said was wrong, but it felt appropriate to apologize.

"No, it's fine."

"Laura," Billie said through a mouthful of food. "Tell Jessica something that would freak her out. Do it!"

Laura looked annoyed.

"Mel collects data and Laura correlates everything to real cases out in the world. She knows crazy things about all of us. It's all public record."

"Mostly," Laura said, taking off her glasses to clean them with a tissue. "Billie, I've found that a lot of people don't care to know how much of their personal information is out in the world."

"So you know things about me from the internet?" Jessica asked.

"It's how we found you," Laura said. "But I don't make it my business to snoop."

"Tell me something," Jessica said. She tried to make the request sound casual, but she felt exposed.

"Trust me, Jessica, people never like to hear the things they've revealed online, even if they say they do," Laura said.

"Please?"

Laura looked up and searched her memory. "Uh. Once you were on your own, you lived in seven apartments over the course of thirty months. You walked out on four lease agreements."

Jessica stopped chewing. Her stomach turned. Suddenly, the idea of eating raw fish that was trucked or flown into the middle of a desert seemed like a horrible idea.

"Sorry—too personal?" Laura asked.

"No," Jessica said as she forced herself to swallow. She tried to smile and look like everything was still normal. She hadn't told anyone about those broken leases. After a couple of moves, she thought that she had successfully left them in the past.

"Tell her something even more personal," Billie said.

"I don't think she wants to hear..."

"No," Jessica said. "Tell me."

Laura's eyes didn't break contact with Jessica's. They were playing a game of chicken, but only Jessica had something on the line.

"Tell me," Jessica said again.

"Your family called your brother pumpkin when he was born because he looked orange. Your mom made you stop because she was allergic to pumpkin and she didn't want to even joke about being allergic to her baby."

Jessica stopped breathing. If someone told her that Laura had just dug that fact out of the deep recesses of her own brain, she would have had no reason to doubt it. As far as she knew, the short-lived nickname had been something only three people in the world had ever known. They hadn't even ever told Peter about it because they knew it would make him sad.

"Wow," Billie said. "Looks like you really found something there. You wouldn't believe the things she found out about me. Laura was able to tell me the first time I smoked a cigarette and where I stole it from. I mean, there are things that I'm certain don't exist anywhere online, but somehow Laura finds them."

"I need to use the restroom," Laura said, excusing herself.

"You look shook," Billie said to Jessica. "You okay?"

"How did she know that?"

"It's government databases probably. They record everything about everything, pretend to lock it away, and then they act all surprised when someone like Laura stumbles on the keys. They talk about only analyzing metadata, but what that really means is that the people who they have doing the analysis aren't smart enough to correlate things to real people. Trust me, Laura might be the smartest person you've ever met. At least about computer things, she's smart. She does seem to have some issues with gauging boundaries."

"No," Jessica said, looking down at her sushi. "I mean, I asked."

"Yeah, true. I think she should have known that your brother was off limits though."

From over at the bar, Dylan said, "Hey, the rain is stopping in fifteen minutes."

A couple of people clapped. Vivian, standing over by the window, made the sign of the cross.

"You want to stay with me tonight?" Billie asked.

"Upstairs?" Jessica asked.

"Yeah, that loveseat in my room folds out. You still look a little shaky."

"Actually, that would be really nice, thank you. I have a bag out in my car."

"I'll tell Ullman to get it for you."

"He doesn't have..."

"Trust me, he likes to feel useful."

CHAPTER NINE

Billie

Return

"It has been a while since I got into the gritty details of this, so I'm going to go slow," Billie said.

Jessica shifted in her seat. Billie was such a private person—so closed off—it was difficult to watch her trying to open herself up enough to talk.

"I moved from the suburbs to Boston when I was eighteen. By twenty-one, I had a boyfriend and a place to live. I was twenty-five when everything went to hell. I had a good job. I started counting traffic for the city, but I had worked my way into the traffic projects department. Everybody hates Boston traffic, so our department was the butt of every joke, but I didn't care. They paid well. My boyfriend worked a couple of jobs, depending on the time of year. In the summer, he used to work on highways in the night crew. It paid less, but it wasn't as hot and it wasn't as dangerous. Sometimes, during the summer, we would only see each other for ten minutes a day. I would come home and wake him up, and then he would be out the door."

Billie thanked Dylan as he handed her a drink.

They had another full house for the meeting. Jessica glanced around and realized that, for once, she knew everyone's name.

"I got out of work on a Thursday and ran for the T. It was raining, of course. I didn't know it was supposed to rain. By the time I got back to my building, I was soaked and freezing. As soon as I woke up Len, I knew he would be out the door. When it was raining, they always tried to push the clock—I don't know why. I was already resenting the fact that we wouldn't get any time together. I would have just a few minutes with him, and I would be freezing and wet, just thinking about jumping in a warm shower the whole time I was with him. Then, I got inside and he was already out on the fire escape in his coat. He used to go down the fire escape and meet his friend in the alley behind our place."

Bilie sighed.

"I'm trying to tell you this just like it happened. Anyway, I yelled at him that he could at least have a conversation with me before he took off. I told him to get inside and say goodbye to me. He didn't say anything. I went to the bathroom, figuring that I would skip right to the warm shower. The whole time I'm taking a shower, I was cursing Len under my breath. When the toilet flushed and I was nearly burned, I shoved the shower curtain aside and yelled at him directly."

Jessica squirmed in her seat again. Billie was back in that moment and it was terrible to watch.

"I asked him why he got undressed again. He said he didn't know what I was talking about and told me he had to get going. He gave me a kiss and I closed the curtain. My brain just chewed on the problem while I thawed out in the shower. He had been out on the fire escape in his coat, then he had come back in, undressed, and used the bathroom. There was only one way that it made sense—it wasn't Len that I saw out on the fire escape. The more I thought about it, the more it made sense. Len wouldn't have worn a long coat like that. He would have had on his hooded windbreaker. That had to be some other creep who was standing out there on the fire escape, looking at me through the window.

"I wrapped myself in a towel and went out to the living room while I yelled to Len that there was a peeping Tom out there. I found Len in the bedroom. He was on the bed, face up with his arms and legs out like a starfish. He was cut right down the middle. I didn't know very much about anatomy, but even I knew that there were things missing from inside him. There wasn't all that much blood, but there were definitely organs missing. I didn't know what to do, so I just slipped into the closet and pulled the door shut. The only Iight was coming from under the door, and most of that was blocked when my towel slipped off."

Billie wiped her forehead with her hand. She clenched her jaw and almost sneered before she continued on with her story.

"One of the reasons I was good at my job was because I knew how to blend in. They would try to put instruments on the streets to measure traffic and they would be vandalized or stolen. Cameras would be painted or broken. In some neighborhoods, the only way to get rush hour traffic counts was with real human beings, clicking clickers for every car that passed. And you couldn't just ask anyone to do it. You had to have someone who was dependable, who would blend in, and who could hold her own when she was harassed by the people who did their business on the streets. That was me. Nobody messed with me.

"For a while, the lady who managed our building thought I was a prostitute. The clothes I wore to get my job done didn't leave her any other explanation. I explained, but eventually I had to show her a pay stub for her to believe me. I also showed her the commendation my boss gave me the year before. Other people tried to copy my methods, but they didn't understand. The clothes were only part of it. The clothes helped you get in the right headspace, but I also had to turn myself into someone who would legitimately live on the streets of the neighborhoods I worked. It was easy for me—years before, I had done just that.

"So, hiding in that closet, I automatically reached for Len's jacket. I knew just where it was, and what I would look like when I put it on. I grabbed a hat from the shelf too. I transformed myself into my version of the guy I had seen on the fire escape. I entered his frame of mind as I slipped my bare feet into my boots. All I needed was a knife, and I knew where Len kept one.

"When I stepped out of that closet and saw my boyfriend again, it was through new eyes. I wasn't horrified by the disembowelment. I saw it and I could appreciate the craftsmanship of it. The act had been committed during the course of my shower, resulted in very little spilled blood, and I hadn't heard any of it from the bathroom. There was real skill demonstrated in that. I stepped close to Len's body and found the big knife he kept in his bedside drawer. He said it was a hunting knife, but Len had never been hunting in his life. In my hand, wearing the costume of a killer, the knife felt right.

"It was my turn to hunt. I crossed the living room to the window that led to the fire escape. I turned to look at the apartment through the killer's eyes. Taking everything in, I saw the my home as an outsider and imagined seeing a tired woman come through the door, sopping wet, grabbing a towel from the linen closet next to the door. The memory of myself dried her hair while she looked out at the fire escape and said, 'Is it too much to ask that we have a conversation for two minutes before you run off to work?' Then, I watched her throw down the towel and head for the bathroom. A moment later, my imagination supplied the sound of the shower coming on.

"I retraced the killer's steps into the bedroom. When Len woke up, the killer would have slipped behind the door. Sure enough, I saw drops of water on the floor there. The killer had dripped rain on the floor while they waited for Len to go use the bathroom and then return to the bedroom. That's when the killer struck, taking Len from behind and guiding him to the bed. My imagination couldn't come up with an explanation of how to extract all of Len's blood without spilling it everywhere, but I had a good sense of what the killer did next. They would have returned to the linen closet next to the door."

"Why?" Wahid asked, interrupting Bille for the first time.

Billie took the question in stride. "That's where I left my bag when I came in. The killer assumed that once I found Len I would run for my bag to get my phone. Hiding in the linen closet provided the best place to lie in wait. Sure enough, as I approached the closet, I saw a small puddle of water gathered beneath the door. I could hear my own heartbeat pounding in my ears as I slowly reached out my hand. At the precise moment my hand touched the knob, my apartment door rattled in its frame and then flung inward."

Billie looked down at her hands.

She took a deep breath.

"It was the police. They knocked the knife from my hand and tackled me to the floor. On the way down, my head struck a wooden chair and I barely knew what was going on for the next ten minutes. Every time they shouted a question at me, I would just repeat it back trying to figure out what they were saying. Everything I said was used against me in a court of law, just like they warn you. But, in my case, they weren't admissions, they were just me repeating a question I couldn't get my head around. 'Did you kill your boyfriend?' and I would say, 'I kill my boyfriend?' The only thing they didn't have was Len's blood on the knife I was holding."

She paused for several seconds. Jessica tried to hold back her question, but it just came out.

"They accused you of killing him?"

Billie shook her head with a dry laugh. "They *convicted* me of it. It only took the jury a few minutes to come back with the decision. My lawyer tried to get me to plea. He tried to coax me into saying that Len was abusive. I wouldn't do either. I would have rather spent the rest of my life in jail than blame Len or take the blame for his murder."

"How did you get out of prison?"

Billie gave her a sad smile and shook her head. "That's not part of this story. There were a couple more things I pieced together from the evidence that the police collected. They found a tiny trace of Len's blood in the linen closet, so I know the killer did go there after he killed Len. The killer was probably waiting in there while I went to the bedroom and then made their escape while I was putting on my disguise in the bedroom closet.

"The neighbor across the alley, a really old guy, saw a couple of things. He saw the killer standing on the fire escape, come inside, and attack Len. He testified that the shower was on when Len was murdered, but nobody believed me that I was taking a shower during the stabbing. The police had no explanation as to where Len's blood went. As far as anyone knows, that's a complete mystery.

"The old guy went to his kitchen to call the cops and must have still been there when I came out of the shower and hid in the bedroom closet. Nobody saw the killer go back down the fire escape. That's it. That's all I know."

"Do you need a break before more questions?" Vivian asked.

Billie shook her head.

"No. Go ahead."

Questions

Jessica barely paid attentions to the questions that came at Billie.

"Did they think that the wounds on Len matched the knife you were holding?" someone asked.

"There were some superficial similarities, but they admitted that most of the wounds weren't an exact match. My layer argued that the police never found the real murder weapon, but that didn't sway anyone."

Billie was rubbing her forehead, like the questions were giving her a headache. Jessica wanted to go to her, but didn't think that any gesture would be well received.

"Was the window to the fire escape normally locked?" another person asked.

Billie only nodded.

When the questions were finally over, Billie practically sprinted for the door to the terrace. Jessica intended to follow her out there, but Dylan and Mel were already going that direction. Jessica had never been out to the smoker's terrace before, and she thought she would feel out of place is she tried to join them now.

People dispersed different directions. It was uncomfortable to wait on the couch for the smokers to come back inside. After a couple of minutes, Jessica gave up and decided she would give Billie space. There had been no dates mentioned in Billie's story, but Jessica guessed that it had to have been years since the incident. It was hard to guess. Something about the way that Billie had told her story, it felt like something that had just happened.

Jessica saw Ullman in the foyer.

"Thank you," she said, "for welcoming me in the other night."

He didn't seem to know what she was talking about.

"In the rain?" she added.

His face softened a little.

"Of course."

She nodded and headed for the door.

"Are you staying the night?" he asked as she pulled the front door open.

"No. I have work tomorrow," she said.

Jessica had her hand on the car door when someone appeared from the shadows. She sucked in a breath and put a hand to her chest.

"You scared me to death," she said to Dylan.

"Sorry. I heard you were leaving and I wanted to stop you."

"What? Why?"

"I thought maybe you would stay with Billie tonight. She has a hard time when she tells her story and I know it would really mean something to her if you stayed."

"Me? I thought you two were tight."

Dylan shook his head. "The whole time she has lived here, the only people she has ever had in her room were Simon and you. Ullman hasn't even been in there and he and Billie are practically brother and sister."

"Oh?"

"You might not think of her as a friend, Jess, but I think you might be her *best* friend."

"I had..." Jessica shook her head instead of finishing the sentence. "Yeah, I have a bag. I guess I can stay."

"Good. Thank you. I'll stick around for a little bit as well."

Jessica opened her trunk and found the bag packed with her overnight stuff.

"I had no idea that she and Ullman were so close."

"You are, apparently, terrible at judging who Billie is close to," Dylan said with a laugh.

Jessica shrugged. They approached the door and it opened from the inside. Ullman held it open and welcomed them with a sweeping arm. Dylan walked fast towards the private wing and Jessica rushed to keep up. He stopped at the stairs.

"Good luck," he said, looking into her eyes and then glancing away.

"Good luck?"

Jessica climbed slowly. When she glanced back, Dylan was already gone. At the end of the hall, Billie's door was closed. She knocked, hoping that she was at the right door. Eventually, she heard feet cross the floor and the door clicked and swung open.

"Hey, Billie, you mind if I hang out for a minute?"

Billie looked her up and down before her eyes settled on the bag.

"You planning on staying for a while?"

Jessica blushed as she came in and pushed the door shut with her foot.

"I just haven't had a chance to stake out one of the rooms yet. I thought you might want to talk after that story."

Jessica set her bag down and then settled into the chair near the window.

"Not really," Billie said. "I kinda left it all out on the field."

They sat in silence for a moment before Jessica thought of something to say.

"I remember how infuriating and terrifying it was when the cops wouldn't believe me. I lost my family and then they heaped on the misery. I couldn't have felt more alone."

Billie nodded.

"I know you said it wasn't part of your story earlier, but I'm still curious how you managed to get released from prison," Jessica said.

Billie reached over to the nightstand and grabbed her pack of cigarettes.

"You want to go up to the roof?"

Roof

The air up on the roof was something that Jessica had never experienced. Hot air was rising from the surface beneath her feet, and it was being consumed by the cool night air. It felt like the world was evaporating beneath her and it might sweep her up into the blackness above.

She hugged her arms around herself and shivered.

Billie got up from her deck chair and walked back over to the access door. Leaning inside, she came back out with a sweatshirt and tossed it to Jessica.

"Thanks."

Billie sat down again and lit her cigarette.

"I'm guessing that they make you tell your story periodically," Jessica said.

In the glow of her cigarette, Jessica saw Billie raise her eyebrows in a silent question.

"You seem so reticent to talk about yourself, but something made you do it. Do they make you tell your story for each new arrival?"

"Nobody makes me," Billie said. "It's difficult, but it's something that I have to do. Keeps me grounded."

Jessica covered her mouth and stifled a laugh.

"What?" Billie demanded.

"I would describe you as many things. Grounded isn't at the top of the list."

"I'm grounded," Billie said.

"I think of grounded as, like, centered, peaceful, and balanced.

You're more the strong, defiant type."

"Thank you," Billie said with a nod.

"And angry. Maybe with a few impulse control issues."

"You're just stereotyping me."

"Could be," Jessica said. "Probably."

They both laughed. The flashing lights of an airplane passed overhead. The glow of the city lights made a dome over the buildings in the distance. While they sat in silence, Jessica pulled her legs up and folded them under herself.

"The hardest thing to accept is the loss of the future," Jessica said. "I can only guess at the way life would have been, and that just means that I'm free to completely idealize it. I would have gone to college, moved back to maybe twenty miles away from Dad's house and found a little apartment and a starter job. I would have met someone and maybe started a family of my own."

"That's dumb," Billie said.

"In what way?"

"You could still do all those things. It's ridiculous to pine for things that you could have if you chose to have them. Just do it if you want to do it."

"How can I, knowing the trauma and loss that might live around every corner?"

Billie laughed.

"Everyone in the world has those same risks, Jess. Just because you've experienced them already doesn't make you more susceptible. It's arguable that you've already survived the worst thing that could ever happen to you. If that's the case, then you should feel completely free to take any chances you want. People don't win the lottery twice. Goes the other way too."

"That's like building a sand castle on the same beach that a hurricane swept away. Stupid."

"And, yet, people do that every single day. It's not getting knocked in the dirt that defines you—it's whether or not you get back up."

"This is a strange pep talk from the woman who is hiding here, perpetually frightened to go out in the world."

"Who better to give you advice? If I was over it, I wouldn't be able to empathize with you," Billie said.

"I don't think that's the way it works," Jessica said.

Billie shrugged.

They fell silent again.

Eventually, Billie said, "I'm guessing they sent you to keep an eye on me. You don't have to, you know. I'm not a danger to myself right now, I'm just tired."

Jessica considered what Billie was saying. She thought she had a pretty good idea what it meant.

"Tell me what happened after," Jessica said.

"There is no after. This is all *after*," Billie said.

"Whatever," Jessica said.

"Tell me about your aunt."

"Huh?"

"I noticed the way you glossed over that part of your story. You tell me about that."

"Not much to tell. Technically, she was my great aunt—but not really. My grandmother on my mother's side was really my step grandmother. So she was my step great aunt. She and my grandmother had moved down to Florida to live with their mother, who died before I was born. They lived on the gulf side. I had only met her a few times. She didn't even come to Mom's funeral. I guess she was my godmother. Honestly, I don't even know how they tracked her down. She wasn't on my father's Christmas card list. I barely recognized the name when they said that she agreed to take me in. They put me on a flight and I arrived in Tampa. Part of me wanted to be excited, but it was like I was seeing everything as a pinpoint of light in the distance. I was so withdrawn into myself that it actually affected my vision."

"Yeah," Billie said. "We fixate. Perception narrows."

"Yes," Jessica said. "I had to do everything. I had to go to the high school on my own. I learned the city bus route. I didn't want to ride the bus with all the underclassmen or admit that I didn't have a car. It was weird. I don't think I had a single conversation with anyone that whole time. Then, my aunt had a stroke. I came home and found her staring at nothing. It was raining that day. I almost ran out of there. Instead, I called for an ambulance and held her hand while we waited. She recovered a little in the hospital and then she died."

Billie nodded. "What then?"

Jessica sighed.

"I just kept on. I had her checkbook and I forged her signature to pay the bills. She had already made the arrangements for her own funeral. Eventually, the lawyers sold the house out from under me in order to settle the estate. Everything went to charities except for some money set aside for my mom. The first time the lawyers contacted me, it was because they were trying to find contact information for Mom. I gave them the address of the cemetery back in Milford."

"She didn't leave you anything?"

"I don't know. I think she intended to, but maybe didn't get around to it. It didn't matter. By the time they kicked me out, I had graduated and I was ready to move on anyway. There was too much rain in Florida."

"All things considered, seems like a pretty soft landing," Billie said.

"How so?"

"You made it through high school and slipped into adulthood without being shipped off to a foster home or orphanage, right? You never really had to suffer as the ward of someone who wanted to hurt you."

Jessica frowned. "I lost my whole family and then found out that there was no such thing as extended family. All of that in the course of two years. You call that a soft landing?"

Billie shrugged. "Kind of. Yes."

Jessica thought about it for a minute and then started laughing.

"What?" Billie asked.

"Nothing. Everything."

"You holding something back on me?"

Jessica nodded. She knew she couldn't speak. The words weren't going to come out. She struggled so hard to make a sound that tears sprang from her eyes and rolled down her cheeks.

"Spit it out," Billie said.

Jessica's voice came out as a croak. "Aunt Carol told me something."

"What?"

Jessica shook her head. "It was nonsense—I know that. Her voice was so slurred that I couldn't even really tell what she was trying to say. I would just make up words that somewhat matched the sounds coming out of her and if they made sense I would pretend that's what she intended to say."

"What was it?"

"Before the ambulance came, I was petrified. I held her hand and through the window I watched the rain spilling over the gutter. She said, 'Drowned,' and I told her we were going to stay inside, where it was nice and dry. I cautioned that we would have to go outside for just a second so we could get in the ambulance, but then we would go to the hospital where everything would be dry again. Aunt Carol only blinked and frowned. Half of her face was already sagging. When she frowned, she almost looked symmetrical again. Aunt Carol said, 'Drowned in blood,' and I almost let go of her hand."

Jessica clamped a hand over her face, gripping her own temples to prevent the headache that was beginning to throb.

"You're kidding. Are you sure that..."

"No, I'm not sure of anything. I told you that. She said it again, 'Drowned in blood,' and I knew that she was talking about the guy from the rain. I asked her if she knew what happened to my family and she turned and pointed her eyes at me. I don't mean that she looked at me—I'm not sure she was able to actually *look* at anything. Her eyes were unfocused, but pointed right at me. She said, 'They never wanted you.' That was the last thing she managed to tell me before the ambulance arrived. Later, she recovered a little in the hospital but she couldn't tell me what she meant by that. She didn't remember saying it."

"Do you have a guess?"

"At the time, the only thing I could think was that she was just completely out of it. Clearly, her blood vessels were clogged or whatever, right? You can't expect someone to express themselves in that state. It's just nonsense words. Later, when I couldn't sleep because I was alone in that house for the first time, I began to wonder if she meant my parents. Mom always used to say that I was a beautiful gift to her that she never had the audacity to hope for. She was like that. Mom always used to say really flowery things like that. But, of course, I analyzed that expression after she was dead. She never had the audacity to hope for me. That probably meant that I was unexpected. That's another way of saying that my parents weren't trying to have kids and that I was a mistake. Then, after I was several years old, they gave into the concept and decided to have my brother and sister."

"What kind of cancer did your mom have?"

"Ovarian."

"So, maybe she just meant that they told her she probably wouldn't have kids. That's another explanation for why you were so much older than your siblings—they were trying the whole time and it took a while."

"But, then Aunt Carol said they never wanted me."

"That could mean so many things, or nothing at all," Billie said.

"Yeah. You're right. In fact, later I started to believe that maybe she just meant 'they' as in the guy."

Billie nodded.

"Or, maybe 'they' means whoever is behind the guy."

"Behind?"

"Like some force that sends the guy around to kill."

"You think there's some kind of, what, meeting or something where people decide who should live and who shouldn't?"

"No, I mean... Who knows, right? I'm just trying to think of all the things that Aunt Carol could have meant. It's probably silly to read meaning into the last words of someone whose brain is literally dying. Then again, it's possible that she had insight that a healthy person could never have. There are parts of the brain that exist to only make sense of things in the reality that we've learned. When those parts are turned off, maybe we see things clearly for the first time."

"Maybe."

Benefactor

They had been silent for several minutes. Jessica was contemplating her memory of her aunt. As her breathing became more labored and she stopped responding to questions, the doctors provided no explanation. Then, one day Aunt Carol just slipped away.

"I remember the day I gave up," Billie said.

Jessica turned and watch Billie light another cigarette. She used a cheap plastic lighter—nothing like what the guy carried.

"Gave up on..."

"Living. I had been in prison for nearly three years and I had been stabbed two times and punished both times. They were light stabbings. If someone means to kill you, they'll stab you forty or fifty times. If you just catch one or two to the gut, then they just wanted to give you a message."

"What was the message?"

"I don't know. That's probably why they stabbed me two different times. I just didn't get the message. It would have been three or more if it wasn't for Simon."

"He was the guy who used to own this house?"

"This house and many more," Billie said.

"He protected you?"

"Yeah. He did everything. Before Mel and Laura, Simon had an agency on his payroll and all they did was look for people like us—people who were victims of the man. I wasn't the only one who was falsely accused of murder. When he found one of us in jail, Simon fought to get us out. I was in protective custody when

Simon's people tracked me down. I was pulled from a hospital bed and transported to a different facility where I sat across from a pair of old women who asked me about that day. At first, I didn't want to say anything. I had already been convicted and I knew that nothing I said would change that."

Billie blew smoke up towards the stars.

"Simon came in and dismissed the pair of women. At this point, I still didn't have any idea why I had been pulled into another interrogation or who Simon was. He pulled his chair around to be closer to me. I told him that I needed to get back to my bed. I still had sutures and sitting up was pulling on them. He ignored me and just stared. He told me, 'The man smells like rotting leather and something cool and sweet, like a bubbling creek you would find running through the woods. But underneath there's always that rotting leather smell that reminds you he belongs to death.' That's when I guessed that Simon was another victim. He had come to see if I was too. From his description, I knew precisely who he was talking about, but I said, 'I never smelled him. I never got that close.' Still, I knew in that moment that we had both seen the man. I had to trust Simon. He was like me. The thing was, I had to prove to Simon that I was authentic too."

"Prove to Simon? You were the one locked up," Jessica said.

"Right, but what if I made up the stuff about the man. I had to give Simon some detail to prove that my story was authentic. I thought and thought, but I didn't have any real evidence. If I had, I wouldn't have been sitting in jail. I told Simon my story from the start and he only stared at me. There was nothing in my description that validated what he suspected."

"What did you do?" Jessica asked.

"I gave up," Billie said. "I threw up my hands and just gave up. I said something like, 'I have nothing more to tell you. Just let me go back to my bed. As soon as I heal up, I'll just go stand outside in the rain and wait for him to finish the job. That was enough for Simon to take a chance on me. Next think I knew, I had a brand new legal team with all kinds of motions and appeals. I think that was all for show. The legal process wasn't what got me out of prison—it was Simon's pull. I never set foot in another court. I was granted probation, but I never had to talk to a single probation officer. The legal system contains rules for normal people. For those as rich as Simon, everything was only a suggestion."

"He brought you here?"

"No," Billie said. "I came here on my own. Getting out of prison was huge—probably saved my life—but what really stuck with me was how I saw Simon change his mind as soon as I mentioned the rain. To me, down in my soul, I knew that the man had come with the rain or the rain had come with him. That's not something I had ever expressed to the police or any lawyer though—why would I? The weather on the day of the murder was purely incidental. The only pertinent fact about it was that I tracked the man by the puddles he left behind. But in my mind, the rain was everything. So I told Simon that I would stand outside in the rain and wait for the man to finish the job. That's when he knew that I was telling the truth. Back then, the connection between the murder and rain was much more of a secret."

"Are some of the others here people that Simon rescued from prison?"

Billie shook her head.

"Nope. I'm the only one here. Maybe being in prison changes a person, or maybe the murders themselves changed them, but the other people that Simon had released didn't turn out as pleasant and well-adjusted as me."

"Oh."

"You remember how I described wanting to be the hunter when I saw what happened to my boyfriend?"

Jessica nodded.

"I had this impulse to dress up like him and almost *become* him. It was weird how quickly that idea took hold of me. In fact, during my trial I almost thought the prosecution was justified. Part of me really believed that I had killed Len. Everything else seemed like a fantasy I had concocted, but I could almost remember slicing him open."

"No," Jessica said, rejecting the images that popped into her head. It was too easy to picture Billie straddling her boyfriend and brining the knife down.

"No, it wasn't me. I'm just saying. Well, I think that the majority of the others who were falsely accused and prosecuted indulged even more in the fantasy that they were to blame. In fact, one of the guys that Simon got released became a copycat."

"What?" Jessica asked, sitting up straight.

"Yup. He chased storm fronts coming east across from Colorado. He rode a motorcycle and when it started raining he would leave his bike in a ditch and walk to the nearest house. He wasn't a successful copycat, thank god. The first house he invaded, a woman clipped him with a handgun when he broke in. He jumped back on his motorcycle and continued the chase. He wounded a guy in Kansas, but that guy survived. Finally, on his third attempt, he was caught when he stumbled on some steps and broke his ankle. The police grabbed him limping down the road."

"That's horrible. Is it possible that this is all..."

"Just copycats? I don't think so. It's easy to tell the real victims because there's always a part of the story that can't be explained. Like you, with the power outage."

"And phone."

"Right. There's a supernatural element to the real incidents. The copycats are also apprehended pretty quickly. That's why Simon had to stop trying to get people exonerated though. Almost all of them turned bad anyway. If they weren't killers before, they became killers when they went through the whole process."

"Maybe that's the point," Jessica said.

"What do you mean?"

"I'm not particularly religious, but what if this guy is, like, a demon or something. Maybe he's being directed by Satan to destabilize our society or just terrorize us in general. Maybe part of the terror is to turn us into killers too. His demon goes around killing. In the process, a certain percentage of people turn into killers who mimic him. It's like a virus or something."

"That's crazy," Billie said.

"Is it any crazier than what happened to you?"

Billie thought about that for a minute. She stubbed out her cigarette.

"I guess not."

Kitchen

Jessica covered her mouth when she failed to stifle another yawn.

"You working tomorrow?" Billie asked.

They were sitting in the kitchen. Between them, bowls of sticky, melted ice cream were sitting. Jessica's head buzzed from the sugar.

"Yeah," Jessica said. "Do you work?"

"No. I don't even leave this house anymore."

Jessica had already suspected that Billie never left the property.

"I can't go without a job for long," Jessica said. "I need to have something to fill my time or my brain kinda goes off the rails. There was a time when I lived in Arizona. The insurance company finally paid out my father's policy. I got lucky because my aunt was already dead. That sounds weird to say it like that. If Aunt Carol had been alive when my father's policy paid, then she would have gotten the money because she was my guardian. Then, when she died, all of Dad's money would have gone to charity. I assume that's what happened to the money from the sale of the house and everything."

"That sucks."

Jessica nodded. She propped up her head with her hand.

"So, it was just dumb luck that they took so long to verify that his death qualified. Anyway, with all that money I decided that I didn't have to work. Before long, I went crazy. I started hanging out with these guys at the gun store. Everything to them was a giant conspiracy. It sounds cliché to say that these heavily-armed guys were all into weird conspiracy theories, but it happened to be true. It doesn't take long before those ideas start to make sense," Jessica said.

"Like a virus?" Billie asked.

"Huh?"

"You said maybe the murders would spread like a virus. Is that where you got that idea?" Billie asked.

"Oh. You know? Maybe that is where I got that idea. I remember one night I confessed what happened to me. I expected that they would be floored by what I was saying, but they all took it in stride. Half of them were just nodding, knowingly. One of them said something like, 'Yeah, these paranormal murders are on the rise.' Then he blamed it on afro-latin rituals or something. He just folded my thing into one of his bigger theories and started spouting off, expanding his mythos to incorporate what happened to me. I can't even begin to explain how frustrating that was. Those things legitimately happened to me and he was rolling the murder of my family into some half-baked twisted ideas that he had read or heard about. It's a good thing I wasn't holding a gun at that moment. I might have shot him."

Billie laughed.

"I had started to hang out with those guys because I felt so alone," Jessica said. "Then, when I realized that my experiences were so unlike theirs, I felt even more alone. I moved soon after that and the first thing I did was get a job. I figured out that I needed to be surrounded by people who were pissed that they had to work on the weekends, or pissed because they didn't get a promotion. I wanted to leave all that weirdness behind. Give me a room full of people who want to talk about what a jerk the boss is, and I'm happy."

"You wanted regular drama," Billie said.

"Exactly. To stay sane, I need regular, normal-person drama going on. For me, a job is an escape from crazy fringe ideas and fear. It resets my expectations. I remember when Mom was in the hospital. Dad's boss visited one time and told Dad that he could take some time off to get everything squared away. But there wasn't all that much to do at home. Dad said he had to keep going in and us kids had to keep going to school. We had to stick to normal life so we didn't get lost in the other stuff."

Billie contemplated that idea.

"That's probably smart, but I don't think I could do it," Billie said.

"I'm not saying *you* should. This is just something I figured out about myself."

Billie nodded.

"Speaking of which," Jessica said. "If I don't get some sleep, I'm going to be useless tomorrow."

"That will help make you like everyone else."

Jessica smiled. "That's true. Everyone drags around like zombies half the time. They all seem to have a pretty intense social life. If I don't see you in the morning..."

"I'll catch you for Dylan's night. He usually likes to tell his story after I've told mine."

"Should I brace myself?"

"No need. If anything, Dylan's story is almost lighthearted compared to everyone else's."

Jessica sat confused about that as Billie took their bowls to the dishwasher.

CHAPTER TEN
Dylan

Running

Dylan took a deep breath. For once, he wasn't sitting at the bar. Dylan sat between Joe and Wahid on one of the couches and it seemed like the rest of the furniture had all been pointed to face him. Jessica found herself directly across from Dylan. Every time he looked up, he was staring into her eyes.

"My partner, at the time, was out of town on business. I was alone. Back then, I wasn't all that okay with being alone. I needed someone I could pop in on and ask a question or share a thought. So, as I moved around the house, tidying up, I was well aware that I was alone that night. And then I wasn't."

Dylan's shoulders rose as he took a breath.

"It was raining, hard. I was already looking forward to taking a swim at dawn. Our swimming pool would smell so clean, almost electric, the morning after it rained, and the water would be cooler than normal. I knew that by the time I got out, my whole body would feel minty fresh. That's why I turned on the pool lights when I was walking through the living room. I wanted to see the water splashing on the surface of the pool, lit with blue from below.

"When I turned them on, I saw Phillip standing there between me and the pool."

Dylan looked up into Jessica's eyes and explained, "My therapist told me to give my fear a name instead of just referring to him as an archetype. So, instead of calling him 'The Man' or 'The Killer', I gave him the name Phillip. I knew a kid named Phillip in school. He was weak and a complete pushover. So, I call the man in the trench coat Phillip."

Jessica nodded. She conjured the memory of the man lighting his hand-rolled cigarette and tried to apply the name Phillip to him. For her, it didn't stick.

"I yelled through the glass doors and told him to go away. I saw that he was smoking out there and I imagined that he would toss his cigarette butt into the pool when he was done, and that was the end of my patience. How could I feel minty fresh in the morning if I was swimming in an ashtray? I picked up the phone and said, 'I'm calling the cops on you. Go away.' He turned and walked off into the night, so I put the phone down. I had my reasons for not wanting to call the cops. Another time when I was staying alone, I called them because of a noise. It turned into a whole thing.

"Instead, I just texted my friend Arthur and told him I was coming over. He was like me—he liked to have other people around. But, unlike me, he couldn't live with anyone for long, so he really enjoyed my occasional visits. I put on a raincoat, but decided I didn't want to mess with an umbrella. Before I left, I turned on all the lights in the house, inside and out. Our neighbors hated it when we left on the lights that pointed down at the driveway, but I figured that was a good thing. They would keep an eye on the place for us out of spite."

Dylan looked down at his feet. He was hunched over, resting his arms on his thighs.

"It was raining so hard out that it wasn't all that easy to see. I glanced at the neighbors' on the way by. It looked like they had replaced the linen sheers on the front window. There was a big new splash of burgundy in that window. As much as I hated the linen look, I *despised* the splash of burgundy. Of course, you can guess that it wasn't the neighbors who had done the redecorating. It was Phillip.

"I heard someone walking behind me. Just the way she walked, I recognized Holly. Have you ever had one of those friends who has a bounce in their step that's contagious? Holly brightened up every room she walked in. When I spotted her, I slowed down and called out when she was still several paces away. A tall man confronting her on a dark street in the middle of the night? I knew it would scare her. But even before I was yelling to her to be heard over the rain, she was running towards me. She asked, 'Dylan, is there someone following me?' I glanced over her shoulder and shook my head. I told her that I didn't see anyone and then I mentioned Phillip. I told her that there was a creepy guy lurking around the neighborhood. She was headed down to meet friends for a drink. I knew the place so I said I would walk with her and then double back to Arthur's house."

Dylan had a sad smile when he paused.

"I loved that about our little neighborhood. We were out in the suburbs, but there was always something happening. We had a couple of restaurants that were open all night and some shops too. Whenever you had the urge to get out, there was always something to do, and you always saw someone you knew. While we walked, she called her friend who worked for the police. She told her about the guy and then handed the phone to me to give a description. I didn't have all that much to say. He was wearing a long trench coat, maybe gray. He had a cowboy hat on that was so soaked through that it was drooping down on the sides. I told her about the cigarette. I got the distinct impression that Holly's friend didn't really care. We were just going through the motions.

"We got to Arthur's place and we could pretty much see the bar from there. Holly said I didn't have to keep walking with her. I insisted, and then she insisted. I guess we both thought that the guy was back behind us still. I told her I would wait and watch and she couldn't stop me. She left with a wave and a smile. I knew she was a tiny bit nervous because she moved her bag up her shoulder and clamped it to her side with her arm. I leaned against Arthur's wall and pulled out my phone. While she crossed the street and walked up the block, I was checking my messages.

"You can probably guess the next part. When I looked back up, Holly should have been opening the door to the bar. Instead, I didn't see anyone. The whole street was empty—not even a passing car. I was about to yell her name when the door behind me opened and I nearly screamed. It was Arthur, standing in his doorway, covered in paint. When he was in a manic period, Arthur would paint for days. Then, he might go two or three days and barely get out of bed. He yelled at me to come inside or go away, and I told him we weren't doing either thing. I told him to grab a coat and we were going to look for Holly. If it had been any other name, he probably would have told me to get lost, but everyone loved Holly. He put on a yellow raincoat, a matching hat, and these ridiculous black boots. He looked like he was trying to sell fish sticks. When I told him so, I thought he was going to turn around and go back inside."

"Pardon," Wahid said. "How far from your friend Arthur's to the door of the bar?"

Dylan looked up and narrowed his eyes. "Imagine, like, you come out of a door, go down half-a-bock to the stop sign, and then kinda across the street and one door down. It was a t-intersection, and Arthur's street dead-ended into the one the bar was on. I'm terrible with distances, but maybe fifty paces?"

"Thank you," Wahid said. Jessica saw Joe scribble something down in his notepad.

"He asked where she was going and I pointed at the bar. We headed there first. I wasn't sure who she was going to meet, but I figured that we could at least look around and see if she just ducked inside when I wasn't watching. We didn't see her, so I went to the bartender and asked if he had seen her. I described her pink hat. I couldn't remember her coat, so I figured it was not noteworthy. He said that as far as he knew nobody had come in for the past ten minutes, so I asked if anyone seemed to be waiting for someone. He pointed at a booth in the corner."

Joe scribbled again in his notebook and Dylan glanced over to see what he was writing. Joe showed him the page and then Dylan continued.

"The way that bar was set up, I knew that the bartender would split his time between front and back, so I wasn't too sure that he would have seen Holly. I went and introduced myself to the couple in the booth and asked if they were waiting for Holly and had they seen her. They said yes and no. So, I knew she hadn't made it inside and I told them so. They were on their feet in an instant and the four of us headed for the door. The woman called Holly's phone—I should have thought of that immediately, but I didn't. The guy called the cops. I told them about Phillip, although I hadn't named him yet, of course. I forgot to tell them about Holly's cop friend who we had already talked to. He was wearing a black London Fog, and she was wearing this raincoat that was red, gray, and black, like in a V-shape.

"We split up. The couple went right and Arthur and I went left. We alternated yelling for Holly. Arthur pointed down the driveway between the bar and the auto parts store next door. I followed him. In the darkness, his yellow coat almost glowed. I'll admit, I was starting to panic. I kept telling myself that there was nothing to be worried about yet, but I didn't believe that one bit. I knew that she was in deep trouble if we didn't find her fast.

"Arthur yelled something, ran a few paces, and then bent down to pick up something from behind a dumpster. I wanted to scream. Whatever he had found, I didn't want to see it. When he stood up and turned to me, I covered my face and only watched between my fingers. He had a big smile on his face and pointed at the thing he was holding up.

"He said, 'My horn!' I've been looking for this for a month. I dropped my hands. He was holding up one of those old brass horns that's in a circle with a rubber squeeze bulb. When he squeezed it, it made a weird wheeze. I yelled at him that we were supposed to be looking for Holly, but he wouldn't stop talking about his dumb horn. He said he used to have it on his door instead of a bell. In his opinion, it was way less intrusive. When I yelled the second time, I must have been visibly more upset because he stopped and really looked at me before saying, 'I'm sure your friend is fine, Dylan. We'll find her.' It was one of the most genuine, direct things I had ever heard Arthur say. He was usually so disconnected from reality. Seeing the situation through his eyes for a second actually made me feel a tiny bit better. The whole thing was a little ridiculous. My pants were soaked through up to the knees from the splashing rain. My hair was a bird's nest under my hat. We were standing in the darkness between two buildings looking at an old horn. And all of that because of Holly.

"That's when Arthur pointed back towards the street and said, 'Her?' I turned and looked and, yup, it was Holly. We ran towards her."

Jessica's eyes were wide, listening to the narrative. She wanted to believe that this would be how the story ended. Everyone would be safe and Arthur had even gained something for the adventure. She reminded herself that if that was the case, they wouldn't all be gathered to listen.

"She nearly bolted when she saw us running towards her, but I shouted her name and she froze. I asked where she had been and she seemed confused. 'I saw my friend Angela's car over there,' she said, pointing. Apparently, Angela had just broken up with her boyfriend and Holly sat in her car for a few minutes, steaming up the windows as they talked about the breakup. She had muted her phone, she said, so she didn't hear the phone calls. The three of us then had to track down Holly's friends, who had gone the other direction.

"Holly was calling them as we walked. She had her phone pressed to her ear under her hat, but said she couldn't hear anything. She ducked into the doorway of the bar and we waited. Arthur spotted them up the street. I wasn't about to let Holly split with us. At that point, I felt like the whole thing was just a misunderstanding, and that there really wasn't any particular danger, but there was still a thought in the back of my head that things had nearly gone spectacularly wrong. We waited another second. Holly said, 'They aren't answering,' and I said, 'Let's go get them.' They weren't that far away."

Dylan coughed and cleared his throat.

"Give me a minute," he said.

Blood

After going to the bar for a glass of water, Dylan coughed again and then made his way back to his seat between Joe and Wahid.

Joe patted him on the back when Dylan coughed again.

Dylan thanked him and cleared his throat one last time.

As he started again, his voice was scratchy and weaker. His eyes looked troubled.

"They didn't turn around when we ran after them. Holly yelled their names. I yelled for them to stop. The two of them, shuffling slowly, just kept going down the street. I recognized her from the red, black, and gray raincoat, but the more I looked at the man, the more I wondered. When he left the bar, he had been wearing a black London Fog coat. I remember thinking about how they were so out of style that they might just be wearable again.

"But the coat didn't look right. It looked almost gray, like stone. That's when I remembered Phillip and I had a realization —it wasn't Holly's friends walking away from us. It was Phillip, the homeless man who had been smoking and looking in through my sliding glass doors. The woman was leaning on him as they shuffled and I thought that maybe he had drugged her or someone taken her hostage. I slowed a little, but Holly and Arthur kept going. I had to keep up. Holly reached them first and put a hand on the woman's shoulder as she called her name again.

"That little touch was enough to upset their delicate balance. It wasn't Phillip—it was indeed both of Holly's friends. They stumbled and fell to the ground at Holly's touch and we realized that they were mortally wounded. The man and woman were both holding their stomachs to try to keep in their insides, which were falling out. It was insanity—horrifying insanity. My brain wanted to ice over and simply shut down at the sight. Holly covered her face with her hands and let out a quick, piercing scream before she went silent.

"Arthur let out a single honking wheeze from the horn he was still carrying—the one that had been stolen off of his door. I turned to look at him, wondering why he had squeezed his horn. He hadn't There was a knife protruding from his chest. It had gone all the way through his body and pierced the rubber bulb of his brass horn. In some weird reflex, he was smiling as he gurgled and the rain washed away the blood leaking from the corner of his mouth."

Jessica's eyes were wide and she covered her mouth as she listened to the terrible turn the story took.

"I don't know how Phillip snuck up behind us and managed to stab Arthur without any of us knowing. The only sound had been the wheezing horn and Phillip was gone. Holly screamed again as Arthur dropped to his knees and then pitched forward onto the sidewalk, just a couple of paces from Holly's friends. I grabbed Holly's hand and ran back towards the bar. She resisted at first and then kept pace with me.

"I was about halfway back to the bar when I realized that there was no strength in Holly's grip. Glancing back I saw that I was holding a hand that was connected only to a forearm. The rest had been severed and there was no sign of Holly."

Dylan covered his eyes with his hand and continued his story.

"I mean, what can you think in a situation like that. It was so absurd that I had to believe that I was trapped in a nightmare, right? Things like that don't happen in reality. I ran into the bar, screaming my head off. The place was empty. Later, I heard that everyone had simply gone home. The place hadn't been packed when I went in before, but there had been plenty of people there. I heard one woman say later that she and her date had just decided it was time to go and they left. It was as simple as that. Nobody talked about what really must have happened. Deep down, they must have sensed that evil was coming.

"I ran to the bar, thinking I would go past it and into the back —still looking for someone to help me wake up from my nightmare. That's when I saw the bartender. He was behind the bar with his throat cut. It didn't look right to me. I remember thinking that someone would struggle if their throat was being cut. There was no blood on anything except the front of his shirt and his throat was cut really deep. I didn't want to look at him, but I couldn't help it."

Dylan coughed again.

"It's just... Have you ever had one of those dreams where you realize that it's a dream because of the absurdity of what's happening? I had been halfway convinced before that moment, and then the bartender was what really kicked it over the edge. As far as I know, I'm still in that dream."

Dylan was silent for a moment. Jessica wondered if his story was done.

Before anyone could ask their questions, Jessica leaned forward and whispered, "I've had that same feeling." Dylan didn't look up. Jessica sat back and blushed, feeling self-conscious.

Joe put a hand on Dylan's back and asked, "So, that's where you were?"

"Yes," Dylan said. The ambiguous question prompted him to finish. He straightened. "Yes. That's where I was when I heard the door swing in. I spun, thinking it would be some fresh horror coming through the door. It was two uniformed officers, shaking the rain from their coats. From their perspective, they were just responding to an ambiguous call about a missing person and they arrived to find an empty bar.

"One of them asked, 'Did you call in about...' he stopped asking when he saw the look on my face. All I could do was point to the bartender. They immediately went into high alert. One covered the door while the other approached with his hand on what I assumed was his gun holster. As soon as he spotted the bartender, he reached under his coat and triggered his radio, I guess. I didn't understand a word of what he called in. By then, I was going to pieces. Until that moment, I managed to hold everything at arm's length because I was still struggling to believe what I was seeing. Having that officer take control of the situation gave me permission to let it sink in and I couldn't handle it. It's a strange feeling to have sanity ripped out from under you like that.

"Fortunately, I don't think they considered me a suspect for a single second. I began to blubber about Holly, Arthur, and Holly's friends. They couldn't make sense of it. It was like we didn't share a common language. They had their police talk and I had my panic-induced nonsense. There's no way to translate between the two. I dragged them out to the street and pointed. It was raining so hard that we couldn't even see the bodies down the block. I heard sirens coming.

"Finally, one of them got the idea and asked, 'Are you saying there are more victims?' I nodded and shouted and they walked down the street with me. They never checked to see if any of the people on the sidewalk were alive. I thought that would be the first thing they did. In fact, I was ashamed of myself that I had assumed the others were dead instead of trying to help them. I was remembering things all wrong though. There hadn't been time to go back. I had run for my life and then the police had arrived moments later.

"But there was still something wrong with the scene. I distinctly saw Holly's hands clutched to her chest as her lifeless eyes were being pounded by the rain. That's when I remembered that I had seen one of her arms severed. It made no sense, so I decided to keep my mouth shut about that. Either I was crazy or the world wasn't as rational as I once believed. I couldn't risk having anyone else know that there was such a wide gulf between me and reality. They lock up people like that."

Dylan let out a long breath and sank back into the couch.

"Just to clarify," Vivian started, "did you ever see him after that brief encounter outside of your sliding door?"

Dylan shook his head.

"No. Not once. And I know what you're thinking—they could

have been killed by anyone. But I *know* that it was Phillip."

Jessica couldn't hold her question back any longer. "You call him Phillip—where did that name come from?"

"Therapy," Dylan said. "My therapist encouraged me to give him a name so he wouldn't just be an archetype. He was a real person so I'm supposed to call him by a name, even if it's just a name I made up."

"That's right. You said that. Sorry," Jessica said, blushing again.

"No worries," Dylan said. "I'm the only one who has named him, as far as I know. Calling him Phillip is just my coping mechanism."

"You mentioned the neighbors," Wahid said, prompting Dylan.

"Yes," Dylan said with another sigh. "It took almost a week before anyone noticed their absence. Someone came by—a relative or something—and banged on their door. When my partner and I went out to the porch, they came over and said they hadn't heard from Townsends in a while and asked if we had seen them. We said no. I don't remember who spotted the flies in the window. We stood there, speculating until the police came, entering my life again. I recognized some of them. They had interviewed me several times to find out everything I knew, and here they were again.

"I was surprised that none of them made the connection. I put it together instantly. It was obvious to me that Phillip had started with their house, murdered the family, and then came to look through my window. I opened my mouth to suggest the police look for Townsend blood out near our pool, but that would have been stupid. For one, the blood would have been washed away by the rain. Two, the police had already done a cursory search after I told them about Phillip the first time.

"I kept my mouth shut and my theories to myself. Presumably, if the wounds had matched those of Arthur and Holly, they would have said something. I think I'm the only one who made the connection."

"What did your partner think of all this?"

"Nothing, really. Things that didn't happen directly to him might as well have happened on the moon. He was a bit of a narcissist. When I talked to him from the police station, pretty much begging for him to come home, he started telling me about *his* day, like we were just exchanging stories about our lives."

Dylan shook his head at a memory.

"If you're right," Jessica said, "then it seems like you might not have even been the target."

"Do you have a question?" Hilda asked.

"Did you ever feel like he was coming after you?" Jessica asked. It was the only thing she could think to say. After the question left her lips, she wished she hadn't asked it.

"Actually, looking back, no. Even though he chased me, I didn't feel like he was out to murder me. I felt like the designated witness, if that makes sense," Dylan said. "I felt like the lone audience member of a horrible movie."

After a pause, Vivian asked, "More questions?"

Jessica glanced around. A couple of people shook their heads. Joe was still scribbling in his notebook.

Wahid cleared his throat and then said, "Once again, I think it's interesting to note the differences between Dylan's experience and that of the rest of us."

"More similar than different," Billie said.

"Perhaps," Wahid said. "But the fact that there were two completely unrelated sets of victims that night—those witnessed by Dylan and those not."

Hilda shook her head. "I've never been convinced of that distinction. All of the crimes were laid out for Dylan to witness, either directly or indirectly. He spotted the blood on the curtains and discovered the body of the bartender. One could argue that he didn't witness any of the murders directly. He simply found the evidence."

"After the man prompted him to action by appearing outside his sliding door," Billie said.

"Precisely," Hilda said.

"The knife," Jessica said. "Didn't you say there was a knife protruding from the artist's chest?"

Dylan nodded. "Yes, from Arthur."

"What happened? Did the police find that?"

"Yes. They think that knife came from the bar and matched the bartender's wounds and those from Holly's friends. There were no fingerprints or DNA other than from the victims."

"What about Holly's wounds?" Jessica asked.

"Those were from a different weapon."

"So that's a performance too," Jessica said to herself. Imagining the neighbors, who weren't found for another week, it was clear to her that those wounds would match Holly's, but were probably made with something non-descript, like a knife that anyone would have in their butcher block. It was the same with her family. There was one special cut—she thought of it as a *marquee* cut—and that was when the guy had decapitated her father. That weapon had been found. Every other cut was made by a more generic weapon that had never been recovered. Presumably, the guy had taken that weapon with him.

Jessica turned and found Christopher.

"Christopher, you saw a long weapon that you couldn't really describe come through the gap between the doors, right? It impaled your friend?"

"His name was Grant," Christopher said.

"Jessica, we try to focus on one story at a time during these sessions," Hilda said.

"Wait though—aren't we trying to find similarities?" Jessica asked.

"Among other things," Hilda said.

"Give her a chance," Vivian said.

Hilda nodded. Nobody else objected, so Jessica turned back to Christopher.

"Grant's wounds didn't match any of the others, did it?"

"They said it was inconclusive, but someone let slip that it appeared the same weapon that killed Grant was the one that cut off Terrence's hand. Something about the cleft. I didn't follow,"

Christopher said.

"What did you say about the performance?" Joe asked Jessica.

"I was just thinking that it was the same as my father. There was one wound that didn't match the others. I've thought that his..."

She swallowed hard. "Pardon me, this is difficult to talk about. The decapitation was like a brutal performance. The goal of that was to terrify me, not just kill him. With the other, simpler killings..."

Jessica shook her head to clear the thought of her brother and sister.

"With the other killings in my family, they were done without ceremony with a simple weapon."

"Product versus process," Mel said.

"Yes," Laura said, nodding. "Some killers derive pleasure from the process of the act, and others simply desire the product—the death, or the body."

"Do they ever do both?" Joe asked.

"Both at the same time is very rare. Sometimes they graduate from one to another through the course of a career," Laura said.

"A more nuanced classification divides killers into visionary, mission-oriented, hedonistic, and control-oriented," Hilda said, ticking the types off on her fingers as she listed them.

"Regardless," Laura said, "it's unusual to find more than one pattern in a single incident."

Hilda thought about that and then nodded.

"Isn't everything about our little group unusual?" Billie asked.

Late

"Don't go. It's early," Dylan said reaching a hand towards Jessica.

He and Billie were hardly talking. The whole evening, Jessica had felt like she was intruding. At one point, she had intended to stay over at the house, upstairs in the guest wing. But, contrary to that thought, she had just said her goodbyes and stood up to leave.

"It's not early," Jessica said, looking at her phone. "It's almost one."

"You working tomorrow?" Billie asked.

"No."

"Then it's early," Billie said with a laugh. She held up her drink to toast Jessica. After a sigh, Jessica found her seat again. They heard a door deep in the house close and they turned to see who was coming down the hall. Jessica could only imagine that it was Ullman. She thought he was the only other person on the premises.

She was the only one surprised when Christopher entered. The way they greeted him, Billie and Dylan seemed to be expecting Christopher.

"Here," Billie said, "saved you a seat."

With the four of them seated in tall leather chairs, the central area of the library was full.

"I thought Ullman didn't like people drinking in here," Christoper said.

"He doesn't like a lot of things," Billie said with a big smile.

Jessica wondered if Billie was opening up, or maybe if she had just misjudged her at first. She barely seemed like the same person who had appeared so sour at Jessica's first meeting.

"Dylan was just talking about how we make him feel 'othered'," Billie said.

"Shove it, Billie," Dylan said with a wave.

"I'm sorry—is that or is that not what you were just saying?"

"In a manner of speaking, that's what I was saying, but I wasn't making a big, public declaration of grievance or anything. I was just talking out loud."

"I'm sorry," Christopher said. He looked serious and sincere. "I hope I didn't make you feel uncomfortable."

"It wasn't you," Dylan said. "You would be the last one I was worried about."

"Oh?" Christopher asked.

Billie leaned forward to explain. "See, Dylan thinks that we don't take his experience seriously because he barely knew the people who were murdered. Holly was just an acquaintance, he didn't even like the neighbors, and Arthur was just a guy who lived down the street and never slept at night. He doesn't even know the bartender's name."

"Or the names of Holly's friends," Dylan added. "I knew once."

"But even you, Christopher, had a pretty deep relationship with the victims in comparison. And Jessica here is a gold star victim. She lost father and siblings. Nobody beats that except maybe Joe."

"Isn't Wahid in the same boat?" Christopher asked. "Just co-workers?"

Billie waved away the thought. "He suffered because they reported to him. He felt responsible."

Christopher looked up. "What about Vivian?"

"Exactly!" Dylan said. "She barely counts. I'm surprised we even let her sit in the circle with the rest of us."

Jessica thought about Vivian's story—there was no doubt that Vivian had been deeply wounded by the loss of her animals, but even she had expressed the same idea. Her losses just didn't seem to compare to everyone else's.

"This is unfair," Jessica said. "It's not a competition."

"I'm not saying it's a competition," Dylan said, "just that there should be some criteria required for sitting in the circle."

"I thought there was. We're all witness to murders committed by that man," Jessica said.

"I don't think you can technically *murder* an animal," Dylan said.

"Of course you can," Christopher said.

"Whatever," Dylan said with a flip of his hand.

"Wait," Jessica said, "were you *physically* hurt? I wasn't, but Vivian was. She said that he cut her. Doesn't that make her even more of a victim?"

The room was silent for a moment.

Billie said, "That's a really good point. I've seen that scar that Vivian has. It's pretty bad. I think that if her boyfriend hadn't showed up, she would have been cut right in two."

Dylan sighed and looked away as he adjusted himself in his seat. "I had... forgotten that part," he said. "So, maybe I'm wrong. At least I can admit when I'm wrong."

"If you have to make a big deal of it like that," Billie said, "then it's probably something you don't do very often, Dylan."

Dylan smiled and laughed.

The mood seemed to change with his laugh. Dylan had been entrenching himself in a hateful position, but Billie had called him out.

Jessica turned to Christopher, "So, do you stay here often?"

Billie and Dylan both burst out with laughter.

"What?" Jessica asked, blushing once more.

"That was, like, the most awkward pickup line ever uttered," Billie said.

"It wasn't a pickup line. I was... I've stayed here a lot in the past few months it seems. I'm here so much, I sometimes forget the way back to my apartment, and I've never seen Christopher outside of the group meetings."

"It's okay," Christopher said. "I didn't take it as a line. I actually just came back for my laptop."

He pointed over at the table near the window. "I was writing before the meeting and I left it behind."

He looked so sheepish and apologetic about an honest mistake that it made everyone laugh again.

"Well, stick around, Christopher," Billie said. "Maybe we'll have some fun."

Later

"I don't think I have a shot," Christopher said. His eye was practically glued to the scope.

"Of course you do," Billie whispered.

The slate roof under them was still uncomfortably hot. Jessica relished every gust of night air that came their direction. It didn't happen often enough. She watched as Christopher wiped a bead of sweat from his forehead and then tried to find his target in the gun's scope.

After a slow exhale, Christopher squeezed the trigger. The sound was a sharp crack that reverberated out into the night. Below, they heard an agonized shout.

"You missed," Billie said.

From below, they heard Dylan shout, "You didn't hit any of them. Don't shoot, I'm going to get some of them off the bottom."

"Ms. James," a deep voice said from behind them.

Jessica spun to see who had spoken, she rolled towards the edge of the roof and Christopher's hand shot out to steady her.

Ullman was standing over them. The lights from the pool below cast his face in shimmering blue.

"What's up?" Billie asked.

"We've discussed water balloons in the pool before," Ullman said.

"You said we shouldn't *throw* them. You never said anything about shooting them with a pellet gun from the roof."

"How old are you?" Ullman asked.

"Thirty. How old are you?"

A glare was his only answer.

"We're going to clean up all the pellets and rubber," Billie said.

Jessica's eyebrows rose and she looked to Billie. When she had proposed the idea, Billie had assured them that the pool had a special vacuum filter that would automatically clean up the pellets and the broken bits of balloon. At the time, it had sounded too good to be true.

"Be sure you do," Ullman said. He reached out a hand. It was clear what he wanted. Christopher clicked the safety and then handed the pellet gun to Ullman, who strode back towards the stair well. When Ullman reached the door, he glanced back. Billie waved at him and then covered her mouth as she laughed.

"What's happening?" Dylan called from below.

"Ullman shut us down. He thinks we're too old to have fun," Billie yelled.

"Did you tell him that we're practicing for the zombie apocalypse?" Dylan yelled.

Shock spread across Billie's face. She looked genuinely disappointed when she said, "Oh! I should have told him."

For some reason she couldn't explain—probably sleep deprivation—this struck Jessica as terribly witty. She snort laughed and then Christopher and Billie laughed at her.

On the ground, Dylan yelled, "What's happening now?"

They laughed harder.

Fountains

"I really never have," Billie said.

Billie was standing on the front landing of the mansion. She still had one hand on the doorframe, like a lifeline back to her safe place.

"Come on," Jessica said. "This was practically your idea."

"Who wants to see a bunch of water shot up in the air?" Billie asked.

Dylan approached Billie slowly and then put out his hand. "Come on, Billie, live a little."

She sighed, rolled her eyes and took his hand.

They ran and caught up with Christopher, who was unlocking his car. Jessica took the passenger's seat while Billie and Dylan piled in the back.

"Where's the ashtray?" Billie asked.

Christopher turned around in his seat and pointed at Billie and Dylan. "No smoking in my car."

They laughed.

Christopher drove down the hill at a safe pace. Jessica thought about her father. If he had lived, he would have been at least ten years older than Christopher. There were similarities though. Christopher wasn't exactly carefree, but he hadn't really said no to anything yet. In fact, when Billie had talked about going to see the fountains, Christopher had volunteered to drive.

"You're sure they're going to be running?" Billie asked. "I

thought they stopped at midnight."

Jessica looked at the clock on the dashboard. It was almost three in the morning.

Dylan reassured her. "I told you, it's a test run. Only a few people know about it, but they're going to do the whole show."

"And how did you find out if nobody knows?" Jessica asked.

"I happen to know the people who know," Dylan said.

The way he said it made her laugh. She settled into her seat and looked at the fancy houses they passed. Some security lights were on around the grounds, but the lights in the houses were all off. Everyone was either out or asleep. Both options were likely, she decided. It seemed like a lot of people made their own strange hours. The air was on, keeping the temperature regulated, but Jessica opened her window a little to feel the night air.

Dylan and Billie were fighting over something in the back seat.

Jessica closed her eyes and for a moment imagined that she was back with her family. The kids were being rowdy in the back, but her father was unperturbed. They were out on an adventure with no responsibilities except to see new things. She drifted off to sleep with that thought and woke up when the car pulled to a stop.

"I knew it," Billie said. "We came down here to look at unlit pools of water. There's not a single fountain going."

"Give it a second," Dylan said.

The lights and water came on a moment later. Jets sprang up into the sky. In the distance, Jessica heard faint music playing. Billie left her car door open and ran to the edge of the fountain so she could watch. Dylan was right behind her. Bringing up the rear, Christopher and Jessica walked slowly, watching Billie wave her arms as she watched the display.

"She's older than us," Christopher said.

"Sorry?" Jessica asked. Billie was a couple of years older than Jessica, but based on his story, Christopher had to be at least twenty years older than either of them.

"I mean metaphorically," he said. "Sometimes I feel like my

maturation was frozen in time because of what I witnessed. The murderer took away what was left of my college years and stole the intervening decades."

She held her tongue—the truth was that she had suspected what he was saying from the moment she saw the way he told his story. Everyone else kept insisting that Christopher had a fine life and easily managed to compartmentalize his trauma. They were wrong.

"Maybe I should stop hanging around, going to meetings," he said. "Every time we get a new person in the group, I have to tell my story again and it tears off the scab for the millionth time."

"Sorry," Jessica said.

Up near the fountains, Billie and Dylan jumped each time the big jets made a rainbow in the lights.

Christopher slowed and turned to Jessica. "No need to apologize. I don't resent you or anything."

"No, I didn't take it that way."

"It's my choice to come each time, and it's my choice to tell my story over and over. I'm just beginning to think that it's maybe a mistake to keep going."

"That's what I thought you meant!"

Christopher opened his mouth to answer, but he was silenced when Billie turned and yelled to them.

"Get over here," she called.

Jessica rushed forward and heard Christopher right on her heels. Dylan was leaning against the barrier, looking across the fountains. Billie pointed as Jessica ran up.

"What is it?" Jessica asked.

"You see?"

It was difficult to see anything except the spraying water lit from below by yellow and white lights.

"There!" Billie pointed. Jessica finally thought she saw what Billie was pointing at. Across the water, on a bridge, she saw a solitary man standing. His long coat made him look out of place. A chill ran down Jessica's spine.

"That could be anyone," Christopher said. He seemed to

immediately know who they were talking about. Jessica scanned the rest of the bridge. There was only one person. The fountains died down and she lost sight of him.

"Where did he go?" Dylan asked.

The next jets of water rolled from right to left, making it look like a giant sea monster was traversing the lake. Billie's finger swung to point at a new location.

"Right there!"

"He's getting closer," Dylan said.

"Nonsense," Christopher said. "It's a long way around this pond, it would take quite a while for him..."

The fountains sent a thick mist into the air and they lost track of the man again. The next time they saw him, he was so far to the left that there was almost no jetting water between them and the man. Jessica tried to calculate how far he had gone, and how much distance he still needed to cover before he would be right on top of them.

"We can only see him through the water," Dylan said. "Is that the secret? He can only be seen through water? Is that why he always shows up in the rain?"

"No," Jessica and Christopher said at the same time.

"I saw him in my living room," Jessica said.

Nobody said anything for a few seconds. They simply stood there, frozen in place, wondering where he would appear next.

"Is this real?" Dylan whispered.

"Yes. We have to get out of here," Billie said.

Jessica looked to Christopher to be the voice of reason. It was impossible to believe the man would show up here, on a clear night, just because there was water from the fountains hanging in the air. Then again, everything about the man seemed impossible when she gave it any thought.

Christopher said, "Maybe we should."

As soon as he took a step back towards where the car was parked, it broke their paralysis.

Jessica, Billie, and Dylan all ran. Christopher brought up the rear.

They were three quarters of the way to the car when Jessica had a horrible thought. If Christopher fell to the knife of the man, it would seal the fate of all of them. Christopher had the keys.

The marker lights on Christopher's vehicle flashed and Jessica nearly screamed. He had hit the button to unlock the doors.

Billie and Dylan opened the nearest doors. Jessica followed Billie into the rear seat and slammed the door behind her before she leaned over the seats to look in the cargo area. It was empty. Billie let out a yelp when the driver's door opened and Christopher slid behind the wheel.

"Go, go, go," Billie whispered.

Jessica took her hand. They both leaned towards the center as they peeked between the seats in the direction that they had last seen the man.

"What are you doing?" Dylan asked. "Turn around and go the other way."

Christopher shook his head.

Jessica wanted to scream at him, but was too afraid to even open her mouth. There was something about the way that Christopher was gripping the wheel—nothing was going to dissuade him. Billie squeezed her hand tight as Christopher accelerated.

The road they were on looped around the pond and then crossed the bridge where they had seen the man standing. Through her window, Jessica could see the fountains leaping and splashing. But Jessica kept her attention focused dead ahead. That's where the man was—she could feel it. She steadied herself, putting a hand on the seat in front of her. The motion of the car was beginning to make her feel like she was floating.

"No," Dylan said.

Jessica flicked her eyes to the side and understood what was troubling him. The fountains had gone into a display where mist came up from the water. Lasers danced on the clouds of water, projecting some image that they were at the wrong angle to see. None of that mattered. What mattered was the wind that blew the mist across the road in front of them.

Christopher gripped the wheel so tightly that the plastic squeaked. One of Jessica's hands was in a death grip with Billie. Her other fingers dug into the seat in front of her. They all stared forward as Christopher continued to accelerate towards the blowing mist.

Billie gasped.

It took another moment before Jessica saw him.

Standing right in the middle of the road, the long jacket made him unmistakable. Their headlights reflected off the long blade held in his left hand. Mist from the fountains swirled around him.

"Turn around," Dylan said.

"I'm sorry. I can't," Christopher said. The vehicle accelerated. The engine screamed. Jessica felt so dizzy that she could barely stay upright.

Billie relaxed her grip on Jessica's hand and she said, "Do it."

The idea was like a virus. As soon as it entered Jessica's ears, it took root.

The vehicle rocketed towards the man.

He disappeared when a patch of clear air blew through the spot where he was standing, and then he was back, fully visible through a thin veil.

Jessica whispered, "Faster."

She forced herself to keep her eyes open.

They hit.

The sound was horrible crunch and snap of bones crushed by metal. The vehicle bounced as the man was plowed under the frame and ground between steel and pavement. Then, an instant later, the sound was gone.

Christopher didn't let up on the accelerator. His car burst through the mist into clear air and Billie whipped around in her seat to look through the back window.

Jessica joined her. They saw a shape crumpled on the pavement in the edge of the mist. It was a formless mass—she couldn't see any of the details of the man.

"Slow down. Just a little," Dylan said.

They were racing towards an intersection.

Christopher let his foot off the gas, but didn't touch the brake. They shot right through an intersection. Christopher muscled the wheel with both hands and guided the protesting tires into a turn. With the fountains behind them, obscured by buildings, he finally let the vehicle slow down a bit. He ran a red light or two, but the streets were mostly empty.

Jessica was finally able to catch her breath and her head stopped spinning.

The car pulled over and slowed to a stop.

"What are you doing?" Dylan asked.

"We have to find out if it was real," Christopher said as he opened his door. As soon as he was out, Dylan reached across and slammed the door shut again before hitting the button to lock them.

Billie pressed her face against her window to watch Christopher as he inspected his vehicle.

A few moments later, he came back to his window and knocked twice.

"Unlock the door," he said through the glass.

Billie reached between the seats and unlocked the doors to let him in.

Christopher started driving again before he spoke.

"No real damage that I could see. There looks like there was some moss or something up under the radiator, but I'll wait until later to check it out."

"I don't think you should," Billie said. "I think you should get every part of him off this car before you do anything else."

"Okay," Christopher said.

"Let's get back to the house," Dylan said with a sigh. "I'm hungry as hell, all of a sudden."

"Yeah," Jessica said. She hadn't intended to say anything, but she couldn't help but agree.

"Don't bother going back to the house then," Billie said. "I saw Hilda and Mel heading for the kitchen earlier."

Dylan moaned.

"What's that mean?" Jessica asked.

"Sometimes the two of them clear the place out. They use Simon's pantry like a grocery store," Billie said. "Have to wait for Glen to restock."

"Trent makes a wonderful omelet," Jessica said, echoing something she had heard earlier.

"That sounds good—where's Trent?" Christopher asked.

"Take a left up here."

Diner

"This really is wonderful," Billie said, looking at a piece of her omelet between her fingers.

Dylan covered his mouthful of food and said, "Gross."

"Me? You're the one spitting egg everywhere."

They laughed. Jessica was now sure that her lighthearted mood was mostly from sleep deprivation, but she didn't care. Together, they had gone on an adventure and come out the other side. They had faced their worst fear.

The waiter came by with a pot of coffee in one hand and a pitcher of water in the other. Christopher took more coffee. Jessica held up her water glass.

"Compliments to the chef," Billie said, holding up her piece of omelet.

The waiter yelled over his shoulder, "Compliments, Trent."

A voice came from the back, "Thank you."

"There's never anyone in here," Jessica said. "Why do you guys stay open all night?"

He shrugged and said, "They pay me. I come in."

That made the table laugh again. The waiter shrugged and walked away.

"I met Joe and Vivian here when I was new to town," Jessica said.

"He's a strange one," Christopher said. "He found me down in Texas. Do you know he doesn't sleep?"

"Everyone sleeps," Dylan said.

Christopher shook his head. "I don't think Joe does. He just wanders around, tracking down the people that Laura turns up in her searches. Sometimes he's gone for a few weeks. Then, within the next few months, we have an influx of the folks he met during his travels. He's like the Pied Piper of murder witnesses."

"He didn't track me down," Billie said.

"I like to call us Foes of Phillip," Dylan said.

Jessica whispered the name to herself and shook her head.

"You don't like it?"

"Doesn't roll off the tongue," Billie said. "Philanderers?"

Christoper snorted and a little coffee sprayed from the mug pressed to his lips. He was chuckling as he mopped himself up with a napkin.

"Phil's Specters," Jessica said.

"Stop it," Dylan said, putting up a finger. He tried to hide his smile. "I spent a year in therapy assigning the name Phillip to that demon and I will not have that name mocked."

He couldn't keep a straight face.

Billie picked up her utensils and used them for the first time. She cut some of her omelet and held out her pinky as she placed it delicately in her mouth. The sight of her trying to look like she had manners made Jessica smile.

Billie pointed with her fork through the window.

"I see that moss you're talking about, Christopher. He might not have done any damage to your car, but you've got remnants of him in your grill."

"Maybe we should collect that and have it analyzed or something," Jessica said.

"I think I'd rather just go through a carwash and be done with it," Christopher said.

"Fair enough," Jessica said, but something about that idea bothered her. "I don't know though. Maybe they would figure out the... I don't know, the chemical composition or something? Maybe someone could tell us how to kill the man once and for all."

"Tried that," Billie said, pointing her fork at Jessica. "Not going down that path again."

"Sorry?" Jessica asked.

Christopher gave Billie a worried look and shook his head a little.

Billie sighed and rolled her eyes. "Like I told you before—we're not supposed have side chatter."

"Side chatter about what?" Jessica asked.

"We just have parameters," Christopher said.

"For a good reason," Dylan added.

Christopher nodded.

Jessica felt confusion morphing into anger.

"I'd love to know why this group has so many stupid secrets," Jessica said. "We've all been through this horrific trauma. Why do we all have to have all these little pockets of information that nobody will share? Vivian said it was superstition, but I'm starting to think that's not even true. I was supposed to hear what happened six months ago, but it still hasn't been addressed. It seems like you guys hold stuff in because you think keeping a secret to yourself will somehow give you power. You know what? It doesn't give you power at all. All it does is fuel your fear."

Billie's eyes went wide for a moment and then she went back to her food.

"That sounds like it has been building up for a *while*," Dylan said with a hand gesture towards Jessica.

"We are superstitious," Christopher said. "You're right about that. I think you understand why."

"But everyone has spent so long making sure they have nothing left to lose," Jessica said. "What good is it to be so unencumbered if you're still so precious about everything?"

Christopher took in a breath and let it out slowly as he nodded.

"Yeah. Yeah. So, the thing is, before you came to Vegas, Simon paid for a bunch of research and he came up with a plan."

Dylan looked down at the table and propped up his head with

a hand to his forehead.

"More than one plan," Billie said, pointing her fork at Christopher.

"Yes. True. He came up with a couple of plans. Everyone knew about one of them. When we talked it all the way through, most of us agreed to give it a try. This was last year, down in Mexico."

"Cozumel," Dylan added.

Christopher turned and looked at Jessica. "It's an island off the east coast of the Yucatán Peninsula."

She nodded.

"In the rainy season, they don't have much tourism. Simon found a hotel that was going to be demolished and he convinced them to hold off for a few months so he could rent out the whole thing. All of us who signed up were given a plane ticket to Cancún and instructions on how to get down to the ferry from Playa del Carmen. We traveled separately."

"Incognito," Dylan said.

"I wasn't allowed to go," Billie said. "Even Simon's lawyers couldn't get me a visa, but Simon could have snuck me down if he wanted."

"We arrived just before rainy season," Christopher said. "Simon told us that his people thought they had determined the correct set of circumstances to summon the man, but he wouldn't tell us details."

"Couldn't," Dylan added.

"Right—he said that he couldn't tell us or else it wouldn't work."

"Precisely what someone with delusional disorder would say," Billie said.

"You knew him better than I did, but I don't think he was delusional," Christopher said. "Anyway, part of the nature of the plan was that we weren't really allowed to know the plan going in. It was a leap of faith that I was willing to take."

"Me too," Dylan said.

"We were down there a few days and then the rains came like they were on a schedule."

"Every day," Dylan said. "El Norte."

"Some of the people working in the hotel called the daily storm El Norte," Christopher explained. "My Spanish is rusty, but they said that the rains in the spring are just like gentle fingers, caressing you. El Norte is different. Those rains are like cold needles. In a moment's notice, the sky would go dark. In Playa del Carmen, the kids on the beach would cover their soccer ball with sand and run into the ocean to get away from the rain. They would submerge themselves with just their eyes and noses above the water."

"You're avoiding the subject," Jessica said. It was the middle of the night—she didn't feel like hearing another long-winded story. "I keep hearing these whispered allusions to some sort of incident where someone tried something to rid the world of the man. What happened?"

Christopher looked her directly in the eyes. "I'm willing to tell you my recollection, but I will do it at my pace."

Jessica rolled her eyes and looked up at the ceiling. Dylan hadn't touched the coffee that he had ordered earlier. Jessica reached across the table and slid it over towards herself.

Vacation

"I arrived before most, made my way to Playa del Carmen, and I got a preview of El Norte while I was staying at a little beachside hotel. I think I was the only one out on the beach that afternoon. The storm came out of nowhere and took me by surprise while I was watching the boys play soccer in the sand. A moment before the rain, they buried their ball, like I said, and ran into the ocean. I could hear them talking about 'el hombre' and I thought maybe they were talking about the man, but in retrospect, I believe they were discussing me.

"When the rain came, I understood why. El Norte comes down like daggers of ice. I was soaked and stinging before I got back to my room. I had to chase an iguana out of my shower before I could get warmed up. When I got out and dried off, I saw welts on my body where the rain had hit.

"That was my introduction to El Norte, so you can understand why I was careful not to be caught in it again. The next time it rained, I was over on Cozumel with the others. The hotel Simon rented had seen better days. They were tearing it down for good reason. It was six floors of tired-looking rooms. We all stayed on the second floor. Obviously, there were plenty of rooms for us to each stay alone, but part of the plan put me and Joe together. I had to sleep with a sheet over my eyes because Joe stayed up all night, working at the desk."

"What was the plan?" Jessica asked. She couldn't believe all the useless stage setting that Christoper was giving her. In the context of a meeting, people had to get up the momentum to reveal their trauma, so the slow build was inevitable. In this case, it felt like Christopher should be able to simply answer her question.

Christopher seemed to ignore her.

"Simon's instructions were clear. We weren't to talk about him, watch for him, and, to the best of our ability, not even think of him. The idea was to fully act like we were just there on vacation. The more someone asks you to not think of a thing, the more your brain returns to it. I got the impression that Simon had that in mind when he issued the instructions. We were nine little antennae, broadcasting to him day and night.

"People naturally gathered down in the tiki bar when it started raining. We sat in wicker furniture, looking out under the palm frond roof at the ocean. It was pounded by the sharp needles of rain. You could feel the anticipation in the group. Everyone had the sense that he was coming."

Jessica had never been to Mexico, but she felt like she could picture it perfectly. She reached out and grabbed the table in front of her to ground herself in reality.

"We had gathered and, in a sense, prayed for him. Now he was going to fulfill those prayers. Everyone knew that Simon had a plan for how to deal with him when he arrived, but he couldn't share the details."

"Why?" Jessica asked.

Christopher only shook his head.

Dylan ended up answering. "I always assumed that the same way he could feel us calling to him, he would know what we were planning. There has to be some kind of psychic connection, you know? If any of us knew what was in store, then Phillip would sense it and stay away."

Christopher nodded. "That's as good a guess as any, I suppose. The first time I saw him, it was out of the corner of my eye. Over the bar, and through a pass-through window, I could see the hotel's kitchen. Amongst the dark shadows, I saw a shape looming in there. I believe that he was being cautious, and that gave me a lot of hope."

"Why?" Jessica asked. "If he was being cautious, didn't that mean that maybe he suspected something."

"Yes," Christopher said, "but think about it. The only reason he would be cautious was if he was vulnerable in some way. A force that's truly unstoppable has no reason to ever show any caution."

"Oh."

Jessica nodded. As the idea sunk in, she started to feel a little hope herself.

"Simon's people had told me one thing. It was on a little notecard that was tucked into my plane ticket. The card simply said, 'Dave chose well.' He was one of the people who was murdered in the dorm, and all I could think about was the thing he chose as his weapon—a fire extinguisher. From those three words, I came up with an explanation. I believed that the researchers had maybe discovered a vulnerability with the man and that something about a chemical fire extinguisher could hurt or stop him. After all, Dave had survived his initial encounter with the man. When I got to the hotel, I made note of every fire extinguisher I saw. There were several around the tiki bar. If he tried to come at us, I was going to jump up, grab a fire extinguisher, and get ready to defend myself."

Christopher pointed to Dylan.

"I didn't realize that he was stalking us yet, but my note just said, 'Turnabout.' I don't know if Simon's people knew this, but when I was a little kid, I used to stalk my mother with my squirt gun. Getting closer and closer, I would try to squirt her in the ear. I know—terrible, right? At the last second, she would always grab my gun and say, 'Turnabout is fair play.' They meant that I had to grab Phillip's knife and use it on him. I was sure of it," Dylan said.

"Everyone's note had different instructions," Christopher said. "Except for maybe Simon and Ullman, we all thought we had the key to defeating him, and that it was up to us. That's why I didn't indicate to anyone else that I saw him. I thought that I might have to let him close in on one of the others. I was using them as bait."

"So the whole point was to try to kill him?" Jessica asked.

Christopher nodded.

"And you were pretty sure that it was possible to kill him?"

"Obviously," Billie said.

"Why is that obvious?" Jessica asked.

"No, I mean it's obvious that they *thought* they could kill him, not that they could."

"Oh," Jessica said. "What made you think that, Christopher?"

"I don't know. I guess because I feel like everything dies eventually. I don't really believe in immortal beings or whatever. I guess I don't believe in occult or paranormal stuff either, really. I mean, of course I know that there are things that are beyond the scope of what science can define, and if that's what you call paranormal, then fine. But I guess I don't believe in ghosts or demons or religion really."

"Okay," Jessica said. "So, everything is mortal, so he must be mortal."

"Yeah. That's fair."

"That's what I thought, too," Dylan said. "After Cozumel, I wasn't so sure."

"So, you saw him lurking. What happened?" Jessica asked.

Christopher sighed and sipped his coffee.

Arrival

"From the stories," Christopher said, "and my own experience, I thought it was likely that the man would ask for permission to come in out of the rain. There were a few staff members working around the hotel. Simon's people had given them our names and pictures. Nobody else was supposed to be let in. But, since he was already in the kitchen I thought it was likely that he had been invited in and he might have already claimed victims."

"Claimed," Dylan whispered, shaking his head.

"I saw him moving through the shadows, going towards the bamboo door over near Vivian. Through the slats of bamboo, I could see the shape of him, getting ready to make his entrance. As soon as the door began to swing, I was up. I ran for the fire extinguisher. I had the sequence of moves planned in my head and it all worked perfectly. Vivian saw me coming and shrunk back as I raced forward. The man was halfway to her when I hit him with the extinguisher. It shot out a dusty burst of some kind of gas and the man froze in it as Vivian scrambled away.

"I barely saw Joe approaching from my left. He threw some liquid at the man's feet. I was angry at first. It seemed to me that my solution was the right one, and Joe might ruin it, but Joe had his own instructions. Joe tossed a lighter. It looked exactly like the one that the man carried, and it was lit. The thing bounced once on the floor and then *whoompf,* fire blossomed around his feet. That's when Dylan came in."

"I didn't even see the flames," Dylan said. "I was only looking at his left hand and the knife he was holding at his side. I was completely focused as I stepped up. I could see the whole thing in my head, clear as a movie. He would raise the blade, I would twist to the side, my arm would come down and my knee would come up. He would let go of the knife or his wrist would break as he tried to keep his grip. I practiced the move so many times that it's still my first instinct whenever anyone reaches out to shake hands."

"It worked perfectly, too," Christopher said. "Dylan smashed the man's arm, the knife popped out of the man's grip, and Dylan snatched it out of the air. It was perfect."

"I should have swung for his neck, but his arm was closer. The blade passed too easily through his forearm. It broke the bones and flesh with one good hack. I still think if I had decapitated him it might have stopped him."

Jessica immediately pictured her father's severed head and tried to dislodge the image by focusing on their words.

"That's when I saw the flames. I stepped in the gas too, and my shoe caught fire," Dylan said. "I backed up. I should have pressed forward."

"Maybe if they hadn't given us conflicting missions," Christopher said. "I understand why they couldn't have us coordinating between—he would have known—but to have one person coat the man with fire suppressant while another tries to light him up... That was dumb."

"But that may have been why it was so easy for me to chop the end of his arm off," Dylan said.

"Yeah. Impossible to know. Anyway, I backed up a pace because it seemed like the fire extinguisher was a bad idea if Joe was trying to light him on fire. I saw that Vivian was chanting, Mel was gathering himself like he was going to try to rush the man, and Wahid was stomping on an overturned chair, trying to dislodge one of the legs. Everyone in the bar was attacking in a different way and the man almost looked frozen until Mel tackled him."

"He should have given the fire time to work," Dylan said.

"I don't know if it would have," Christopher said. "He was fully dusted from my fire extinguisher. The real chaos began when Mel plowed into the man. The fire spread to some of the table skirts and Mel and the man crashed back through the bamboo door into the kitchen. I put out the little fires quickly with short bursts from the fire extinguisher."

"I was somewhat obsessed with the hand that I had hacked off of Phillip's arm," Dylan said. "The fingers were still moving and it twisted on the floor. I freaked out a little and hacked at it with Phillip's own blade. It didn't seem like flesh exactly. There was no blood and little resistance to the knife."

Billie shivered at that description.

"The fires were out and I looked up to see Joe following Mel and the man into the kitchen. I looped around the other side of the bar. That's when I spotted Simon, Ullman, and Laura on the far side of the kitchen. I had a pretty good sense of what they intended to do. There was a pantry with a metal door. I had the idea that they wanted to herd the man into there to trap him. It occurred to me that it would be dry in the pantry and maybe that was the secret. My fire extinguisher dust was totally dry. The fire from Joe would dry him out. Then, if we could trap him, maybe being completely dry would kill him. I tried to banish the realization from my head. I was still worried that if too many of us knew the real plan, then the man would know it too."

"Dry," Jessica whispered to herself.

She held up a hand. "Wait—the dry thing—how did you figure that out?"

"I don't know," Christopher said. "It just popped into my head when I saw them over near the pantry. Maybe because my grandmother used to call her pantry her 'dry storage'. She had a root cellar, where she kept her canned stuff, and potatoes, and whatever. But she also had a pantry for dry storage. Mel was trying to grab the man, but I think he kept slipping out of Mel's grip. The fight was moving and they were knocking over pots and pans and big metal trays. Vivian came to the door. She was still chanting."

"I followed behind her when I was done chopping up the hand. I didn't like holding his knife. It felt alive in my hand, like it was squirming," Dylan said.

"I think Joe would have tried to catch the man on fire again, but he didn't want to burn Mel," Christopher said. "Now, Mel says he wasn't aware of the plan, but as soon as he saw Simon standing near the pantry he decided to try to drive the man in that direction. Every time the man slipped from his grip, he herded him that way. I swept to the right to block the man's escape. I just pointed the fire extinguisher towards him and that seemed to steer him. Joe went the other direction and Dylan brought up the rear."

Dylan nodded at that.

"With one final tackle, Mel practically carried the man into the pantry. That's when we heard Mel scream. I thought the worst—I figured that the man had stabbed Mel with a second weapon. It turned out that Mel had just gotten a really bad cut from one of the shelves."

"It pretty much impaled him," Dylan said.

"Ullman was the one who rescued Mel. He pulled him out by his feet," Billie said.

They looked to her.

"That's what he told me," she said.

Christopher nodded. "Yes. That's how I remember it as well. Ullman pulled Mel out and Simon and Laura slammed the metal door shut and put their backs to it while Ullman fed a metal rod through the lock hasp."

"The blade went crazy," Dylan said. "It twisted and shook in my hand. At first I thought it was just trying to stab me. Even disconnected from him, it wanted to draw my blood. When I dropped it, the knife jittered and rolled on the floor. That's when I knew it was trying to return to Phillip. I scooped it up in a big metal pot that was drying on a rack and clapped a lid over it."

"We had him," Christopher said. "We had the man trapped in the pantry, banging on the door, and Dylan stood over near the stove with the knife in the pot, ringing like an alarm clock. Simon said that we should prepare ourselves for a long wait. We had to stand guard as long as the man was making noise. He was staring at Dylan's pot while he talked. The sound of the blade clattering around in there was distracting. Finally, Laura asked a question that was beginning to form in my head as well. She asked, 'Is that part of it? Is the knife supposed to be doing that?' Simon nodded slowly, but looked unsure."

Christopher took another sip of coffee. The cup trembled a

little when he set it back down on the table.

"Simon told us, 'My researchers predicted and modeled several scenarios. In most of them, we were successful when Dylan secured the knife away from the main body.' It was encouraging until Dylan said..." Christopher said.

"I left the hand," Dylan interjected. "I cut up the hand, but left it under one of the tables in the bar."

"So, Joe and I glanced at each other and agreed that we would go back through the door with another pot and find the hand. Simon told us he didn't think it was necessary, but he didn't forbid us from doing it either. We didn't make it out of the kitchen."

Christopher went to take another sip of coffee to clear his throat. It just made him cough more. Billie pushed her water across and Christopher switched to that.

Jessica couldn't stand the delay.

"What do you mean, you didn't make it out of the kitchen?"

Loss

"We were just about to go through the bamboo door when the noise stopped. The banging and the rattling inside Dylan's pot stopped exactly at the same time. Everyone looked to Simon—I thought that he was the one who knew what was supposed to happen. His eyes were wide and he just shook his head. Ullman said that it might already be over."

Dylan interjected. "It turned out that Ullman was the one who actually knew the plan."

"The butler?" Jessica whispered.

"He's *not* a butler," Billie said.

Christopher took over the narrative again. "The idea was that Ullman wasn't connected and Simon trusted him completely, so the researchers had explained their findings to him to coordinate. Anyway, Ullman said something like, 'It could take minutes, hours, or days. We won't know until we look.' Then, Vivian said, 'Well, we're not doing *that*. It would be incredibly stupid to do *that*.' Most everyone agreed. Simon was staring at the pot that Dylan was holding in his arms though."

Dylan nodded. "I knew he wanted to look inside. I kinda thought it was a good idea too. Honestly, when the noise stopped it felt like the pot got lighter. I was pretty convinced that we were going to open it and there would be nothing in the pot. I took it to the counter and set it down, but kept my hand clamped on the lid."

"Why didn't you just go look for the pieces of the hand?" Jessica asked.

Christopher pointed at her. "That's exactly what I said. If the man had disappeared, I thought there was a chance that the hand had too. Joe stopped me when I tried to go through the door. He said that maybe we ought to stick together for a minute. I had to admit that splitting up seemed like a terrible idea after what I had been through before. We went to where Dylan was standing. Everyone gathered in a circle except for Laura. She kept her back to the pantry door. She didn't trust that the bolt would stay in place, I guess.

"Simon started to tell us one of the theories about the man, but Ullman stopped him. He said something cryptic, like, 'We don't yet know which fuel stokes the fire.'"

Dylan nodded, agreeing with Christopher's memory, and added, "I was still wondering if the pot was empty, but I had a good idea. I picked it up—one hand on the bottom, and one on top—and I shook it."

"Something rattled around in there, but it didn't sound like a knife," Christopher said.

"Wait, hold on," Jessica said. "How big was the pot and how big was the knife?"

Dylan held his hands out, maybe a foot apart, and said, "It was a great big boiling pot, like you would use to boil a ton of pasta. It was black enamel, with flecks of white."

"Like a lobster pot?" Billie asked.

Dylan shrugged.

"It didn't clank. It made, like, a muffled sound when Dylan

shook it."

"And it was pretty light," Dylan said.

"Laura told us to wait and think about it, but we had to look. Dylan set the pot back down and lifted the lid. The rest of us peered inside. The knife wasn't in there anymore," Christopher said.

"There was thick fog and some water," Dylan said.

Christopher said, "Simon asked where the knife was. Dylan, you just shook your head."

"How could I know where it went? At one point I was holding the knife. It started to shake and twist in my sweaty grip, so I put it down. Then, I scooped it up in the pot. There was no way it could have fallen out. I mean, just add it to the list of bizarre things that happen when Phillip is around, I guess."

"So the next question was, obviously, if the knife was gone was the man still in the pantry? I was pretty sure he wasn't. Like I said before, I'm not into supernatural stuff, but even I have to admit that the man seems to move around faster than traditional physics can account for. Given that, and the evaporation of the contents of the pot, it stood to reason that we couldn't be sure that the man was still in the pantry. Ullman had been right. The only way to know for sure was to open the door and look."

"Laura did *not* agree," Dylan said.

"No," Christopher said with a nod, "she didn't. Her point was that there was no harm in waiting. If he was out, he would probably attack us and we would know. If he was in, then it was probably because he couldn't get out. In her opinion, there was no good reason to look. Ullman came up with one quickly though."

"Quick enough that it didn't seem like an idea he had in the moment," Dylan said.

"Exactly," Christoper said. "I thought the same thing. One of the researchers had probably warned Ullman that if we got the upper hand, we shouldn't stand idly by because it would give the man time to gather his strength. He said that there was a real danger in allowing him to gather strength. None of us had a way to refute that, so we took it as fact."

"Stupid," Billie whispered.

"Yeah. In hindsight, sure," Christopher said. "At the time, it didn't seem outlandish. There was a fresh fire extinguisher in the kitchen, so I traded the one I had partially used for it. Joe had picked up his lighter and had more of the gas or whatever he threw the first time. We were all as ready as we could be. Laura called for a vote and lost. Everyone except her wanted to push our luck. Simon was just about to open the pantry door."

"That's when I yelled for them to wait," Dylan said. "I thought I had the perfect idea. We could test the fire."

"The hand," Jessica said.

"Exactly," Dylan said. "We found the pieces. Christopher grabbed them with tongs and put them in my pot. Joe doused everything with a tiny bit of his gas and then lit it. It caught fast and burned bright."

"Like a flare," Christopher added.

"Yeah. I could feel the heat on my face and it twisted and writhed, like it was in real pain," Dylan said. "It burned in layers. The skin peeled away, flaring with bright orange flame, and then the rest of the tissue burned a deep red. When it was down to just bones, they burned blue. The bones were still grasping at the air as they burned away. The whole thing only took a minute or so."

"Laura asked if the rest of us could smell what she smelled. I rushed over there are and caught a hint of it on the air. The burning hand hadn't really smelled at all, but over near the pantry door it smelled almost like burning hair, or some hot chemical reaction. Simon latched onto that, saying it proved his point. I wasn't sure what point he thought it proved. It seemed to me that a minute before he had been saying that the man would be either dead or gone. The hand had still seemed alive even when it was nearly burned away."

"Was there any residue left in the pot?" Jessica asked.

Dylan answered, "No dust or ashes, but some white scorch marks."

"We took another vote—who wanted to open the door. Every went around. I think it was fifty-fifty. Vivian, Mel, and Wahid sided with Laura. Those four definitely wanted to wait, maybe indefinitely. If we were attacked, then we knew the man was out. Otherwise, we would assume that he was entombed in the pantry. If that was the case, they wanted Simon to have the whole thing sealed in concrete forever."

"Wait," Jessica said. "Was that really an option?"

"Trust me," Billie said, "with Simon, *everything* was an option."

Christopher continued, "The rest of us wanted to check to be sure. Pragmatically, I thought if the hand could burn away, then so could the man. We needed to give Joe a second chance now that, hopefully, the fire extinguisher dust was no longer an issue. It all came down to Ullman, who said that he wouldn't vote. Without him, we would have been left not doing anything, I guess. We beseeched him. Simon asked for an informed opinion. I thought that was disingenuous because it implied that somehow the researchers really knew anything. They had done their homework and told Ullman whatever they had told him, but to think that they really had an answer was..."

"Stupid," Dylan finished.

Christopher nodded. "Naive, I was thinking, but sure. After consideration, Ullman said we should open the door and be ready for whatever we saw. Everyone looked to Joe, which made sense. He would attack with fire. Simon asked Laura to step away from the door. After making her objections one last time, she consented. Simon told us that anyone could leave if they wanted. That was a particularly silly notion. Who would leave the group? Anyway, the door creaked when it opened. I held my breath. Smoke rolled out of the pantry and spread across the floor. It smelled terrible—almost like burning plastic or something."

"I kept turning around and looking at the bamboo door," Dylan said. "I was afraid that while we were all concentrating on the pantry, something would get us from behind."

"Once the door stopped creaking, it was completely silent in the hotel kitchen. Simon reached up to scratch his cheek and I could hear his fingernails moving over his stubble. He was the closest to the pantry, so he had the best angle to see if there was anything hiding back behind the shelves. He took a half-step forward and then shook his head. He said, 'I don't see him.' Without taking his eyes off the interior of the pantry, he waved Joe forward and said, 'Light it up—just in case.'

"I moved forward as well, thinking that we might need the fire extinguishers so we didn't accidentally burn the whole hotel down. Joe just had a little more gas in the plastic container he was carrying. He tossed it through the doorway and then threw the plastic jar in after. Holding the lit zippo in his hand, I remember the way he looked to Ullman and then to Simon. Ullman had the information, but Simon was the one who Joe looked to for authority. He was our leader."

"Just because he funded the trip?" Jessica asked. She didn't mean for her question to sound like a commentary, but it did.

"The whole thing was his idea and his mission," Billie said.

Jessica nodded quickly.

"Simon told him to do it, and Joe tossed the lighter in. Light from the flames grew immediately. This time, all the light was yellow. From where I stood, I couldn't see anything but the shelves of food and the fire. We could hear it beginning to consume some of the cardboard packaging. Something, probably a can being heated, started to hiss. I waited with my hand on the fire extinguisher's lever. Glancing up, I looked for a smoke detector. My heart froze in terror for a second when I imagined that there might be sprinklers in the ceiling. I didn't see any—Simon would have already thought of that."

"I remember the smoke," Dylan said. "There were layers to it. White, puffy smoke came out and rose to the ceiling. The darker stuff rolled along the floor."

"Simon said the man wasn't in there and waved me forward to douse the flames with the fire extinguisher. Before I could take a step, Vivian screamed something."

"She yelled Simon's name," Dylan said.

"Right," Christopher said. "He jumped back, but he wasn't quick enough. I was behind him, so all I saw was the blood stain the back of his shirt from the exit wound. The man had been hiding somewhere in the pantry and he had lunged out with the smoke and murdered Simon."

"I saw Phillip bolt for the window," Dylan said. "He was so fast, but other than that he looked completely human. He jumped up on one of the prep counters and threw himself up at the high window. His torso disappeared through and Mel almost managed to grab one of his legs before he got away."

"A bunch of us caught Simon before he fell. Vivian had her hands pressed to the wound on his chest. Ullman was on his special phone immediately, calling in the doctors who were waiting just outside the compound. The kitchen flooded with people, securing the site and tending to Simon."

"So stupid," Billie said.

Recovery

"I don't get it," Jessica said. "What part is stupid?"

"The whole thing," Billie said.

"I thought you said you would have gone."

"Yeah, but I wouldn't have gone along with his dumb plan. There had to have been a way to lure him out without putting everyone at risk. You don't try to stop a runaway train by standing on the tracks."

Christopher rubbed his forehead with his right hand. "We've been through this."

"I'm not blaming you guys," Billie said. "Believe me. You just... You don't know everything that I know."

"Like what?" Dylan asked.

Billie looked down at the table. She had her head propped up with her hands, like the thoughts in there were too heavy to carry with just her neck.

"You've been holding back something, Billie," Dylan said.

"Why don't you spill it. What are you hiding?"

When she looked up, Jessica could see misery in her eyes.

"You guys. How did you never figure out Simon's real plan? He didn't go down there to stop him. I'm sure he wanted someone to kill the man, but that was never Simon's real mission. He just wanted that murderer to finish what he started. Simon wanted the man to finally put an end to the guilt that he was carrying around. There was no explanation as to why Simon survived the first attack, when his family was killed and he couldn't live with that guilt anymore."

Christopher said something next, but Jessica didn't hear it. She had spent enough time in grief counseling groups to hear plenty of people express survivor's guilt. It had never occurred to her to try to die by the hand of the man though. That idea was completely new to her. But something in the back of her head told her she was wrong. Maybe she hadn't acknowledged the thought, but it was there.

Dylan was saying something about the doctors who came into the hotel kitchen when Jessica finally formed her thought into words.

They all stopped talking and listened to her.

"Is that what we're all doing?" Jessica asked.

"What?" Christopher asked.

"We didn't come to Vegas in order to share stories with other people who had been through the same trauma. We came here to put an end to our guilt."

"Speak for yourself," Billie said.

"Okay, fine," Jessica said. "I'm starting to think that maybe I came here to end my guilt. I was commiserating with plenty of people out in California. I didn't have real friendships, but I had a pretty good support system. The thing that I was missing was a way to get back to that guy. I think part of me believes that the only way I'll be back with my family again is if he takes me too. That's the one thing that I don't have in common with them anymore."

After she spilled that revelation, Jessica sat there with her mouth open. She had voiced her dark thought, but the truth of it was still spilling over her. The idea made her feel cold.

"We saw him tonight," Dylan said. "You didn't run to him. You were afraid, just like the rest of us. If anything..."

Dylan looked to Christopher. A moment later, they were all staring at him.

"No," Christopher said. "No, I'm not suicidal. The only reason I wanted to drive towards the man tonight was because I thought there was a legitimate chance I could hurt him by running him over. None of us have a story where someone hit him with a car. I had to know if it would work. Just because it failed doesn't mean that I was trying to hurt myself."

"I believe you," Billie said. She reached across the table and touched Christopher's hand.

He thanked her silently.

"Well, I'm not so sure," Jessica said. "About me, I mean. I'm wondering now if the only reason I chased Joe was to maybe... I don't know."

"Don't think about it," Dylan said. "We all have dark thoughts —intrusive thoughts. There's no shame in that. Just don't act on them, okay?"

Jessica nodded slowly. She looked around the diner. There was nothing really familiar about the place, even though she had spent several nights sitting in one of the booths as she waited out other sleepless nights. Her life was filled with places and things that she used as a substitute—a temporary placeholder. Somewhere, her real life was waiting for her, but she didn't know how to find it.

"Jessica?" Christopher asked.

That night that her family had been murdered, her life had ended as well. She was certain that everything that had happened since was just a dream that her dying brain had concocted. If she thought hard enough—forced herself to remember—she would realize that the man had killed her too.

"Snap out of it, Jess," Billie said. To punctuate her command, Billie pinched Jessica's arm.

"Ow!"

"You okay?" Billie asked.

"I'm fine."

"You didn't look fine. You looked like you were having an existential crisis."

"Why the hell would you say that just from looking at me?" Jessica asked. "I was just thinking about things."

"Relax, Jess, I was just concerned."

"I'm fine," Jessica said. Her tone made the statement an obvious lie. She took a breath and turned back to Christopher. "So, that was it? The guy appeared, stabbed Simon, and everyone gave up on the plan? Doesn't sound like much of an effort."

Dylan put up his hands to object. "After what happened with the knife in the pot that I was holding, we had to check to see if he was still in the pantry."

"And I was standing right behind Simon," Christopher said. "I'm certain that the man wasn't in that pantry. I don't buy the idea that Simon stood there and just let himself be stabbed."

"That's not what I said," Billie said.

"We thought he was trapped," Christopher said. "If not in the pantry, then *at least* in the kitchen. Nobody could have predicted how quickly he could slip by us and escape through a window that was at least seven feet off the floor."

"Based on everything we've heard," Jessica said, "that doesn't seem outlandish at all. He gets in and out of houses and locked attics with no problem at all."

"Well, I would have thought that he was visible in the pantry," Christopher said. "I don't know how I could have predicted that he would be there but not visible."

Jessica raised her voice. She couldn't contain her frustration any longer. "The *knife* turned into a *hand* inside a pot that Dylan was holding. That happened right in front of your eyes, right? If that can happen, why would you be even slightly surprised that he would be there, not be there, or materialize out of nothing?"

"It just..." Christopher started. "I guess you had to be there."

"No thank you," Jessica said. "Next time you have a trip based primarily on denial, I'll stay back with Billie. I can't believe you would go and try to summon him with just the assurance that you can't know the plan or he'll know it too. Who would sign up for that?"

"I would have," Billie said. "I'm not suicidal, but I'm not going to run away from him either. Next time I face him, I'm going to make him pay for stealing my whole life. He took everything but my pumping blood, including my freedom. I don't let that kind of thing go."

"Fine," Jessica said. "You do that. So, Simon died in the hotel kitchen?"

"No," Dylan said. "They had set up a small operating theatre next door. They wheeled him over and he died in surgery. They got to him very quickly and they seemed like they were prepared to deal with anything, but they couldn't save him."

"I talked to the doctors enough to know that there was something unusual about the injury," Christopher said. "They told me that the tissue appeared to be fighting their every effort to close the wounds. No matter what they did, Christopher just kept bleeding."

"Great," Jessica said. "There's another advantage for him, as if he needs it."

She pushed down on the table and stood up.

The others began to make their way to their feet. Dylan held up the check and they all pitched in cash to cover the tab. While he took it to the register, Jessica walked outside and looked up at the clear sky above. She blinked and stared until she saw a couple of stars or planets. Billie came out and stood beside her.

"I'm sorry—I didn't mean to make you feel crazy," Billie said.

"I just don't like people making assumptions about me," Jessica said. "It seems like a lot of people would rather just make assumptions instead of actually listening to what you have to say. If you're just going to guess, I'd rather have you not think about me at all."

"Fair. Okay," Billie said.

Jessica heard Christoper and Dylan come through the door.

"If you guys don't mind," Christopher said, "I don't want to go back to the house with possible remnants of the man on my car."

After what they had said, about the knife somehow morphing into a hand, Jessica had to agree. There was no telling what was stuck to Christopher's car, or what it might transform into if they just ignored it. Once she climbed into the back seat, it didn't matter where they went anyway. She was drifting off to sleep as soon as he started the car. She imagined having to climb the steps back at the mansion and wondered if she should just crash on one of the couches in the lounge. It would be easier.

Machinery

The rhythmic sound of machines woke her up. Something was jostling and bumping at the vehicle. Jessica lifted a hand and massaged her neck. A few minutes asleep had already put a kink in her muscles. The air was sweet with strange perfume.

"What are we..." Jessica started to ask. As her eyes adjusted, she saw the pink and blue foam on the windows and figured it out.

Christopher turned around in his seat.

"Car wash to get off the moss and dirt from..."

"No!" Jessica's scream interrupted him.

Billie reached out and grabbed her arm. There was panic in her eyes, but also confusion.

"Stop it!" Jessica screamed. "Honk the horn. Honk!"

"What?" Christopher asked.

Dylan turned around and eyed her. None of them understood. That's when Jessica saw him through the windshield. He was standing between the flapping brushes on the right side of Christopher's vehicle. Soap dripped from the tired brim of his hat.

Jessica raised a trembling hand to point as her mouth opened and closed, unable to make any more sounds. They turned and saw. The car kept rolling forward. Now, the right side of the hood was passing him. Dylan was nearest to him. He scrambled backwards for a moment, trapped by his seatbelt until he thought to unbuckle it.

Christopher finally got the message about the horn. After pounding on it several times, he pushed into the horn with his full weight and they heard the sound of the horn over the spraying water.

The man didn't move.

The vehicle lurched as Dylan knocked the shift lever into reverse when he tried to climb over it.

Through the soapy window, Jessica saw the man's arm raise.

The long knife sliced through the gasket between the door and the frame, cutting the air in front of Dylan's knee. When the knife retracted, Dylan climbed between the seats, spilling into Billie's lap as she struggled to get out of his way.

The vehicle bucked when Christopher stepped on the accelerator. The tires tried to jump out of the car wash's tracks.

Jessica saw the knife enter the vehicle again, this time between the passenger's door and the frame pillar. When the tires spun and caught, the vehicle bumped backwards and the knife disappeared again. Under them, the rollers pushed the tires forward as Christopher wrestled the gearshift out of reverse. Jessica pulled her arms in close to her chest and inched away from the door. She tried to imagine where the knife would infiltrate next time.

Next to her, Dylan was rolling over the seat into the cargo area as Billie yelled at him. She screamed when she caught a shoe to the face and pushed his leg away.

The knife shot between the top of the window and the frame, just above Jessica's head. It explored up and down, seeking her as she shrank in her seat and turned her head to avoid it. Next to her, the window was opaque with colorful soap. The blade retreated and came back at her side, almost finding her shoulder. Jessica twisted away.

She kept her focus on dodging the knife, but heard the engine roar as Christopher tried to fight the transmission into drive. The next jab came at her feet. Jessica lifted them, hovering them over the floor as it sawed from front to back, sniffing her out. The metal was alive—Jessica was sure of it. The blade might be blind, but it could definitely taste, and it wanted to taste her blood.

Christopher finally got control of the transmission and the car jerked forward.

She heard a horrible scream from outside the vehicle. The sound seemed to come through the frame and seat beneath her, rather than through the air. It was the scream of a wild animal in pain. She spun in her seat to see if she could glimpse the man through the rear window.

Instead, she saw Dylan's huddled form. He was crouched behind the rear seat with his arms covering his head. When the car jerked and swerved, Dylan rolled. Jessica had to grab onto the seat as vertigo washed over her. The world spun. She couldn't focus on anything.

Out there, in the spinning world, Dylan screamed and then the tires joined the noise.

Jessica felt her stomach lurch and struggled to keep her food down.

Billie was yelling for Christopher to drive faster and go to the hospital.

Every time Jessica opened her eyes, she felt like she was tumbling backwards. Her eyes rolled up and then jerked back down uncontrollably. Nausea rose and fell. She tried to focus on her breathing and then she screamed when a hand closed around hers. Sandwiched between clawing fingers and the back of the seat, she couldn't pull her hand free.

In and out—she put all of her attention on breathing as the seat bucked and rolled under her. She reminded herself that it wasn't happening. The world wasn't spinning, just her equilibrium. If she simply stayed perfectly still, her balance would return. That's when the car whipped around a turn and she slid across the seat. Billie caught her and held her upright.

"Where are you hurt?" Billie asked.

Jessica started to answer and then realized that Billie was

talking to her. Behind them, Dylan moaned. Jessica heard a siren in the distance.

It took all of her concentration to keep herself from vomiting. The way the world was flipping and flopping, she didn't know which direction was up. She had the horrible feeling that if she vomited, most of it would be sucked back into her lungs the next time she tried to take a breath. People died that way—Jessica was sure of it.

When the car finally came to a stop, she didn't really believe it until she heard one of the doors open and fresh air washed into the vehicle. The air smelled toasted and hot, but it was better than the recycled perfume from the car wash soap.

Behind her, she heard Dylan moan again and the hand loosened its grip on hers.

She had to risk it. Jessica opened her eyes and found the door handle, practically spilling out onto the pavement. There were bright lights glittering off of a million shiny surfaces. Through glass doors, she saw a man in blue scrubs pushing a gurney towards Christopher's vehicle.

Billie said, "He was stabbed. Right there."

Dylan moaned.

Another hospital person arrived and then took control, easing Dylan onto the gurney and then lifting into its locked position so they could roll it inside, chased by Billie.

"What happened?" Jessica asked.

Christopher was leaning into the back of his vehicle. He touched a dark spot on the upholstery.

"I think he stabbed him right through here," Christoper said. His fingers had found a hole in the carpet.

"Why?"

He looked up at her. "Are you okay? Did you get hurt too?"

"Christopher, why would you go through a car wash? After everything..."

"I didn't know," he said, shaking his head. "I've been through a thousand car washes. How would I know?"

CHAPTER ELEVEN

Jessica

Work

The machine roared. The metal conveyor belt shook and the green plastic tray pushed its way through the rubber flaps. A little steam escaped from the giant dishwasher as the glassware emerged. Jessica peered into the darkness, wondering if those tiny points of light were reflections in the man's eyes.

When a hand touched her shoulder, she jumped and nearly screamed.

"Whoa," Sadie said, laughing. "What's going on with you?"

Jessica pressed a hand to her chest and felt her own heart pounding. She took a deep breath.

"Nothing. I'm fine."

"You look like you need a hot shower and about twenty hours of sleep," Sadie said.

Jessica tried to smile. She hadn't been able to sleep for more than an hour at a time ever since Dylan was stabbed. As for the shower, the closest she had come was a cold bath the day before.

"I'll be fine," Jessica said. "I'm just... I'm dealing with some things, you know?"

"You worried about your friend?"

Jessica searched Sadie's eyes, trying to remember when she

had told Sadie anything personal.

"I'm just being nosey. Don't mind me. One of my spies told me that they saw you in the hospital, visiting some guy who used to work here."

"Oh," Jessica said.

"Don't look so surprised. I told you, I'm a super connector. There's nobody that I don't know or know someone who knows someone, you know?"

Jessica shook her head.

"You need me to cover you? I'm clocking off now, but I can take one of your shifts if you want a break," Sadie said.

"Actually, that would be really helpful," Jessica said. She started untying her apron. "I'm supposed to have four more hours. Can you cover me?"

Sadie glanced at her phone to check the time, or maybe her messages. Jessica was already heading for the lockers.

"I don't mind," Sadie said, "but I'll have to tell Millan, you know?"

"Thanks—I appreciate it!" Jessica said over her shoulder.

Hospital

She spotted Billie in the corner, near the head of Dylan's bed. Jessica hated the fog of depression that Billie brought with her when she visited.

"Hey," Jessica whispered.

Billie looked up and nodded. Dylan's eyes were closed. One of the monitors pulsed slowly. He had to still be asleep.

"How are you doing?" Jessica asked.

"Fine," Billie said. "They keep trying to chase me away, but I'm fine."

"I can give you a ride home if you want."

"No."

Jessica went to the bench by the window and turned her body so she could see Dylan but also keep an eye on the skies. They were on the third floor, and there was no rain in the forecast, but she didn't plan on taking any chances.

"Have they said anything?"

"The last woman said, 'Still not out of the woods.' I told her that Dylan had never been near the woods in his life. They have all this medical jargon at their disposal. Why do they insist on stupid metaphors?"

Jessica shook her head.

"What's going on with the group?" Jessica asked.

An angry sneer passed over Billie's face for a moment and Jessica knew that the news had to be bad.

"They think they can kick us out—that's the infuriating part," Billie said. "I mean, I *live* there. If they think that Ullman is going to let them keep meeting in the place that I live... It's just crazy."

"Billie?" Jessica asked, trying to gently interrupt. She put up her hand, like she was a student asking to use the restroom. When Billie stopped, Jessica whispered, "Can you backtrack in the story a little? Last I heard, Christopher was going to call a special meeting to tell them what happened."

Billie glanced at Dylan. The sight of his sleeping face must have convinced her to lower her voice and control anger.

"So, yeah, Christopher went and told them all what happened. They listed out the rules that we broke, and they formally kicked us out. There was even a motion on the table to disband everything permanently, but I heard that the vote failed by a narrow margin. I have no idea what they thought they would accomplish by disbanding everything permanently. Can you believe that it got four votes? I'd like to know which of them thought that they could disband everything just because they didn't like what some of us said. How arrogant would you have to be to think you can control the words that come out of my mouth?"

"Hold on," Jessica said. "What rules?"

"They have rules. We weren't supposed to disclose what happened in Mexico. We weren't supposed to have a branch meeting where stories were told outside of the group setting.

Once we saw him, we were supposed to immediately inform the others and instead we went to eat at that diner. We broke like, half-a-dozen rules if you take all that garbage seriously."

"I didn't know about those rules," Jessica said.

"Maybe you didn't know about all of them, but you definitely knew about some. Don't you remember your first night in the group?"

"Barely," Jessica said. "I spent the first good chunk of time trying to remind myself of everyone's name and then I was so lost in Christopher's story that I think I forgot about everything else."

"Well, Joe read a bunch of rules."

"Wait, though, the first time I met Vivian, she told me her story and it was just me, Joe, and her. Isn't that one of the rules?"

"Did she tell you the whole story or just a couple of details?"

"A couple random details, I guess."

"See—that's okay, according to them. It's not a complete gag order, they just don't want an entire story recounted, like when we told you about what happened in Mexico."

"Oh."

"And they'll tell you it's because there might be connection between talking about him and manifesting him, but that's a lie. It's really about control."

The sheet over Dylan's leg twitched. Billie and Jessica both froze, looking at him to see if he would move more.

After nearly a minute, Billie shook her head.

"We know you can hear us, Dylan. You were awake yesterday. What's going on in your head?"

Dylan didn't respond. As far as Jessica knew, none of the doctors had offered any explanation as to why Dylan was dropping out of consciousness for stretches of time.

They turned at the sound of a knock on the doorframe.

Christopher took a step inside the door and stopped. He folded his arms across his chest and tilted his chin towards Dylan.

"Any change?"

"He's still being stubborn," Billie said.

Jessica offered, "None that we know of. But they might be holding back information on his condition because we're not family."

"I thought you told them you were his sister," Christopher said to Billie.

"I did, but a couple of days ago, when jerkface was awake, he told them I wasn't. He told them it was an insulting insinuation."

Christopher smiled. After a second, Billie smiled too and then laughed behind her hand. She reached out and touched Dylan's arm.

"Wake up, Dylan, okay? Or I might tell everyone I'm you're wife."

The sheet twitched from Dylan's foot jerking to the side a little. Jessica's eyes went wide.

"That might just be working," Jessica said.

Billie leaned closer. "Actually, that's not a terrible idea. Maybe I can get a pastor in here and convince him to marry us while you're still unable to object."

They stared at the sheet, but Dylan didn't move again.

Christopher sighed and took a step towards the door.

"I'll see if I can get any more info," he said before he backed out of the room.

"Just us," Billie said. "Since they booted the four of us, only a couple of people from the group have even bothered to visit. It's like they blame us for the attack."

"Well..."

"Jessica, stop. It wasn't our fault."

She shrugged. "I'm not defending the rules. I barely understand them. But there was a feeling that night that we were almost chasing danger, you know? I mean, we could have taken the hint when we saw him at the fountains. Instead, we just kept pressing forward."

"Living our lives, you mean? We shouldn't have to hide away and avoid certain subjects. We shouldn't live in fear our whole lives. That's what the others are advocating. I would probably get locked away in an asylum, but I'm almost convinced that it's time to find the right investigative reporter and just spill my guts. This whole thing could be a ten part documentary, or a podcast or something. We could turn our misery into millions and maybe something would finally get done about these crimes."

"Nobody would..."

"Right—nobody would believe me. There are tons of scandals that were covered up for decades because of that same rationalization. That's just the coward's way out, Jessica. It's a victim's mentality. What if the whole support group only exists as a support system for cowardice?"

Jessica shook her head.

"It's about coping and grief," Jessica said.

"Well, maybe it should be about *doing* something, Jessica. Did you move out here to cope, or did you hope that you could actually *do* something?"

Jessica blinked and looked up at the ceiling.

"I guess I moved here because for a tiny fraction of a second it felt like Joe saw me and understood me. I went years and years thinking that there was nobody in the world who could understand what I went though and then he walked in and sat down in my meeting. With just a few words, I knew that he would understand me."

"And now, because you broke some unspoken, ludicrous rule, he has banished you."

"I'm sure it wasn't Joe."

"Are you? They claim that nobody runs the group, but let me tell you something, Simon used to run the group. Ever since his death, there has been a power vacuum and Joe is the one who is trying to insert himself into that. Do you know that he tried to get control of Simon's endowment?"

"His what?"

"Simon set up some kind of financial trust in order to maintain a few of his houses and pay some salaries. There's one branch that just funds our group. It pays for Mel's server time and Laura's team of researchers. It covers Joe's travel expenses when he goes to talk to people. There's a legal team who step in and defend people like me—those who are accused of murder. Joe found out about the advisory board and tried to get himself installed on it. He was this close to taking control of the whole thing."

"Why?"

"For the money, Jess. It's all about power and money with people like that."

"He never struck me as..."

"Well open your eyes."

Jessica leaned back in her chair. She looked at Dylan and took a deep breath. After she let it out, Jessica folded her arms over her chest. Billie was distressed. It was important to remember that and let her talk it out. It *wasn't* important to take everything she said seriously.

"You don't want to believe. That's okay. Here..." Billie said. She pulled a folded paper from her pocket. "Look at this."

Jessica held it to the light and read the paper. She check the letterhead and then the signature.

"How did you get this?" Jessica asked.

"Because, unlike Joe, I *am* on the advisory board. The worst part is, he petitioned them not to fund Dylan's care and he *knew* that I would see that document." Billie glanced at Dylan, maybe remembering that there was a possibility that he could still hear them, even though he was unconscious. She lowered her voice to an angry whisper. "Joe argues that the group determines its own membership, and membership dictates benefits."

"We get healthcare because we're in a support group?"

"No, not for everything, but that's not the point. Simon set up limited care for everyone who went to Mexico last year, and that's still in place. Because Dylan was stabbed by *him,* his care should be covered. Joe wants it revoked. Do you know what would happen to Dylan if Simon's estate wasn't paying for all this?"

Jessica shrugged.

"I can't say for sure either, but I do know that he wouldn't be getting this level of care," Billie said.

Jessica thought about what Billie was saying. She looked down at the paper again. Joe's language seemed completely unsympathetic to Dylan's plight. If what Billie said was true, and Jessica had no reason to doubt her, Joe shouldn't have any say at all in the matter.

"So, what are you saying we should do?" Jessica asked.

"You don't have to help if you don't want to. I'm going to find a reporter and put them on this story. Just from listening to everyone over and over, I know enough details to make a plausible case. If we can get national attention to these attacks, then maybe we can finally get someone to do something about them."

"Like what?" Jessica asked. The image that popped into her head was of trucks full of soldiers chasing rainclouds across the Great Plains.

"This is my point," Billie said. "I don't have the answers, but someone in the world might. How will we know that until we shed more light on the situation?"

Jessica nodded.

Interview

Jessica stared at the woman's smiling face, trying to figure out what was wrong with the expression. Taken individually, all the components of her features were correct. The smile was reflected in the creases next to her eyes. Her eyebrows were raised slightly, expectantly. Every few seconds, as Jessica spoke, the woman nodded encouragingly. The whole picture suggested that this woman was on Jessica's side.

"Let's jump back to the morning of the alleged attack, can we?" Mindy asked.

"Alleged?"

"Sorry—so sorry! That's just an old journalist's habit. Please excuse me," Mindy said. She calibrated her tone, making her voice precisely one notch softer and more sympathetic. "Let's jump back to the morning of the attack, okay?"

"I was dizzy, so I was lying on my back when I heard the rain start."

"This is first thing in the morning?"

"No. I mean, like I said, this was when the rain started. It was before noon, but not, technically, first thing."

"Can we start at *technically* first thing?"

Jessica took a breath and glanced around the room. The room was in a hotel, but it wasn't *technically* at hotel room. It had to be some kind of small meeting room that could be rented separately, Jessica figured. She wondered if maybe there was a blackjack or poker table that would be wheeled in for private gambling. They were using two of the high-backed chairs near the window for the interview. Jessica had a cup of tea sitting on the table next to her. It had been there so long, untouched, that it was undoubtedly cold.

"Sure. First thing, I woke up. I tried not to 'load up.' That's this thing I used to do when I was a teenager. When I woke up in the morning, I would stay in bed for a few minutes, thinking about all the things I had to do that day. Dad said that I would come downstairs for breakfast with dark clouds already swirling over my head because I had loaded myself up with stress already. So, I had a little poster that I made for myself that said, 'Don't load up.' Whenever I woke up, I would look at that and try my best. Sometimes I wondered if maybe it had the opposite effect though because it just made me concerned about not being concerned."

"Interesting," Mindy said. "Where is it now?"

"Sorry, what?"

"The poster you made for yourself? Where did it get to?"

"I suppose I threw it away before the move."

Mindy tapped a button on her computer. "The move to Florida."

"Right."

"Okay—back to that morning in bed, sorry."

"So, I woke up. I tried not to load up, and then I got dressed. I would do morning stuff before I took my shower, and I hated walking around in a robe, so I always got dressed twice."

"If I could—let's back up to the dark clouds."

"Sorry?"

"You said that your dad mentioned that you would come down for breakfast with dark clouds over your head. Where do you think they came from?"

"They're metaphorical," Jessica said.

"Yes, I get that. Why were you carrying so much stress?"

Jessica frowned. "I'm just guessing, but maybe because I lost my mom when I was a little kid and I felt like I had to basically be a mother to my brother and sister while, at the same time, trying to do well in school, get my extracurriculars, and not disappoint my father."

"That's a lot of weight to carry."

"Hence the dark clouds, I imagine," Jessica said.

"You don't need to imagine—they're your dark clouds. You can attribute them to anything that makes sense to you."

"What are we doing?" Jessica asked. She waved her hands in front of her face, calling a stop to the questioning.

"I'm trying to get a clear picture of that day," Mindy said.

"I've already told you three times what happened."

"Sometimes we get the clearest picture from the subtle differences between repetitive tellings," Mindy said with another genuine-looking smile.

"Repetitive is right," Jessica said.

Mindy folded down the lid of her laptop for a moment. She had done this several times already. Each time she folded the lid down, it felt like she was saying, "This next statement isn't part of the interview. It's just me being your friend."

Mindy said, "I know it's not an easy process, but sometimes we don't even know the parts of the story that we habitually leave out. Sometimes, that's where we find the biggest clues. Just lose yourself in the memory. Tell me everything and try to answer the questions. Remember, I'm on your side. All I'm trying to do is help you get to the truth. Once we find that, we'll know."

"I already know the truth," Jessica said.

"Then humor me. Help me get there too, okay?"

Jessica took a deep breath and thought about Billie, who had already done her interview with this lady. It had to have been twice as hard for Billie. A court had deemed Billie guilty and incarcerated her for murder. Mindy must have really latched onto that. At least Jessica was never really accused of anything. The fake smile and penetrating eyes of Mindy were the strongest accusation that Jessica had ever faced.

"Fine," Jessica said.

"So, you woke up and looked at your poster."

"Right. I tried not to load up and I pulled on some clothes before going downstairs."

"How were you dressed?"

When Jessica hesitated, Mindy said, "Again, I'm just trying to form a really clear picture to chase out any details."

"Whenever I would get up, I would wear jeans, an old sweatshirt, and slippers to go down and do chores, eat breakfast, and whatever. Then, when that was done, I would go back up and shower and change into clothes for the day. So, at this point, I was wearing jeans, an old sweatshirt, and slippers."

"What kind of sweatshirt?"

Jessica was growing tired of fighting the silliness of the questions, so she just answered.

"It was green with UVM in gold letters. That's where Mom went to college."

"You must have missed her very much."

"Of course I did."

"So, it wasn't your day to make breakfast?"

"No. Some days, Dad would work all night. On those days, I would tiptoe down and make silent breakfast for my brother and sister. They loved it. It was a game to them to try to be perfectly quiet so we wouldn't wake Dad. They never succeeded. Julia would drop a fork or Peter would start coughing on orange juice. Whenever either of them made a noise, they would both start to laugh. Before I could stop them, they would be laughing and then Nigel would start barking. Even Nigel knew we were supposed to be quiet. I guess he picked up on my anger when the kids would laugh, and so he would start barking to try to make them be quiet. It almost always got out of hand. Actually, to say 'almost always' is a lie. It *always* got out of hand. I don't remember a single day when we managed to be quiet. Before breakfast was finished, Dad would always be slamming doors and grumbling about how we woke him up."

"So, why do it?"

"Huh?"

"Why go to all that effort if it always ended the same way?"

"Courtesy? Dad worked late to provide for us. The least we could do was try to let him sleep."

"Couldn't he just go back to sleep after you all left for school."

"I believe that's what he did."

"So, why all the wasted effort?"

Jessica shook her head. "I don't know. Go dig up Dad and ask his corpse. He wanted us to be quiet so we did our best."

"Did it feel like your best?"

"Can we stop? It doesn't feel like you're asking about that day anymore. It feels more like unqualified therapy."

"Fair enough. So the day of the attack was a quiet day."

"Yes. Dad worked all night, so it was a quiet day. It was also a Saturday, so after I got everything going, I went back up to lie down. Making breakfast, I got pretty dizzy."

"You've mentioned the dizziness several times."

"Right. I get dizzy when death is close. The doctor said it's a stress-induced panic attack. The blood pressure change causes vertigo."

"Is that what you believe?"

"Sure. Anyway, I was lying on my bed when the rain started."

Mindy's fingers were tapping the keys of the laptop quickly. Her attention was focused on the screen. When she finally looked up, Mindy's fake smile was gone. It had been replaced by fake empathy.

"This is not unqualified therapy, I promise, but can I ask you about your mental state as you listened to the rain?"

"Why?"

"I would rather not plant ideas, but I have the feeling that your mental state that morning might be pertinent."

Jessica frowned. Mindy's answer had raised more questions than it answered.

"Please?" Mindy asked.

After a sigh, Jessica said, "I suppose I was feeling anxious and angry."

Mindy nodded.

"Anxious because of the dizziness and because there were several important tests coming up at school. I didn't need one more thing to go wrong, and the vertigo was, like, just one more issue that I had to deal with along with everything else. The anger was because I felt like I wasn't getting any support from my family. Sometimes it felt like the more I had going on, the more they required from me."

Jessica had to stop. Sadness and guilt welled up and choked her. She gripped her temples between her fingers and leaned over, trying to let the emotion pass, but it kept multiplying.

In a barely audible whisper, Mindy asked, "Do you feel angry now?"

When Jessica shook her head to say no, tears escaped the corners of her eyes. The sorrow was a dull ache, way in the back of her head. The guilt took over, filling her heart and pumping with her pulse.

"Can you see him now?"

"What?" Jessica asked. Her eyes flew open. "What do you mean?"

"Sorry," Mindy said, holding up her hands. "I was just wondering if putting yourself in a vulnerable emotional state would allow you to manifest him in some way."

"Me? What?" Jessica asked. "You understand that he is not

something that *I* manifested, right? He's an outside force. I'm the victim, not the cause."

"Of course," Mindy said.

"I need a break," Jessica said. She stood up and looked at the two doors on either side of the room. "Which way gets me outside?"

Mindy pointed.

Break

She managed to get outside before her tears really began to flow. Jessica took a deep breath in and it shuddered out of her. Folding her arms across her chest, she closed her eyes and pointed her face at the sun, letting it warm her. The interview room had been far too cold.

In her pocket, her phone buzzed.

It was too bright to see who was calling.

"Hello?"

"Hey," Billie said.

"It's you," Jessica said. "What's up with this stupid reporter? Where did you find her?"

"I used the research group. They tracked her down. Her credentials are impeccable. She is open to anything, but not hung up on anything spiritual or any metaphysical woo-woo stuff. She has a reputation of digging deep and getting to the bottom of..."

"Well, she got to the bottom of my patience pretty quickly. I don't think I can take much more of her weird questions."

"Just stick with it, please?"

"I don't understand what she's trying to get at. What kinds of questions did she ask you?"

"Tons," Billie said. "Honestly, there were a lot of things about the interview that didn't make sense to me either until we got to the end. You have to trust that she's going somewhere with the questions. Just give her some leeway and she'll bring you around, okay?"

Jessica stared off into the distance. Waves of heat made everything far away seem distorted and in constant motion. No matter how long she lived in the desert, she didn't think she would ever get used to that.

"I don't mind talking about him. I would understand it if she was asking me to describe everything I knew, everything I had seen... It's just..."

"Jessica, think of it this way—we don't know what we don't know. Maybe there's some reason we were attacked out of everyone in the world. Maybe if she can connect all those threads together, we'll actually get somewhere with understanding why he came to us and why he left us alive. Remember, this is just information. It can't hurt you to discuss it, right?"

"I guess. I'm not going back in that room though."

Billie laughed over the phone.

Jessica smiled for the first time that day.

"There's a lanai up on the tenth floor. Tell her you want to finish the interview there," Billie said. "She'll have access to it."

"Good."

Lanai

Jessica stared out at the horizon and then turned her eyes to the journalist. It was warm on the lanai, but the fans above and an occasional breeze made it more than comfortable. Mindy looked off-balance and uncomfortable in her chair.

"Where would you like to start?" Jessica asked.

"Good. Yes," Mindy said, tapping a key to find her place. "Let me just..."

"I think you were asking if I could see him? I can't now and I couldn't downstairs either. I've only ever seen him twice—once at my house and once a couple of weeks ago when we saw him on the other side of the fountains and then in the car wash."

"Sounds like three times," Mindy said.

"Sure. Call it three. Anyway, back to that first day, like I said I was feeling anxious and angry. Now, thinking back, it makes me feel guilty. There have been so many times when I realized all the countless ways that my father and siblings supported me and grounded me in the world. It's silly that I ever felt like they were a burden. But I have to forgive my teenage self for those feelings. I had friends who didn't have a care in the world—at least that's the way it felt to me. They had two parents and no little brothers and sisters to take care of. Their parents worked regular, nine-to-five jobs and were home for dinner every night and breakfast every morning. Of course, I realized later that nobody has a perfect life. My life was a challenge, but I had a lot of advantages. Back when I had two parents, one parent, and then none, I still had plenty to be thankful for. I still do. Anyway... What's the next question?"

"Tell me about the expression on your father's face."

Jessica felt cold again.

"Sorry. When?"

"When the attacker decapitated your father I think you said his face was smiling, or grimacing?"

"I never did."

"Sorry," Mindy said, tapping her keyboard. "I might be confusing my interviews. I thought you said that it looked like your father's face was smiling and that maybe he was smiling because you finally had to take all the responsibility yourself."

"What?"

"That wasn't you?"

"No. I never said that and I never felt that way. I don't know where you got any of that from."

"Like I said, I'm probably just confusing my interviews."

Jessica waved her hands in front of her face. "Wait, wait, wait. You've only talked to, like, Billie, Christopher, and Dylan. None of them had decapitation stories, and none of them had responsibility heaped on them by their fathers. Who could you possibly be confusing me with?"

Mindy closed her laptop a little. "I'm so sorry. Please—I was only trying to prompt you where I thought you had left off earlier. Let's back up. Can you tell me once more what happened when you returned home from the... Bissons'?"

Jessica blinked and studied Mindy.

"What's that smell?" Jessica asked.

"Smell?"

"Are you a smoker?"

"I have been in the past," Mindy said.

"When we took a break did you smoke?"

Mindy shook her head.

"Were you around someone who was smoking?"

"I might have been. Truth be told, my sense of smell is not that great. It's entirely possible that I passed through some cigarette or cigar smoke. As you're probably aware, there are a number of smoking rooms in the casino attached to this hotel and others, although I've read that the number is decreasing."

Jessica stood up and moved a little closer to Mindy.

"Are you allergic or something to smoke? If so, I'm very sorry. My room is a few floors down. I could change my clothes if you can spare a few..."

As Jessica got closer, Mindy's eyes didn't leave her. Still, Mindy's fingers were busy. Without looking at the laptop, Mindy was closing applications and shutting things down. Jessica got the feeling that there might be something on the screen that Mindy didn't want her to see. She didn't waste any time. Jessica lurched forward and snatched the machine from Mindy's lap, quickly retreating to the balcony.

"What are you doing?" Mindy asked, chasing after her.

Jessica got to the balcony first. She held the laptop at arm's length, dangling it over the drop.

"Tell me what's on here," Jessica said.

"My notes and my drafts. What would you think that I..."

Jessica interrupted. "Just now, you were closing something you didn't want me to see. What was it?"

"Just my notes from other interviews. I maintain confidentiality until the story is written and I get a chance to fact check and provide a copy for the subject to review. I'll do the same for you, obviously, assuming that you don't destroy all my work."

"Why are you asking me questions designed to make me upset?" Jessica asked. The laptop slipped a bit and she barely caught it. Mindy put her hands to her chest as the laptop swayed over the descent.

"It's a time-saving trick," Mindy said. "I get you into a vulnerable emotional state and then I back off a bunch to regain your trust. I find it helpful with traumatized young women. I'm an older woman, successful enough, and they want me to respect them. After the initial anger, I usually get a quick revelation that would take ten times longer if I just tried to build trust slowly."

If Mindy was lying, Jessica couldn't see it in her eyes. For the first time, she actually trusted everything that Mindy was saying.

"I'm sorry," Mindy said. "I know that my methods are a little cruel at first, but usually the payoff is worth it—for me and the person I'm interviewing. They often come to a better understanding of their own pain and that gives them peace. It's like tearing off a bandage."

Jessica adjusted her grip again and was preparing to hand over the laptop when another question popped into her head.

"Were you lying about the cigarettes?"

"No," Mindy said. There was a tiny flinch just before she answered. The smallest squint betrayed her.

"That's a lie."

Mindy took a deep breath.

"You're right. I still smoke. Billie told me that you're not a smoker and I thought it was easier to simply lie."

"What's your brand?"

"Sorry?"

Jessica let the laptop slip a bit and spoke very slowly. "What brand of cigarette do you smoke."

"I just..." Mindy said, shaking her head. "I guess I don't really have a preference. I just take whatever is..."

Jessica let the computer slip a tiny bit more. It was pinched between the very tips of her fingers.

"Hand rolled. Criss Cross pouch," Mindy said quickly.

"Let me see your lighter."

Mindy shuffled quickly back inside and returned fast with her bag. Jessica adjusted her grip—the laptop really had been a second away from slipping from her fingers. Mindy didn't notice. She only had eyes for the contents of her purse. She held up her lighter. It was a green plastic disposable lighter.

Jessica pulled the laptop back to safety and set it on the table.

"We're done," Jessica said as she headed for the door.

Mindy called after her. "I know my methods are questionable, and I apologize for that, but I hope you can see the big picture here. I'm trying to get to the bottom of this for you, and I will use every trick I have to do that."

Jessica slammed the door, cutting off the rest of Mindy's excuses.

CHAPTER TWELVE

Jessica

Alone

With all the blinds drawn and the air conditioner on full blast, Jessica couldn't tell what time of day it was. Sometimes, over the din of the fan and the television, she could hear someone walking around upstairs. When that happened, she put a pillow over her head and tried to nap. Her appetite dwindled at the same rate as her food supply. Working her way through the cabinet, she ate whatever was in the next can or package.

Jessica didn't dare to answer the phone. She expected to receive an angry call from Ms. Millan about the missed shifts. It never came. Apparently, Jessica wasn't the first employee to fade away from their job at the "meat grinder," as Dylan called it.

At the end of the cabinet, Jessica was completely out of food. Standing in front of the counter, she shook a little salt onto her finger and licked it. The taste only made her stomach rumble harder. Cinching the drawstring of her sweatpants helped for a little while. Pressing on the outside of her stomach somehow made it feel fuller within. When her hunger came back, the pain made her double over.

In the stack of mail on her table, she found a flyer for a pizza place that had twenty-four hour delivery. Jessica found a way to order through the website and then sat next to the door, dozing while she waited for the knock. When it came, she was too weary to stand up. She reached up, turned the knob, and said, “Leave it there, thanks.”

“Are you sure?”

“Yes.”

The guy took way too long fumbling with the bag and setting the pizza down on the hallway floor. The tiles of her apartment hall always looked dirty and dusty, no matter how much they were cleaned. She understood his hesitancy, but still hated him for how long it took. Jessica forced herself to hold still until she heard his retreating footsteps. Then, she reached through the gap around the door, turned the box to an angle, and pulled it into her lair.

She sat there, just enjoying the smell for a minute before she opened it. The quantity of the food was daunting. Her stomach knew its limits. She had to go slowly or she would get sick. Choosing the tiniest slice, Jessica nibbled on the end before she dared take a full bite. Her mouth had lost all of its toughness. The heat of the melted cheese immediately claimed a layer of skin from the roof of her mouth. The crust cut her lip.

She fell asleep halfway through the first slice.

Guest

Her hand closed around the piece of pizza when she heard the sound. She stuffed some cold pizza into her mouth. Some forgotten instinct told her to hoard the food in case the sound was from another predator.

“Jess?” a voice called. It was followed by a knock at the door.

Jessica realized that her door was still open a crack. She hadn’t bothered to close it after grabbing the pizza.

Until the voice called again, she couldn’t put a name to the sound.

“Jessica?” Sadie asked.

“This isn’t a good time,” Jessica tried to say. The words came out slurred. It was like she had been silent for long enough that she had forgotten how to speak. Jessica realized that she had been holding some of the pizza in her mouth. She swallowed and tried to answer again, but Sadie was already pushing her way in.

"No," Jessica said.

"I'll just come in for a..."

Sadie stopped when she saw Jessica sitting there in sweat clothes, dining on floor pizza.

"What are you doing?" Sadie asked. "Are you on a bender or something? You're not going to OD, are you?"

"Close the door," Jessica said. She meant to say, "Leave and close the door behind you," but only the abbreviated version came out. Sadie took the order as an invitation to come in all the way.

"I was hoping you moved," Sadie said. "When I heard you stopped coming to work, I thought about how you said you moved every few months or whatever. I was hoping to find your place empty. I never thought..."

"I'm about to move," Jessica said.

"Really? Because it looks like you haven't moved in days," Sadie said. "This places smells like the women's shelter. What's with the TV? I'm turning this down."

She stepped over Jessica, who was still trying to get to her hands and knees so she could make it to her feet. Sadie was picking up trash and tossing it over the counter into the sink when Jessica flopped down into a chair. With deep regret, Jessica realized that she had left the pizza over on the floor. She was starting to think that she could handle another piece. With the thought, her stomach woke up again.

"Could you hand me that?" Jessica asked, pointing.

Sadie stopped two or three times to pick things up on her way. The dirty clothes, she tossed towards the bedroom. Trash went in the sink.

"If you're going to do that, the trash can is in that tall cabinet."

"Do I look like *your* maid? I'm just picking up stuff so I don't step in it. What is this? What drugs are you on?"

"Nothing," Jessica said with a sigh. "I've just had a rough couple of days."

"Couple of *weeks*, Jess. We're about to have you legally declared dead."

"Go ahead."

Sadie picked up a few more things, deposited the pizza on the coffee table in front of Jessica, and then took a seat on the edge of the couch cushion, carefully glancing around first to make sure she wasn't sitting down in something.

"Oh, how's it going with what's his name?" Jessica asked as she helped herself to another slice. It was cold and not good, but at least there was no need to worry about burning her mouth further.

"Bagged and tagged," Sadie said. "I'm working on another guy now. His name is Seth Fewell. Terrible name, but good looking. I think I'll try for something longer term next."

Jessica nodded.

"Do you want help with whatever you're dealing with here?" Sadie asked, gesturing towards Jessica in a general way.

"No," Jessica said. "I'm fine."

"You're not fine, but I won't try to help you if you don't want it. I know for a fact that people in your condition can't be helped until they want to be helped. I had a boyfriend who overdosed. We all tried to get him to see what was up, but he just refused. I think he wanted to die. You, on the other hand, have never struck me as the type of person who wants to die."

"I'm not," Jessica said.

"But you also don't seem to be the type of person who wants to live. That puts you in a weird place."

Jessica's stomach cramped. This time, it wasn't from hunger. Her stomach was rejecting the new food. She got up too fast, headed to the kitchen for water, and had to brace herself on the counter to wait out the head rush. For a moment, she thought that it was vertigo. The idea passed quickly. The water felt wonderful washing down her throat.

"So, what is it?"

"What's what?" Jessica asked between breaths. She had finished the water so fast that she was panting. Jessica moved quickly back to her chair to give her stomach time to settle down.

"What have you been taking? You look like a human skeleton, you're not going to work, and standing up made you look like you were going to pass out. I'm struggling to put all those together into a single picture."

"I told you, I'm not taking anything. I've just been a little, I don't know, depressed? My friend got stabbed right in front of me. Actually, he was literally behind me, but we were in the same car. Then my grief group kicked me out, and then some reporter hassled me. It has been a tough... month? I'm not sure how long it has been, but it's been tough."

"And hiding here helps you?"

"No. I'm not saying that I'm doing the best thing, but it's all I'm capable of."

"Come on. Let's get you out of here. You need some fresh air," Sadie said as she stood up. "You think there are clean clothes anywhere in this place, or do we have to do laundry?"

"I'm not leaving."

"Lady, you couldn't resist me if you tried, so I suggest that you follow orders."

"Thank you for your concern, Sadie. I appreciate it."

Sadie sat on the edge of the couch again. "Jess, I know what's good for me and I do what I want. People see that and they immediately think that I'm selfish. You know what? They're absolutely right. But I'm also very caring. People don't believe that those two qualities can coexist in the same person."

Jessica let her eyes close. She was attempting to retreat into sleep, the same way she did when the upstairs neighbors were being too loud. A hand closed around her wrist.

"Right now, I've decided to help you. Believe it or not, my help doesn't require your consent."

"What about all that stuff about not trying to help me if I didn't want help?"

"That's just my excuse if things don't turn out. You turn up dead on your bathroom floor and I'll just say, 'I tried to help her, but she wasn't ready to accept it.' We all have our coping mechanisms."

Jessica smiled and then wheezed out a quiet laugh.

Sadie stood back up and began to kick clothes towards the bedroom door.

"You have a shower here, right?"

"Of course."

"Don't say, 'of course,' like that when it's pretty obvious that you haven't been in the presence of a shower this month. You can't *of course* that question."

"Yes. I have a shower. The bathroom is right there."

Sadie pushed open the bathroom door with one finger while her other hand went up to pinch her nose shut. Reaching in to flip on the light, her eyebrows went up.

"Not terrible. I expected worse. Get in there and scrub off some of that crud while I find you something to put on."

Jessica let her eyes slide shut until Sadie pinched her ear.

"Did that sound like a request?"

Out

A thin layer of clouds glowed bright pink in the evening sun.

Leaning out from under the awning, Jessica shook her head and wrinkled her nose with a sneer.

"No."

"It's *beautiful* out, Jessica. Don't fight me. We're just going to walk around the block."

"Why?"

"We're trying to drag you back into reality, remember?" Sadie asked. She literally grabbed Jessica's arm and dragged her until Jessica gave in. With barely enough energy to walk, Jessica didn't have nearly enough energy to fight.

"It's hot."

"It will do you good. My grandmother used to always say that air conditioning will give you pleurisy."

"What's pleurisy?"

"I have no idea. I always assumed it has something to do with the lungs, but I never bothered to look it up. Could be a toe fungus for all I know. Anyway, this guy, Seth Fewell."

"Terrible name, but good looking," Jessica said.

"Exactly. You know him?" Sadie asked. She didn't pause long enough for Jessica to respond. "I saw him at Genie's house. I don't think I ever told you about her. She's a meddler. All I did was whisper something about Seth and then he was calling me. Honestly, I don't even know why I answered the phone. When I figured out who was calling me, I told him, 'No, thank you.' The next day, he called again."

"I thought you said he was good looking."

"Of course he is. Wait, have you seen him or not?"

Jessica looked up. They had only made it halfway to the corner and her legs were already feeling heavy. Between the walking and incessant onslaught of words, Jessica didn't think she was going to make it.

Sadie was still waiting for an answer.

"No. I haven't seen him."

"Well, good looking or not, I figured I would go ahead and block him. I don't need to be chased around. I can't believe Genie gave out my number like that."

Jessica spotted a bench near the bus stop. She veered in that direction.

"So, then, I made it my business to spot him out in the wild again so I could get *his* number."

"Didn't you already have it from when he called?"

"No. I deleted it. Fortunately, I was able to figure out where he worked and then I scouted around to see if I could guess where he would hang out. I arranged to run into him outside of his gym one evening."

Jessica lowered herself to the bench. Sadie was so busy with her story that she barely seemed to notice and she sat down next to Jessica.

"He asked me why I ignored him and I said I wasn't aware that he had called. He told me that we had talked, which was basically a lie. I had only said three words to him. That's barely a conversation. Anyway, I told him to give me his number and he shook his head, saying he would only type it in himself. I must have been feeling crazy because I let him. He put that number in and then immediately called himself. When he flipped the phone around, it showed the last time he called me. All proud of himself, he held it up like a magician showing me the card I picked, you know?"

Jessica shook her head. She was barely tracking the story, but it seemed like the right response.

"I grabbed my phone back and turned and walked away. He will hear from me when he hears from me. If he calls me again, I'm going to walk away."

Jessica was looking down between her knees at the sidewalk. Somehow, the clothes that Sadie had picked out felt too tight on her skin. Shifting her shoulders, the straps of her top were rubbing her raw.

"Are you even listening to me?"

Jessica shook her head.

Sadie leaned back and sighed.

"What happened to you? When I met you, I thought you were one of the more stable people around here."

Jessica laughed towards the ground.

"My friend Winnie, back in Colorado, she built her life from scratch. As soon as she got her driver's license, she just walked away from her family and modeled her life after how she thought things could be. Some people watch TV and they get mad at how those people have these idealized lives and these petty problems that regular people would never worry about. Instead of doing that, Winnie just decided that she was going to be a normal person with normal issues. Her life is like that now. She's like one of those people you see on TV. Nothing bothers her for more than thirty minutes at a time. A problem pops up, it turns out to be a simple misunderstanding, and she laughs and moves on."

Jessica sighed.

"That's kinda the way I thought you were. You moved here to get away from something, but I figured that you were the type who just shook it off and kept going."

"Sometimes your problems follow you," Jessica said. She raised her head and propped her elbows on her knees.

"That's why I change my number every couple of years. If I don't give you the new number, you can consider yourself dismissed. That's what I tell everyone."

"I remember," Jessica said. On the windows of the shop across the street, there was glare from the sunset. Jessica thought she saw moving water beyond the window, like they had an indoor fountain or something. She imagined walked across the street and pressing her face to the window, and wondered if she would see the man on the other side of the glass.

Sadie was deep into an explanation about how she chose the people who would get her new phone number. Jessica interrupted.

"I took a shower, right?"

"You must have. The water was running and you came out with wet hair and a *lot* less dirt. I didn't watch or anything, but I have to assume you showered."

"Huh," Jessica said. She touched her own stomach and then reached around to touch her back, half thinking that she would find oozing blood.

"Are you going to tell me what's going on, or what?"

"I can't. You won't believe me."

"So what?"

"Huh?"

"Jess, I *already* think you're crazy. My opinion of your sanity is not going to decrease one bit, no matter what you say. You could sit there and tell me that there was a family of martians living in your right nostril and I wouldn't bat an eye at this point."

Jessica smiled and reached up to touch her nose.

"I've told you all of my business. You know what kind of sociopath I am. Sharing goes both ways, or didn't your mother teach you that?"

Jessica looked down, surprised at how fast the tears spilled from her eyes.

"No," she managed to say with a voice that sounded too thick to be her own. "No, she never taught me much of anything."

Walking

When they started walking, Jessica found it easier to talk. The words left her mouth and stayed right where she had dropped them. By continuously moving, Jessica was able to leave all those crazy notions behind her. With only a couple of clarifying questions, Sadie kept quiet and simply listened. She didn't scoff at any of Jessica's crazy claims.

Except for the group meeting at Simon's house, Jessica had never told anyone all the details at once. Sadie was a normal, everyday person, and she still seemed to accept the idea that Jessica had been hunted by a supernatural man who traveled with the rain. If their roles had been reversed, Jessica wouldn't have been able to keep quiet like that. The questions would have popped out of her mouth on their own.

"So, that's it. Billie, Dylan, and Christopher are aligned with this reporter. They're trying to get a documentary or something made, thinking that it will bring attention to the problem. The others won't talk to me because I broke their unwritten rules. I might as well move back to Pasadena again. Back then, I was okay with feeling alone because I didn't think there was any other way to be. Now, it's a major loss. I'm on my own."

Sadie turned a corner. Jessica glanced around, trying to figure out where they were. The whole time she had been telling her story, she had let Sadie dictate all the twists and turns. Jessica patted her pockets and realized that she had left her phone back in her apartment. If Sadie ditched her, to find her way home she would have to start asking strangers where she was.

"Juice?" Sadie asked.

"Huh?"

Sadie was pointing at a window that looked like an ice cream parlor. When she nodded, Sadie led her inside. They sat on high stools and ordered juice that looked like a milkshake but tasted vaguely of dirt. The juice gave Jessica a head rush by her second sip.

"Because they're cooperating with the reporter, you can't talk to Billie and them?"

"Well, yeah, I mean that's the way I feel about it. It's like they hired her and all she wants to do is try to get me to admit that I'm to blame for my own attack, you know?"

"Did the reporter do the same thing to Billie?"

"I don't know. I assume that she only targeted me."

"Why?"

Jessica shook her head. "I don't know."

"And this group you got kicked out of, did they say it was forever, or just a punishment? None of them will talk to you?"

"Honestly, I haven't talked to them about it, or anything, for that matter."

"It's important for you to have them to talk to?"

Jessica nodded. "In that group was the only time I felt safe in years and years."

"Yeah," Sadie said. "I get that. And you won't fight for it because you don't feel like you deserve to feel safe."

"What?"

"That's what people do," Sadie said. "If there's something they want and they feel like they deserve it, then they fight for it. The only thing keeping you from doing that is yourself. You won't let yourself fight because you're afraid that you might get it back."

Jessica shook her head and drank some more of the foul-tasting juice. It was starting to grow on her. The ginger was spicy in a weird way, but it made her stomach feel more settled than before.

"No," she said. "I'm just being realistic. I'm not going to hurt myself by banging my head against that wall they put up. I'm simply protecting myself from their unfairness."

Sadie nodded. "You didn't look like you were protecting

yourself when I came and dragged you out of that apartment. You looked like you were punishing yourself. Or maybe you were just wallowing. Whatever it was, it wasn't protection. You can't heal by refusing to take care of yourself."

"And *you* can't grow by actively making the same mistakes over and over. Why do you feel like you don't deserve a mature, adult relationship, Sadie? Why are you offering me advice instead of analyzing your own choices?"

"We see ourselves reflected in others," Sadie said. "When I tell you stuff, although I'm being perfectly accurate, I'm also telling it to myself."

"So you're going to change?"

"Eventually," Sadie said. "Right now I'm kinda having fun."

Jessica shook her head. "Hypocrite."

"Probably. But I'm also making the world a better place. The men that I toy with *deserve* to be toyed with. They need to walk a mile in my shoes before I'll dance with them."

"Why not just find a nice guy? Why do you have to keep finding the ones who *deserve* to be toyed with?"

"Right now, I'm having fun," Sadie said with a shrug.

It could be debated, Jessica decided. There was something desperate about the way that Sadie pursued men that definitely suggested it wasn't all fun. On the other hand, it wasn't making Sadie miserable. She would figure out her issues eventually, and she would learn why it was so important to her to be the aggressor. From the outside it was simple to characterize Sadie's behavior.

"Okay," Jessica said.

"Okay, what?"

"You said that I was wallowing. What am I supposed to do about it?"

Sadie shifted in her chair so she was facing Jessica.

"There you go, you're halfway there. I'm no expert, but in my opinion when someone is punishing themselves like you are, they're avoiding some kind of confrontation. What is the confrontation?"

The simple answer that popped into Jessica's mind didn't bring any dread with it. The specter of the man had hovered over her for years—it was a comfortable anxiety, if that was a thing. Fishing around for the real issue, Jessica thought about the reporter. The interview with Mindy was what had driven Jessica into hiding. The smiling woman with questions that were slipped into her like daggers—Mindy was who Jessica was avoiding.

Jessica nodded. "I know what it is."

"Heroin?"

"What? No," Jessica said.

"Oh, right," Sadie said, snapping her fingers. "Heroin is what you're using to avoid the fear, right? You're hiding by turning off your brain."

"I'm not taking heroin."

"Ketamine?"

"No, Sadie, listen to me—I've been hiding because I've been avoiding facing the questions that the reporter was asking me. Somehow she was able to hit on really deep questions that I ask myself in the middle of the night and it made me furious and uncomfortable to hear them from someone else's lips."

"Oh. That's all? How old is this lady? Just put on a trench coat and chase her down the street at night. That will make you feel better."

Jessica laughed. "You're terrible at giving advice."

"You know, a *lot* of people tell me that," Sadie said, crossing her legs.

"I have to go back to the interview and answer the questions. Even if it makes me uncomfortable, I have to do it."

"That's a good start," Sadie said. "And if that doesn't work, tell me where she's staying. I know kitchen people all over this town. I'll get someone to put a fun surprise in her food."

"Thanks," Jessica said as she stood up. Turning left and right, she remembered that she had no idea where Sadie had led her. The slow way that Sadie stood up and stretched before she started walking—it almost seemed like Sadie realized that she had the upper hand and was taking full advantage of it.

Jessica didn't mind. Dominance games weren't important to her.

They didn't talk much as they walked and Jessica stayed half a step behind and to the left to allow Sadie to take the lead. Jessica looked at the shops they were passing and wondered if the bakery they passed was worth returning to. The smell of baking bread lingered outside the shop, but it was mixed with the faint odor of melting plastic. Jessica was still hungry enough that anything might taste good. Through the window of a bar, she saw a TV mounted up on the wall. On the screen, a waterfall cascaded over some rocks and splashed around a woman holding up some kind of lotion. Behind the woman, through the curtain of water, Jessica saw the shape of a man in a long coat. Maybe it was just a rock formation. Maybe it wasn't.

"I know him," Sadie said.

"Huh?"

"That bartender you were staring at? His name is James or Larry or something. My friend went out with him."

"Oh," Jessica said.

"I want to meet a man with a strong name, like Ash."

"Ash?"

"Or Quentin."

Jessica shook her head.

"Seth Fewell. It just doesn't sound right," Sadie said.

It took Jessica a minute to remember who Sadie was talking about—one of her future conquests.

"Okay," Jessica said.

CHAPTER THIRTEEN

Jessica

Coffee

Jessica spun the paper cup until the seam was facing away from her. She took a sip. The coffee was cold, but that was okay. Lifting her phone, she checked the time again. It was pretty clear that Mindy wasn't going to show up. Jessica should have expected that. On the phone, Mindy had been noncommittal, and she seemed like the type of person who would be definitive if they intended to show up.

Jessica took a deep breath and prepared to get up.

Out in the garden, Riley was watering some tall plants that had been clipped to form a topiary. Jessica had been sitting there for twenty minutes and Riley hadn't looked over once. After a brief internal debate, Jessica decided to leave that confrontation for another day.

Just before Jessica stood, Mindy came around the corner. Her bag was clamped between her arm and her side. She took her chair without offering a smile or a hand to shake.

"Thank you for meeting with me," Jessica said.

Before answering, Mindy pulled a recorder from her bag and clicked it on.

"Do you mind if I record this conversation?" Mindy asked.

Jessica nodded and Mindy said, “Please say it aloud.”

“Yes, I don’t mind if you record this conversation.”

“Thank you.”

After a few seconds, it was clear that Mindy was waiting for something. Jessica’s first instinct was to apologize. She suppressed that impulse.

“You were asking about the expression on my father’s face after he was decapitated,” Jessica said.

Mindy looked naked without her computer in front of her. The device had acted as a barrier to hide behind. Now there was nothing between them except the small device with slowly increasing LCD digits and a tiny red light.

“It was surprise, I guess,” Jessica said. “Honestly, my memory of his face isn’t really that clear. I know that I saw him, but it’s possible for me to imagine many different expressions on his face in that moment, so I’m not quite clear about what I’m remembering and what’s just an invention of my imagination.”

Mindy nodded.

Jessica took another sip of cold coffee.

“What about your brother and sister?”

Jessica shook her head. “I never saw them again in person. Later on, I wondered why they never had me identify the bodies. I guess maybe that’s something that happens more on TV than in real life? I don’t know. The funerals were all closed casket. I caught glimpses of pictures, but it was like my brain shut off when the photos passed before my eyes. I refused to associate those images with my memories of Peter and Julia.”

“So they never saw your father.”

“No, of course not. They were hiding up in the attic during the attack on my father.”

“In fact, there were no witnesses who saw your father’s return to the house. The next time anyone would see your father, he was already dead.”

“Of course,” Jessica said. The questions were infuriating, and they were probably meant to be. Mindy was trying to elicit an emotional response from Jessica in order to drive her to some new revelation. Jessica decided that the only way to endure the interview was to assume that Mindy wasn't being manipulative at all. Instead, she would imagine that Mindy was simply the dumbest person on the planet, and had no idea how insensitive the questions were.

In the distance, Riley was talking with one of the gardeners.

"Did the police test your clothing for blood spatter?" Mindy asked.

"I don't think they did. It was raining and I had been outside so much. I'm not sure there would have been any results from the tests. They did offer me a change of clothes though, so maybe they did something and just never told me. Do you have information that they performed tests?"

"I'm afraid I don't have my notes in front of me," Mindy said.

Jessica got the point of that innocent-sounding statement. Mindy didn't bring her notes because they were on her computer, and Jessica might threaten to destroy it again.

"Your neighbor said that he never saw any sign of the alleged attacker, is that correct?"

"Yes, that's correct. Mr. Bisson showed up when I was in the yard and he insisted that we stay put and wait for the authorities. He wouldn't even go up and check on my brother and sister."

"Do you think that if he had, he would have been able to prevent their murder?"

"No," Jessica said with a sigh. "I think that the man had already killed them. Every moment of what happened that night went precisely to his plan. There was never any intention to kill me. I was simply the witness. I was meant to watch it all happen without any ability to prevent it. I was meant to run to the neighbors' and bring back help after it was already too late. My father leaving and returning was all part of it. Julia and Peter hiding but being killed anyway was all part of it."

"It was orchestrated," Mindy said.

Jessica nodded and Mindy pointed at the recorder.

"Yes," Jessica said. "It was all orchestrated."

"With all this control, is it possible that there was an attacker but he wasn't the one who *actually* performed the murders?"

"I didn't actually see any of the cuts with my own eyes. When I ran into the house, my father's body was still bleeding and the only person there was the man, but I can't say that I actually saw him swing the blade, you know?"

"So, there were three of you in the room, including your dying father."

"Right."

"And, presuming that your father didn't manage to cut his *own* head off..."

Jessica swallowed.

"Right," Jessica said. "Since there were only three of us, and Dad couldn't have done it to himself. And, given that I know that I didn't kill Dad, I can only draw the conclusion that the man did it. Plus, a strong indicator is that the man was still holding the blade that was dripping with Dad's blood."

"A blade that was never recovered."

"Right."

"Or witnessed by anyone else."

"Right."

"In fact, the man was never witnessed by anyone else."

"Not at that time, no."

"There was another time?"

"Yes—I guess it was several weeks ago that Dylan was attacked."

"And it's your assertion that it was the same man."

"It is," Jessica said.

Mindy tented her fingers below her chin and stared off at nothing.

"I'm not trying to second-guess your methods," Jessica said. "But this has all been covered dozens of times. You've heard my story directly from me, and I know that you've read my written statement as well as all the police reports. Is there really something you expect to extract from these questions?"

"Yes," Mindy said. "There is. I have a few more."

"Certainly."

"In college, did you have any sexual partners?"

"I did."

"Did you break up with them, or they with you?"

"Both. I dated one guy for a year who broke up with me because he said he needed more time to study. He later dropped out. Then, I dated another person who I broke up with. He was too clingy for me."

"Did any of them ever comment on your trust issues?"

Jessica took a deep breath. "Sure. The clingy one did."

"And what was your response?"

"I broke up with him," Jessica said. The answer wasn't perfectly truthful. There had been a pretty big gap between him bringing up the trust issues and when she eventually broke up with him. But she didn't feel that the question deserved a perfectly truthful response.

"Has anyone else in your close sphere been attacked with a knife while you knew them?"

"Yes," Jessica said.

Mindy's eyebrows went up.

"Dylan? You've interviewed him, remember? He was attacked with a knife in the back of Christopher's vehicle while I was only a few inches away from him."

"It's your understanding that he was conclusively attacked with a knife?"

Jessica cocked her head. "Yes. Why?"

"The hospital report was not conclusive on what caused the injury."

"That's because of Billie," Jessica said as she put together what must have happened. "When we arrived at the hospital, Billie was afraid that the police would want to know how Dylan got stabbed."

"So, you contend that the same person who attacked your family also attacked Dylan."

"Sure."

"You don't sound confident."

Jessica took a deep breath and focused on distancing herself from the emotions that were trying to claw their way to the surface.

"I'm very confident about what happened, but it doesn't seem that you're really interested in that. Your statement referred to the attacker as a person and I've been clear that I can't verify that he was a person. Last time, we settled on 'the man' or 'the entity' as shorthand. You're either not listening, you have a terrible memory, or you're once again trying to get a rise out of me. My answer might have sounded unsure because I was unsure of your intentions, not of the answer."

Jessica delivered this response with calm clarity.

"Good," Mindy said. "Very good."

"Sorry?"

"You're ready."

"For what?"

"Do you remember when we first spoke? I mentioned that I would like to record some of our interviews to present in my podcast?"

Jessica shrugged. "Sure. I thought you decided against that."

Mindy shook her head. "It was always the plan, but you weren't ready. Now, you're ready. Can you meet me at this address in the morning?"

She handed a card over to Jessica. The street name didn't mean anything to her geographically, but it sounded fancy.

"Okay."

"Wonderful."

Garden

The sun and heat were a physical weight, pressing down on Jessica's shoulders as she walked the garden path. She spotted Riley's hat over the roses and wound around the corner to catch up. By the time Jessica was on the next path, Riley was disappearing behind a hedge. Jessica had to jog to follow.

"Riley!"

Riley's face was covered with tiny pinpoints of light that

filtered through the brim of her hat. The corner of her mouth turned up into a smile when she saw Jessica. The sight made Jessica slow and nearly turn around to run away. In that moment, Riley's smile made her look just like a photo of Jessica's mother.

"Hi, Jessica, I thought I saw you on the patio."

"Yes, I think you did," Jessica said.

Riley's smile faded.

She attempted to fill the awkward silence. "If you'd like to join me in some gardening, I have some more gloves and a loose shirt. It helps a lot with the heat. I'll..."

"No, I'm good. Can you do me a favor?"

"Of course."

Jessica pulled the folded paper from her pocket and held it out.

"What's this?" Riley asked as she reached for it.

"Please have someone from the group read that at the next meeting. I mean, they probably won't but, give it to Joe or Vivian I guess. They can decide."

Riley stared down at the piece of paper.

"What is it?"

"I just want everyone to know how silly it is to think of yourselves as a support group and then boot someone out because of some rule that doesn't make sense in the first place. We all have our own ways of dealing with trauma and sometimes we need the freedom to express ourselves in the moment when we're trying to cope. Hard and fast rules are..."

She trailed off when she saw that Riley was unfolding the paper. As she read, Riley shook her head and then said, "No, Jessica."

"Great. I'll just leave it for..."

"No, I mean, no. You have the wrong idea. Who told you that you were kicked out of the group? Didn't Joe come to talk to you?"

"What?"

"After Dylan was attacked, Joe said he was going to track you down and see if you were okay, and then Joe was... Didn't he talk to you?"

"No."

"I'm so sorry, Jessica. You must have thought we were monsters. What gave you the idea that we didn't want you to come back?"

"It was..." Jessica motioned towards the house and then decided not to finish naming the culprit. "Wait, where's Joe?"

"He had to travel to see his nephew in Ohio. There was some family emergency or something. Vivian knows more, I'm sure. I only heard second hand."

"Oh."

"I guess I just assumed that he had talked to you and that you decided to take some time away. We're meeting tomorrow. Please come—everyone is thinking about you. All of you were never not welcome. I know Dylan is still recovering. Billie seems to be taking a hiatus, and I've only seen Christopher a couple of times since the whole incident."

"Wait, Christopher has been back?"

Riley nodded. "Yes. He missed a week or two, but yes."

Jessica reached out and Riley handed back the note.

"We'll see you tomorrow then?"

"I'm not sure."

Confrontation

"That was amazing," Mindy said as she took off her headphones.

"Yes," Jessica said. Everything had flowed out of her. All the tiny details that Jessica would always remember in the middle of the night had been seamlessly integrated into her narrative for the first time. Telling her story into the microphone had been like removing a heavy coat and taking a deep breath of fresh air for the first time in a decade.

"That was really something—completely natural, unimpeachable, and matter of fact. Your story is really going to tip the scales of anyone even remotely skeptical."

Jessica pushed back from the desk and placed her headphones on the chair as she stood up.

"We'll send you a copy after we finish post production, but I promise you we're not going to have to edit a thing."

"Please redact the name Bisson," Jessica said. "In the past they haven't wanted to be connected with my story."

"Okay. Yes, we can bleep that name if that's acceptable?" Mindy asked the question while looking through the glass at someone in the control room. The man nodded and gave a thumbs up.

"Whatever," Jessica said. She headed for the door.

As soon as the heavy door closed behind Jessica, she was surprised by someone emerging from a shadowed doorway on her left.

"Sorry. Didn't mean to jump out like that," Billie said.

"What do you want?" Jessica asked.

"I just wanted to thank you for doing that interview. I know it was an emotional grind. Mindy has such a strange, jarring technique, but it's *so* effective. I hope you're not mad at me for keeping quiet about what it would be like. After I figured out her strategy, I knew it would be slightly traumatic, but the results outweigh the ordeal, don't you..."

"That's not why I'm mad at you, Billie. I think you know why I'm mad."

For a moment, Billie's features just showed confusion. The expression rapidly changed to anger.

"I don't like guessing games, Jessica."

"You told me that we broke the rules so we were kicked out of the group."

"I never said that."

"Yeah, Billie, you did. You also told me that Joe was getting Dylan's healthcare revoked. I visited Dylan last night. He said his bills were all paid by Simon's trust."

"Yes, but not through the group policy that Simon set up for everyone who went to Mexico. Joe got the board to switch him over to a different policy so he wouldn't be on the group one anymore."

"Who cares?" Jessica asked. "His bills were paid. His level of care didn't change. None of that stuff you talked about actually happened. Why did you tell me all that?"

Billie folded her arms.

"You needed the right frame of mind to do what you just did. If you hadn't felt betrayed and cast out, you wouldn't have been honest and believable in the interview."

"Why is that important? Do you know how terrible it feels to find out that my friend was just manipulating me in order to make some stupid interview better? Do you have any idea how depressed I've been for the last month? I could barely leave my apartment."

Jessica tried to push down her anger. Once she let one emotion take over, she wouldn't be able to control herself. The last thing she wanted to do was break down in front of Billie.

"This is going to change everything. You'll see. You're not in the right position to understand, but eventually you'll see."

"I don't care, Billie. I could not care less about what you're doing with Mindy. She's as bad as you are, in my opinion."

"You've already signed the releases. Your interview will be produced and released."

"Billie, I *don't care.* I don't want to have anything to do with you. Got it?"

Instead of answering, Billie turned and walked back down the hall, towards the rear exit.

Jessica went the other direction.

CHAPTER FOURTEEN

Hilda

Robbery

Jessica wiggled in her seat, trying to get comfortable. It felt like she had been waiting forever. Her heart jumped when she saw Billie cross the hall, but Billie didn't join the meeting. The attendance was the lowest that Jessica had seen. Dylan was still pretty much keeping to himself. Between his injuries and his anxiety, he didn't leave home much, from what Jessica could tell. She wasn't at all surprised to see that he was absent.

Christopher was a no-show as well. According to Riley, Joe was visiting his nephew.

When Wahid arrived, there were only four of them, including Jessica, sitting on the couches. Jessica thought that more people must be coming, but dismissed the idea when Hilda started the meeting.

"Let me start by welcoming Jessica back," Hilda said with a smile. "I'll just go ahead and start, if that's okay with everyone."

"Of course," Jessica said. Wahid and Riley only nodded.

When Hilda spoke again her voice was emotionless and quick, like she was reading aloud the warnings on the side of an aspirin bottle. Until she addressed Jessica directly, Jessica was wondering if Hilda was joking.

"First, I want to stress that this story is a work of fiction. All of the details given about crimes I will claim to have committed are complete fabrications. Any places or people who I describe are constructions of my imagination. There is one true thing I will tell you, and it's that I'm sorry. Jessica, this is the first time you'll be hearing my story and you should know that I blame myself for the trouble that all of us have encountered. I believe this all originated because of me, but let me start at the beginning."

Jessica tried to process everything that Hilda had just said as she sat there and blinked. She wanted to ask Hilda to back up to the beginning and start over. Before she could open her mouth, Hilda had already moved on.

"I have a knack for recognizing patterns. It started when I was a little girl. My father loved jigsaw puzzles. My mother tolerated them. I could look at the hole where a piece should be and I found that I could describe, or even draw, the piece with amazing precision. The shape of the piece and its markings were all dictated by the pattern of the whole. This was just something that I did instinctually. It took no training or coaching."

Jessica glanced over and saw that Ullman was walking slowly towards the bar. It was the first time that she had seen him in the room during one of the meetings. She watched carefully as he took a seat a the bar.

"When I started dating, the boy down the street asked me out and I quickly learned more than I should have about his family. They had a business with many workers. They paid those workers in cash on Wednesday at noon, and the cash moved to the accountant's offices on Tuesday night in preparation. These are not things that were said openly in my presence. Details like this would simply crystallize in my head as I overheard general conversations in my boyfriend's house."

A thousand questions popped into Jessica's head as she listened. The group was so small, it felt informal enough that she could interrupt and ask for more background information. How old was Hilda? What kind of business did her boyfriend's father run? Where did they live? Jessica kept her questions to herself, mindful that the group had rules that she had, apparently, missed in the past.

"My parents weren't financially stable, and a dread would settle on our house every month when the bills were due. Nobody had to tell me these things. I understood the pattern. My father's brother would help out when he could by sending envelopes of cash. Nobody spoke about it, but he would drop the envelope right in our mail slot every few weeks. If my father tried to acknowledge the gifts or thank his brother, my uncle would get flustered, so it had been years since the gifts were mentioned and I was certain that the amount of cash was never discussed. That gave me an opportunity to inject more cash into coffers."

Jessica couldn't help herself. "Wait, how old were you?"

Hilda shifted back into her disclaimer voice.

"As I said, this is a work of fiction, but the character I'm describing here would have been nineteen."

Jessica nodded.

"So, I formed a plan and executed it. I skimmed enough money to keep my household afloat for two months. It was noticed by my boyfriend's father, blamed on one of the accountants, and dealt with appropriately. I have no regrets or guilt. The accountant was hurt enough to send a message about embezzlement, but not so much that it would scare off their other employees. Their business was full of cash and thieves, so they valued their accountants very highly.

"It would be a while before I was comfortable taking money from that business again, but I found that there were several other opportunities relatively close. A young woman back then was an unlikely suspect, so I could move around pretty much at will. With a little care, I never felt even remotely unsafe as I skimmed from this business and then the next. Sometimes the amounts I extracted weren't even noteworthy. The accountants were precise, but the people providing the cash expected some amount of loss in their payroll. I wasn't the only person with their fingers in the till.

"The day everything went wrong, it wasn't an oversight or a failure in planning. It was just bad luck. Luck is one thing that doesn't follow any pattern. You can't predict it. It was early in the morning, very early. I left my house around four, so I must have arrived at the location around four-thirty. There was a single desk lamp on and the cash was in an unlocked safe built into the back wall. I knew the safe would be unlocked because I had visited the office before, when the safe was empty and unlocked. When I discovered that they didn't keep it locked when it was empty, I decided to disable the lock and see if they bothered to fix it before the next cash drop. They didn't.

"I counted out what I needed and closed the safe door. When I stood and turned, I saw a man in the doorway. It wasn't *the* man. It was one of the accountants. He was a little guy, shorter than me, with bushy gray hair that made him look like a little elf or something. In each of his hands, he held the hands of one of his daughters. The oldest daughter was nearly as tall as he was.

"His youngest daughter turned to her father and grasped his hand in both of her. She pleaded up to him, saying, 'Please, Papa, don't. Please don't.' I was confused by this until his older daughter started begging too. She was a little more composed and she said, 'Papa, please don't kill her. You don't need to kill her.' That's when I knew what kind of trouble I was in."

Hilda paused to clear her throat.

"There was a clear division of labor in this particular organization. They had people who worked with their hands, people who were involved in violence, and the people who handled the money. None of those groups had any crossover responsibility. They wouldn't have kept a violent accountant on the payroll. I knew that this accountant wouldn't be a dangerous person. Not physically, at least. The daughters clearly thought the opposite, and they certainly knew him better than I.

"He turned to his oldest as he let go of her hand and he said, 'Take your sister outside.' The youngest immediately forgot about me and said, 'But, Papa, it's raining. I don't want to get my new shoes wet.' He silenced her objection with a stern glance.

She was frightened of him.

"I started to wonder if it would be safer to try for a window or try to barge past him. He might be dangerous, but he was also pretty small. I thought there was a chance I could muscle my way by. I also considered screaming for help, but dismissed the idea. Anyone who might hear me would be as least as dangerous as the accountant. It didn't take any time for me to settle on a window escape. I thought I could unlock it, throw it open, and just crash through the screen before he navigated between the desks to stop me. His eyes jumped to the window as well, so I bolted for it before he could act.

"I didn't waste a single movement and everything went perfectly. I went headfirst through the screen as I tried to imagine how I should position my body in order to hit the ground correctly."

Wahid put his hand up.

When Hilda nodded to him, he asked, "How far to the ground."

"Not far. Two meters, perhaps? About my height."

"And why didn't you see him through the screen?" Wahid asked.

"Who?" Jessica asked. She thought she could guess the answer, but the question just popped out of her mouth.

Hilda answered Wahid first. "I didn't see him because the rain had infused the screen and clouded it over. Do you know what I mean? When rain hits a screen, sometimes it sticks in the little squares and makes it difficult to see what's outside?"

Then, Hilda turned to Jessica to answer her question.

"Wahid jumped a few seconds forward in my story. Of course the man outside the window was the man you know. He was the man who comes in the rain and in a moment you'll understand why I apologized to you at the beginning of this story. But, for the moment, I need to take a small break."

Hilda cleared her throat, stood up, and maneuvered to the bar. She and Ullman moved into a tight huddle as Hilda approached. The two of them had a whispered conversation that concluded with Ullman nodding and putting a hand on Hilda's shoulder. When she returned to her seat, she took a moment to compose herself.

Escape

Jessica was still looking over at Ullman when Hilda started her story again.

"As I crashed through the screen, I recognized that there was a man in my path. I took in a thousand details in a fraction of a second. His hat was soaked through and showed a lattice of cracks and fissures where it seemed that the material might fall apart at any moment. His shoulders were slumped under the weight of his coat. There was a patch of moss on his right shoulder. His head was turned downward so I couldn't see his face beneath the brim of his hat, but I saw his hands. They were raised, almost as if he intended to catch me, except in his right one he held a long knife.

"The skin was gray and flat. It was opaque and wrinkled. The closest comparison I can make would be the skin of a decaying shark. Even in the rain, I picked up the smell of the man. It was sharp woodsmoke mixed with organic rot. With that one glance, I forgot about the hairy accountant and that threat of violence I was trying to escape. I pulled up my legs to catch on the window frame and stop my descent. The action slowed, but did not stop me. I was still tumbling through the window and imagined I would flip over and be impaled on the wet man's knife.

"The accountant grabbed my ankles. His hands felt strong enough to crush my bones to powder as he hauled me back through the window. The wet man took a step back as I was pulled away from him. My fear transferred over easily from the knife to the accountant, who threw me to the floor. I scrambled away until my back hit the wall and he stood over me in a wide stance. The accountant scowled down at me as he unbuttoned and then rolled up each sleeve. The arms he revealed bulged with muscles and thick tendons straining against skin.

"I saw the future. I would be beaten to death by this little accountant. I proclaimed my innocence and begged for his mercy. I told him I would give back all the money and more. As he cocked back his fist, gibberish was spilling from my mouth. I said, 'What about your little girls and the man with the knife? They're all witnesses.' His arm stopped mid-swing and he narrowed his eyes. 'What man? What knife?' he asked."

Hilda took a moment to wipe her mouth with her hand, pulling her lower lip down briefly as she stretched her jaw.

"I blabbered something about the man with the knife outside of the window and he dashed for the sill to look out. He began to mutter something misogynistic about me but his rant was interrupted by a scream that came through the doorway. It was the scream of a little girl. The accountant ran, calling out his daughter's name."

"What was the name?" Wahid asked.

Hilda shook her head. "Don't remember. I was too focused on getting out of there alive. I approached the window quickly but cautiously, looking for any sign that the wet man was out there waiting for me. When I couldn't see him, I acted fast. I lowered myself down as much as I could, pushed off, hit the ground, and rolled. There was only one way out of that compound, so I stuck to the side of the building as best I could and tried to dash between the bushes. I heard another scream. When I got to the corner, I had no choice. I was going to have to sprint for the fence. Sometimes I have difficulty staying in the moment. My brain is always moving onto the next plan. Even as I peeked around the corner, I was already trying to think how I would deal with the fact that the accountant had seen my face. Would I have to move away? Was the wet man working for the accountant's boss? Would *he* come after me?"

Hilda put out her hands and shut her eyes for a moment. It appeared that she was still trying to plan her next move even though the events she was describing happened decades before.

"The accountant was on the metal stairs, under the awning, holding one daughter in his arms. I could tell by the way he was pressing his palm flat against her neck that he was trying to slow the flow of the blood that was everywhere. The wet man had his other daughter. She stood on her toes because the man was holding her up by her hair and had his knife to her throat. I couldn't help myself. Now that I knew that the wet man and the accountant weren't working together, I saw an opportunity for a clean resolution. I could rescue the girl, helping the accountant, and win his absolution. If we took out the wet man in the process, I would walk away perfectly free. Or, I could run. I should have run.

"Instead, I spotted a metal pipe and grabbed it as I flanked the wet man. He still hadn't spotted me as I approached him from behind. The accountant saw me and communicated everything with his eyes. He was desperate for help. I raised the pipe and approached. I can only imagine what it's like to hit a real person with an iron pipe. Hitting the wet man was hitting a stone.

The pipe hit the back of the wet man's head and it rang like a bell in my hands. He dropped the girl and I dropped the pipe. He turned slowly to me and I forgot about the accountant and the girls. I forgot about the money I had stolen and all my plans. Everything left my head. I was frozen in fear and hypnotized by the dark holes in his face and the glittering eyes that looked out at me.

"My mouth hung open and the rain fell. I don't know how I remained standing because it felt like all the strength had left my muscles as he eyed me. His hands worked at something and then he raised a limp cigarette to his lips. When he lit it, the flame defied the rain and the cigarette burned. I waited for my fate. For once, I wasn't plotting and planning. My mind wasn't churning through some problem. It was peaceful—almost pleasant. The accountant broke the peace with a scream and he swung my pipe directly into the wet man's face. The cigarette exploded into red and blue sparks and I snapped back to reality.

"I stumbled backwards and my feet tangled. I fell to the pavement as the accountant swung again and again, beating the wet man down to his knees and then until he was slumped over.

It sounded like the pipe was hitting solid rock. I saw that the girl I rescued was now cradling her sister. She had taken over for her father, holding the wounds. The sound of her cries barely registered over the falling rain and the clanks of the pipe.

"When the wet man stopped moving, the accountant slowed. He backed up, keeping his eyes on the wet man but speaking to me. He said to me, 'You can run now. This curse will follow you, but you can run.' I said I would help his girls if we could be even. He told me that we were even, and told me again to run, so I did."

"Wait, he said there was a curse?" Jessica asked. Everyone turned to her. She shrank in her seat. The attention didn't shift back to Hilda until she spoke again.

"Yes, Jessica, he told me that the curse would follow me. As I ran home, I hoped that it was simply an odd metaphor. Perhaps he meant that he, the accountant, wouldn't hunt me down, but he couldn't vouch for what his bosses might do. That answer made the most sense to me. The accountant could absolve me because I had helped him, but he couldn't protect me from punishment for stealing. I returned home, got cleaned up, and waited for repercussions. It had always been my plan to play dumb. I was a normal suburban girl who nobody would ever suspect of robbery. My best ploy was to stay put and act innocent.

"I had to cover up quite a bit when my boyfriend arrived before noon to invited me to a picnic at his house. I wore pants down to my calves and a long sleeve shirt. I was lucky—that summer faded, soft fishermen's shirts were the fashion for young ladies, so my outfit was impractical but explainable. My head throbbed, so I wore sunglasses and sat in the shadows while my boyfriend talked with his father. The picnic turned into somewhat of a social event as different people dropped by and sat in. They talked in code, saying that a competitor's employee had unexpectedly quit that morning. I was certain they were talking about the accountant when someone said that he took his daughters with him.

"My heart pounded as I listened to them discuss the incident in their abstract way. My boyfriend's father asked a visitor about the special friend, and whether he had taken care of the rodent problem. In my interpretation, *I* was the rodent, and the wet man was the special friend. The visitor laughed and said yes, the rodent and his daughters had been removed from the equation.

"The different businesses I had stolen from had banded together and hired the wet man to track me down. As far as I could tell, the accountant was dead and everyone assumed that the wet man had killed him in the act of committing another theft."

Jessica whispered, "I don't understand."

Hilda's eyes were gentle and kind. "I'm sorry, I'm probably butchering this story. I've told it often and most people have heard it before. What's your question."

"You're saying that your boyfriend's father *hired* the rain man?"

Hilda nodded. "I believe so. More accurately, they hired someone to summon him. In their line of business, where violence was a normal part of each of their operations, they would have gone outside their circle to take care of someone like me. If any of them used their own muscle, it would have presented an imbalance. So, when one of them saw the pattern and discovered that each of them had lost money in the same kind of tiny robbery, they decided the best response was to hire someone to summon a solution."

"So they know, or knew, where he came from? That's great, right? If he was summoned, can't he be banished?"

Hilda blinked and gave Jessica a sad smile. "Maybe. Do you have another question?"

"What happened to the accountant?"

"When I left the scene, it appeared that he had everything under control. I discovered that I was wrong about that. Apparently, both he and his daughters died that morning. Perhaps if I had stayed to help, I could have stopped it, but when he told me to leave I took his advice. I regret that."

"I'm sorry," Jessica said.

"Me too. So, sitting behind my boyfriend's house, tucked in the shadows, I watched the various bosses come by to discuss the situation and learned more with each coded conversation. The accountant and his daughters were dead. Most of them assumed that he was the 'rodent'—meaning the thief who had been stealing from each of them. My boyfriend's father was unconvinced. He was too smart. I think he understood how unlikely it was that an accountant for one business would be able to sneak in and steal from other businesses. He would have been recognized immediately. They were all aware of the staff of their competition."

"Why is that?" Wahid asked. Jessica was glad—she wondered the same thing but felt that she had exhausted her quota of questions.

"Staff of rivals were, to some extent, untouchable. They couldn't be recruited or harmed. That's the other reason for outside help to discover the thief. If it had been the accountant who was stealing, nobody would have been able to take care of the problem except the accountant's own people. So everyone knew everyone in the business. My boyfriend's father listened, but after his last visitor left, he was clearly puzzled. I could see it on his face. He knew that the thief had escaped, and he probably thought that the accountant was merely a distraction."

Information

"My boyfriend thought things were getting serious. I maneuvered him into inviting me to dinner and family functions. If things had kept going, I could have made him propose to me, but that was never my intention. At that same time, my parents were unable to make their mortgage payment and they lost the house. There was an uncomfortable moment when they asked my uncle for help and he confessed that he didn't have any money either. He apologized for not sending much money the past couple of years and confusion erupted.

Fortunately, neither side was eager to discuss the issue, so it fell away without anyone discovering that I had been keeping things afloat.

"My boyfriend's father was relentless. He had constant secret meetings at his house with various people as he tried to narrow down his list of suspects for the robberies. His competitors—the other bosses—were mostly satisfied that the problem had been dealt with. The accountant was dead and the robberies had stopped. One day I was over at their house, embroidering kerchiefs with my boyfriend's mother and sister, when a long black car pulled up out front. A man in a tan suit stepped from the passenger's seat and opened a rear door. He helped a little boy down from the seat and then walked a step behind the boy up to the door. I heard the doorbell and my boyfriend's sister went to answer. My boyfriend's mother asked me what I had seen—she noticed that I had watched all this through the window. I described the boy and asked if it was a nephew or cousin or something. She said no—the boy was a consultant and then laughed at my confusion.

"It wasn't easy to eavesdrop on that conversation. I excused myself to use the restroom and then crouched at the top of the stairs so I could listen over the balcony. The boy's voice had the pitch and timbre of a child, but the vocabulary and pace of someone old and weary. All I heard was that the contract was still open and that the weather wouldn't change until it was properly closed. I had to scurry out of there lest I be caught listening in. Later, on one of my more harrowing adventures, I searched the files of my boyfriend's father and came up with a phone number for the boy's handlers. It took me months to arrange a meeting for myself, and by then I had broken up with my boyfriend."

"A boy arranged for you to be hunted?" Jessica asked, shaking her head in anticipation of the answer.

"He wasn't a boy," Hilda said. "That was how he was masquerading at the time. I came to find out that he had no true form. He could inhabit different hosts pretty much at will, although they always had to be someone innocent. Children were his preferred vessel."

"But he called the rain man to you? He was the one who summoned him?"

Hilda nodded. "I believe so, yes."

Jessica sat up on the edge of her seat. "This is huge then, right? Isn't this the answer? Why isn't this everything we're talking about? Who cursed my family, I wonder?"

Wahid reached out and almost touched Jessica's arm, but she pulled back from the gesture.

"Did Simon's people research this?" Jessica asked.

"Of course," Hilda said.

"What did they say? Is there any truth to it?"

Hilda nodded. "There's more to the story. And, if you remember, my apology is still ahead as well."

Jessica took a deep breath and tried to find some patience. She hated the casual attitude that everyone seemed to have. She hated the idea that they had been sitting on this enormous piece of information and hadn't said anything to her about it before. Everything had to be on their glacial timeline.

"Please, go on," Jessica said.

Hilda nodded.

"Those months were horrible for me. I was constantly looking over my shoulder, wondering when I would be hunted down. As I said, I broke up with my boyfriend. I was going crazy trying to maintain that relationship and cope with the stress of not knowing what was happening. I didn't want to call the phone number until I knew who it belonged to, but I decided that I didn't have any choice. On a payphone, downtown, I heard a young voice answer and ask what I was seeking. I said told the phone that I needed information. The voice agreed to meet.

"At the time, I was a waitress at a fairly large restaurant. I arranged the meeting for a day I was working and booked the reservation secretly for a dark corner in my section. I wanted to get my eyes on the child who had apparently summoned something to murder me. My tactic didn't work at all. As soon as

I approached to take the child's order, the little girl motioned to her guard and the man grabbed my arm and forced me to sit."

"So it was a little girl now?" Jessica asked.

Hilda nodded. "Yes. At the time, I thought maybe it was an associate of the boy I had seen at my boyfriend's house. During that conversation I decided that it was a presence that could move between hosts. It told me that it knew I was the one who had called and that it also knew I was the thief. My denial was met with reassurance. It said that the older business was not the topic it came to discuss. I had asked for information of how to free myself from the curse and it wanted to know what I could trade. I didn't have anything and I told it so. A chill ran through me when that girl studied me with her tired eyes and said that I had much to trade. I shook my head and told her that my family was poor. We were living in a small apartment and could barely make ends meet. I should have been in college. Instead, I was working as a waitress so my parents could keep the lights on.

"The presence inside that little girl informed me that it didn't care about my worldly possessions. It had access to riches that I couldn't imagine. I figured it out before I was told. The presence wanted another host. It wanted to live as an adult again and taste the full flavor of life. To do that, it needed to find a very particular host. It wouldn't take the host forever, and in exchange it offered whatever I desired."

"You would be the host?" Jessica asked.

"Yes. I was innocent in all the ways it required. To take a child as a host, it could trick the child. To inhabit an adult, it required consent. So, with me it had the rare opportunity with innocence and leverage, as long as I agreed. We agreed on a year of service where I would be a passenger in my own body. I couldn't have understood the torture of watching myself move around the world without any control. My wariness led to one other concession—when I started my service my parents would have a financial windfall to take care of their needs. I went to that meeting simply looking for information and I ended up with what sounded like a solution to all my problems."

Hilda glanced over at Riley.

"What?" Hilda asked. "What's that look for."

Riley threw up her hands. "Nothing. You know me. I'm just... This is the part in your story where I get a little... I don't know."

Hilda raised her eyebrows.

"I'm sorry. Please continue."

"My service was to begin promptly. I had a couple of days to put my affairs in order and inform my family that I had decided to go on a trip. This was coincident with my father being selected for a generous grant, so they wouldn't need my help with their finances anymore. I told them to be careful with their windfall and I packed my bags. They dropped me at the train station and I was picked up at the next stop by my new employer. My bags were put in storage and I was swept away to a ceremony. A priest presided. The little girl was stretched out next to me and my body was filled with the presence. I thought it would be like sitting in the passenger's seat as someone else drove. I was wrong. It was like I was shoved down into a dark well and someone was standing on my shoulders and kicking my head. I knew instantly that I would never survive that way for an entire year.

"After what felt like a month of discomfort, I sensed quiet and I came to understood that the presence had gone to sleep. It occurred to me that only a single day had passed. There would be three hundred and sixty-four more to come. That's when I began to plot and plan to find a way to break the contract. I worked tirelessly to retake control of my body. I felt the strain in my soul and imagined that it wasn't harming me, only making me stronger. When the presence awoke again, I stayed quiet. I don't think it suspected a thing until, after weeks of training, I felt ready to battle it.

"My first attempt was a dismal failure. The presence had unimaginable power and it beat me back down into the far recesses of my consciousness. Had the fight gone on much longer, my mind would have been snapped like a twig. I vowed to not attack again until I was sure of victory. When it went to sleep again, I doubled, tripled, and quadrupled my training."

Wahid rose his hand. "What did this training consist of?"

Hilda took a breath. "The best way I can describe it was like an extreme form of meditation. I would focus my entire being on one thing—for example the texture of the cloth touching my knee. I would examine the report of every single nerve ending in the area and repeat that interrogation again and again until I had mastered that square inch of skin. Then, I might do the same thing with a muscle in my abdomen. I was integrating every piece of tissue with my mind in a conscious way. Normally, that type of activity is strictly governed by the subconscious mind. My notion was that the presence had control of the subconscious, so I would have to make the link with my conscious mind in order to attack the presence from both sides."

"Where did you come up with this idea?" Wahid asked.

"It was something I deduced from the ceremony."

He looked like he wanted to ask a follow-up question but instead shook his head and gestured for her to continue.

"I lost track of time," Hilda said. "I would train or think about training constantly and I tried to ignore what the presence was doing with my body. Under its control, my body lost its innocence and part of my left foot. I discovered the missing toes one night when the presence was asleep. I tried to inhabit my own spine and discovered a flurry of activity running up my spinal cord. The messages were of pain, swelling, and a call for resources to fight infection. Inside my own mind, I wept at the loss. Plunging into a depression, I began to realize that nothing would ever be the same. I had traded my dominion over my own body—the only thing we can ever truly own. For a while, I did nothing but weep invisible tears as the world continued around me. I couldn't sense it or communicate with it, but the world marched on.

"The only thing I could really feel was the contempt of the presence. It had beaten me, and it didn't hide its gloating over that fact. My rising anger eventually fueled me into another takeover attempt. This time, I was successful. When it was asleep, I started with the toes. I stretched myself into those muscles and nerves. I drove out the presence, forcing it to contract, little by little, until it only had a hold right in the core of my body. That's when it woke up and the fight really began.

"It clawed and fought but I was filled with rage and immensely strong from all my training. I could extend myself cell by cell, driving it out of my flesh until it occupied only my heart. That's when the real standoff took place. Silently, it communicated with me that my time was almost through. Eleven months had passed, and if I gave the presence just another week to find the next host, it agreed to vacate early. It had no leverage with which to negotiate and I told it so. That's when the presence showed me the leverage it really had. The presence stopped my heart for a few seconds and I felt my strength wane. I don't understand the link between the soul and the body, but it's there. As my flesh starved for oxygen, I felt my conscious mind begin to dissipate and dissolve. The presence proved that it was willing to kill my body if I didn't agree to its terms.

"At any other point in my life, the presence would have won that gamble. Had I been younger and more timid, I would have conceded. Had I been older and wiser, I would have chosen the compromise. As a young woman at the height of my hubris and power, I decided that I would accept nothing less than victory. Perhaps it was only arrogance that led to my decision. Perhaps I thought I could drive out the presence before it could stop my heart forever.

"I was wrong. As I pushed the presence out of me, it managed to halt my heart before it was driven away. I found myself in full control of a dying body. I gasped for air. My muscles were barely able to comply. The captain of a sinking ship, I could still sense the presence and I knew what it was thinking. It taunted me and offered me one last chance. It would release its grip on my heart if I submitted to two more months of occupancy. But I sensed panic behind the offer. My body dying was hurting it as well. Maybe it would continue on in some other form, but it didn't have another host ready or another priest to perform the ceremony.

"At the last moment, before my consciousness dissolved completely, I felt hands on my chest. One of the guards hired by the presence to protect itself was performing CPR on my body. As my blood was pushed artificially through the compression, I felt my control coming back fully. I was able to wake up my autonomic nervous system and it took over once more."

Hilda got up and went to the refrigerator behind the bar. She opened a bottle of water for herself and handed another to Ullman who took it with a nod of thanks.

"That was it," Hilda said. "I won. It's not often that one can fight a superior strength and win, but I was young, determined, and dumb enough to pull it off."

"You forgot the apology," Wahid said.

"Oh. Of course," Hilda said as she took her seat again. "Sometimes I get so caught up in the fight that I forget the last thing the presence communicated to me. At the time, I thought it was just one more empty threat tossed out in defeat, but I've since reconsidered. The presence warned me that if it was banished from this world, anything it summoned would become untethered. Of course, it had claimed to summon the wet man who killed the accountant, and the implication was that he would continue to stalk me. At that point, I was breaking our agreement so I had no expectation that the terms would be upheld."

"Untethered," Jessica whispered.

"Yes," Hilda said. "I suppose that the presence could have banished him, just as it summoned him. Once I dispatched the presence from this realm, the wet man was loose. That's why I owe everyone here an apology. Without me, the wet man wouldn't be roaming through this reality, choosing his own new victims through his own inscrutable process. Questions?"

Jessica raised a finger and waited for Hilda to acknowledge her.

"What have you been able to learn about the presence?"

"Very little, I'm afraid. There were people who had dealings with it, and claimed to understand its origin. When I would dig deeper, the motives for their claims were always questionable."

"But it summoned the rain man, right? Surely there must be someone who knows how that happened. Did you manage to track down the priest who presided over the ceremony to transfer the presence into you? Maybe he had a part in the summoning?"

Hilda shook her head and frowned. "Nothing I was able to uncover suggests that there was anyone else there when the presence summoned the wet man. I'm afraid that I have no leads as to that origin."

"Something—anything—a name or a place. Did you go back to your boyfriend's father? Maybe he has some insight into how the man was chosen? Did he ever go after you again? You were in Mexico, right?"

"No. I was not. Any other questions?"

Riley raised her hand.

Hilda rolled her eyes and sighed. "Go ahead."

"Why does your story keep evolving, Hilda? That's all I want to know. Why is that the first time you told it, you were barely a witness. As you tell it now, you were some genius thief and the triumphant victor over some mysterious demon that possessed your body for nearly a year. I remember the first time we heard your story. It ended when you ran away from witnessing a man and his daughters being attacked."

"We've been over this," Hilda said. "Ullman, would you mind reading the statement from my lawyer."

"It's not necessary," Riley said.

"No, you've questioned the veracity of my statement. That type of challenge is expressly forbidden in this group, as I'm sure you remember. Because I anticipated your attack, I've invited Ullman to act as a proxy for my attorney. Ullman? Please read the statement."

"Forget it," Riley said, standing up. As she walked away, she said, "Make up your own rules to suit your fabrications. None of the rest of us feel the need to embellish, you know."

The end of her rebuttal came as she rounded the corner to the hallway. Jessica squirmed in her seat. She couldn't remember the last time she had felt so uncomfortable.

"I suppose we're adjourned?" Wahid asked.

Jessica nodded. Hilda stood and went the other direction, towards the kitchen. Ullman followed her.

Wahid sat there for another few seconds. Jessica waited until she was sure that Hilda was out of earshot.

"What was that?" Jessica asked. "Did Hilda make that stuff up?"

"It's not our place to wonder," Wahid said. He slapped his hands on his knees and stood with a grunt. "Goodnight, miss. Take care. Good to see you again."

"Thanks. You too."

Sitting

Jessica rapped lightly on the doorframe and waited for Riley to invite her into the sitting room. Riley lifted her reading glasses, peered at Jessica, and then waved her in.

"You alone?" Riley asked.

"Yeah. Just me."

"She's right, you know," Riley said. "I don't have any business questioning someone else's story. It's just weird for me because I was there when Hilda made it up. It's difficult to sit idly by and watch her weave more details into the fabrication."

"Why would she make it up? Are you sure she didn't just slowly remember it?" Jessica asked as she took a seat.

"Remember? How is that something a person could forget?"

"Well, she did start the whole thing with a disclaimer about how it was all made up, right?"

"As if that absolves her."

"No, I mean maybe it's one of those things where she remembers but distrusts her own memory. She's telling us things that she can't wrap her head around, so she has to distance herself from them."

"You're way too generous," Riley said. "All that business about how her lawyer won't let her incriminate herself so he makes her give a disclaimer at the beginning? She doesn't have a lawyer. Talk to Ullman sometime. All that is pure theater."

"Huh," Jessica said, slumping into her chair. "Why would she do that?"

"Attention, maybe? She wants us to feel like her story is more important than everyone else's, so she put herself at the beginning of everything and tries to take the blame."

Jessica sensed someone in the doorway. She turned and caught a glimpse of Billie walking away. Riley got up and walked quietly to the door, peeked through, and then shut it.

"What happened with you guys? I thought you were becoming best friends with her and Dylan."

"My mistake," Jessica said. "I knew I shouldn't trust her. She's the kind of person whose whole demeanor screams not to trust her, but I did anyway. Sure enough, she validated my original impression."

Riley sat down again. "See, that's almost precisely the way I feel about Hilda. It's so rare to find that perfect combination of wit and intelligence in a person and you just know that you're going to be close. Then, they turn out to have a massive character flaw and you keep smashing your head against it."

Jessica nodded.

They were silent for a moment. Jessica discovered that there was still a part of her that wasn't ready to dismiss everything that Hilda had said, despite Riley's opinion.

"I can't stop thinking about that 'presence' that Hilda described. If any of that is even remotely true, it seems like it could give us a big lead on the origin of our trouble."

"Agreed, but think of it this way—if any of Hilda's story were remotely true, then Simon's people would have uncovered information about it. I talked to Simon before the Mexico trip. He said that his people looked and looked and couldn't fine any connection. They also looked into the alleged crime families that Hilda said she robbed when she was a young woman. They found no trace of that as well. Either all of that nefarious activity remains covered up to this day, or it never existed at all. One of those explanations makes a lot more sense."

Jessica narrowed her eyes. "But would he tell you?"

"Sorry?"

"Maybe this was a lie too, but I was told that Simon didn't give anyone all the real information before Mexico because it would have been dangerous to have in anyone's head."

Riley looked away as she thought about that.

"Ullman would know," Riley said as she stood.

Jessica jumped up and jogged after Riley as she stalked down the hall, past the meeting area, and down into the other wing. They found Ullman in the kitchen helping Glen wrap sandwiches on the island. Wahid and Hilda sat at the table at the far end of the kitchen. Riley planted her hands on the countertop and squared her shoulders with Ullman.

"What did Simon's people find out about Hilda's claims?" Riley asked.

Ullman's hands stopped wrapping and he raised his eyebrows.

"Simon told us there would be disclosure when we returned. It's understandable that all that stuff got lost in the shuffle after everything that happened. But here I am, asking for full disclosure. What's the truth behind all that?" Riley asked, gesturing vaguely over her shoulder towards Hilda.

Jessica shrank back from the confrontation. It was difficult to watch. Hilda was the oldest of the group, as far as Jessica could tell, but at that moment Riley had a very commanding, matriarchal presence that was impossible to deny.

"I can provide you with all the declassified research in the secure library," Ullman said after blinking slowly.

"Just sum it up for me, Ullman. Is she full of it, or is there something there? I can understand if Simon didn't want us to know before Mexico, but that's ancient history now. If she was adjacent to the origination of this monster, I believe we all have a right to know that information."

"What origination?" a voice asked. Jessica turned to see Billie standing near the door to the back stairwell.

Taking a step back, Jessica folded her arms across her chest and glanced back and forth between Ullman and Billie.

"Ms. Symonds wants to investigate the veracity of the narrative provided by Ms. Muller."

"The stuff about her being a cat burglar?" Billie asked.

"No," Riley said, "the stuff about her being possessed by a presence that called the rain main into existence."

Hilda must have heard some of what they were saying. She stood and approached fast.

"What's the discussion over here? Ullman, I'll remind you of your oath."

Ullman put up his hands and shook his head in a gesture to proclaim his innocence.

"This is the scenario we discussed," Ullman said. "As I told you, I have to respond to direct queries on this topic."

"Nonsense," Hilda said. "You're my attorney. You can't reveal our conversations."

"I won't, but I have to disclose the information our research team uncovered."

"No," Hilda said. "Not here, and not now."

"Of course," Ullman said. "I'll set the date."

"I want to know every fact you intend to disclose," Hilda said. "You owe me that."

Ullman gestured to Hilda and they split away from the others to have a private conversation over near the ovens.

"What does that mean?" Jessica asked Riley. "What date is Ullman going to set?"

"Confidential meeting," Riley said. "In the secure library."

"And he'll tell you what Simon didn't want to tell you before Mexico?"

"He'll tell all of us," Billie said. "That's the way it works."

CHAPTER FIFTEEN

Jessica

Secure

Jessica glanced around, trying to remember if she had ever seen everyone in the same place before. She decided that she had—at one of the meetings they had all been present. It was different seeing them in the secure library. They were all crammed into a fairly small area.

Until that night, Jessica hadn't even known about the secure library. When they talked about it, and told her the time of the special gathering, she had assumed they were talking about the library down the hall from the regular meeting space. It wasn't until Ullman met her in the foyer and led her through a nondescript door that she realized there were stairs that led down to a fortified room below ground.

Billie was leaning against a wall when Jessica arrived, so she had taken a chair on the opposite side of the room. Joe sat down next to her. The back of his neck and forehead were sunburned. He smelled of some kind of lotion.

When Ullman escorted Christopher into the room and shut the door, they were all present.

Ullman moved to the head of the room and waited for their attention.

A few side conversations petered out and silence fell.

Ullman cleared his throat.

"Following the recollection of Ms. Muller several nights ago, a question arose that needs to be answered from our benefactor's archive. I will ask you to remain silent as he answers the questions in his own words."

Jessica's eyes went wide as she tried to piece together what was about to happen. Ullman hit a button and a panel in the ceiling slid to the side to let a screen descend. There was the image of a concerned face frozen in the paused video. Jessica realized that she was seeing Simon's face for the first time. An older man with a deeply-wrinkled face, he looked more kind and weary than she would have expected.

With the press of another button, Ullman started the video and the man on the screen came to life.

"Hilda's encounter?" Simon asked. His eyes moved to the side, getting a queue from someone before he returned his gaze to the camera. "This is about Hilda's encounter. The question has probably come up about the veracity of Hilda's story. No offense, Hilda, but it doesn't surprise me that people might think you're making stuff up. Even with everything we've all seen, it's a tough... At any rate—yes, a lot of what is verifiable about Hilda's story has been verified."

Hilda folded her arms across her chest.

"Some of it, obviously, could not be verified. Private conversations with only one survivor are never... Anyway—you get the point. We obtained a diary that shouldn't exist. Here's a tip—if you're in the business of committing crimes, don't write those crimes down. From that diary, we tracked down a special 'consultant' who made introductions between shady people and the type of person who might solve 'problems' for those shady people. It appears that there was a bounty on Hilda, although the people who put out that bounty referred to her just as the thief. They didn't know her identity, but they had figured out her methodology. I don't have to say allegedly. This is all hearsay from me, or so they tell me."

Riley turned to Hilda and nodded. Hilda didn't acknowledge the silent apology.

"It seems that when they had trouble but didn't have a name to go with the crime, these people used an outside consultant of the, let's say, *paranormal* variety. These people were all very superstitious and some of them were of the opinion that Hilda was a ghost. You need a ghost to fight a ghost, I suppose. Anyway, many of them feel that the thing that killed the accountant and his daughters was the paranormal force they had contracted. Others, myself included, feel that the two events may have been unconnected and the attack on the accountant was merely coincidence."

Jessica glanced at Hilda again. The shock was apparent on her face.

The video of Simon kept going.

"The *curse*, for lack of a better word, contracted against Hilda should have resulted in her getting sick and wasting away. She was bleeding the businesses, so they considered it to be a just punishment to bleed her in response. Stabbing should have never entered into it. It's anyone's guess why Hilda didn't waste away. Maybe she did negotiate with the paranormal force, maybe it just didn't exist in the first place. There's too much speculation in our lives, I won't introduce more."

Ullman hit a button and the screen jumped to a different scene before it froze.

Several conversations broke out around the room. Riley went to crouch down next to where Hilda was sitting. After a moment, Hilda took Riley's hand and they seemed to be having a pleasant exchange. Next to her, Joe was leaning over and talking with Wahid.

Ullman stood at the front of the room and waited patiently for several seconds before raising his hand.

"If I may—I'm supposed to play one other clip after."

He had to repeat his request again before people finally quieted down and Riley moved back to her seat.

"Thank you," Ullman said. He stepped aside and started the

video again.

"I didn't want to tell you any of this before our trip because of the dangerous nature of information. Sometimes, the less you know the better. I have to assume that you're seeing this because I'm unable to deliver this information in person. I don't regret anything. I want you to know that. I have only myself to blame or thank, depending on how you look at things. I hope you're all well."

The video went black.

"How many?" Joe asked.

Ullman looked to him with raised eyebrows.

"How many videos are there like that? Am I right in assuming that there are all kinds of answers that he recorded videos of? That last bit was like a canned coda, right? How many other little videos do you have?"

Ullman shook his head. "I'm not aware of the number."

"Show them all," Billie said. "We deserve to see them."

Even across the room, Jessica could see the smudge in Billie's makeup. She had been crying.

"I agree completely," Ullman said. "I'm afraid that we only have access to videos that are in direct response to a question that has been asked. Ms. Symonds asked a question about Ms. Muller's narrative and we were entitled to see the response to that inquiry."

"Who makes that decision?" Joe asked.

"I believe you know the answer to that question."

Joe stood up and approached Ullman. Jessica heard some of what Joe said. To Jessica, Joe sounded demanding and entitled. She didn't know all that much about Ullman, but had the sense that this tactic wouldn't be fruitful at all. Glancing around the secure library, Jessica wondered what was contained in the books and binders that lined the walls. Of the books, most of spines were marked with only numbers. Entire shelves held nothing but thin, spiral-bound volumes.

She looked back up when Joe asked, "Fine. Is there any ongoing research into the nature of the killer?"

Ullman's eyes went to one of the lower shelves on his right. He crouched and opened a three-ring binder, propping it open with one hand as he scanned the table of contents with another. Before he stood and turned back to Joe, he snapped the binder shut again and put it on the shelf.

"I'm afraid not."

Wahid raised his hand. "Was there ever significant research into his nature?"

Ullman crouched again, opened a different binder, and scanned the contents. Jessica noticed that the shelf containing these binders was different than the others. It had a door that could swing down and lock away the contents of the binders.

Whispering a number to himself, Ullman used a remote control to dial in that code. It appeared on the screen, digit by digit, and then Simon's face changed. When Ullman hit another button, Simon began to speak.

"As you can imagine, we've done a lot of research into the origin and the essence of this thing. The closest comparison that we can come up with is a Tulpa. I urge you not to dive too deep into your own research on this kind of thing, because just the act of focusing on it can be dangerous. It's like Tinkerbell, in a way. The more you believe in it, or even think about it, the more power it has."

Simon froze.

"I don't understand," Vivian said. "We're not even supposed to think about it? Why are we getting together all the time and rehashing our stories?"

Ullman returned to his index and found another number.

When Simon spoke again, he addressed her question. "There's a certain amount of risk involved in gathering people at my house. Honestly, we may be doing more harm than good. But, I had the statistics people run the numbers and we can't show that the number of attacks has increased since we began our meetings. If I had to guess, we're only increasing the risk for ourselves, not for the world in general. And, because the suicide rate was so high for people who didn't talk about it, I considered the risk to be acceptable."

"If that's true," Mel said, "then doesn't it disprove the idea that thinking about him gives him power?"

Jessica wondered if Mel was feeling guilty about his own preoccupation. From the little she had talked to him, it sounded like he spent most of his time gathering statistics on the rain man. It would stand to reason that he was bolstering the man's power just because of Mel's efforts.

Ullman went to his binders and didn't come up with a number this time.

"I'm sorry. I don't have an answer on file for that question."

Several people tried to rephrase the query, but hit the same wall.

Christopher asked what evidence existed to support the Tulpa idea. Ullman checked the binder and stood again with no numbers on his lips. Vivian took a different approach and tried to find out if any of Simon's videos addressed the comparison between the killer and a Tulpa, or whether there were any other proven examples of Tulpas in the world.

Jessica pressed her hands to the side of her face and listened to all the fruitless questions as her frustration grew. She couldn't believe that their future safety—their peace of mind for the rest of their lives—was boiling down to a stupid guessing game when Ullman clearly had access to all the available information.

When she looked up, Jessica realized that Billie was looking directly at her. The stare wasn't angry or challenging. It was almost pleading. Jessica cocked her head as she tried to figure out what Billie was attempting to communicate. They didn't have their cellphones—devices weren't allowed in the secure library. Billie glanced over to Ullman and the back to Jessica with raised eyebrows.

Jessica gave her head a tiny shake to indicate that she didn't know what Billie was trying to say.

Billie's hand shot up.

Ullman was in the process of being yelled at by Joe. When that concluded, he turned to Billie to address her.

"Can I speak with you a moment in private?" Billie asked.

Jessica thought that if any of the rest of them had asked, Ullman would have immediately turned them down. He had a special relationship with Billie though. After mulling it over for a moment and then looking back into Billie's pleading eyes, he nodded. The two of them headed towards the door. Just before they reached it, Billie leaned back and glanced to Jessica before shooting her eyes over to the shelf with the binders.

That's when Jessica understood the plan.

Question

As soon as the door clicked shut, Jessica jumped out of her chair and threw herself to her knees in front of the shelf. She had formed a basic guess about the different binders by watching which one Ullman pulled in response to the various questions. The third one was for historical questions. The fourth seemed to be about their stories in particular. The fifth one contained the index for inquiries about the future.

That's the one she reached for.

"What are you doing?" Joe asked.

Vivian shushed him.

Laura, who was closest to the door pressed her ear against the metal. She whispered, "Keep looking. I'll tell you when he's coming back."

"This is absurd," Joe said. "The board can be petitioned and they will relent if enough of us express, in a rational way, the..."

"Joe, shut up," Vivian said.

Jessica kept scanning the index. There were answers about a possible military response to the threat. She saw an entry for how long the trust would be funded after Simon's death–Joe would probably be interested in that answer, if he didn't already know. Laura hissed something just as Jessica saw an entry that jumped out at her. She slammed shut the binder and shoved it back into shelf just as the door opened. Jessica flopped back into her seat as Billie led the way, walking backwards and continuing to talk to Ullman.

They were all too quiet.

Ullman glanced around at the silence as he followed Billie in.

"We have a couple more minutes," Ullman said as he took his place in the front of the room. "Are there any other questions."

Several people turned to Jessica.

She tried to act innocent as she asked, "If the Mexico expedition failed, were there any other efforts planned to deal with the rain man?"

Ullman stood, staring at her.

"I'm guessing that Simon wouldn't have informed the others because he wouldn't want the man to know, right? But were there other plans underway that could be set in action?"

Ullman kept his eyes on her as he moved to the shelf, only looking away when he pulled the appropriate binder. He flipped the page that she had just been looking at.

Standing up, he whispered the number to himself as he punched it into the remote control.

Simon's face on the screen changed. In the previous videos, by comparison, he had looked almost jovial. On the screen now was the image of a person about to discuss something very serious. Ullman hit the button and Simon came to life and sighed. Billie raised her hands and covered her mouth as he started to speak.

"This is a tough one for me. It's impossible for me to answer this one without admitting to myself that you're seeing this after I died. I hope that you're okay and that wherever I am I'm not missing you too much."

Simon's eyes looked straight into the camera and Billie was off the side. Still, it seemed like he was looking directly at Billie as he gave the camera a sad smile.

"I know you'll understand," he said with a deep breath after. "Anyway. The question though, is, what's next? Mexico must have failed or nobody would be watching this. Is there another plan that I kept secret to keep the plan strong? Yes. The answer is yes. I'm assuming that you're listening to this because you've decided that it doesn't matter whether or not everyone knows about the plan, and maybe you have a point. We kept Mexico absolutely secret, and that didn't work."

Joe grunted and Vivian shushed him again.

"I'm afraid that, for the most part, it's more of the same. It's a big trap and we're the bait. In Mexico, we've got a bit of a shotgun approach in the works. Each person will bring something from their story into the mix and hopefully the combination will put him away. But, like I said, if you're watching this then I have to assume that I was right and it *didn't* work."

Simon shook his head.

"No, I can't say that. I have to take responsibility for making the final decision, so if Mexico fails it's on me. I've always run my businesses by getting the smartest people together, getting their advice, and then making my own decision in the end. That's not unusual. I think that approach describes every successful... What am I doing?"

Simon smiled, looked down, and then back up to the camera.

"I'm avoiding the question because I don't want to think about it. Okay, here you go—my people have set up a house. It's up in the Pacific Northwest. Whenever we decide to pull the trigger, a group will be shuttled up there and the trap will be set. I don't see the point in compartmentalizing the information this time. Everyone knows that approach already, and we have to assume it failed in Mexico. So, before they leave, the group will have access to all the theories and ideas that my team generated. They warn me that all this swirling information will make the trip that much more dangerous, so I hope you consider carefully before you sign up. This mission is going to be small. Four, or possible five people will go. Please, consider carefully before making the decision. No matter how miserable you think your life is now, don't forget that it could be worse. I miss my family every day, but that doesn't stop me from appreciating the new family that we have."

The video cut off suddenly with Simon waving his hands in front of the camera and then going still.

Ullman stared at the screen for a few seconds before turning back to the group.

"Any other questions?"

The room erupted.

Debate

"We should have know about this months ago," Joe said as he paced. "This is nonsense."

"This is where we're at right now, Joe," Vivian said from the couch.

After a little debate down in the secure library, they had moved up to their normal meeting room. None of them had reason to believe that the metal door and concrete walls of the secure library was any safer than anywhere else, so they had come up to where they were more comfortable. Jessica sat at the far end of the bar—away from Billie, but closer than she had been to her in a while.

There were five sealed packets on the coffee table in front of Wahid. He reached forward and fanned them out. Returning his hand to his lap, Wahid absentmindedly wiped his fingers on his pants.

"I don't think anyone who went to Mexico should go on this trip," Laura said.

"Nobody expects you to go, Laura," Riley said. "Relax."

"I'm not saying that because I don't want to go," Laura said. "I just think it's a bad idea. If there's any truth to the idea that he can sense what we know, then we need to be careful about what preconceived notions the participants might have in their heads."

"You seriously think that matters?" Christopher asked. "We all know exactly what happened, and this wouldn't be the first encounter for anyone here. If you're right, then we should be talking about hiring mercenaries or something."

"That wouldn't work," Wahid said. "If this is anything like Mexico, it will be built with former victims in mind."

"Don't pretend there's any logic to apply here," Mel said.

"That's unfair," Wahid said. "There are details that we're not privy to. Unless and until we find out the reasoning..."

"Does it matter?" Hilda asked. "Does any of this debate matter? The only question is whether or not anyone is going to risk their life to see if this plan is better than the last."

"We should open the envelopes and see what's expected. Nobody should make a decision until they understand the plan," Wahid said.

"That's not how this works," Laura said.

"Now you're pretending to know how this works?" Mel asked.

"Why are we arguing?" Vivian asked. "If anyone wants to go, they'll go."

"After what happened in Mexico," Christopher said, "it would be incredibly stupid for us to jump in without more information. Mexico was Plan A, and it was pretty much a suicide mission."

"I'm going," Jessica said. It didn't seem like anyone heard her. The yelling continued. Over on the other side of the couches, Joe still paced back and forth.

Billie turned to glance at her when Jessica stood up from her stool and said, "I'm going," again. She moved to Wahid and took the seat next on the couch next to him so she could lean over the envelopes. On the corner of each, she saw tiny print.

She read them to herself.

"Low effort, medium risk, mildly physical."

She put that envelope to the side and kept looking until she found one that read, "High effort, high risk, very physical."

Jessica settled back into the couch and studied the envelope. It was thick enough to contain at least twenty or thirty sheets of paper, she imagined. The flap was sealed. With a deep breath, she worked her finger under the corner of the flap and then tore it across the top with her finger.

Jessica realized that the room had gone silent.

"What?"

"You're committing to this?" Wahid asked.

"Yes. I said I would go."

Billie jumped down from her stool and grabbed the top envelope. "I will too."

"I'm not asking you to," Jessica said.

Billie sneered at her. "I didn't say you did."

"Fine," Dylan said. He winced as he walked towards the table.

"No," Billie said. "You're still recovering."

"So what?"

"She's right," Vivian said. "Plus, what Laura said earlier is true—I think people who went to Mexico should consider carefully if it's wise to go on this one."

"That narrows it down quite a bit," Riley said. Jessica slid down so Riley could sit on the edge of the couch between her and Wahid. Once there, Riley sorted through the envelopes and picked one out. She retreated to a chair and balanced the envelope on the arm. Billie had her envelope clutched to her chest. Jessica's envelope was open but the contents remained unexamined.

"I know you're all thinking I should be next," Hilda said, "but I refuse. I have a variety of reasons and I don't think I have to explain myself."

"I don't believe that anyone was thinking that," Wahid said.

"No, I kinda was," Riley said. "It's symmetry, you know? She was there at the beginning, right? Maybe it can't end without her. Plus, we're out of volunteers, right? Everyone else went to Mexico."

Joe moved to the table and took one of the two remaining envelopes. He backed away, holding his envelope in both hands as if he expected someone to try to take it from him.

"There's no rule about Mexico people not going, so I'm going," Joe said.

"One more then," Wahid said. "It says 'optional' on it, but I suppose if we're not going to..."

"That belongs to me," Ullman said from the archway. "I should have said earlier. The optional one is mine." He moved with authority and pulled the last envelope from the table.

"No," Laura said, "this isn't right. This isn't the way this is supposed to be. Don't you all see it?"

"It's what we're doing," Joe said. "Maybe none of it is right, but it's what we're doing."

Room

Jessica jumped when she heard the knock on her door. It had been a long time since she had stayed in the mansion. She was no longer accustomed to living in a group setting.

"Yeah?"

The door opened a crack and Billie asked, "Can I come in?"

"Fine."

Jessica stared down at the papers that she had organized in front of her on the bed. All the travel documents and itinerary were on the left. The stuff regarding her role was right in front of her. The background information was in a pile on the right. She planned to spend the most time with that. As Billie came into the room, Jessica had an impulse to pile up all the documents so that Billie couldn't see them. She decided it was a silly impulse—Billie probably had a lot of the same information in her own packet.

"I thought maybe we should clear the air before we go," Billie said.

"We."

"Yeah. We're going to have to focus on the job, you know?"

"Sure. Let's talk about the air, Billie. Why does it need to be cleared?"

"You know, the whole thing with the group and the reporter," Billie said.

"Uh huh. And..."

Billie rolled her eyes and leaned back against one of the chairs.

"And, it was wrong of me to lie to you, okay?"

Jessica shook her head.

"You know what this group meant to me when I showed up here. I was alone, Billie, and I was trying to rebuild my ability to trust relationships again."

Billie looked down at her hands. She was rubbing her palm with one of her thumbs. Jessica remembered doing that. At one point, when Jessica went to grief meetings nearly every day, she just about wore a hole through her skin with all the rubbing she did.

"You didn't just take the group away from me, you took our friendship and threw it away."

"It was for a reason," Billie said.

"I don't care."

"The reporter is coming on the trip. They're going to document the whole thing. I already talked to Ullman and he said that..."

"Billie, I don't care about that."

"I know. You've made that clear," Billie said.

The room fell silent for a moment. Jessica returned her attention to the page in front of her on the bed. It listed three potential jobs and seemed to suggest that any of the three would be waiting for her as soon as she arrived. The date at the top of the documented declared that it was more than a year old. She had no idea how they could arrange for three different ready-to-fill jobs and then hold them for more than a year.

"Are you going to forgive me or not?"

"Forgive, yes? Trust you again? I don't know how I could do that. It wouldn't be fair to myself."

"I had reasons, you know. Not just that stuff about wanting to get you to open up to the reporter. I was scared out of my mind that Dylan wasn't going to pull through from his injuries, you know? I couldn't bear the thought of losing him. He was the one that I bonded with, aside from Simon, and then after Simon died..."

"I feel for you, Billie. But I can't just decide to trust you again because I can sympathize with your pain. I feel like you should understand that and you shouldn't be all up in my face demanding that I return to the way things were. This isn't my fault."

"Yeah," Billie said as she stood. "You're right. I want you to know that I'm sorry. I made a mistake and I'm sorry. That's really the beginning and the end of it."

Jessica nodded.

Billie left and pulled the door shut behind herself.

CHAPTER SIXTEEN

Jessica

Trip

When they landed, the pilot informed the cabin that it was a wet day. Jessica heard the rain beating down on the roof of the jet bridge as she rolled her bag towards the gate. Through the airport, she had tried to prepare herself, but couldn't force herself to step out through the doors to find a cab.

"Jessica?" a cheerful voice called.

She didn't even bother to turn around, thinking that they must be hailing someone else.

"Jessica—I thought that was you."

Mindy came up alongside her.

"Oh," Mindy said, looking through the glass doors. "This must be difficult for you. You want to share a cab? You're headed over to the house, right? I got a hotel room around the corner."

For a few seconds, Jessica tried to think of all the possible scenarios that might be likely. Twice now, she had been a witness to the rain man. If that happened again, and the driver was the only other person around, the cab would crash. There might be a significant benefit to having another potential victim around.

"Sure," Jessica said.

She followed Mindy out to the covered platform and then down the row to the next available cab. Jessica waited for Mindy to put her bag in the trunk and then shoved it forward to put her own in back. When Mindy gave the driver the name of her hotel, Jessica then read off the address of the house and asked to be dropped off first.

"Nervous?" Mindy asked when they were underway.

"Not really. No."

"This whole thing is designed to force a confrontation, no? I would think that would make you nervous."

Jessica looked through her window. There was too much green. Her time in Vegas had conditioned her to harbor disdain whenever she saw a lot of green. It meant that someone was wasting water. They passed by a patch of trees that were practically covered in vines. To her eyes, it was an overload of plant life. It barely seemed real.

"Was it a tough decision to sign up? Billie said that there was a lot of hesitation before the slots filled up. I think someone told me that you were signed up for the high effort role. What does that entail?"

"I'm not going to talk about it," Jessica said.

The cab merged onto the highway and Jessica watched as the cab driver changed lanes to pass a van. They passed close to the other vehicle and Jessica studied the van's window through the rain, wondering if that driver would be wearing a drooping hat or smoking a wet cigarette.

"That's probably the best approach, actually," Mindy said. "From what I've heard, it sounds like maybe the killer has a psychic connection or something with his victims. Any discussion might tip him off, I guess."

"Nobody knows anything," Jessica said. "Speculation is dangerous."

"Interesting. Why do you think that?"

Jessica turned back to the passing scenery, mad at herself for engaging at all.

For a couple of minutes, they rode in silence. Jessica could almost feel Mindy gearing up to ask a question. Maybe it was a smell that the reporter gave off.

"When do you start work?" Mindy asked.

"Who told you I was going to get a job?"

"Nobody. I mean, you just did with your defensive response, but nobody really. During one of the interviews you said that you always get a job right away when you move to a new place so you can avoid getting paranoid and falling in with the wrong crowd."

Jessica frowned and sighed.

"I'm not moving here."

"But you are getting a job, right? Was that one of the terms spelled out in your packet?"

"I'm not going to talk about it."

"Doesn't matter, I guess. I'll have plenty of opportunities to see for myself, right? We have a whole team who will document everything that happens. It's going to be a great conclusion for the story."

"That's a terrible idea. Someone is going to get hurt."

"Maybe," Mindy said. "I was *very* upfront with all the people who applied. They all have a good sense of what they're walking into. Nobody will be blind to the possible danger. Compared to what some of these people have been through, the chance to document a serial killer was an opportunity that they jumped at."

"He's not a serial killer," Jessica whispered. The driver kept glancing in the mirror. She didn't want to freak him out even more.

"What would you call him then?"

"He's not a person, remember? This thing is like a wildfire or a tornado. Anyone who would purposely put themselves in that path should be committed."

"Isn't that what you're doing?" Mindy asked.

"I've been in the path since I was a kid. This is my chance to finally jump out of the way."

The driver veered right and took the exit for Harmony Hill. When he took a left, the road plunged deep into a sea of tall trees that blocked off the view of the sky.

"One last act of penance, trying to absolve yourself of the burden you carry?"

Jessica glanced over at Mindy, wondering how she could possibly be dumb enough to get everything so wrong. Mindy wasn't dumb. She was doing it again—trying to manipulate Jessica into some kind of revelation with maddening questions. Jessica looked at Mindy's handbag and wondered if the conversation was being recorded. Instead of answering, or saying another word, Jessica put on her headphones.

The trees opened up and they passed through fields dotted with cows. Taking another turn, they started down a road with houses every hundred yards. It quickly transitioned into a legitimate neighborhood. Jessica saw a convenience store and recognized the sign. She had never been to a "Croc 'N Shop" but it was one of the job interviews she had coming up. They took another turn and passed by a bank and a school. Jessica recognized the street name when the driver turned on Marsten Road. It was in her new address. The house was easy to spot as they rounded the turn. It was a gray victorian, plucked straight from a nightmare.

Mindy tapped Jessica's shoulder. She was holding out a business card.

"The number for the front desk of my hotel. Call if you need anything."

"Thanks," Jessica said. She put the card in the trash bag hanging from the seat in front of her as the driver pulled up in front of the nightmare house. Jessica got out and shut the door behind herself before Mindy could follow. The driver popped the trunk and got out to help. When she had her bag on the pavement, Jessica gave the driver a tip and told him that Mindy would take care of the rest of the fare. He turned around in the road and then disappeared back towards town as Jessica stared up at the house.

A light drizzle began to fall.

Jessica rushed towards the house.

House

When Jessica turned the key in the deadbolt, it met no resistance. She pushed the door open with her foot and listened to hinge groan as the house opened its mouth to swallow her up.

"Hello?"

There was no answer. Leaning to the right, she couldn't see any lights on in the place. The interior was all a gloomy gray color that matched the clouds behind her. From where she stood, it looked like the house had been fully furnished about a hundred years before and not changed since. Breaking up the floral wallpaper in the hall, there were paintings of people who looked like they had been plucked from a Bram Stoker novel.

Taking a deep breath, Jessica carried her bag inside and toured the first floor of the house, turning on lights as she went. The bulbs came on slowly, like the electricity was coaxing light from reluctant filaments. Jessica started to make a mental shopping list—new light bulbs was at the top of the list. In the kitchen, she came up with a few more items. She would get a microwave, a teakettle, and some cheap silverware that wasn't all tarnished. The packet had included a gift card for living expenses. Jessica intended to use hers to dispel as much of the creepiness as she could.

When she finished looking around the first floor, she climbed the stairs to find the bedrooms. She chose the one at the end of the hall that had a view of the town below. It was farthest from the stairs and looked like it would get the morning sun, if the sun ever came out again. Outside, the rain had picked up. Jessica added bedsheets and curtains to her list. She pulled down the heavy dark curtains that were hanging in front of the windows and stuffed them into a garbage bag while she coughed from the dust.

She set the bag out in the hall and began to unpack.

From downstairs, she heard a woman's voice call, "Hello?"

"Upstairs," Jessica yelled back. Piling her shirts into one of the drawers, Jessica was staking her claim. She wanted to make it clear that this was her room.

Riley rapped on the door frame.

"Hey," Jessica said. "Did you come in on the two-fifteen flight?"

"No. I actually flew in last night but I was given a hotel room for one night," Riley said, shaking her head. "It's all very... confusing, I guess. We can ask Joe when he gets here. I'm curious to know if they did the same weird arrangements for Mexico."

"Weird arrangements?"

"Well, I mean, why did they give us all separate flights, and why did I have to stay in a hotel before coming here? It seems unnecessarily random."

Jessica opened another drawer to put away her pants and found a new set of sheets still wrapped in the drawer. She crossed bedding off of her mental shopping list and opened the package.

"I'll give you a hand," Riley said, moving to the opposite side of the bed.

"Let me know if you need anything from town," Jessica said. "I'm going to walk down later."

"I have a car," Riley said. "They didn't get you a rental?"

Jessica thought about that. "I didn't see anything in my packet. Maybe I missed it. No, wait, I distinctly remember some mention of taking a cab."

"See? Random."

Jessica nodded. When they finished making the bed, Riley went back to the hall and lifted her bag.

"So, we just pick a room? Is it like at Simon's house? Any open door is available?"

"I guess," Jessica said closing her door behind herself. "There are six rooms up here. From the outside, it looked like there were windows up on a third floor as well, but I haven't seen stairs to get up there."

A chill ran through Jessica as she thought about the house she had grown up in. There was probably a hatch in the ceiling of one of the closets. Kids might try to hide up there, but they would be found anyway.

"This one looks nice, right?" Riley asked as she flipped on the lights in the room right next to Jessica's.

"Right next to the bathroom. Billie will probably take her famous middle of the night showers and wake you up."

"I'm a heavy sleeper," Riley said. She went in the room and put her bag on the bed.

Jessica paused in the doorway. "If you have a car, maybe we can go grocery shopping later? Everything in the fridge looks processed and salted."

"It's a deal," Riley said. "Should we wait for the others or just go on our own?"

Jessica thought about trying to drag Billie through a grocery store and then shook her head.

"I figured we would all just fend for ourselves, you know? We're probably going to have different schedules and habits. No need to add friction."

"Good point," Riley said. "Let me get settled and I'll track you down."

Jessica nodded. She left Riley there.

Town

The yard was much more charming than the house itself. The rain had slowed to a light mist. Aside from her sneakers and the cuffs of her jeans, Jessica didn't get too wet while she toured the yard.

There were a couple of overgrown flower beds that Riley would probably attack the moment she spotted them. A bulkhead on the side of the building probably led down to the cellar. Jessica had toured the first floor pretty thoroughly and hadn't seen stairs going down. They had to be somewhere. She made a mental note to look for a cellar door. It would be a good idea to know all the entrances and exits of the creepy house.

At the back edge of the lawn, she saw a footpath that cut back and forth down the side of the hill. On the other side of a small patch of woods, the Croc 'N Shop stood. The packet hadn't given her a rental car, but it had specified the number of hours she was supposed to work per week, and the Croc 'N Shop was one of the employment options.

Jessica checked the time and glanced up at the house. She could see Riley moving around in the bedroom, probably trying to make the place livable. Jessica started down the hill. It was a quick, steep walk. The trail ended at the back of the parking lot. Jessica passed a young woman leaning against the side of the building, blowing clouds from her vape. Her shirt had a cartoon crocodile—the logo of the store.

"You worked here long?" Jessica asked.

"Two years."

The vape cloud smelled of apples.

"What's the worst part?"

"Ten to seven shift. Nobody comes in after midnight and the only thing to do is dust and front the stock."

"You allowed to read?"

The woman shrugged and blew another cloud.

"You can, but I don't. Victor hates it."

"Victor's the manager?"

"Nope. Chelsea is the manager. Victor is the ghost who lives in the stock room. If he knows you're reading, he knocks stuff over."

Jessica nodded and thanked her. She headed for the door. An electronic chime announced her entrance and a guy behind the counter mumbled something. Jessica found a bottle of iced coffee and a small bag of chips. When he was ringing up her purchase, she asked him the same questions. He had the same answers, including the one about Victor, but he didn't mention reading. He said that Victor hated it when people talked on the phone.

Jessica was starting to form an opinion of the manager, Chelsea, already. It sounded like she was the type of person who kept people motivated to work through fear. And instead of instilling fear of getting fired, she made her people fear a ghost named Victor.

The vaping woman was gone when Jessica went back out. Jessica leaned against the wall and ate her chips, trying to imagine what it would be like working there.

"Boredom, probably," she whispered to herself. Through the trees, she could see the top of the house on the hill where she was staying. With the peaks of that house nearby, it was almost plausible to think that the Croc 'N Shop might be haunted. The old victorian house had a menacing presence up there.

Her phone buzzed. It was a message from Riley—she was ready to go.

Jessica texted back for Riley to pick her up at the Croc.

She went back to her chips and iced coffee, leaning against the building as the drizzle picked up again. There was just enough overhang from the store to keep dry. Around the corner, she heard the electronic chime and the vaping woman came around again.

"You can't loiter," the woman said.

"Okay. I won't," Jessica said. "My friend is picking me up in a sec."

"Are you the new person?"

"Sorry?"

"We heard there's a new person starting tomorrow. Is that you?"

Jessica shrugged. "Could be. Who told you?"

"Chelsea said she heard it from corporate. Chelsea thinks you're a spy."

"A spy?"

"Supposedly, every now and then they send someone down to make sure that all the franchise rules are being followed. Are you the spy?"

"Not that I know of," Jessica said. She offered her bag of chips and the young woman took one while eyeing Jessica with suspicion.

"I'm Erika, by the way. With a K."

"Jessica."

"If you are the spy, and you're, like, undercover or whatever, you can tell me. I won't tell Chelsea."

"Okay."

"Thought so." Erika took another offered chip.

Jessica saw a car turning in and then spotted Riley behind the wheel. She gave the rest of the chips to Erika and said goodbye.

"See you tomorrow," Erika said.

"Sure thing," Jessica said waving.

"You know her?" Riley asked when Jessica got into the passenger's seat.

"She's my new co-worker. I start there tomorrow."

"You already have a job?"

The rain was just enough to warrant the windshield wipers. They slapped away the drops.

"Don't you?" Jessica asked.

Riley laughed.

Shopping went fast. They stopped at a Target first, where Jessica got lightbulbs, curtains, silverware, a trash can, and a bunch of cleaning supplies and toiletries. Riley bought a pair of umbrellas and gave one to Jessica as a gift when they were walking out.

Grocery shopping was more difficult. Nothing was where Jessica expected to find it. She was staring at a freezer case, trying to find a decent-looking burrito, when someone tapped her on the shoulder. Jessica whipped around and nearly knocked over a display of hotdog rolls.

"Sorry!" Billie said. "Sorry. I'm so sorry. I didn't mean to frighten you."

Jessica had never seen Billie look so meek and timid.

"No, it's fine, Billie. What's wrong?"

Billie shook her head. "I don't have any money. I tried to use that card that was in my packet. I figured that I didn't want to show up to the house with nothing to eat. But I did the checkout thing so I wouldn't have to talk to a cashier person, and then my card wouldn't work."

Jessica sighed. "Did you call?"

"Call who?"

"There's a number on the card. You have to activate it."

"Oh?"

"Where's your stuff?"

"I left it at the machine. I was going to run out, but then I saw you and I thought... It's okay. I'm sure there's food. I'm going to sneak out of here I guess."

"Billie," Jessica said, shaking her head. "Come on."

Jessica grabbed a couple of burritos, put them in her basket, and escorted Billie back towards the front. She waved and apologized to the bagger who was starting to collect Billie's things from the self checkout area. Jessica combined her groceries with Billie's and they put everything on Jessica's card.

"I'll pay you back," Billie said as they sat on the bench near the door.

"It's all Simon's money. No need."

"I guess."

"Are you okay? You look terrible," Jessica said.

Billie looked down at her hands as she picked at a cuticle with one of her fingernails.

"I'm... It's okay. I guess it's been a while since I tried to be self-sufficient out in the world. I didn't realize how sheltered I was at Simon's. The flight was a nightmare—the security stuff. Getting my car was awful. Driving. I was never that good at driving and then trying to figure out where I was going. I stopped here because I couldn't find the right road."

"There's Riley," Jessica said, standing up. "I'll tell her that I'm catching a ride with you. I know where we're going."

House

"What is this place?" Billie asked, looking up through the windshield.

"It's fine," Jessica said.

She grabbed her bags from the back seat and headed towards the house. The door was unlocked again. Jessica's eyes scanned around as she walked towards the kitchen. She was looking for any sign that Ullman or Joe had shown up—that would explain the door.

In the refrigerator, she put some things away in the different drawers and slots, but kept the food for her dinner segregated on one half of one of the shelves. Ullman and Billie were probably accustomed to simply taking whatever they wanted, so Jessica reminded herself to not be too upset if something disappeared.

When she shut the refrigerator door, Jessica saw Billie standing near the sink.

"Rooms are upstairs," Jessica said. "Riley and I closed the doors to the rooms we chose."

"It's raining," Billie said.

Jessica nodded. "Yeah, plenty more coming too, according to the forecast."

"You're not worried?"

"Isn't that what we're here for?"

"I thought that we would have some time to prepare," Billie said.

"I don't think that's how this is going to work. I'm not sure that a lot of preparation is in the cards."

"I'm starting to wonder if this is a good idea."

Jessica smiled and shook her head. "Of course it's not."

They heard the front door. Jessica moved quickly through the living room, assuming that it was Riley. She slowed when she saw Ullman, loaded with baggage, trying to squeeze through the doorway. Billie passed Jessica and practically ran to help.

"I thought you weren't going to make it," she said.

"I nearly didn't," he said.

"I can't thank you enough," Billie said.

As Billie helped Ullman carry in his bags, Jessica slipped past them with a smile and went out to the porch. Riley was pulling up. Jessica waited for her to park before she ran out into the rain to go help unload. They got everything to the porch and then started to bring it all inside. With all of Riley's groceries moved to the kitchen table, Jessica walked around with her big package of light bulbs, taking out the yellow, flickering bulbs and replacing them with impossibly bright white ones. More light did help to cheer the place up, but it also highlighted all the cobwebs and dust.

Jessica went back to her bag—she had predicted this problem. With her brand new broom and dusting cloths, she began to work through the first floor, cleaning up the obvious issues.

"You don't have to do that," Riley said when she caught Jessica dusting the side table in the living room.

"Just makes it a little less dreary," Jessica said.

"I mean, you don't have to do that all by yourself."

Riley joined her and the two of them tackled the room together. They moved some of the furniture in the living room and it almost looked inviting. Next, they tidied up the hall and worked down to the kitchen. Billie was sitting at the table, talking to Ullman as he chopped and sautéed. Jessica and Riley worked around him to freshen up the room as he cooked.

"Glen gave me a recipe for tonight," Ullman said as they worked. "I hope you'll join us for dinner?"

Riley answered for them. "That sounds lovely. Count us in."

Jessica took a seat when she needed a break. It felt like she had been on her feet all day, although it also seemed like she hadn't really done anything. It was all busy work to fill time. There were things she didn't want to think about and staying busy was the only way that she could avoid the intrusive thoughts.

"That must be Joe," Billie said.

"Sorry?" Jessica asked.

"That noise? Didn't you just hear the door."

"I did," Riley said. "I'll go see if he needs help."

"I'll come with," Jessica said, getting back on her feet.

Riley slowed in the hallway. "That's odd. I heard the door too, but it doesn't..."

Jessica almost ran into Riley when she froze in place.

“What is it?” Jessica asked, angling to see around her.

Billie was at her back an instant later. “Is something out there?”

“I think so,” Riley said.

Jessica couldn’t stand it any longer. She twisted past Riley and went to the door so she could look through the vertical window on the left side. There were three cars out front. It seemed that everyone had a received a rental car except Jessica. She thought about the writing on the packet that she had picked out. It had read, “High effort, high risk, very physical.” This was the path that she had chosen.

When she stepped out to the porch, she realized that the temperature had dropped several degrees. Her breath fogged out of her mouth. She walked the length of the porch, looking down either side of the building. There were footprints in the wet grass, but they seemed to only be between the road and the front door.

From the doorway Billie asked, “Do you see anything?”

“No,” Jessica said. “What did you hear?”

“The front door,” Riley said. She was standing in the shadows behind Billie. “It sounded like someone opened the front door.”

Jessica glanced out at the lawn again, studying the wet grass.

“Didn’t Mindy say that her crew was going to set up some perimeter cameras on this place?”

“Yeah,” Billie said. A moment later her phone was in her hands. “I’ll make sure they get on that right away.”

“Good,” Jessica said.

Night

Joe showed up right as they were sitting down to dinner. They set another place for him and then Billie had to jump up when her phone announced that the camera crew had arrived. The house bustled with activity for the next hour. The crew put cameras all around the first floor while the five housemates ate and then cleaned up.

In the den, they had monitors set up on the desk. From there, Jessica could see every angle of the yard surrounding the house. It was dark out, so all the views had a strange gray glow as they picked up details that Jessica couldn't have seen with her own eyes.

"Is there some kind of motion detector on these or something?" Jessica asked one of the team.

"They're always on," the man asked.

"Yeah, but is there some audible warning or something it could make if someone comes near the house?"

"They're not set up that way. If we put an alarm on these, it would literally go off every time a moth passed in front of the lens."

Jessica frowned.

"Is that a problem?" he asked.

"I was hoping that these would help keep us safe, not just document our murder," she said.

Startled by her answer, the guy finished coiling his cables and rushed back out to the equipment truck.

Jessica found Riley on the stairs.

"It's early, but I'm going to go up to my room and relax," Riley said. "It's been a long day."

Jessica nodded. "Did the others move in yet?"

"Billie is unpacked. I don't think Ullman or Joe have even set foot upstairs."

"They're probably going to be banging around until three in the morning," Jessica said.

Riley nodded and smiled before she resumed climbing the stairs. "Good thing I'm a heavy sleeper."

Joe was reviewing paperwork in the living room. Jessica took a seat opposite him and watched as he flipped through documents, peering at them through the glasses perched on the end of his nose.

"I'd like to know who wrote this," he said.

"What is it?"

"This is, supposedly, the history of this house. I don't believe for a minute that any of it is real. It seems like heavily plagiarized fiction." He held up a photo of a portrait. "This man built this house by himself as a gift to his wife but she died of tuberculosis less than a month after they moved in. His daughter then died by falling down the stairs. The housekeeper was the only witness and later she was accused of pushing the daughter to her death. There was scant evidence of the crime but the housekeeper was nonetheless hanged."

"That's horrible."

"It gets worse. The man's son moved back in with his new wife to help take care of the father as he was aging and then the son was called to war."

"Which war?".

"I'm guessing the first World War. Hard to tell. The son gets drafted or whatever and his wife lives here with her father-in-law until the two of them meet a grizzly end."

"What happened to them?" Jessica asked.

"Murder. It's unclear if it was an itinerant guy or a friend of the family. Both were convicted. The son came back from the war not knowing that everyone was dead except his baby daughter. The whole thing is like a soap opera."

"What makes you think it's not real?"

Joe took off his glasses. "I can't find any backup for these stories. I tried to research them before I left Vegas and I came up with nothing. I asked Laura to look into the names and dates and she said she thought it was fiction. That's when I realized all the parallels to different stories. There's a..."

He was interrupted by a crash from the kitchen. Jessica ran to see what had happened. She found the room empty. Only the lights above the sink were on. The rest of the kitchen was dark and quiet.

"What was it?" Joe asked.

"No idea," Jessica said. She wove around him and went down the hall. Mindy's people had left one person to monitor the cameras. A young woman sat behind the desk. She was just about to take a bite of a sandwich when Jessica came through the doorway. The young woman quickly wrapped the sandwich back up and hid it in her lap.

"What just happened?" Jessica asked.

"Sorry?"

"Can you..." Jessica began as she turned a monitor so she could see it too. "This camera, here. Can you look to see what made a noise in the kitchen?"

"I'm not allowed to stop the camera," the young woman said.

"I'm not asking you to. Just show me the video from two minutes ago up until now."

"Oh," the young woman said. "I don't think I know how to do that."

"What are you here for?"

"To make sure everything keeps running."

"How are you supposed to make sure everything keeps running if you don't know how to run it?" Jessica asked.

"Hey, Jessica?" Joe asked from the doorway.

"What?"

"Can I talk with you a second?"

Jessica shook her head and followed Joe out into the hall.

"I'm sure she's just here to make sure that nobody tampers with anything. They didn't give her any actual training, and they're probably not even paying her. Production companies use these interns like sentient doorstops."

"Then I'll do it myself," Jessica said.

She went back into the room where the intern was just about to take another bite of her sandwich.

Jessica said, "Mindy is outside. She needs to talk to you."

The girl wrapped her sandwich quickly, put it in her bag and then rushed for the door, ducking by Joe.

"That was mean," Joe said.

"Whatever."

The mouse woke up the one screen that wasn't showing any cameras. Jessica found a folder of video files and saw that they were broken up by the hour. The current one was still growing in size, but Jessica was able to open it and find the part of the video where she turned on the lights in the kitchen, looking for the source of the crash. She backed up the video a minute and turned up the sound.

Joe joined her as she watched.

It was difficult to see in the dim light of the room, but something on a shelf moved and then tumbled into the sink. Its impact was the source of the sound.

"What was that?" Jessica asked.

"Vase," Joe said. "Wedding vase."

"What's a wedding vase?"

"It's from one of the stories. Come on—I'll read it to you."

Jessica looked at the screen again and watched the clip one more time. The intern came back and Jessica closed the video and gave her back her seat.

"Did you find Mindy?" Jessica asked.

"Yes. She said she didn't need to talk to me."

"Oh," Jessica said. "Sorry."

Vase

"Here it is," Joe said, adjusting his glasses to the end of his nose. "Every day, Mary arranged fresh flowers to put in the vase in the kitchen window. She knew that Frederick would arrive home by train and then climb the hill on foot, looking up to catch a glimpse of her. He always talked about it in his letters. If she didn't happen to be in the window when he arrived, she wanted him to see something pretty in her stead."

Jessica went back to the kitchen. The light was still on in there. There was nothing in the sink. Returning to Joe, she shook her head.

"That can't be it. There's no vase in the sink."

"Of course not, it was shattered on the evening of her death," Joe said. He traced the text with his finger as he read, "Mrs. Stapleton, coming by to drop off a loaf of bread for her neighbors, was the first to notice the missing vase of flowers. The discovery led her to peek through the kitchen door. That's when she saw the young woman in a pool of drying blood on the kitchen floor."

"Awful," Jessica said. "So the vase was gone?"

"Shattered," Joe said. "Presumably during her murder. Maybe she was going to dump that day's flowers, or maybe she accidentally knocked them over when she was attacked. Either way, the vase was found shattered in the sink and the young wife was dead on the floor. Searching the rest of the house, a group found her father-in-law murdered as well. They came up with two suspects for the crimes—a bum and a neighbor. The bum was convicted and executed. Later, when new evidence turned up, the neighbor was also convicted. Doesn't say if he was executed or not."

Joe flipped over the piece of paper.

"Wait," Jessica said. "You think that a ghost vase made the noise we heard?"

"I think that we both saw something fall from the shelf and land in the sink. That object made the noise we heard. Because there's no trace of that object, I suppose we have to assume it was a ghost vase."

Jessica shook her head. "What does any of this have to do with the rain man?"

Joe shrugged. He picked up another document from the table and leaned back to read it.

Jessica stood up.

"Now what?" Joe asked.

"Sorry?"

"You look like you're ready to go fight someone."

"No, I'm just putting something together," Jessica said. "The intern said that Mindy wasn't looking for her, but I saw her cellphone in her bag when she put her sandwich in there. That means that..."

"Mindy is outside," Joe finished.

"Exactly."

Jessica headed for the door. She paused to grab the umbrella that Riley had bought for her and stepped out into the night. The light from the house disappeared quickly in the rainy dark. She stumbled down the stairs and found her way across the yard until she spotted the cars. Walking down the line, she found a van with light leaking around the curtains in the windows.

Jessica knocked and waited.

Mindy opened the door and Jessica saw screens that duplicated the video feeds from inside the house. Mindy waved her inside. There was just enough room for two people. Jessica shook out her umbrella and took the empty seat.

"You must have imagined that I was watching, right?" Mindy asked. "This can't be a surprise."

"No, nothing like that. I just wanted to find out what you know about the whole haunted house thing going on here."

"How do you mean?"

"Someone has gone to a lot of trouble to make us believe that the house is haunted and I'm curious as to why. The door keeps unlocking, we've heard sounds from upstairs when nobody is there, a cold wind blows through the kitchen sometimes, and now we've heard a crashing vase that seems to show up on your video."

Mindy nodded. "What makes you think that someone is behind it?"

"What's the other explanation? Simon's people discovered a house infested with ghosts and arranged for us to stay here? Why? Is it connected to why we're here or is this all coincidence? I tend to believe that it's connected because they gave all the supporting information to Joe in his packet."

Mindy glanced at her screens. Joe was still in the living room. The intern showed up on a separate display so Mindy could monitor her. They didn't see anyone else on video. Riley, Ullman, and Billie had already gone upstairs, and there were no cameras there. Mindy looked back to Jessica.

"I guess I tend to think that there's a reason why they chose this house. I don't know if the things you've seen and heard are real or fabricated. I'm not a big believer in things that I can't prove."

"Me neither."

"But I suppose it doesn't matter what's causing those things. Maybe the point is to put everyone in a certain frame of mind. Like, maybe you have be a little scared."

"Why?"

"Bait, maybe?"

"Bait?"

"You're witnesses, right? Wasn't there some movie or TV show where some evil entity fed on fear? If the thing that attacked you is like that, then wouldn't fear be the perfect bait?" Mindy asked.

"I'm more inclined to assume that you're behind it all because you're trying to get the most interesting footage for your documentary."

Mindy laughed. "I'm afraid my business doesn't work that way. We're not above stretching the truth to get the right response, but we never show evidence of the unexplainable. As soon as you do that, the video becomes the story. We have to hint at things without really ever showing them. We're about the witnesses, not the events."

"That's somehow both relieving and way worse than I thought," Jessica said.

"I understand what you mean."

Jessica stared at the screens, waiting for something to happen on one of them. The intern finished her sandwich. Joe put down one document and picked up another. On the exterior views, the most interesting thing happening was rain dribbling from one of the gutters.

"Can I offer you some advice?"

"I won't take it," Jessica said.

"That's fine. I just think that you might want to stop trying to find the trick. You signed up for this. That means that part of you must have trusted that it was all set up by people with a specific goal in mind. Hopefully, that goal matches yours and that's why you agreed to come. Instead of trying to figure everything out, just go along with the mission you've already chosen."

Jessica opened the door and her umbrella.

"If I find out that you're behind this..."
"You won't. I'm not. I'm just documenting," Mindy said.

CHAPTER SEVENTEEN

Jessica

Work

Jessica was exhausted by noon. Her co-worker, Erika, took breaks at least three times an hour. When Jessica heard the electronic chime, she had to put down whatever she was doing and head for the register. It was pretty much a given that Erika would be outside vaping. An older man bought a pack of cigarettes, a bag of chips, gum, and a single can of beer. She waited for him to leave before she went back to cleaning the inside glass of the hot dog machine. According to the list, it hadn't been done in since the weekend and it was supposed to be checked off every twenty-four hours. Jessica had already burned herself three times.

The chime sounded and Jessica rushed back to the register.

Billie stood at the counter.

"What do you need?" Jessica asked.

"Is there an application?"

"Are you supposed to get a job here?"

Billie shrugged. "I don't know. I'm bored. I saw you and I figured that if you could do it, so could I."

"It was in my packet," Jessica said. "I had to pick from one of the three jobs listed there. They're part of my role. Did you have a job in your packet?"

"I'm supposed to wash," Billie said. "I took everything to the laundromat and I was done in ninety minutes."

"Are you allowed to do that?"

"The laundry got washed. What's the difference how it got done?"

Jessica shrugged. "I don't know. I honestly have no idea what the scheme is."

Chelsea came out from her office.

"May I help you?" she asked.

Billie took one look at her and seemed to come to a quick decision.

"Yeah. I'm looking for work."

"You can submit an application and I'll read it tomorrow. Are you on break, Jessica?" Chelsea asked.

Jessica sighed. "No."

"See you at the house," Billie said, turning to leave.

When the chime sounded to mark her exit, Jessica went back to the hot dog machine. There was something satisfying about completing each task and checking it off the list, even if she was the only one doing everything. She could feel Chelsea's eyes on her, watching her work. Then, when she glanced over, Chelsea had gone back into the office.

Erika appeared from the stock room, making Jessica jump.

"Chelsea hates visitors," Erika said. "You can get away with a lot, but not visitors. You should tell your friends to meet you by the dumpster if they need to talk to you."

"She's not my friend."

"Whatever. I have to do inventory on the drinks. Cover the register, will you?"

"Okay," Jessica said.

Through the glass and between the rows of beer, she could see Erika back there, sitting on a stack of cases, looking at her phone.

Jessica laughed and stood up straight to stretch her shoulders back. That morning, after introducing herself to Chelsea, she had been given a shirt, a badge, and a few basic instructions about the cash register. She hadn't filled out any paperwork or shown her ID. It was a fake job, meant to fill her time or maybe put her into some particular mental state for whatever strange experiment was taking place up on the hill. They were actors in a story.

Jessica was the worker.

"But who's to say I'm a *good* worker?" she mumbled.

Jessica pulled a cup from the dispenser and poured herself some soda from the fountain. She sampled a couple of them before deciding that the machine tasted like mold. The chime rang. Before rushing to the register, Jessica grabbed a beer from the refrigerator.

She opened it and took a sip while she rang up the customer. Chelsea came out from the office and eyed Jessica. In response, Jessica lifted the can to toast her. Bracing herself for confrontation, Jessica didn't break eye contact with her new boss. Chelsea only shook her head and went back to her office.

The chime rang again as Jessica set her beer next to the soda fountain. There was a cleaning procedure to flush out the syrup lines and a different one for the water supply. Jessica started at the top. From inside the stock area, Chelsea called, "Are you going to take care of that customer?"

"It's your turn," Jessica said.

Dinner

The house was filled with bright chaos when Jessica returned. She shook out her umbrella and called a greeting. Joe answered from the living room. Riley responded from the hall. Jessica took off her wet shoes before stepping inside.

"What's all this?" Jessica asked.

There were papers pinned to the north wall and carefully arranged on the sofa and the coffee table.

"Research," Joe said. "I spent the morning at the library and found the sources for a lot of this stuff. The stories are true, it seems, but the names and dates were all slightly altered. It's like they wanted us to know parts of the story, but not the whole thing. Riley says I'm allowed to do anything I want to this room for the next two days, and then I have to clean up and move on. I think I can get it all organized by then."

"Riley?" Jessica asked.

"Yeah," Riley said from the doorway. "I've decided to go one room at a time and I'm starting with the hall. I'll try to leave a path to walk, but it might be easiest to go around the other way for now."

Jessica followed her and saw tarps covered in shreds of soggy wallpaper.

"This is your job now?" Jessica asked.

Riley laughed. "It's my interpretation of what my packet indicated I should do. I like to keep busy, and Ullman has taken over the garden. It's too dreary and damp out for me anyway. Better to stay inside."

"You need help?" Jessica asked.

"No. I'm not being serious about it. I'm just trying to honor the process."

Jessica shrugged. She climbed the stairs, wondering if she had honored the process—whatever that was supposed to mean. A hot shower helped to strip away some of her weariness. Dressed in comfortable clothes, she was ravenous by the time she descended again. All she could think about was the frozen burrito waiting for her. Instead, she smelled garlic and onions.

Ullman and and Billie were busy in the kitchen.

Without a smile, Billie said, "Have a seat. We're making dinner for everyone."

"I was just going to have a burrito."

"Too late. We made enough for everyone."

Jessica considered arguing the point. After being around people all day, it seemed like a good idea to put something on a plate and retreat to her room for some quiet time. The aroma of the food swayed her. It looked like Ullman was getting ready to start dishing it out. Jessica did as she was told and took a seat near the window. Nestled into the corner of the porch roof, she saw the glowing red lamp of one of the cameras and wondered if Mindy was outside in the van.

"How was your day?" Joe asked as he sat down across from her.

"Busy but dull," Jessica said. "Don't ever eat or drink anything that comes from the Croc unless it's in a sealed package."

Joe laughed. "I'll take your word for it. Although, when I was a kid we used to stop by this little store on the way home from school. They had a pinball machine and a..."

"Wait," Billie said, "there was electricity when you were a kid?"

"A pinball machine and this cooker that made hotdogs. I used to get one every Monday. It was my reward for having survived the return to school yet again."

Jessica shook her head. "The number of grease-soaked flies that I cleaned out of the hotdog machine today. You wouldn't believe how many bugs you probably ate when you were a kid."

"Do you mind?" Ullman asked. "We're working on presenting a lovely, bug-free, dinner. Could we save that kind of talk for another time?"

"Glen teaches you three recipes and you're a gourmet?" Billie asked.

Riley entered and took one of the free chairs just as Ullman brought plates over to the table. Fork in hand, Jessica forced herself to wait for the others to take their seats before she started shoveling food into her mouth.

"When is something supposed to happen?" Billie asked.

Ullman raised his eyebrows and looked at Billie. To Jessica, it seemed pretty clear that they had already talked about this and maybe decided to not raise the issue.

After dabbing his lips with a napkin, Joe said, "I believe that the idea is to set up the right conditions—or, right as far as we can guess—and then wait."

"We have the right weather, and they seem to have given us tasks to occupy us," Riley said.

Joe nodded. "In Mexico, I guess we were supposed to be doing vacation stuff, but it was torturous to sit around and wait. At least they have us doing something here."

"Speak for yourself," Billie said. "I wasn't assigned anything and that lady at the Croc 'N Shop barely glanced at my application. Someone told her that I was a convicted felon."

That last statement came with a pointed look at Jessica.

"It wasn't me," Jessica said, shaking her head. "It's the truth, but I wouldn't go around telling people about it."

"Exonerated," Billie said.

"Not, like, legally," Jessica said. "Regardless, I wouldn't say anything. After all, I *know* you didn't do it."

Billie shook her head.

"I don't believe there's any rule that says you can't help one of us," Joe said. "I'm sure Ullman could use an extra set of hands out in the gardens, right?"

"Maybe you're not supposed to do anything. Maybe your boredom is part of it," Riley said. "One of the packets was marked low risk and low effort, right? Maybe there's a perfectly good reason to have someone in that role. If that's the case, I would say just go with it and experience what you experience."

Jessica looked through the window at the camera and thought about what Riley was saying. The advice fit nicely with what Mindy had said. Billie was struggling to figure things out instead of just going along with the mission. It was more clear than ever that people had worked to set up a specific scenario. If they didn't trust that, then they had no business being there.

On the other hand, Simon had trusted his people to set up the Mexico scenario, and that had ended in his death. The gravity of their undertaking landed Jessica with sudden clarity. She put down her fork.

"Joe, in Mexico, was it clear when things began to go sideways?" Jessica asked.

Joe's eyes shifted left and right and then over to Ullman.

"I don't think we should be talking about Mexico," Joe said.

"We're here, risking our lives," Jessica said. "I think we should be able to talk about anything we want."

"Do we want to risk tipping our hand?" Riley asked.

"Our hand?" Billie asked. "Are you kidding? We don't have a hand. Last time, you were given tools to defend yourselves. This time, you guys were given busywork and chores. We don't have anything to hide."

"She's right," Ullman said. "The secrecy in Mexico was, at best, ineffective. It was arguably counterproductive because everyone was so compartmentalized that they couldn't work together. I don't believe we have any such mandate on this trip."

"In the video, I thought that Simon verified that there's a psychic element to the stalking," Joe said.

"Verified that there was a theory about it, but then he admitted there was no evidence to back that up," Riley said.

"Back to my question," Jessica said. "Was there a point in time when it was clear that everything was going sideways."

Joe didn't answer.

Ullman stood up and began gathering empty plates.

"To me," Ullman said, "it was clear from the start that everything was off track. They took elements from the survival stories and tried to combine them. All they really did was ignore the one thing everyone had in common. You were all witnesses. Everyone except for Simon, that is."

He headed for the sink with dishes and came back for more.

"In the end, we all ended up as witnesses again," Ullman finished.

"Except Simon," Billie added.

Evening

Stretched out on her bed, Jessica curled her toes until her feet cramped up and then straightened them again. She did it over and over, enjoying the discomfort, until it stopped working. She kept picturing Vivian that first night they had met. At the time, Vivian seemed very meek and afraid. Later, Jessica had revised that opinion. It was the construction noise. That first night in the diner, Vivian and Joe had been staying up because the construction noise sounded like thunder. Jessica couldn't judge Vivian for being timid at that sound. After all, it had rattled Jessica too.

Her window was open just a crack. It let in a humid breeze that smelled of thick vegetation. It had been years since she had enjoyed that aroma. Jessica hadn't realized how much she missed it. The window also let in the low rumble of distant thunder. Every now and then, the breeze would kick up and she heard rain pelting the window. They were camped right at the edge of a cliff and the ground was unsteady beneath them.

"Hey," Bille said.

"What's up?" Jessica pushed up to a more vertical position as Billie came in and sat down.

"I think this is it," Billie said.

"This is what?"

"Listen, this isn't fear talking or anything, but I want you to know that I really am sorry for the way I treated you. I was trying to manipulate you for my own reasons and telling myself that it was for your own good. I know that was wrong."

"Thanks for saying it, but I know that's how you feel. I'm still going to reserve the right to be angry with you for a little while longer," Jessica said.

Billie nodded. "I'm not sure we have that much more time."

"Why would you say that?"

Billie looked down at her hands and then over at the window when another rumble of thunder growled outside.

"I'm starting to think that the people who set this up knew precisely what they were doing," Billie said. "All the conditions were put in motion to summon him quickly and efficiently, and we played our parts perfectly."

"Good."

"You really want a confrontation?" Billie asked.

"I admit that I was scared earlier. The reality of everything was setting in. But I'm tired of being scared. If he's coming, let him come."

"That's easy to say."

"True," Jessica said. "But, think of it this way, regardless of what happens to us, Mindy is going to capture the whole thing. I mean, it looked like she had everything very well documented and it's all being transmitted to some databank somewhere, right? Along with the interviews, this story is going to get out there."

Billie nodded. "That's true."

"Maybe once all the murders are connected, something will get done. That was the part that always bothered me the most, I think. My whole family died and people tried to take care of me and make sure that I was okay. That was nice and all, but what I really wanted was for someone to acknowledge that this wasn't normal."

"Yeah," Billie said.

"It must have been even worse for you because they accused you."

"Right," Billie said. "He was really in my head. It was terrifying the way I reacted. I felt like I immediately had to become him. It was the only way that I didn't feel like a victim. When they first hauled me in, I didn't protest or claim my innocence."

"Really?"

"I think that's why they worked so hard to convict me. Just by the way I was acting, I convinced them that I was the killer. If a cop thinks you're guilty, they move heaven and earth to make sure that you go away for it. There's nothing that they won't do to secure that conviction."

"I suppose that's good, in a way," Jessica said.

"It's not all that difficult for them to convince you that you really were guilty."

After a pause, Billie continued, "I would have done anything for Simon, and it wasn't because he got me out of prison. It was because he finally made me realize that I didn't belong there. I would have done anything for him but I shouldn't have let him talk me out of going to Mexico. I could have stopped him from being stupid."

Jessica just listened. She wanted to say that Simon had chosen his own path. From what Jessica had heard, it seemed like he understood the risk and maybe embraced the danger. It wasn't her place to say that though.

Instead, she asked, "What's with Ullman? What kind of loyalty would make him come to this situation for a job?"

"It's not just a job. He and Simon were like family."

"Sounds like Simon had that way with people."

"A few people," Billie said. "The most broken of us."

Jessica laughed and Billie jerked her head up, ready to take offense.

"Sorry. I wasn't laughing at you. I was thinking about jobs and my sudden revelation today. I was working my heart out for these people I just met and it occurred to me that it was my own fault. They were taking advantage of me, but it was only because I was letting them do it. When I walked in there, it was like I had a big sign around my neck that said, 'Abuse my good nature.' I have this thing where I need approval so bad that I sacrifice my own well-being to get it."

Billie nodded and then glanced over at the window.

"You want to get some ice cream?" Billie asked.

Jessica shook her head. "It's raining and I wouldn't imagine there's anything open."

Billie smiled.

Ice Cream

"He's a magician," Jessica said.

"I know," Billie whispered.

"Who is?" Riley asked from the doorway.

Billie slammed the freezer door shut and turned to press her back against it, like she had been caught shoplifting.

Jessica saw Billie's guilty face and then laughed when Billie tried to shrug it off.

"Ullman," Jessica said, slipping a hand by Billie to open the freezer door again. "I haven't had this mint ice cream in years, but it was alway my favorite. Somehow he guessed my flavor, see? He even put a piece of tape with my name on it."

"Wait—before you look," Billie said, "what's your favorite flavor?"

Riley looked up and away while she thought. "I don't get it much, but I used to like that kind with all the chunks of candy bar in it. What did they call that?"

"Candy Sundae?" Billie asked.

"Could be," Riley said. When she looked to the carton that Billie was pointing at, her face lit up. "Yes! That's it. Wait, it even has my name on it?"

"Magician," Jessica said.

Billie pulled the cartons from the freezer, pressing them against her chest and rushing them to the counter. Jessica found the bowls and spoons. After protesting that she didn't need the sugar before bed, Riley finally joined them in dishing out the ice cream. They took their bowls over to the table and sat in the dim light coming from the stovetop.

"Billie says this is it. He's coming tonight," Jessica said.

Riley sighed. "Honestly? It wouldn't surprise me. I know we just got here, but it feels like everything was concocted in just the right way to make conditions perfect."

"How so?"

Riley shrugged.

"I don't know. I guess it's just a feeling. This is a ready-made script and we were all dropped right into these perfect roles. Joe's the one focused on the past instead of the present. You're off toiling, trying to contribute at the expense of yourself. I'm the one trying to make the perfect nest. Billie's the brooding one, unable to see her advantages."

"Ullman?" Billie asked.

"The caregiver. He's trying to make the rest of us happy through our stomachs," Riley said, holding up her spoon.

Jessica laughed. The sugar was going to her head.

"Wait, so in your scenario, who lives?" Jessica asked.

"I hate to say it," Riley said. "But it's clearly not me. The one building the nest never lives. If I had to guess, I would say it's the brooding one."

Billie shook her head. "No, this time all of us live."

The window next to her was closed, but Jessica felt a cold breeze anyway. On the wind, she smelled cigarette smoke and Jessica dropped her spoon into her bowl.

Riley locked eyes with her.

Without turning, Riley asked, "Billie, when was your last cigarette."

"I don't know. Why? Are you keeping track?"

Riley didn't answer.

"I thought Ullman was the caregiver. I guess it would have been a couple of hours ago," Billie said. "Why? What's up with you two."

Jessica stood.

"I'll go make sure Joe and Ullman are up."

Riley nodded. Standing up, she waved her hands over her head and turned to the corner of the room. As Jessica left the room, she heard Riley saying, "If you guys are watching, something is about to happen."

Alert

Ullman and Joe had adjacent rooms. Jessica was able to knock on both doors at the same time. She knew there would be no answer. It was too easy to picture the two men already gutted and dead in pools of their own blood.

When Joe's door clicked and snapped open, Jessica gasped.

"It's happening?" Joe asked.

Jessica nodded.

"I thought so," Joe said. "Where's Ullman?"

Jessica pointed at the door and Joe just barged in. Jessica followed him and the two of them almost crashed into Ullman as he hopped on one foot, pulling on a shoe.

"You okay?" Joe asked.

“Of course,” Ullman said. “We think it’s time?”

Jessica realized that they were both looking at her.

“We smelled tobacco smoke but Billie hasn’t had a cigarette in...”

“Nearly two hours,” Ullman said.

“Right,” Jessica said.

With a head nod, Joe led the way and they formed a tight line towards the stairs. As he walked, Joe’s head swiveled every direction, taking everything in. Jessica did her best to imitate him and scan every detail of the stairwell as they descended. At the bottom of the stairs, Billie jogged by on her way to check the lock on the front door.

“Have we spotted him yet?” Joe asked.

Billie shook her head. “It’s too dark out there.”

“Cameras,” Jessica said, pointing to the den and then leading the way.

“Where’s the intern?” Joe asked as they entered.

Jessica went straight to the monitors. She passed her finger over them as she peered at the images. Some of them only showed black. In others, she saw artificially bright video of the different sides of the house. There was nothing moving outside except the leaves and the falling rain.

“One of us should keep an eye on these,” Joe said.

“We’re not splitting up,” Billie said. “Remember Christopher’s story—nobody leaves the group.”

“Where’s...” Ullman started to ask.

Billie seemed to jump to the same realization. She ran to the door and yelled, “Riley!”

From the hallway, they heard a surprised yelp.

“Don’t do that,” Riley said. “You nearly scared me half to death.”

“Everyone stays together,” Billie said.

“That’s fine,” Riley said. “You ran out of the kitchen to go lock all the doors. I was right behind you.”

“I’m staying in here. I want to watch the cameras,” Jessica said. There was no sign of the intern, but it still seemed rude to take that chair. Instead, she dragged one of the other chairs around to the side of the desk so she could sit and watch the screens.

Joe pointed and then Riley was handing another chair from the hall. Ullman brushed the wallpaper dust off of it before he sat down. Billie leaned up against the wall and bounced her toe on a squeaky part of the floor as Joe paced. Slipping by Jessica, Riley wasn't timid about taking the intern's empty chair. She sat down and scanned the camera feeds with Jessica.

They watched the feed for several minutes. Jessica had to force herself to blink when her eyes began to dry out from staring.

"He likes the element of surprise," Billie said. "He's not going to come when we're standing around waiting. He'll let us get tired and drop our guard and then he'll come."

"I disagree," Joe said as he approached the window. "I don't think he goes for surprise so much as a building sense of dread and fear. It's like manna to him."

Riley kept her eyes on the screen and said, "If we take Hilda's story as gospel, then he's actually a mission killer who is untethered from his mission."

"What does it matter what we call him?" Jessica asked. "We can try to put motives on his actions, but we're just telling ourselves a story to try to rationalize chaos."

"It's dangerous," Ullman said. "If we feel like we understand the situation, then we might ignore contradictory evidence."

"Yes," Joe said, "you're right. All that matters is that we stay ready. Billie has a point though—we can only stay hypervigilant for a limited amount of time. Some of us should be actively focusing and some of us should be trying to meditate or take our minds off of the situation so we can rotate shifts."

"It's been thirty seconds," Riley muttered.

Jessica ignored her and said, "I'll take first shift on video."

"I will too," Riley said. "There are a lot of screens here. I'll watch the ones on the left and you take the ones to the right."

Joe let out a surprised grunt and they turned to see the intern standing in the doorway.

"What's going on?"

"Where were you?" Joe asked the young man.

"Bathroom? Is something going on?"

"Grab a seat," Riley said. "We're on high alert."

The intern looked like he wanted to ask a bunch of questions, but kept quiet and moved to the corner of the room over near Billie.

Jessica forced herself to stay focused on the screen. It was difficult to keep her attention there, when Ullman kept straying near the window. She didn't have a view of the house outside that window—that was on one of Riley's screens. Jessica kept expecting something to crash through the window and impale Ullman. Another possibility was something sharp stabbing through the wall and getting Billie. Jessica thought carefully about the layout of the house and realized that there was a closet on the other side of Billie's patch of wall.

The only way the rain man could get Billie was if he was already inside the house. Jessica had a camera view of the hall, but not the closet door. There was a gap between the camera that looked at the front door and the one pointed from the kitchen. Between them, they picked up both entrances to the hall, but not the closet door itself.

"Wait," Jessica said. A terrible thought occurred to her.

Joe must have heard the fear in her voice. He stopped pacing and approached.

"What?"

"There's a closet door here, right?"

She pointed to the left of one of the camera views.

"And it would be to the right of this view here."

"Yes," Riley said, taking her eyes off her own cameras for a moment to glance at where Jessica was pointing. "I was using a ladder for the wallpaper removal. I stashed it in that closet earlier."

"What was in the back of the closet?" Jessica asked.

"Wall," Joe said. "Wainscot up to a chair rail, just like the hall."

"If there was a stairway down to the cellar, wouldn't it be right about there? It would be under the other stairs, right?"

Joe shook his head. "I checked out the cellar yesterday. I couldn't even get over to that section as far as I could tell. I'm not sure there ever was a cellar under that part."

"Or it was walled up," Jessica said. She glanced over at Billie who had her ear to the wall. "What if he was already downstairs the whole time."

"There's a vent in the kitchen," Riley said. "Maybe we smelled the smoke coming from the vent and not through the window."

"I didn't smell anything," Billie said.

"Your sense of smell has been ruined by smoking," Jessica said.

Billie shrugged and put her ear back to the wall.

"I was pretty thorough when I checked the cellar," Joe said.

"Right, but you said that it didn't even look like there was a cellar under this part. Why wouldn't they have a cellar under the whole thing?"

Joe stiffened as he considered the question.

Discovery

Gathered in the hallway, they stood in a tight group in front of the closet door. Riley reached in and pulled out the ladder and a few tools that she had stashed in the closet. Jessica passed them to Ullman, who stacked everything against the wall.

"When would he have come in?" Joe asked. "The cameras would have caught him, right?"

"Stop thinking about this rationally," Billie said. "You're going to get us killed."

When she had removed everything that she had put in there, Riley dragged out the stuff that had been there when they arrived. In the back of the closet, she removed a pair of boots, a dusty briefcase, and then a footlocker. Finally, they were looking at the empty closet. Riley took a step back and put her hands on her hips.

"I don't see where..." she started to say.

Joe moved by her and started pulling at the molding and then the wainscoting. Next, he started pushing on it. Joe jumped back when the whole wall creaked and a crack opened on the left side.

"Hidden door," he said.

"Mystery solved then," Billie said. "He's in a hidden part of the basement, and he got there through this secret door. Maybe he snuck past the cameras, or maybe he has been there for a week. Let's burn this house down and cook him alive."

"If he's alive," Jessica said. "And if fire has any effect on him."

Joe nodded. "We can't assume anything. I'm all for burning, but not blindly."

Riley grabbed the handle of a long scraping tool that Ullman had leaned against the wall. She used it to push open the hidden door even more. Jessica could see the stairs that led down into the darkness.

"In Mexico, we tried to dry him out," Joe said. "That might have worked, but it wasn't quick enough. I think burning is still a good idea."

"Perhaps," Ullman said. He grabbed the ladder and unfolded it. Climbing a couple of steps, he was able to reach one of the cameras that Mindy's team had mounted in a corner. The light was still on. Jessica figured it had to be battery operated and wireless. Ullman took some of the painter's tape from Riley's stash of tools and then borrowed the scraping tool she was still holding.

Jessica figured out what he intended to do.

"I'll watch the monitor," Jessica said.

Ullman nodded.

Jessica saw one of the screens dipping and swaying as Ullman began to extend the camera down the stairs. It took a second for the image to adjust to the dim light. When it did, she saw spiderwebs stretching between beams and ancient stair treads with decades of dust. If the man was down there, he hadn't used the stairs to get there.

The view twisted as Ullman reached farther into the darkness.

"Turn to the left a bit," Jessica called. The view jerked and stabilized. She could see the room at the bottom of the stairs.

"Flip it over," she yelled. She had the terrible thought that he might be under the stairs, ready to strike out with a knife between the treads. Ullman figured out what she was asking for and spun the camera so she could see the stone foundation behind the stairs.

Jessica jogged back to the hall.

"It looks clear," she said. "If he's down there, he must be around the corner."

Ullman pulled the tape from the camera and said, "Watch again, please. I'll toss it down."

Jessica nodded.

The intern followed her back into the den. The two of them stared at Ullman's face through the screen.

"Ready?" he asked.

"Yes."

The screen blurred and flipped when Ullman tossed the camera down into the darkness. It finally came to rest at a strange angle. At first, the camera focused on the dirt floor directly in front of them. Then, as it switched into low-light mode again, more of the view came into focus and they could see the angle of the wall and part of the area around the corner.

"Great throw," the intern whispered.

Jessica moved closer to the monitor, trying to see detail in the blob of blackness in the center of the image. For a moment, there was a flare of orange in a tiny dot, and then it faded. Something with a reflective edge moved and slipped to the side, trying to get out of the line of sight of the camera.

The intern gasped.

Jessica reached towards the screen, wishing there was some way to make the image clearer.

It went black.

Jessica exhaled.

"Anything?" Joe asked from the doorway. "We smell cigarette

smoke."

"He's down there," Jessica said. "Let's get some lights."

Basement

Ullman clicked on the light and tossed it down the stairs. It hit the dirt floor, lighting up a small radius. Riley handed him a second one and he tossed that too. They each put on headlamps. Jessica spun around when she heard a clicking sound. Billie took a long drag from a fresh cigarette and blew the smoke up towards the ceiling.

"What?" Billie asked after she exhaled. "He's allowed to smoke inside and I'm not?"

Billie glanced around at everyone glaring at her.

"Fine," she said after another drag. She stubbed the cigarette out on the wallpaper and then said, "What?" when Riley grunted with disgust.

"Weapons?" Joe asked.

"Did that help in Mexico?" Jessica asked.

"It's arguable, but I would say yes," Joe said.

Jessica turned to Ullman.

"I don't know if we did him any harm or not," Ullman said.

"This time, we weren't given any kind of hints about weapons. So why are we here?" Jessica asked.

They all just looked at her.

She started towards the door at the back of the closet.

"Wait," Joe said. "What's your plan?"

"I have no plan. Maybe no plan is the plan," she said. Jessica clicked on her headlamp and pointed it down the stairs. One of the lights down there was out. The other one still lit up a small circle on the dirt floor. Her foot touched the top stair and the house shook with a crack of lightning and the immediate rumble of thunder. Jessica didn't hesitate. She took the next step, swinging her head to probe the light into the corners. After a few steps, she spun around to make sure that the man hadn't doubled back to hide under the stairs. She saw Billie at the top of the stairs, ready to take her first step down.

Just like when Jessica had started down, there was another crash of thunder and lightning as Billie began to descend.

Waiting at the bottom of the stairs, Jessica put out a hand to steady Billie when she slipped on one of the treads. Billie took her hand and they stood together as the others descended. Ullman came last. The intern was still at the top. He took one look at the five of them and then disappeared back through the closet to the hall.

Jessica took a deep breath before she stepped to the side to look around the corner.

Her light was swallowed by the darkness surrounding the man. An orange glow lit up his features—deep grooves in a stone pallor—when he took a long pull from his cigarette. Exhaled, the smoke plunged towards the floor and folded around his legs.

Jessica felt the world begin to tip. She had endured enough vertigo to know that the feeling was a lie concocted by her senses, but she couldn't prevent her legs from trying to adjust to the false narrative. Her hand shot out, searching for a wall to brace herself against and it found Ullman. On her other side, Billie grabbed her arm and kept her upright. She felt one of Riley's hands land on her shoulder. The five of them stood firm in the face of evil.

"What arc you?" Joe asked. His voice came out dry and raspy.

The man took another deep inhale from his cigarette. The tip glowed red but the hand-rolled cigarette didn't seem to be burning down at all. The new smoke rolled out from his nose and cascaded over his chin on its way to join the cloud at his feet.

"I just need a place to get dry," he said. His voice was a deep rumble of thunder.

"Why did you kill everyone I cared about?" Riley asked.

Jessica noticed that the orange glow was reflected in the man's eyes even when his cigarette was nowhere near his face. It was hard to make out any details of his features. It was like trying to look directly at a faint star in the sky. The more Jessica focused on him, the less she was able to see. Tilting her head, she let her headlamp and eyes wander down to his left hand, which hung at his side. It was empty—there was no sign of the long blade that had nearly killed Dylan.

"I need a place to get dry," he said.

"Where did you come from?" Ullman asked.

"I need..."

"A place to get dry," Jessica finished for him. Her vertigo was fading. She pulled her hands from Ullman and Billie and ducked away from Riley's grip. "We can stop trying to get answers from this thing now. It's not able to think—it's just a killing machine that has been disconnected from its original purpose. All we need to do is figure out how to send it back to where it came from."

"How do you propose..." Riley started to say.

She trailed off when Jessica took a step forward.

Jessica kept her eyes locked on the man's left hand even as the right came up to lift the cigarette to his face. With one more step, she saw the weapon. It was like it materialized in response to her approach.

"I think we already know the answer," Jessica said. "Dylan proved that the knife can sever parts from it. All we need to do is get the knife away from it and dice it up."

"It came back," Joe said.

"One problem at a time," Jessica said. She moved to her right, beginning to circle the man. There wasn't much space to work with. The walled-off portion of the secret cellar formed an L shape and the man was tucked into a corner where his weapon could reach everywhere. In college, Jessica had taken a self defense class. Her instructor had always said, "The loser of a knife fight is declared dead on the scene. The winner is declared dead in the ambulance."

The man's knife was long enough that Jessica thought she might actually find an advantage in the small space. As she approached, she put her hand on the stone wall and the pressed herself flat against it with another step.

Billie started to move the other direction, to flank him on the other side.

"Careful," Jessica whispered. Billie was farther away from the knife hand, but that would give him extra room to swing for her.

As Jessica took another small step, she kept her eyes locked on the amber glow of his. In her peripheral vision, she saw Billie stop and then heard the scratchy click of the lighter again as Billie lit her own cigarette. The man turned his head to watch Billie and Jessica slid farther down the wall.

"Give me one of those," Joe said, stepping up.

Billie flipped the cigarette she had just lit towards Joe. It bounced off his hand with a small shower of orange sparks and he picked it up from the floor. After taking a drag, he spit to his left. The man's attention seemed fully occupied by them as Billie lit herself another cigarette.

Jessica was almost close enough to be stabbed if the man was quick.

Riley stepped up next to Joe.

Moving forward another inch, Jessica saw the amber glow of his eyes twitch in her direction. Billie must have seen it too, because she said, "Hey, over here."

As she called, Billie flicked her cigarette towards him and it bounced off of his chest. That was the moment she should have moved—Jessica knew it but she hadn't been able to make herself do it.

"It has only the power we grant it," Ullman said.

The idea was too good to be true. Jessica decided that she had to believe it anyway. The only way she was going to find the courage to act was if she told herself that it was possible to win.

The man's right hand began to lift again so he could take more of the strange smoke into himself.

"Don't you know that will give you cancer?" Billie asked. She had yet another cigarette between her lips and her lighter flared. Jessica's headlamp was focused on the man's left hand. The edge of the blade reflected the cold light back to her. The knife twisted a little, like it was aligning itself with Billie as she said, "That's what we ought to do, just wait for him to get sick from those hand-rolled cancer sticks."

As she finished the taunt, Billie took another big step to the man's right, drawing his attention.

Jessica lunged forward.

Fight

She had no intention of trying to disarm him. Jessica's only thought was to grab his wrist and hang on so she could become a part of his every movement. Locked in her grip, maybe he wouldn't be able to stab at Billie.

Her hands grasped something that gave like cloth but had the texture of weathered stone. She formed her grip just as he began to swing his arm towards Billie. The extra weight of her didn't stop him, although it slowed him quite a bit. Instead of being impaled, Billie was able to slide beyond his thrust and attack from his side.

With a primal scream, Billie jumped up and wrapped an arm around the man's neck, shoving her cigarette into one of his glowing eyes.

Dragging Jessica off of her feet, he reached across himself to stab at Billie.

Joe threw himself at the man's legs and Jessica unintentionally kicked him in the head as the man began to tip. There was another scream from Billie. This one contained more pain than rage and Jessica felt a spray of warm liquid in contrast to the cold dampness of the man.

She was losing her grip as the man thrashed.

Another headlamp approached and strong hands closed around Jessica's when Ullman joined the fight. The two of them managed to pull his arm back from Billie. Although injured and still screaming, Billie didn't let go. Riley focused on the man's fingers, trying to pry them from the weapon as Joe managed to pull the legs out from underneath him.

All of them began a slow topple towards the back wall. For a moment, Jessica thought that her vertigo was returning. The lights were streaking across the ceiling and the whole world began to shift. She realized that the man was falling and picking up speed.

Riley screeched out a victorious yell as she cracked one of the man's fingers backwards. The blade twisted and the tip flashed across Jessica's field of vision. Ullman grunted.

Smashing into the stone wall, Jessica was finally dislodged from the man. She pushed up and saw Ullman grab the handle of the long blade, backing away.

"No!" Jessica yelled. "Cut him."

Ullman looked down at the blade in his hand but kept retreating. Jessica tried to chase after Ullman so she could take the knife and do what he was incapable of doing. Instead, she tripped over Joe, who was gripping and twisting the man's leg.

Billie was shouting nonsense as she pounded with her fists.

Scrambling back to her feet, Jessica caught Ullman and said, "Give it to me. It's the only..."

Ullman pointed at Jessica turned back towards the fight. Billie, smeared with her own blood, was pounding her fists on a wet spot of the dirt floor. Riley stomped in a puddle that swirled with mist and Joe sat on his knees with his hands holding either side of his head as he stared down.

"What?"

"He's dissolving," Ullman said. "Perhaps without his weapon he is..."

The thought was cut off by a scream from upstairs.

The five of them froze. Riley helped Joe to his feet. Beneath Billie's mad fists, the wet spot in the dirt floor was quickly disappearing.

"What's happening?" Joe asked.

Riley looked up. "I think he's upstairs now."

"The intern," Jessica said she rushed around the corner. The light at the top of the stairs seemed impossibly bright. It was a different world up there.

"We can't give up now. We finally have the advantage," Billie said.

Jessica heard slow footsteps above.

"Advantage over what?" Ullman asked. "He's gone."

"We could dig," Joe said.

"The floor is already drying. I'm with Ullman—he's gone," Riley said.

"He's upstairs," Jessica said. "Don't you hear him?"

At the top of the stairs, the rectangle of light began to narrow. She heard the creaking of the closet door and then the click of the latch. Jessica didn't waste any more time. She ran for the stairs. Her headlamp bounced and swung as she climbed and slid through the hidden door into the closet. The knob wouldn't turn. When she heard pounding footsteps in the hall and another scream, Jessica threw her shoulder against the door, trying to break it down. She was collecting herself for a third attempt when a hand grabbed her shoulder. Ullman moved her to the side. He raised his foot and kicked the door with a flat foot aimed right at the wood next to the knob. The first kick splintered the wood. The second sent the door flying open. It banged against its stop.

Jessica was the first through, followed by the others. The front door of the house was wide open. Rain was coming down sideways out there, some of it blowing through the open door.

The others caught up with her in the hall as she walked forward carefully, checking the stairwell and the living room to make sure that the rain man wasn't about to leap out at her.

"Where is he?" Riley asked.

"He's unarmed," Ullman said, holding up the long blade.

"Don't be so sure," Joe said. "He has killed with other implements in the past."

Billie nodded in agreement.

"But that knife can hurt him," Jessica said, pointing at the knife. "Based on the story of Mexico, I'm sure of it."

"I was in Mexico and *I'm* not sure of it," Joe said.

"It's not going to matter if we can't find him," Riley said.

Jessica looked down the hall towards the kitchen, through the front door, and then up the stairs towards the bedrooms.

"He'll probably find us," Jessica said. "Let's go back to the camera feeds and see if we can spot him."

When she started that direction, only Billie followed. Jessica stopped.

"What? Is there a better idea?"

Except for Ullman, they stood and stared at her. He was looking down at the knife in his hand.

"I'm not trying to boss everyone around, but I thought we agreed to stick together. If someone has a better idea than looking at cameras, let's hear it. Otherwise, I'm going that direction."

"I don't know if it's a better or worse idea," Riley said, "but it seems like maybe we should consider going after the intern and making sure he's okay."

"I didn't even catch his name," Joe said.

"We could start with the van," Riley said. "They monitor the cameras from there. Maybe they saw where the intern ran."

"I think the man is in the house. He's after us," Jessica said.

"Don't we owe it to the documentary crew and, at least, the intern?" Riley ask.

"Owe them what? We didn't ask for them to come, and we warned them about the risk. If they didn't take it seriously, who's to blame?" Jessica asked. In her head, it had seemed like a perfectly reasonable thought. As soon as the words left her mouth, she realized how cold and uncaring she sounded. The others were staring at her.

"Fine," Jessica said.

Ullman and Riley led the way. Riley grabbed her raincoat from the hook next to the door and that started a trend. Ullman was the only one of them who went out into the pouring rain with no top layer. Billie and Jessica brought up the rear of the group, keeping their eyes on the house as they moved across the lawn towards the road. The wind whipping through the trees made the shadows dance. The light spilling from the windows did very little to illuminate the area around the house. He could have been hiding anywhere, watching them as they walked to the van.

"Mindy!" Riley called as they approached. "You in there?"

Jessica glanced over her shoulder and saw that they sliding door of the van was hanging open. It was pretty clear that there was nobody inside.

"Damn," Billie said when she took a look. "Now what?"

"There's no sign of them. How many people were in the van?" Riley asked.

"I've only ever seen Mindy out here," Jessica said.

"And the intern," Joe added.

"There was another car though," Billie said. "I think there was another car. Nobody else lives around here, so it must have been them, right? They must have left in the other car?"

"Does it matter?" Jessica asked. "We know what we have to do next."

"It matters whether or not we call the police," Riley said. "If we think that something happened to them..."

"Call the police then," Jessica said. "There's going to be blood."

"Hello?" Billie said, pointing at her arm.

"More blood."

"So you're proposing that we go search the house?" Riley asked.

"I think I know where we're headed," Jessica said. She raised a hand and blotted out the lights from the first floor windows so she could be sure about what she was seeing. When the other lights weren't glaring in her eyes, it was easier to see the faint glow from the window up near the peak of the old house.

"What room is that?" Ullman asked.

Jessica said, "The attic."

Attic

"There's no staircase. How do we even get up there?" Billie whispered as they climbed the stairs.

They were all creeping quietly, as if that would make a difference. The stair treads creaked as the five of them made their way to the top.

"We're going to find a hatch in the top of one of the closets," Jessica said.

"Because of the hidden door to the cellar?" Riley asked.

"No, because that's the way it was as my house," Jessica said. "I'll bet anything that he's up there waiting for me to come."

"Why would we go to him then?" Joe asked. "He has the advantage only if we give it. We can wait in a safe place and make him come to us. Like the den, with all the camera feeds. Why don't we go back to that idea?"

Jessica reached the top of the stairs and turned around to address the others.

"Do what you want," Jessica said. "I'm going after him. I don't know what compelled him to stick around, but I'm going to keep the pressure on."

"I'm with Jessica," Billie said.

The five of them formed a circle in the upstairs hall.

"Yes, I'll go with you," Ullman said. He flipped around the blade and presented the handle to Jessica, anointing her as their leader.

Jessica didn't take the knife. "Hang onto that for now."

"Strategically, I don't think this the right move, but I'll go along with the group," Joe said.

They all looked to Riley to hear her vote. Riley was looking up.

"Well, I suspect you're right about where he is," she said, pointing.

Jessica's headlamp was still on. She had forgotten about it until it swept up and circled the dark spot on the ceiling. She hoped that the dark color was merely because it was wet. A droplet was forming in the center though and it was dark brown. Ullman reached out and guided Riley back a step as the drop swelled and then fell. It splashed at their feet.

"Maybe just a leak," Joe said.

"You really think so?" Riley asked.

"No," Joe said.

For a moment, they all stood there, watching the next drop

form.

"One of these rooms..." Jessica said as she moved to the door of her own room. Before she opened it, she knew that it couldn't be in her room. She had inspected the closet thoroughly. Billie was right there with her as she pushed into the room and went to the closet. The two of them looked at the unbroken ceiling and then pressed on the walls to make sure that they all felt solid.

From the hall, Riley said, "I've looked at the closet in my room, but maybe not thoroughly enough."

They joined her in the hall and then followed Riley into her room. The closet had a light on a pull chain. The bulb flickered to life when Riley pulled the chain. She quickly turned it off again. Back in the hall, Joe and Ullman were coming out of Joe's room.

"Stay together, please," Billie said with a nervous glance upwards. Everyone filed into Billie's room and watched as she pushed a small table away from the closet door. Over her shoulder, she said, "I don't like closets."

When she had cleared a path to the door, she stepped back and let Jessica take charge. The fear was contagious. Jessica put her hand on the door and took a breath before she swept it open. Loose clothes tumbled out.

"Some of those were already in there when we got here," Billie said.

On the shelf in the top of the closet, there were shoeboxes stacked right up to the ceiling. Jessica knew what they would find when they moved all those boxes out of the way. He was waiting for them. Every time she blinked, Jessica imagined her dead brother and sister up there with him as well, but that was impossible. Of course, all this was impossible.

"He couldn't have gone this way," Riley said, looking up at the boxes. "How would..."

She trailed off without anyone having to argue with her.

Thinking that there were shoes in the boxes, Jessica pulled one of the lower ones and tried to topple the whole stack. It was heavier than it looked and when it spilled, colored glass jars tumbled. Most hit the pile of clothes, but one struck the bare floor and shattered, making Riley yelp in surprise.

"Help me," Jessica said.

Ullman was the tallest. He moved forward and reached up with one hand to begin taking the upper boxes down. In his other hand, he still held the knife. They formed an assembly line, ferrying boxes away from the closet and stacking them on the desk near the window. Something metal clinked in the box that Jessica carried. She froze when she heard footsteps above. She spun and saw that everyone heard it. For a moment, they all stood still, listening. When the footsteps stopped, they got back to work, clearing the rest of the boxes.

Silently, Ullman pointed up at the door in the ceiling of the closet. There was no handle—just a rectangle of wood in a simple frame. It would have to be pushed up and out of the way. There would be no way to do it safely. Ullman reached up with the knife, intending to use it to push open the door from below.

Jessica reached out and put a hand on his arm.

"Not with that," she said. "It might be our only advantage."

He nodded and moved when Riley came over with a broom. She reached the handle up and was about to push. Joe put up a finger, requesting that she wait. He was looking at the ceiling. A moment later they heard footsteps moving towards the other side of the house. Joe pointed at Riley then, urging her to continue.

Riley gave the broom a shove and Billie clicked on her headlamp, casting it up towards the opening. From where she stood, Jessica couldn't see anything except a couple of dusty, exposed rafters overhead. Ullman, began to circle, trying to see up through the hatch from a different angle. Riley held up a hand to ask him to stop moving. She pressed a finger to her lips and they all listened to the footsteps begin to come back in their direction. Everyone took a step back from the closet. Jessica clenched her fists, expecting the man to drop through the hole, but he never came.

Instead, the footsteps stopped, leaving them to wonder if he was just out of sight.

"What do we do?" Riley whispered. "Going up there would be suicide."

"No," Jessica said, giving her a stern look. "No, he has as much power as we give him. Don't fuel him."

Riley stared back—either not understanding or not agreeing.

Jessica gestured towards Joe, who was next to the desk chair. He understood and brought the chair over. Jessica set it down just inside the closet. Taking a deep breath, she closed her eyes and envisioned what she intended to do.

Opening her eyes again, she said to herself, "High effort, high risk, very physical."

"What are..." Riley started to say.

Jessica jumped up.

CHAPTER EIGHTEEN

Rain Man

Jessica

Her momentum and a little help from her arms brought her up to where her waist was even with the attic floor. Jessica's headlamp landed on the man's knees, a couple of paces away. He was close enough that she could see that the appearance of rock was an illusion. His pants were crusted with dirt and there was moss growing on them, but they moved like stiff cloth when he shifted his weight.

Swinging her leg up, she pressed to her feet carefully. It seemed like if she moved very slowly and deliberately, maybe he wouldn't move either. Her lamp brought her gaze up to his face. The red eyes reflected the light. Jessica reached up and twisted her headlamp to the side a little. That made him look more human.

For a moment, she expected him to say something. His lips moved like they were working up to it. Then he brought up his right hand and unrolled a pouch. His hands worked with fluid grace. The rolling paper appeared and was stretched by two crusty fingers and a thumb as he sprinkled a line of gray tobacco down the length. The pouch was retired as he rolled the cigarette with one hand and brought it to his lips. The lighter rang when he popped the lid and struck the flame with one motion.

When the orange bud glowed, the cigarette crackled.

"Looks like you dried off," she said. There was a wet spot on the floor a few paces away, but the dusty floorboards were dry under his feet.

The man gave her one slow nod in response.

"I suppose that talking to you is like talking to a parrot," she said. "You know how to speak a few words but there's no comprehension behind that speech."

Jessica didn't really believe what she was saying. After all, he had just nodded in response to a question. Unless his nod was unrelated, he must have understood. His eyes studied her and he made no effort to refute her assertion.

The light around her shifted and Jessica glanced down to see Billie's hand come up through the hole and grip the floor. Below her, Ullman and Riley were working to push up her legs. The man's attention was drawn down to Billie as well. Jessica took a step to the side and attempted to draw his focus, saying, "We've heard that you were called here decades ago to settle a debt. The person who held that debt is gone."

He took another drag from his cigarette and the smoke cascaded down his body when he exhaled. Jessica wanted to tell Billie not to breathe in—the smoke was unnatural—but Billie was already climbing to her feet. Joe grunted as he started to climb up. The man didn't move at all. Jessica shifted to her right and ducked under a low collar beam. They were flanking him again. This time, there was enough room to make a circle. Jessica wondered if that would make a difference.

Billie said, "You don't have any business here anymore. The person who called you is dead. It's time to go back to where you came from."

The man's eyes shifted to Billie when she spoke, but he made no sign that he understood.

As soon as Joe was up, he turned to help Riley climb. Jessica tensed and move a little closer to the man, expecting him to attack Joe while he was vulnerable.

Billie saw Jessica's concern and said, "Don't worry about him. He's probably not even able to kill us. He couldn't kill Dylan and he barely drew blood from me in the basement. He doesn't have any power here."

Jessica watched the man closely as Billie spoke to see if her taunts were having any effect. The man merely took another drag from his cigarette and let more strange smoke roll from his nostrils. Riley was on her feet and holding the man's blade. Ullman must have handed it to her so he could climb.

The man was still staring at Billie, but Jessica could almost feel his attention pulled to the blade that Riley was holding. He wanted it back. Ullman was through the hatch quickly and on his feet. Riley handed the blade to him and the man turned to track Ullman as he ducked down and moved to the center of the attic where the ceiling was taller. They were in a semicircle around the man now.

Billie moved forward and Jessica reached out to stop her. She had no idea what Billie was planning to do, but Jessica knew that it would be a bad idea. Before the man could even react, Billie's hand moved like a flash, snatching the cigarette from him. She took a step back and looked at it.

"No!" Riley said as Billie raised the thing to her lips.

Billie inhaled and then looked down at the cigarette as she exhaled the thick mist.

"Weird," Billie said, spitting a piece of tobacco from her tongue. "Stale."

The lighter sang as the man lit another. He was so quick that Jessica hadn't even seen him roll it.

"You have no business here anymore," Joe said. "The purpose that you were summoned to fulfill is gone."

Billie and the man both took deep pulls from their hand-rolled cigarettes at the same time. When they exhaled, the blue mist cascaded down and swirled on the floorboards, too translucent to see by the time it mingled between them.

"We need you to go back to where you came from," Riley said.

"This is fruitless," Jessica said. "He can't understand us."

When she spoke, he turned his head and locked his glowing eyes on her. There was both hatred and comprehension in his eyes.

"Maybe he can't leave on his own," Ullman said.

While the man was looking at Jessica, his back was nearly turned to Ullman.

"Maybe we're going to have to send him."

Ullman raised the knife as he approached.

The man spun so fast it almost seemed like he had turned himself inside out to face Ullman. He raised his left hand to intercept the blade as Ullman brought it down. Jessica knew what would happen. The man would somehow rip the blade from Ullman's hand and use it to cut him to ribbons. She couldn't let that happen. The image of her father's severed head flashed in her mind.

Jessica lunged forward.

Her headlamp reflected the flash of the blade as the man's hand streaked upwards to take possession of it. Ullman's hand slapped into the man's, and Jessica realized that the man couldn't take the blade because Ullman had already released it. It was flying through the air right towards her. Instead of striking at the man, Ullman had tossed the blade towards her.

Instinct told her to dodge out of the way so it didn't slice her on the way down, but she ignored it. Instead, she made her hands into a basket and moved to intercept the path of the knife. The edge sliced through her raincoat and shirt and bit her skin before it flipped over and she got her fingers around the handle.

The man had caught Ullman's hand and bent it down, overpowering him before grabbing Ullman's throat. He was already choking Ullman by the time Jessica screamed and drove the knife into the man's back. The stiff coat looked like stone, but the knife slid through it almost easily, like she was stabbing a snowman. With another defiant scream, Jessica pulled out the knife and stabbed again. The second attack did no more than the first. She could hear Ullman gagging, trying to draw a breath as he beat and tore at the man's grip.

Jessica pulled the blade free as the man shoved Ullman into Billie, who was coming to help.

The man turned to Jessica. His eyes moved between her and the blade in her hands. The sneer on his gray face was pure rage. His hand came up, reaching for it. Jessica took a step backwards. Her feet swirled in the blue mist. Billie and the man had both lost their hand-rolled cigarettes but there was more of the blue mist at their feet now.

When he reached a second time, Jessica swiped at his hand with the knife, instantly regretting the impulse. She imagined that he would do anything to get his knife back, and that would include grabbing its razor-sharp edge.

His glowing eyes were terrifying. That was the last thing Peter and Julia would have seen—his horrible orange eyes. Her fear was trumped by anger—she wanted to punish this thing that had made her brother and sister suffer. She didn't wait for him to grab for the knife again. She held her ground and swung at his fingers with the blade.

It passed through the air between them, accomplishing nothing.

Jessica let out a frustrated yell and backed away as his relentless, slow approach continued. When she banged into a beam, she swayed on her feet for a moment and made a critical mistake, turning away from the others and the hole that led down to the rest of the house.

"Cut him, Jessica," Joe yelled.

She saw that Billie was struggling to come attack the man from behind, but Ullman was holding Billie back. They were cowards. They were just going to stand there and let her die.

"Cut him again," Riley said.

The command didn't make any sense. She hadn't been able to cut him at all yet. The knife in his back hadn't done anything. When he reached forward again, she slashed with the knife, again forgetting that she had resolved not to yield the weapon. It was simple instinct. She kept thinking that the blade would ward him off.

This time, she saw something drop into the blue mist that now covered the attic floor. Pointing her headlamp down at his hand, she saw why the others were yelling. There was no hand at the end of his arm anymore. Although the blade hadn't seemed to make contact, his hand had been severed at the wrist. Blue smoke was leaking from the stump.

Emboldened, Jessica swung again. This time, the knife missed and he clubbed her with his stump, nearly knocking her off her feet. Joe struggled as Riley held him back. Jessica heard her say, "No, Joe."

Jessica felt more alone than ever. She couldn't imagine why they were abandoning her—leaving her to fight this duel alone.

This time, the man reached with his other hand, and Jessica had to dodge and then swing the knife back defensively. Barely making contact, she saw one of his fingers fall. But she had nearly lost her balance. He didn't seem affected by the loss of digits, but it would only take one good hit to knock her off her feet and she would be doomed.

Jessica gripped the knife in both hands and raised it over her head. He opened his arms, like he was waiting for an embrace. Instead of trying to drive the knife into his heart, Jessica redirected her swing and took his left arm at the elbow. She felt a tiny bit of resistance as the knife passed through him. The forearm held on by a strand of crusty cloth for a moment and then it tumbled into the mist as well. Billie shouted encouragement.

The man's head twitched to the side at the sound of Billie's yell and then he punched forward with his stump, catching Jessica off guard. She stumbled backwards, smashing her head into a beam and knocking her headlamp askew.

"Stop it, Billie, don't help him," Riley said.

Jessica didn't know what that meant. She was the one who needed help, and they were too cowardly to do anything.

The man was still stalking forward. He was almost within range as Jessica reached up to straighten her light. Before he could punch her with his stump again, she swung the knife. For a moment, he caught the blade in the crook of his elbow. It didn't seem possible, but he was pulling it from her grip. It took all of her strength to maintain control and saw the blade through his arm to free it. Once she developed momentum, it moved freely again.

He kicked at her leg and she fell into the mist.

Slamming to the attic floor, her headlamp was enveloped by the fog and she heard one of the others gasp. Jessica tried not to breathe in the thick blue fog. It was impossible. Just as his foot came down to crush her, she rolled away and got back to her knees to retreat again.

Jessica turned to put her back to the others so she could retreat towards help.

The man came forward.

When he reached for her, she saw that his left arm was longer than it should have been. His forearm had been severed, but it was coming back. There was no way to win. Giving into to the futility of fighting him, Jessica realized that she had nothing to lose.

She closed the gap between them, resolving to never let the blade stop. It seemed to pass through him easily as long as she never let it come to rest, so she swung it wildly with one hand, taking back the part of his arm that had regenerated and then taking even more.

He bashed her with his other stump and she countered by slicing off more of that limb.

The tide really turned when she swung the blade low and it passed through one of his legs.

The man tilted to the side.

Jessica screamed Julia's name and then Peter's as she slashed at his head and only managed to take a portion of his absurd hat. She yelled for her father and even her mother, who hadn't lived long enough to suffer the sorrow of the family's real death.

His stump cracked the side of her knee and Jessica felt tendons pull and stretch. She went to work on that arm, hacking and slashing until there was nothing left. The mist swirled around fallen pieces of him. Jessica kept at his torso, cutting it across and lengthwise. When she spotted his head, mostly intact, she focused on that. It had more substance than the rest of them. Jessica had to press the knife through with both hands to chop it into pieces.

Her face dripped with blood and tears.

On her knees, searching for bigger pieces of the man to dissect, she saw lights swirling around her and realized that the others were patrolling the attic. Joe kicked something towards her and she saw that it was a boot so crusted with dirt and dust that it almost looked like it was made of stone. Jessica attacked it with the knife, realizing that there as still a foot inside. None of it seemed real. The knife passed too easily through it all.

The mist was beginning to disperse.

Billie brought her a portion of a hand and Jessica diced it up until it dissolved into mist and then that disappeared too.

There was a hand on her shoulder. Jessica shrugged it off but it returned.

Her tears were flowing fast now, dripping from her nose and chin.

Jessica looked down at the knife.

Her headlamp scanned down the length of it. The sharp edge was polished to a mirror. The rest of the blade was stained dark blue, almost black. The handle was wrapped in skin or leather. When she brought it closer to her face to see the inscription on the blade, Ullman reached out grabbed her wrist. Jessica turned the knife and nearly cut him. Nobody was going to take the thing away from her.

He said, “Don’t get any tears on it. No moisture at all.”

“Oh,” she said. She held it out at arm’s length, but still wouldn’t let him take it away.

Joe and Riley were patrolling the rest of the attic, searching every square inch for any sign of the man.

“Where is he?” Jessica asked.

“You diced him up,” Billie said.

“Yeah, but for a second we thought he was gone in the

basement but then he came back."

There was motion on her left and Jessica turned to see Ullman lowering himself down through the hatch.

"No!" Jessica said. "Stick together."

"I'll be right back."

None of the others seemed alarmed that he was leaving, so Jessica swallowed her objections. The knife felt heavy at arm's length, but she didn't dare move. What Ullman said had made perfect sense—she didn't want to get any moisture on it. She was even afraid that she might be sweating into the skin wrapped on the handle.

After a moment, hands appeared in the hatch and then Ullman was pulling himself back up through. He came to her with a large plastic baggie—the kind with a seal at the top. He shook it open and said, "To keep it dry."

"Are you sure it will work?"

"If I'm wrong, I'm wrong. But it's worth a try."

Jessica nodded. She angled the knife carefully into the bag to make sure that the blade didn't cut through the plastic. When he zipped the top shut, she grasped the handle again through the baggie.

"Hello?" a voice called from below.

"Mindy," Billie whispered.

"If anyone's in this house, the police will be here any second."

Jessica looked to Ullman with wide eyes.

Billie was the one who expressed what Jessica was thinking. Pointing at the bag, she said, "We can't let the cops get ahold of that."

Jessica nodded. "Where can we hide it?"

CHAPTER NINETEEN

Jessica

House

When she arrived back at the house, Jessica saw Riley back on her ladder, scraping the last of the wallpaper. Jessica didn't bother to ask why Riley was bothering to do the chore—it was pretty clear that she just wanted something to keep her hands busy.

"Is it safe?" Jessica asked.

"They're upstairs."

Jessica nodded and took the stairs two at a time. She found Billie on the floor next to the door and Ullman sitting in the chair at the foot of the bed. He had a folder in his lap. Neither of them looked towards the pillow, so Jessica didn't either.

"Is it safe?" Jessica asked.

"I checked about five minutes ago," Billie said. "It was still in the bag, completely dry."

Jessica wanted to go flip the pillow over and see the knife for herself, but decided to take Billie's word for it.

"Joe said he found a place to get an airtight ammo can. He should be back any minute," Billie added.

"Good," Jessica said. She sat on the floor near Billie and leaned against the same wall. "You think it will work?"

Ullman answered, "I'm becoming more and more convinced, but maybe it's just wishful thinking. This article is a translation from a translation, so there are parts that don't make perfect sense, but the major theme is that a vengeful spirit can be attached to an object by an element. In this case, it's water. When that object is exposed to that element, the spirit becomes one with it."

"So it wasn't called by the people after Hilda?" Jessica asked.

"Maybe it was, we can't know for certain," Ullman said.

"I *sounds* right thought," Billie said. "I mean, to me. It just goes along perfectly with the rain and him always wanting to get dry."

They were silent for a minute. Since nobody else was there—the police had been gone for a while, and Mindy's crew had been dismissed—Jessica let her eyes land on the pillow. From her position on the floor, she could just see a corner of the plastic bag that contained the knife.

"Where did you get the article?" Jessica asked.

Ullman raised his eyebrows in a silent question.

"You said there was an article that was a translation of a translation..."

"Oh," Ullman said. "It was in my packet. My packet was about half assignments for cooking and chores and half of it was random research. Simon's people turned up a lot of useful information, but it's hiding amidst piles of folklore and delusions handed down through generations."

"We're the experts," Jessica said. "If we took everything that we've encountered..."

"We could put together the definitive knowledge base," Billie said.

"Exactly."

"That's kinda what I was hoping Mindy would do," Billie said. "But I failed to understand that her idea of success is a sensational story that doesn't have anything irrefutable."

"She *doesn't* want something irrefutable? Why is that?" Jessica asked.

"Popularity comes from controversy, and that comes from people choosing sides. If she puts out a video that clearly identifies the perpetrator and the crime, that's just evidence, not entertainment. You need to have some people believe and some people doubt."

"I guess she got what she wanted then," Jessica said. "Nothing important tonight happened on camera. Goes well with all the rest of the tragedy."

"So another act where we collate all this information would just detract from her story. She pretty much told me that."

Jessica rolled her eyes.

They heard a door close downstairs and then a brief conversation between Joe and Riley.

A few moments later, Joe arrived in the doorway with an olive green box in his hand.

"Watertight, airtight, cold-rolled steel, and heavy," Joe said. He set it down to trigger the latch and open it up. "It's lined with foam so the contents won't rattle around while its transported. We could take out the lining but I think it's a good idea to leave it."

"Agreed," Jessica said.

They stood and approached the bed together.

"Did you get a lock?" Ullman asked.

Joe nodded and said, "Bear in mind, the box is well made but it will give out long before the lock does."

"Fair enough," Billie said. "Locks are only to keep lazy people out anyway."

"Who puts it in there?" Jessica asked.

"Let's move this downstairs first," Joe said, latching the box again. "I bought something else too."

Sealed

Riley handed the piece of paper to Jessica. Riley had written it fast. The ink was smeared in a couple of places, but it was perfectly legible.

Jessica read it aloud.

"Warning to the person who has opened this. The knife inside is not valuable at all, but it is extremely dangerous. The blade has been treated with a potent poison that can pass through the skin and even protective gloves. It will also travel through the air, which is why the knife has been sealed in a plastic bag. Please close the case immediately. Any attempts to handle the blade have ended in tragedy."

"Why not tell the truth?" Joe asked.

"Because nobody would believe it and they would probably try to find a way to exploit it. That may be the reason we're all here today," Billie said.

"I think it's the best approach," Riley said. "But I'm just guessing."

"I wasn't criticizing," Joe said, putting up his hands defensively. "Just asking."

"The box is three point six kilograms. The knife is one point one three. Together, four point seven three. We'll mark that on the outside and we can weigh it to make sure that nothing changes, is that your plan?" Ullman asked.

"Yes, but don't forget the weight of the lock," Joe said. He turned to Jessica. "In Mexico, Dylan thought he had the knife secured, but it traded places with parts of him."

"I heard," Jessica said.

"Hopefully, by measuring the weight frequently we will know if that happens again," Joe said.

"I get it," Jessica said.

"Are we taking that on a plane?" Billie said. "Checking it as luggage? How are we doing this?"

Jessica shook her head. "I don't think we're leaving."

"What?" Billie asked.

The way Ullman was looking at her, Jessica imagined that he was surprised as well.

"We still don't know why this house was chosen. We had one confrontation with him and we secured the knife for who knows how long. We've made good strides, but I don't think our work here is through."

Billie turned and walked a few paces away.

"I think she's right," Riley said. "At least for now."

Joe shook his head. "I think we do know why this house was chosen though. Doesn't it make sense to you? They sent us to a place where it was likely to rain and where he would attack us."

"No," Jessica said. "All that research about the people who lived here? What was that about? Why did I have to get a job and Riley had to strip wallpaper. I think we owe it to ourselves to put answers to these questions and understand how the puzzle all fits together."

"Can we get this wrapped up before we continue the debate?" Ullman asked. He was pointing to the ammo case that was still open.

Everyone agreed. The weighed the lock and added that to the sum before they put everything together. Riley's note was laid on top of the bag before they closed the lid and sealed the box. Joe verified that the seal couldn't be broken without removing the lock and then Ullman weighed the whole thing again to make sure of the number before he wrote it on the side of the green metal.

Billie returned and watched the process with her arms folded across her chest.

"I want this to be over," Billie said. "But I'll admit that in my mind I planned for us to be here for at least a month or so before we resolved everything. I guess with that in mind I can stay and help figure things out."

"Thank you," Jessica said.

"I want to make a list of the questions that are left to be resolved," Billie said. "So we know what our goal is. I don't want to live here for a year just debating whether or not we're finished."

"Agreed," Ullman said. "I can go along with that as well."

They all looked to Joe.

"I need to make some calls," Joe said. "I made some promises to my family. I'll have to let them know."

"Do what you need to do," Jessica said, "but remember that this whole thing was planned for five people, okay?"

"Yeah, I know. I signed up for this. I'll figure out a way to honor that."

Work

Jessica waved goodbye to Chelsea and left through the back door. She automatically held her breath as she walked by the dumpster and then kicked into a jog after she passed through the hole in the fence. Running up the hill still stole her breath every time, but it was a good way to shake herself back to reality after finishing a shift at the Croc. The work was sometimes hectic and sometimes monotonous. It was never engaging, except when a customer brought up something interesting. That day, an older man in a gray sweater had brought up something that Jessica couldn't wait to share with the others.

She burst through the kitchen door and found Riley finishing up with the afternoon weighing of the box.

"Still perfect," Riley said.

"Good. You wouldn't believe what I found out today," Jessica said.

"Oh yeah? What?"

"Not yet. Let's get everyone together."

"You'll have to wait until dinner then. Billie's going to be at the library until it closes."

Jessica nodded.

She waved to Riley and headed through the living room. The finish on the hall floor was still curing, according to Riley. It would be a few more days before they were allowed to walk on it. Jessica ran up the stairs and ducked under the plastic that Riley had set up to catch the debris from her latest remodeling.

She checked her clock and decided to shower before a nap. Her schedule was about to shift again and she would have to get all the sleep she could.

Dinner

When she descended, Jessica was still wiping water from her face. After her nap, everything had been foggy. The cold water had helped her get her thoughts back in order. The smell of food woke up her hunger. There was laughter coming from the kitchen. Joe and Riley sat at the table while Ullman stirred something on the stove.

"Smells delicious," Jessica said. "What's for dinner."

Joe and Riley laughed again.

"It's bug spray," Ullman said. "This concoction is supposed to deter the beetles from attacking the lilies in the side yard."

"I told him that they sell perfectly good insecticide down at the hardware store. I almost bought a bag yesterday just to prove the point."

"That's not the way I want to approach this problem," Ullman said, turning back to the stove.

Riley smiled and Jessica covered her mouth to hide a laugh.

A moment later they heard the front door open and Billie call, "I could use some help."

Jessica rushed to go find out what the issue was. Billie had a stack of books under her arm and she was trying to carry two full paper bags as well. She took one of the bags and smelled something more exotic and delicious than Ullman's bug spray.

"Indian," Billie said. "I didn't know what you liked so I got a bunch of different things. We can sample."

"Cool," Jessica said. She led the way to the kitchen, where Joe was up and gathering dishes and utensils to set the table.

"We're all here, Jessica. What was your big news?" Riley asked.

Jessica set down the bag and made sure she had everyone's attention.

"Does the name Victor mean anything to anyone?"

Joe said, "No." The others just shook their heads.

"How about the name Vincent Torre?"

"Of course," Billie said. "He's the one that Joe had me research a couple of days ago."

"One of the under-investigated suspects in the murder of Mary and her father-in-law in this house," Joe added.

"Well, it turns out that Vincent Torre and Victor are one in the same," Jessica said. "And the ghost of Vincent Torre is the one who haunts the stock room of the Croc 'N Shop."

"What? Why?" Billie asked.

"I thought we could ask him that ourselves," Jessica said.

"Our attempts at seances will never be successful," Joe said. "We simply don't have everything we need. Most importantly, unless we come up with a personal possession of Vincent Torre—one that he specifically felt a strong attachment to—we don't even have the prerequisites."

"Not to mention that it's all nonsense," Riley said.

"Yes," Joe said, pointing to her, "on top of the fact that it's all nonsense."

"Well, I believe that I can get us the personal possession and then we can find out one way or the other whether or not it's nonsense."

"How?" Billie asked.

"More importantly," Riley said. "Is this a question that can be answered while we eat? I'm starving."

Jessica smiled and nodded. Billie gave them a tour of each of the containers of food. For about half of them, she had a pretty good idea of the ingredients of the dish. For the other half, she only knew the name, and that was because they were scrawled on the top of the container in grease pencil.

Jessica judged the contents based on how they looked. She ended up with rice and something that had carrots and something else that had peas. She was happy with what she had picked out. Both things were delicious.

When everyone had food and had taken their seats, she jumped into her explanation.

"I was ringing this guy up—older guy, gray sweater—when Erika must have knocked something over in the storeroom. The guy looked over my shoulder in that direction with wide eyes, so

I said something like, 'Don't worry, that's just our store ghost, Victor.' He asked 'Vincent?' and I corrected him. Then, when he was about to leave, I asked him why he thought I said Vincent."

Billie got up and brought a pitcher of water to the table.

"He told me that his family had lived in the area for a million years and that the black sheep of their family was the notorious Vincent Torre. It was widely speculated that he was the actual killer despite never really being investigated for the crimes in this house."

Billie interjected, "The mob thought they had their culprit with the drifter, and then after he was executed there was sufficient evidence to try Gerald Jackson for the same crime."

"Who died in jail while awaiting execution," Joe said.

"Exactly," Jessica said. "So my customer said that his distant relative would have been easily convicted of the crime as well but the legal system's official position was that the correct man had already been punished."

"Twice, it sounds like," Riley said.

Jessica nodded. "With no justice from the authorities, a mob formed and they were intent on making things right. Vincent Torre had a small house down the hill from here, on the plot of land where the Croc 'N Shop now sits. That's where they trapped and murdered him after they extracted a confession."

"That makes sense," Billie said. "I knew that he died under strange circumstances, and that there were plenty of people who believed him to be the real killer. Others were just as adamant that he had nothing to do with it."

"The really interesting thing was the method by which they got him to confess," Jessica said. "My customer said that in his family they talked about Vincent Torre being forced to confess by a demon, although some people said that the demon was simply his own conscience."

"Our demon?" Riley asked.

Jessica raised her hands and shrugged.

"That's one of the things we can ask Vincent. I have a phone number for the customer. He said that he's in possession of

Vincent's most treasured possession—his father's Bible. It's inscribed with the family history dating back to when they immigrated. I asked if we could borrow it to transcribe the information and he said that we can take it for as long as we need it."

"That could be powerful," Joe said.

CHAPTER TWENTY

Vincent

Seance

"Push that back against the cooler," Jessica said.

Ullman slid the rack of chips. It chattered across the tile floor.

Jessica had to wiggle the lock a few times to get it to engage. Since the store was always open, the lock didn't get much use. To the right of Chelsea's desk, she found a switch to shut off the outside sign. Billie had set up the candles. Joe was already sitting in his place at the head of the circle, doing his silent incantations with his eyes shut.

Ullman set down a thin mat for his knees before lowering himself to the floor.

"Cameras are off?" Billie asked.

"Yeah, not that it matters," Jessica said. "I don't think there's any law against having a seance. The worst they can do is fire me."

"I just feel better not being on camera."

Jessica nodded. They took their positions around the circle. Jessica readied herself by getting out a match from her box and setting it on top. On her right side, she had the Bible at her right side and she slid it back a little.

"Make sure that's not in the circle until we get to that part,"

Billie said.

Jessica nodded.

Joe's lips moved silently and Jessica adjusted her legs until she was more comfortable on the hard floor. Next to her, Billie kept fidgeting with her shirt, pulling it away from her bandage.

"Don't fuss with that," Riley said.

"It itches," Billie said.

Joe's silent chants turned into a whisper that grew louder until Jessica could finally make out the words.

"I call upon the spirits. I call them against their will to join us here. I call upon Vincent Torre for those who might know him seek his presence. I remind him that he is bound by the covenant of the dead."

The chant repeated after that. When he raised his finger, they all joined, adding their voices to Joe's. While they spoke, the five of them took their matches and struck them all on the first completion of the chant. Each touched their match to the candle in front of them. The flickering flames lit their faces from below.

On the third repetition, Joe pointed to Jessica and she slid the Bible into the center of the circle. In came to a stop in a spot that looked to be precisely equidistant from each of them—the center of the star that they formed. It jolted to a stop as if it were magnetized to that exact position.

Jessica glanced at Riley who was watching the Bible with wide eyes.

Joe's voice rose to nearly a shout. That was their cue to stop.

When they all finished with the word "dead," the cover of the Bible flipped open.

"Vincent Torre, have you joined us here tonight?"

For a moment, nothing happened.

Jessica heard Riley sigh. They had been through this several times before. The house seemed so lively with strange noises and apparitions, but they never could make any contact, no matter how carefully they followed the steps that Joe had researched.

"The cover flipped," Jessica said.

"It's drafty in here you had just shoved it," Riley said.

"The shove happened well before the flip," Jessica said.

"I'll remind you both that we're supposed to be focused on nothing but Vincent," Joe said. "You have to clear your mind of everything except him and you have to believe in the process."

Jessica glanced over at Riley, but she had already closed her eyes. Jessica did the same.

"Have you joined us here tonight, Vincent Torre?"

When she heard the whisper, Jessica's eyes flew open. The sound had just been the feathery pages of the Bible flipping, but it had almost sounded like a voice saying, "Yes."

"Do you know why we've called on you tonight, Vincent Torre?" Joe asked.

Jessica felt the breeze before she saw the pages flip. Riley was right—the place really was drafty. The wind could almost explain how the pages turned on their own. To Jessica, though, the wind didn't explain the whispery sound that breathed, "Murder."

Joe must have heard it as well because he asked, "The murder you committed, or your own murder?"

"Own," the pages responded.

"Who killed you?" Joe asked.

There was no response.

"He's at the end," Billie said. Jessica saw what she was pointing at. There were no more pages left to turn. From the three short answers, the Bible was already turned to the back cover.

Ullman leaned towards Joe and whispered something.

With a single nod, Joe changed the question.

"*What* killed you?"

The pages flipped back the other direction and the airy response flipped through the entire Bible.

"Wind."

Nobody spoke for a few moments. Jessica looked to Joe, but he didn't seem to know what to say.

"Did it say *Wind*?" Riley asked.

"That's what I heard," Billie said.

"The D was hard to make out, but I believe that is what it

said," Ullman said.

"Again, Vincent Torre, we ask what killed you?"

Jessica felt the breeze and then saw the pages begin to flip. They picked up speed and she concentrated, trying to find some kind of word in the fluttering noise. This time, she couldn't hear anything distinct in the whispering pages. Glancing around at the others, they seemed just as confused as she was. Jessica nearly screamed when something hit her in the back. She spun on her knees just in time to see another small bag of chips fly from a rack and hurtle towards her.

Ullman reached back and steadied another metal rack that was beginning to rock as it was buffeted by the wind. Jessica realized that it was spinning in a circle around the interior of the store, like a tornado. Billie folded both arms over her head to protect herself as magazines and newspapers pelted her.

Riley reached forward and cupped her hands over her candle. Jessica remembered what Joe had said—it took all five candles to open the seance, and at least one of the had to still be burning to successfully close the ceremony.

She looked up to Joe to tell him to start the process quickly—they had to close the seance before the store was ripped apart by the wind. He was already reciting the words. He raised his voice to be heard over the chaos.

"I dismiss the spirits and remind them of the covenant of the dead. Their invitation is revoked. Their presence is no longer wanted. I dismiss Vincent Torre and revoke his invitation. I dismiss the spirits. The covenant of the dead demands immediate compliance."

The wind was still building. One of the shelves behind Jessica toppled.

Billie yelled something but her voice was taken away by the wind.

Finally, Billie reached into the center of the circle and Jessica understood. She had forgotten to take the personal item from the center. Joe was reciting the incantation, so he was forbidden to touch the personal item—to do so would be to invite the spirit into himself.

Billy struggled against the wind to grab the Bible. She flipped it shut and then tugged it from its spot on the floor.

The wind died almost immediately.

Joe finished his speech at full volume and then fell silent, swaying in place like staying upright was a difficult feat.

"I told you this was all nonsense," Riley said. She groaned as she unfolded her legs and started to get to her feet.

"I don't know what we learned," Joe said. "But it was a powerful lesson."

"I think I have an idea. I would prefer not to speak of it here though."

House

As she trudged up the hill, Jessica decided that she had never been so tired. It had taken hours to clean up the store after their seance and then she still had to finish the rest of her shift before Erika came in to relieve her. She wanted nothing more than to take a quick shower and get some sleep, but that wasn't what awaited her. The others would be waiting to hear what Ullman had to say. He had agreed to keep his revelation to himself until she got back.

They weren't in the kitchen when Jessica came through the back door. For a moment, she had the thought that maybe they had all packed up and left her there. Together, they had been through so much. Perhaps surviving a tornado inside a Croc 'N Shop was beyond the limit of their patience.

It was a pleasant thought, she decided. The idea that they could all just give up and move on was a relief from the monotony of their mission.

When she heard the cough from the living room, Jessica's fantasy evaporated.

She headed that direction and found them all sitting around the coffee table. It was like they were having another group meeting, like back in Vegas.

"What's the story?" she asked as she took one of the chairs. It was a struggle to keep her eyes open as she blinked at Ullman.

"I have a list of elements that can bind a Tulpa to an object. One of them is the wind. I believe we accidentally stumbled upon one of those objects last night with Torre's Bible."

"Where is it now?" Jessica asked, sitting up straight. The idea that they might be having this conversation in the presence of the object terrified her for some reason. There was a facet of these mysterious objects that demanded attention. Giving them that attention was dangerous.

"Ullman had me put it in the trunk of my car," Billie said. "I want to get the Bible back to that guy as soon as possible. The other thing is still in its box, upstairs."

Jessica exhaled and felt her heartbeat begin to return to normal.

"Maybe we should destroy the thing in the box," Jessica said.

"There might not be an easy way to do that," Ullman said. "I think there is a better solution."

He took a deep breath and then explained.

"Last night, during the ceremony, it occurred to me that we weren't simply talking to Vinent Torre, we were also talking to the thing that hounded him and murdered him. I believe that the reason this house was chosen was because the creature stalking Torre was the same type of thing that stalked all of you."

"No," Jessica said. "I refuse to believe that."

Ullman looked like he didn't know how to respond to Jessica's immediate anger.

"Jess, it makes sense. Wind is an element. Vincent said he was murdered by wind. Why is it difficult to believe that the tornado was..."

Jessica shook her head. She squeezed her eyes shut and turned her head down towards the floor. Jessica finally got control enough to speak again. "I can't live with the idea that they're still being hounded by him. They have to be in peace now."

Riley spoke softly. "We don't know that Vincent is still being hounded by the wind, Jessica. Maybe the wind was just summoned because we called Vincent to this realm."

"Look," Billie said, "In my opinion, a seance doesn't call the actual person back—we were just, like, shining a light through a glass plate with Vincent's image imprinted on it, you know? We can learn things about him through a seance, but the Vincent is at peace. Your family is at peace too."

"I don't need you guys to humor me," Jessica said.

They were silent for a moment before Ullman continued.

"My real point is that Vincent and you have something in common. It was a different Tulpa for him—bound to a Bible and with the attributes of wind instead of water—but perhaps it sheds light on how to contain your monster."

"He's your monster too now," Joe said. "You've witnessed him twice now, Ullman. You've lost someone to him. You're the same as us."

"Fair," Ullman said.

"I don't understand how this gets us any closer to an answer," Jessica said.

"I would have to assume that someone made that Bible safe somehow. Until we began the ceremony, it didn't seem to be dangerous at all. Perhaps there's a way to secure the knife as well," Ullman said.

Jessica let out a long breath. "Sounds like a long shot."

"How so?" Riley asked.

"We have the thing contained in an airtight, watertight box upstairs, right? We're starting to think that he won't come back if we keep that thing dry. I say we destroy it. We find a volcano and drop the thing in, or convince some billionaire to shoot it into space. Instead, Ullman thinks that maybe there's a procedure that someone used on a Bible a hundred years ago and we can reproduce that procedure in order to... what? We're going to lock the evil into that knife so it can only be released by a seance? Doesn't that seem like a long shot to you?"

"I like the billionaire idea," Billie said. "Do we know any?"

"I'm being serious," Jessica said. "I'm not willing to take any chances with this thing. I'm not signing off on doing anything until we're sure it's going to work."

CHAPTER TWENTY-ONE

Jessica

Work

The bell rang and Jessica looked up from her book.

Erika came right to the counter and put both hands flat on its surface.

"Where's Paul?"

Jessica glanced up at the clock. Paul had gone out ten minutes before to take the trash to the dumpster. It was a job that only took a few seconds.

"Did you look in the back seat of his car? He's probably taking a nap," Jessica said.

Erika rolled her eyes and let out an exasperated sigh.

"Why?" Jessica asked, setting her book to the side.

"You know that girl, Tanya?"

Jessica shook her head.

"She used to go out with that guy who shaves his head. Everyone calls him Dome, but his name is some Russian thing. Anyway, Tanya told everyone that Dome was planning to rob a place, take the money, and moved down to Costa Rica because he thinks he's going to be a surfer or something."

"Erika?"

"And I said, I hope he's not planning to rob the Croc because we keep a shotgun under the counter."

"Erika?" Jessica asked, trying to interrupt again.

"But then Paul told everyone that there was no shotgun and if they wanted to rob the place they should come on a Wednesday afternoon when the manager is away. He even told them that there's only one person on duty on Wednesday afternoons. Guess who that is?" she asked, pointing to her own head.

"Erika, I can see Paul walking towards the donut place," Jessica said, pointing through the window.

With another dramatic eye roll, Erika pushed away from the counter and the bell rang again as she exited.

Jessica had just picked her book up when the bell rang again. She put the book down.

"What's her problem?" Billie asked, pointing through the window. Erika was outside, already yelling at Paul as she stalked after him.

"Paul is trying to get Erika killed again. It never works. I don't know why he still tries."

"He probably has a crush on her. It's the modern day equivalent of pulling her hair."

Jessica laughed.

"You working tonight?" Billie asked.

"No. I'm just covering for Chelsea until she gets back. She had an appointment. Why?"

"Ullman found the guy. Turns out he's only a couple hours away."

Jessica looked away and watched Erika through the window. When she yelled, Erika had a tendency to throw her arms out in random directions. Some people would have flinched away, but Paul was accustomed to it. He simply stood there and listened.

"Jess?" Billie asked.

"Yeah?"

"Do you want to come with us?"

"No. But I will. I'll be home in an hour or so. Does that work?"

Billie nodded. "See you then."

Trip

Jessica stared through the car window at the passing scenery. The three of them—Billie, Riley, and Jessica—were packed into the rear seat.

Glancing to the left, she looked at the box that Riley had on her lap. They had no intention of showing it to anyone. They just couldn't bear the thought of leaving it at the house unguarded.

"Did you see Mindy's footage?" Joe asked over his shoulder from the passenger's seat.

"Yeah," Billie said. "It was pretty much as we expected. They cut in the shot of the camera being tossed to the bottom of the stairs, and then they just showed the closet door with our audio and subtitles. Very mysterious. Nothing illuminating."

"And you told her she wasn't allowed to use it?"

"Of course," Billie said.

"Tell me again how you found this guy, and why you think he knows something," Jessica said.

Joe turned all the way around in his seat.

"We started with Mitch—the customer who talked to you in the store. When we traced his lineage, it turned out that he wasn't actually a blood relative of Torre, but from a side branch. But from his recollection and the family tree in the Bible, we were able to find a living blood relative of Torre. Her name is Sophia, and we didn't tell her about the Bible because we thought it should stay safe with Mitch."

"Yeah," Jessica said. "But the guy we're talking to tonight?"

"I'm getting to it," Joe said. "It took us weeks to make these connections."

Jessica looked through her window again, leaning her head against the glass.

"Sophia didn't know much of anything about the death of Torre, but she had been approached by an antiques dealer at one point who was looking for Torre family artifacts for a client. Everyone assumed that the client was another relative, but based on what Ullman found..."

"We think that the client may be familiar with these types of objects," Ullman said. "And that it's not family history they were interested in."

"So we set a meeting."

"Got it," Jessica said. "We got this guy's name through a relative of Torre."

"That's the short version, yes," Joe said.

The navigation system beeped and then prompted Ullman to turn right.

With a left turn, they entered the parking lot of a cluster of shops. Ullman drove past those and parked near the door of restaurant.

"I'll stay here with the box," Jessica said.

"No," Riley said. "You go in."

"Why?"

"Because I'm already convinced by what Ullman has turned up. I know you aren't. If anyone needs to talk to this person first-hand, it's you."

Jessica sighed. After thinking it over for a moment, she opened her door and stepped out. The air was humid. Looking up at the clouds, she wondered how long it would be before the rain started.

"Sit in front," Jessica said. "Lock the doors. If it starts to rain or anyone comes within six feet of the car, press the horn and don't stop until the battery wears out. Okay?"

"Yeah," Riley said, swallowing. "Got it."

As they walked inside, Jessica scanned the parking lot. She saw a man in a black SUV parked over near the bank. He was staring straight forward at nothing.

"I'm going to stay here," Billie said when she saw the guy. "By the door. With my whistle and a can of pepper spray."

"Yeah," Jessica said, "thanks."

Jessica, Joe, and Ullman went in alone. When Ullman told the hostess that they were there to meet someone, she smiled, pulled menus from the podium, and told them to follow. Jessica glanced over at the bar as they passed. Two guys, not sitting together, were staring up at the TV screen. Something about their expression told Jessica that they didn't really care about what they were watching.

Jessica leaned towards Joe as they walked.

"I don't like this."

Joe just nodded.

In the corner, the hostess led them to a deep booth where a man and a child sat on one side of the table.

"MacGregor?" Ullman asked. Both the man and child nodded. Ullman slid across the bench, making room for Joe and Jessica.

She didn't swing her legs under the table.

Ullman's eyes were fixed on the boy. With a second glance, Jessica understood why. Based on his size and shape, he should have only been seven or eight years old. The boy's face told a different story. The wrinkles around his mouth and eyes and the way the skin sagged under his chin, he could have been in his sixties. He looked too weary to be a kid.

He sounded weary too.

"The object you described to my agent," the kid said. "It's in your possession?"

"No," Ullman said. "But it's secure."

"Good. That's good. An object like that should be kept secure."

"Why do you want it?" Ullman asked.

The boy considered that question for a moment before answering.

"I like to keep things orderly. I can't sleep well at night when things are out of place. You never know what could happen. So, when I know that there's something out there potentially out of place, I track it down. I just want everything secure."

Ullman cleared his throat and nodded. "I've heard that you have an interest in using these things. Maybe they can be used to solve problems."

"No!" the boy shouted. In that moment, he really seemed like a child. It was like Ullman had just told him that it was time for bed and he was objecting.

After collecting himself, he continued.

"No. These things are not tools, and they cannot be controlled. They can never safely be used. It's like trying to swing a sword that has no hilt. Blood will be drawn from every party involved."

"Are you speaking from experience?" Ullman asked.

"Are you mocking me, Mr. Ullman?"

Jessica saw Ullman stiffen just a little at that question. She was certain that Ullman had never used his real name during the course of his research. Somehow, this boy had discovered Ullman's identity. It raised the question of what else the boy might know.

"Stop," Jessica said. "If you really know how to secure one of these items, and your interest is to make them secure, then tell us."

"Why?"

"Because we know of one that's definitely *not* secure," she said.

Ullman locked eyes with her and gave his head a tiny shake.

"He's not going to tell us anything if we're not honest about why we want to know," Jessica said.

"She's right," the boy said.

Joe looked at Jessica and then turned to Ullman. "I'm with her. If we don't trust this guy then let's leave. If we do trust him, then let's tell what's going on."

As Ullman considered Joe's ultimatum, she got ready to stand. She was certain that Ullman would want to walk away. Jessica had no intention of trusting the little person. He was masquerading as a child and he was clearly anything but. That alone disqualified him for receiving her trust.

"Trust," Ullman said. "I'm inclined to trust you, Mr. MacGregor, when you say that you want to establish order. You sound sincere on that point. However, I'm also inclined to believe that you might be the source of the current chaos."

"I'm not the source of anything," the boy said. "I want nothing more than to rest."

"How do these things get loose in the world?" Joe asked.

"When a problem develops, people tend to always believe that there must be a solution. They exert their full effort trying to solve the problem. Then, when it appears intractable, they decide that more power will yield better results. That's when people seek out these objects. There's nothing more powerful than an object bound to a thought."

"Yes, but *who* does the binding? And can they be unbound?" Joe asked.

"All the practitioners of binding are lost," the boy said, shaking his head. "Their magic can't be undone, only bottled up and protected. To that, I've dedicated this past decade. There are only a few still loose. Once I've secured those, I will be able to rest."

"How many exist and how many do you have?" Jessica asked.

"It's impossible to know how many exist," the boy said. "And I would rather not divulge how many I've secured."

"None?" she asked. "Is that about right?"

The boy's guard shifted at her tone. He looked ready to act. In response the boy shot the guard a look and he settled again into his seat.

"I would rather not divulge the exact number, but believe me I've gone to great lengths to rid the world of this chaos."

Jessica looked at Joe and then Ullman. "Let's go. He doesn't know anything."

"That's ridiculous," the boy said.

"You may have possessed one of these things at one point, but you don't anymore," Jessica said. "And I don't believe for an minute that you have any intention of reducing chaos. You thrive on it."

She got up and Joe followed her.

Ullman slid over to the end of the bench but kept his eyes on the boy.

"If you're sincere," Ullman said. "Then now is the time to prove it. Otherwise, you won't see us again."

"I have nothing to prove to you, Mr. Ullman," the boy said. "And whether or not I see you again is not up to you."

Ullman stood.

The guard next to the boy stood and towered over all of them. For a moment, Jessica thought that the guard would try to grab them. He looked powerful enough to take all three of them at once. Maybe it was too public a place, or maybe MacGregor thought there was an easier way to get what he wanted. Whatever the reason, the guard only stood there as Jessica hurried out. The two suspicious people at the bar were gone. Jessica exhaled with relief when she saw that Billie was still at the door and Riley seemed unmolested in the car.

"I wonder if we pushed too hard too fast," Ullman said as he came through the door to the outside.

"Save it for the car," Jessica said. "Let's get out of here."

Billie pushed away from the wall. "I'll drive."

Home

"The boy knew Ullman's name. So they probably know where we're staying," Joe said.

Jessica was looking through the rear window, watching for the black SUV.

"Regardless, I want to know that they're not following," Jessica said.

Billie took a sharp turn at the last second and they all slid over to the left side of the vehicle.

"Give us some warning," Joe said.

"Can't," Billie said. "If I plan my turns, they'll be able to follow us."

"Do you think these people are psychic?" Riley asked.

"Why not?" Billie said over her shoulder.

The tires screamed when she took another turn. They pulled to the curb on an empty street and sat motionless for a moment. Billie pulled into a driveway and turned around.

"Is the Bible going to be safe?" Riley asked. She looked down at the box in her lap. "If we're so worried about this thing falling into his hands, shouldn't we be concerned about the Bible?"

"I can't imagine how MacGregor would have a way to trace

back to Mitch," Ullman said. "But perhaps we should contact him and let him know that dangerous people could be looking for the Bible."

"It's infuriating that we finally found someone who has information about this thing but they're no help in disposing of it," Riley said. "We went through all this to learn nothing."

"We might have learned something," Jessica said.

"What?" Joe asked, leaning forward to look at her.

"MacGregor was a strange combination of someone who looked both old and very young. What does that suggest to you?" Jessica asked.

"Hilda's story," Riley said immediately. "In her latest version she talked about the person who she thought called the man into existence to kill her."

"Right," Jessica said. "So, let's assume that MacGregor is the same person, or same type of person who Hilda ran into years and years ago. If he could call the man into existence back then, why would he need us now?"

"MacGregor either lost the power..." Joe started.

"Or never had it," Riley finished.

"I'm guessing that he never had it," Jessica said.

"So who did?" Ullman asked from the front seat.

CHAPTER TWENTY-TWO

Hilda

Meeting

Jessica sat in the chair at the end of the coffee table, looking straight forward as the others filed in. People seemed to understand that the tone of the meeting was pure business. Maybe they had picked it up from the wording of the request, or maybe it was just a sense that they got from the room.

Dylan and Billie sat together at the bar. For once, they didn't gossip or whisper smirking comments to each other. Jessica had no doubt that Billie had already filled him in about everything that happened. Those two shared everything.

Christopher sat close to Jessica on the couch. He reached out and touched the arm of her chair, saying, "Thank you for going. I'm so glad you came back in one piece."

Jessica acknowledged him with a nod.

When everyone was present, Joe stood up from his seat on the couch. Wahid looked up at him as he spoke.

"Thank you all. I suppose you understand why we weren't able to give updates while we were away. I'm sure they were long months for everyone," Joe said. "Without getting ahead of the story, I'd like to tell you that I believe the trip to have been a great success. I'll turn things over to Riley for the bulk of the narrative."

As Joe sat down, Riley stood. Bending over, she moved the bag from its spot at her feet to the center of the coffee table. Laura's hand moved up to her chin. A couple other people shifted uncomfortably in their chairs as Riley reached into the bag. There was mystery surrounding the trip that the five of them had taken. With that mystery, Jessica saw that perhaps they had earned a little distrust.

People appeared to relax a little when Riley pulled a stack of papers from the bag. She handed around stapled bundles. Jessica was surprised by the thickness when she took her copy. Her own contribution had been just a simple sketch of daily life at the haunted house, with a bit more detail around the encounters with the man.

Flipping open to the first page, Riley led everyone through the outline and quickly touched on the major bullet points. Everyone would be able to take home their copy and study the account at length.

"I don't understand," Mel said. "We always share our stories orally and ask clarifying questions along the way. Why aren't we doing that now?"

"Tonight, I think we have more important things to discuss," Riley said.

With that, she gestured towards Jessica and sat back down on the couch. Leaning forward, Riley gathered her bag and put it at her feet.

Jessica cleared her throat, stood, and tugged her shirt to smooth it.

Ullman moved silently over to the patio door and locked it from the inside. His keys jingled as he slipped them back into his pocket. He gave her a nod to let her know that it was the last door.

The twelve of them were locked in.

"On our trip, we discovered the true origin of the rain man. The person who called him to our realm is in this room."

Reveal

Nobody moved or said a word. All eyes were locked on Jessica.

She had almost hoped that the statement would make the guilty party spring to their feet to decry the whole process, but nobody even twitched.

Jessica stepped around to the back of her chair and leaned against it as she continued.

"This isn't a witch hunt," Jessica said. "We're not here to exact any retribution. Although we believe that the man was conjured on purpose, we don't believe that the person had any intention to hurt innocent people. It was merely an accident that he was turned loose on the world."

Wahid raised a finger with a question on his lips.

Jessica raised her voice and kept speaking.

"However, until we have an honest account of exactly what happened, we can't consider this issue fully closed. Regardless of whether or not we've neutralized the man, we have to spell out precisely how and why he came into this world."

She took a deep breath, offering one more opportunity for someone to speak up and take responsibility.

Jessica looked at each of them, letting her eyes land on theirs for just a moment.

"Okay. Fine. I'll go through this step by step," she said. "Once we had the knife in our possession, we were able to draw some conclusions as to the origin of the man. It's a entity of chaos, tied to an object. When an entity like this is pulled into an object, it appears to be colored by the attributes of it. In this case, it acquired an evil edge designed to taste blood."

Jessica paused and took a step back.

Ullman brought the case to her, setting it at her feet.

Moving deliberately, Jessica took her time putting on the rubber gloves.

"The information we discovered told us that the entity is bound to the object through the use of an element. In our case, the element was obviously water. I know that many of us heard the same request from the man—he simply wanted a place to get dry. This idea was central to the trap set up in Mexico as well. If the man could be dried out, then his power would dissipate. What we found, however, was that it's the *object* that needs to be dried out."

Jessica knelt and flipped the latch on the ammo case. She spun it around and took a deep breath. People seemed frozen in their seats. The ones farther back were stretching their necks to try to watch what she was doing. When she opened the lid, Ullman came to her with a sealed container of water.

"This is rainwater," Jessica said, "although it doesn't need to be. Any type of water should work. We can manifest him now by simply introducing the water to the knife once more."

Jessica raised the lid of the case and prepared to break the seal on the container.

"You have the knife and it's dry?" Wahid asked. "Why would you introduce water to it now?"

"This is a sword without a hilt," Joe said. "It will first cut the person holding it. We've come to understand that if we turn it loose in the presence of the person who called it, the man will only attack that originator. We'll be safe and the originator will fall victim, completing the curse."

"You're sure of this?" Laura asked.

"We are," Jessica said. "Ullman has locked the doors. Everyone except the person who called this into existence will be fine."

"How can you be sure that one of us did the binding or whatever?" Christopher asked.

Jessica looked at him with raised eyebrows.

"I mean, if it's not one of us, won't we be locked in here with him? That's insane."

"We're sure," Jessica said. "We met a person who was trying to acquire the blade and through that conversation we became convinced."

"But you can't be sure," Mel said. "How could you be sure?"

"We're sure," Billie said from the bar. "Go ahead, Jess."

Jessica tilted the container to let the water splash down into the ammo case.

Jumping up from her seat, Hilda yelled, “Wait!”

The call came too late.

Confrontation

The water spilled from the lip of the container, hitting the ammo case and soaking the bare knife within.

When Hilda saw that she was too late, she said, “He’ll kill us all.”

She ran for the hall.

Jessica looked up at the others. Wahid had his hand on his chest and was panting shallow breaths in and out. Riley reached over and put a hand on his arm.

“It’s not the real knife,” Jessica said. “Ullman had a fake one mocked up so we could try to get a confession from Hilda. I guess this is as close as we’re going to get though.”

Billie walked towards the hall, calling, “Hilda, you can come back now. We all know it was you. The house is locked. You’re not getting out.”

“This is messed up,” Christoper said. “I can’t believe you would get us all together and scare us half to death to try to get her to admit to something. There are other, better ways of getting to the truth, you know.”

“And just because she ran out of the room doesn’t mean that she’s guilty of anything,” Mel said. “I almost ran out too. Does that mean that I created the monster.”

“No,” Jessica said. She put the container of water down and returned to her chair. “No. We’re as certain as we can be that Hilda is behind all of this. I don’t think she intended for the man to take innocent lives, but she called him into existence. She has been lying to all of you for years and years. We figured that the best chance we would have of getting to the truth would be to shock her into a situation where she didn’t feel like she had a way out.”

"And you saw what she did," Joe said. "She knew the man would show up and kill us all."

"Doesn't that mean that she's *less* likely of being guilty?" Laura asked. "If she thought that she had a chance of surviving, why would she tip her hand?"

"That's what *I* said," Riley said. "None of this ordeal makes sense to me either, but I figured that we didn't have anything to lose really."

"Assuming you're right," Wahid said to Jessica. "What's our next step?"

Jessica gestured in the direction of the hallway.

"We have an implicit admission. Once she realizes that we're not buying the half-truths anymore, we'll ask Hilda to give us the whole picture of what happened years ago. Armed with that information, I believe we can put everything to rest once and for all."

"What happens if she continues to deny everything?" Laura asked. "It sounds like you don't have any real evidence."

Ullman spoke to the group for the first time. "I believe we have all the evidence that we need. We met with a person who was keen to purchase the knife from us. From Hilda's own description, the person we met is likely the same one she interacted with years ago, when she said that the man was created. If the person we met didn't bind the entity to the knife, that leaves only Hilda."

"So, at the very least we haven't heard the most complete version of her story," Wahid said.

"It does seem to change every time she tells it," Laura said.

"With the exception of Ullman, Hilda knows this place as well as any of us," Joe said. "I suggest we form four groups and start with both wings on the first and second floors. Each group needs someone who has knowledge of all the staircases. I've spent a lot of time on the ground floor of the east wing. I'll lead a group through there and double back through the lower level."

Search

Jessica looked up at the ceiling as the rumble faded away.

"I'm sure it was just construction or demolition," Laura said.

"I hope so," Wahid said.

"Do they have that kind of thing in this neighborhood?" Jessica asked. "I've heard the blasting over near my apartment, but never up here."

"It was either that or thunder, and there's not supposed to be any weather tonight."

Jessica nodded. She reached around and clicked the lock before she shut the door to the bedroom. If Hilda knew what she was doing, it would be simple for her to get through the locked door, but it might at least slow her down.

"I didn't know there were so many rooms up here," Wahid said. "I guess with all the..."

He broke off his statement at a sound from below. It could have been a shout.

"Should we go help?" Laura asked.

"I think we keep going," Jessica said. "They'll call one of us if they need us."

Laura checked her phone and then nodded.

"There are a couple more rooms around the corner up here and then there's a hidden staircase up to the small viewing room."

Wahid shook his head. "I should take advantage of this place. At home, my walls are so thin that my neighbor complains about the crunching if I eat potato chips."

Jessica led the way around the corner.

The door to the next room was almost all the way shut. She pushed it open with her toe and then slipped a hand in to turn on the light. Someone had slept in there recently and the bed was unmade.

"Ullman goes away and the whole house falls apart?" Jessica whispered. "You two cover the door. I'll check it out."

Jessica made a quick sweep of the room. She worked her way

down the left wall, checking inside the wardrobe and under the bed. Both closets were empty. Pausing at the open window, she leaned out and looked at the ground below. Thunder rolled across the hills and made her jerk back. Glancing up, the stars were blotted out by heavy clouds. Their gentle contours were lit by the city's lights.

Jessica closed the window.

"Are you sure there's no rain in the forecast?"

Laura pulled out her phone and used a finger to scroll.

"Well, now they're saying there's a chance of showers."

Jessica nodded and said, "I bet."

They checked the last of the rooms and then Jessica led them to the end of the hall and into the shadows designed to hide the entrance to the staircase. Laura almost lost her balance at the optical illusion. Wahid grabbed her hand and she thanked him.

"Wait here," Jessica said. "I'll be right back."

The room at the top of the stairs was small. She figured she could check it out before the other two climbed. Taking the stairs two at a time, she paused for a moment to take a deep breath before she entered. The lights cast narrow cones at the floor. The room was like a small movie theater, with tiered seats and a big screen behind a curtain. Jessica and Billie had watched one movie there, months before. It took Jessica a moment to find the panel. She used the controls to open the curtain and turn up the lights.

As she walked down the aisle, checking between the seats, thunder rolled overhead. The walls were soundproofed, but the bass still vibrated the air. Jessica reached out and steadied herself. For a moment, she almost felt dizzy.

"Can't be," she whispered.

Jessica ran for the stairs.

"Did you find..." Wahid started to ask.

"We have to get downstairs now," Jessica said. She ran past them and continued down the hall with one hand dragging along the wall in case her vertigo flared again.

"Stay together," Laura said from the end of the hall. "Wait for us."

Jessica reached the stairs and considered sprinting down, leaving them behind. Instead, she waited. Wahid was holding Laura's arm. Jessica moved to the other side and the three of them descended together.

"What's happening?" Wahid asked, breathing hard.

"I don't know."

The long hall on the first floor was empty. Jessica closed her eyes and the world slid sideways.

"That sounded like it came from downstairs," Wahid said.

"What did?" Jessica asked.

"You didn't hear that?"

She shook her head. This time, he led the way. Jessica and Laura brought up the rear. They made their way down the hall and to the staircase, just starting to descend when they heard the next shout. At the bottom of the stairs, Joe and Ullman stood side by side,. blocking off the passage as Hilda beat on Joe's chest with her fists.

"Stop it," Dylan yelled. He and the others were on the other side of Hilda.

Jessica put a hand on Ullman's shoulder.

"Let her go," Jessica said.

"What?"

"Give me the keys."

Ullman looked at her for a few seconds before he reached into his pocket and held them out. Joe wasn't yet convinced. Jessica had to look him in the eyes and ask several times before Joe stepped aside and let Hilda shove past him to climb the stairs. Jessica followed.

At the top of the stairs, Hilda turned for the front door.

"Wait," Jessica called. "I don't have the key for that. You'll have to go out through the kitchen or the back."

She sensed the others behind her on the stairs and hoped that they would stay put.

"Fine," Hilda said, turning around. "I'm parked closer to the kitchen door anyway."

Stomping down the hall, Hilda turned when she saw Jessica pause, propping herself up against the wall.

"Do you mind? I want to get out of this place," Hilda said.

"Sorry. I'm just a little dizzy. I get vertigo when he's coming."

"This is another ploy to get me to believe that I'm in danger. I'm not falling for it this time."

"It's not a ploy. You'll see."

Jessica couldn't have scripted it better. As soon as they started walking again, lighting flashed through the window at the end of the hall and they heard a close clap of thunder follow it. Hilda slowed for a moment before she found her confidence again.

"We've kept the knife dry," Jessica said. "I don't know how, but he's manifesting anyway. Perhaps he's also tied to emotion, not just the object?"

Storming into the kitchen, Hilda shoved one of the chairs out of her way and strode to the door.

Jessica paused again, leaning against the counter as her vision ticked back and forth with her dizziness. When it was at its worst, her vertigo prevented her eyes from locking onto solid objects. Everything swung across her darting eyes for a moment.

She flipped the keys through the ring while Hilda looked through the window, up at the sky.

"It's going to be bad," Jessica said. "Wherever you're going, I suggest you get there fast. When he attacked Dylan, his knife went right through the body of the car. I wouldn't have believed it if I didn't see it."

"He's not coming for me," Hilda said.

"Are you sure? From what we've researched, these things always turn back eventually. That quote that Joe said was pretty common. The man is a blade without a hilt. It cuts everyone involved, and the caller often gets the worst of it."

When Hilda turned to look at Jessica, there was deep fear in her eyes. She snatched the keys from Jessica's hands and stabbed one into the lock. It didn't turn. Frantically, Hilda jerked it out and tried the next one. On her third try, she dropped the whole ring and had to bend to pick them up. When she stood,

Hilda had to wipe tears from her eyes in order to see clearly enough to find the next key.

With a frustrated scream, Hilda threw all the keys at the refrigerator. The metal clanked and the keys slid off into a shadow.

Jessica put her hand on Hilda's shoulder.

"I think we can stop this," Jessica said. "Spells and bindings can be undone. It all starts with understanding how this all came about in the first place."

Hilda leaned against the glass as she buried her face in her hands.

"It was an accident. None of this was supposed to happen."

"I know," Jessica whispered. "It's okay."

When the thunder rumbled again, it rattled the dishes in one of the cabinets.

Jessica led Hilda to one of the chairs.

Confession

Jessica sat across from Hilda, who was looking straight down at the table. When the lightning flashed outside, enough of it filtered through the kitchen windows that Jessica could see the others, standing against the far wall. The silent jury stood and listened as Hilda sobbed and then cleared her throat.

"So many years," Hilda said. "I never thought it would come to this. I..."

"It's okay," Jessica said after Hilda had been silent for a few moments.

"He didn't deserve it," Hilda said.

"Who?"

"Oh... Peter."

The name drove a dagger into Jessica's heart. It was the same name as her baby brother.

"He didn't deserve any of it. He thought that I loved him. I suppose I could have, eventually. I didn't know how much he loved me until he died for me."

"He was the son of the man you were stealing from?" Jessica asked.

The question made Hilda's face harden and Jessica was sorry that she had asked.

"Yes," Hilda said. "I was doing the wrong thing for the right reason. It always seemed like everyone else had everything they needed all the time. It wasn't fair that only my family was struggling to get by. They all professed to be so charitable, but when we were clearly suffering they didn't do anything to help. I only took what they wouldn't notice, and I only did it so we could merely survive."

Jessica nodded and reached over to take Hilda's hand.

"Tell me what happened."

"The accountant saw me. I told you how he discovered me—that was all true. He brought his daughters in early one morning and caught me in the act. I lied about the rest though. It wasn't raining and the spirit didn't come. The accountant caught me and demanded that I return the money I had stolen. I was only to steal from the competitor's and then I had to cut him in. Unless I did exactly as he said, he told me that he would turn me in and I would be killed. I should have known better—he didn't have any leverage over me."

"Why?"

"Because they would have killed him too. Once he let me walk away that first time, he was in just as much danger as I was," Hilda said. "But I believed him and I basically worked for him for months and months. Finally, I couldn't take it anymore. I was dealing with all the risk and I still wasn't making enough money to keep my family's house. My parents had to sell and we moved into an apartment. On top of robbing some very dangerous people, I had to take a job as a waitress just so we could eat."

She sighed and glanced through the window. A fat drop of rain pelted the glass. Hilda wiped her cheek with the back of her hand.

"I told him that I was done, but then he got violent towards me. He knew everything about me and I knew almost nothing. I knew I had to get rid of him, and that I had to do it in a way that was completely untraceable. For that knowledge, I went to Aunt Vim. I had heard the family stories that told of how Aunt Vim disposed of her husband when he threatened her and her children. I thought she would tell me how to poison the accountant. Instead, she told me how to create a Jinx.

"All I needed was one of the accountant's possessions—something that he really valued. Then I had to bind that object to a Jinx and set it loose. Aunt Vim said that once the work was done, the Jinx would return to where it came from. It would be the perfect solution to my problem."

"The possession was the knife?" Jessica prompted.

Hilda nodded. "I broke into the accountant's home when his wife was at the market. Seeing the way that she cared for those girls broke my heart. I told myself that she was a good mother and would be strong enough to continue on without a husband. The accountant had been in the war, and I imagined that his father had given him the knife to keep him safe. I found it in a footlocker under his bed, with pictures of who I assumed were his mother and father."

Hilda glanced to her left and saw the others. For a moment, Jessica thought that she wouldn't say another word. Hilda surprised her when she sat up straighter and continued with a strong voice.

"Aunt Vim's ceremony wasn't difficult or long. We had the knife. I had to choose how to condition the object. I thought that water was the most controllable way to deliver it."

"What does that mean?" Jessica said. "You had to condition the object?"

"The water—it's like you said earlier. You almost had it right. I had to choose how I would train the object. You can't just set it loose in the world. You have to train it how to recognize the target or else everything would be random. Aunt Vim said that I could choose fire, water, air, snow, rock, leaves, whatever. The spirits only understood ancient things, but they understood them completely. I tried to understand Aunt Vim's incantation. The language seemed to be a combination of Latin, German, Chinese, English, and every other language I could recognize. It belonged to everybody and nobody at the same time."

Hilda fell silent. Her eyes moved from side to side, like she was witnessing the past as it played out in her mind.

"What happened?"

Ceremony

"She had everything set up for me when I got to her house. Like I said, it wasn't technically complicated. All of the incantations were written out phonetically for me. It was all ready to go. Vim said she couldn't be with me in the room and I believed her. Once you open the door a crack, there's no way to stop. I wish I had realized that earlier. Later, I could hardly believe what I had done. At the time, though, it all seemed inevitable."

"How so?" Jessica asked when Hilda paused again.

"On the first page of my instructions, Vim had only written out the incantation. I started speaking and immediately knew that I was doing it correctly because I could feel the power of it moving through me. Your whole body vibrates with it. It's like a drug. Flipping the page, I continued with the words while my hands moved to light the candles and crumble herbs over the flames. They grew and changed color, until the candle flames were a dazzling constellation. It was a portal to another place and I felt like I could pick up the entire world and break it in two over my leg. Nothing could have stopped me from continuing. I was on the path."

Hilda reached down and began to unlace her shoe as she spoke.

"On the next page, Vim's instructions were a footnote. Part of me couldn't believe what she was telling me to do. At the same time, I knew it was all inevitable. With the gears in motion, I could either continue to move or be ground to a pulp. It occurred to me then that Vim must have known that I would steal a knife from my victim. She had to have known because in the instructions she told me to use the victim's stolen object to sever my toe."

As she finished the sentence, Vim pulled off her sock. In the dim light, Jessica saw that the woman's foot was tapered in a strange way. The smallest toe was missing.

"I had to give something of myself in order to make my wish into reality. I was helpless to resist the ceremony. I watched in horror as my hands raised the blade and then hacked at my own flesh. I felt all the pain, but I didn't flinch at all. When the toe was detached, I placed it atop the knife and then covered both with a silk kerchief and spoke the final words. When I gathered the kerchief and what was under it, the knife had transformed into something else. I dropped the whole thing in the bucket that contained rainwater. The kerchief was left floating on the surface of the water. The knife and toe were gone."

Hilda exhaled.

"Vim came back into the room at that point. I was exhausted and empty. She said that my role was only half done. I had to go witness the completion of the task and then choose the final incantation. Vim had a wicked smile on her face when she told me this and I had the distinct impression that I had been duped. I thought she was helping me—we had never been too close, but friendly—but at that moment it seemed like the whole thing had been a trick."

Hilda started to pull her sock back on and another flash of lightning burned the image of her white flesh into Jessica's eyes.

"I didn't want to witness anything, but Aunt Vim warned me that my curse would come back to me if I didn't. It came back to me anyway, but I couldn't have known that. I was so distracted by what I had done and witnessed that I moved like a ghost through my own life for the rest of the day. By the time the clouds rolled in, I felt like I was trapped in a nightmare. I never noticed that my boyfriend, Peter, was tailing me. He knew something was wrong and I suppose he decided to keep an eye on me. Maybe he thought that I was stepping out on him, or maybe he guessed that I was in trouble and I needed help. For whatever reason, he was there when I went to witness the murder of the accountant. Unfortunately, he wasn't the only one."

"The girls," Jessica said.

Hilda looked down at her hands as she pulled on her shoe. She kept her eyes down as she said, "Yes, the girls."

After a deep breath, she continued. "He brought them to work. From my hiding place, beneath an awning across the street from the accountant's office, I saw him herd his little daughters inside just as the rain started. It was just like when he had caught me stealing—he brought his daughters to work with him, knowing that the office would be empty. I watched for a moment, trying to decide if I should warn the accountant. I didn't want anything to happen to his children. That's when Peter appeared in front of me, demanding to know what I was doing, and telling me that I had to come with him and get out of the rain. Over his shoulder through the rain, I saw that the man had arrived. I recognized the knife in his hand. The paper with the incantation was folded in my pocket. I told Peter that I had to go and I rushed across the street as my demon banged on the door of the building."

Hilda hugged herself as if she could still feel the cold rain.

"Peter chased me across the street as I saw the horror unfold. The accountant came to open the door. His little daughters were hiding behind him, watching with wide eyes as he tried to shoo away the demon trying to come in from the rain. The knife flashed right as Peter grabbed my shoulder and spun me around. I screamed at him, knowing that whatever was happening with the demon, I had to witness it. That was part of the ritual. I ducked and turned, just in time to see the accountant and his kids falling. They were gushing blood from their wounds."

Hilda's voice caught in her throat. She couldn't speak for a moment as she choked on tears. Riley drew a glass of water and brought it to the table as she sat down quietly with them.

"Peter tried to get between me and the monster that I had summoned. I tore at my pocket, trying to find the final incantation. I had to choose. Aunt Vim had left me with that knowledge. After witnessing the culmination of my efforts, I had to choose whether or not I could live with what I had done. One incantation would banish the demon. The other would command him to take me with him as he returned to hell. Until that moment, I had thought that the answer was obvious. The only reason I was doing any of this was so I could get my life back. Had I simply been suicidal, I could have ended the situation so much more easily. But after witnessing the murder of the accountant and his daughters, essentially at my hand, I understood that the choice was going to be difficult. I wanted everything to end, right there and then."

Hilda coughed and accepted the glass of water from Riley.

"I didn't get a chance to make the decision. Peter threw himself forward, perhaps thinking that he would protect me from the demon. I screamed his name and tried to grab at him, to pull him back. That's when I lost the paper. It fell from my hand as Peter stepped into the path of the knife that was never meant for me. The monster wouldn't have killed me unless I commanded it, but Peter didn't know that. He gave his life and I never really even loved him. I like to think that I would have, given time. We didn't have the time though. I dropped to my knees and found the paper. It was soaked and the ink was running. I tried to recite the incantation, but the syllables were jumbling before my eyes. Whatever came out of my mouth wasn't right. When I finished, I looked up and the demon was still standing before me. He was made of rot and decay, turning to stone before me. The knife in his hand looked to be a permanent part of him. Water dripped from the brim of his hat and cascaded down into my face.

"Someone screamed and I turned to warn them away. I didn't want any more innocent blood spilled. When I turned back, my demon was gone. The rain abated and I was left in a bloody puddle, surrounded by corpses."

Incantation

Wahid joined them at the table. He offered Hilda a box of tissues that he had found on a side table. She dabbed her eyes and blew her nose after thanking him. Christopher stood at the window, looking out into the rain that was intensifying.

"My Aunt Vim was gone by the time I returned to her home. I mean deceased. It was natural causes—a heart attack I guess. Her neighbor found her in the lawn, lifeless face looking up at the sky as the clouds dispersed. At the funeral her face looked perfectly serene. My whole life, her features had been twisted into an angry sneer. I never knew how beautiful she was until I saw her with the weight of all her choices lifted from her."

"So you couldn't reproduce the incantation?" Wahid asked.

"No," Hilda said. "I went through her things and tried to track down whomever might have taught her. It was impossible. Some knowledge is just erased from the world when a person dies. Information doesn't last forever."

Jessica heard the sound of the rain pelting the ground outside.

"It's getting bad out there," Christopher said.

As he spoke a burst of wind sent the rain into the windows making Riley shrink back.

"You saw the syllables though," Wahid said. "Perhaps they're still in your memory somehow?"

Hilda barked out a dry laugh. "You think I haven't tried everything over the years? I've been to a dozen hypnotists who claimed that they could unearth any memory a brain contains. It was all gibberish. I might not remember what was on the paper, but I'm certain that I would have recognized it if anyone had been able to pull it from my memory."

Jessica looked to Ullman. "The researchers? Have they come up with anything?"

Ullman shook his head.

"How does the dealer figure into this?" Riley asked. "You talked about the bosses hiring an assassin and claimed that there was a child who called the demon."

"I twisted the truth," Hilda said. "The dealer was someone that I met when I was trying to find a way to reverse the incantation. He wanted me to reproduce the process and bind more demons to objects for his own purposes. In the end, he invaded my body to find out the secrets. All he learned was that I didn't have any answers. Aunt Vim was the real practitioner and she took her secrets to the grave."

Jessica shook her head. "If she knew, then it must be recorded somewhere. She learned it, and there could be another source."

"Information doesn't last forever," Hilda said. "I believe that the curse weighed on Aunt Vim and she passed it to me so that she could be free of it. It wasn't a power, it was a virus. Once she infected me with it, she was free to go."

"That still doesn't mean..."

Jessica was cut off by a crack of thunder that shook the floor.

"We should retreat from the windows," Ullman said.

"How can he manifest without the knife?" Joe asked. "This doesn't make sense."

"Maybe it does," Riley said. They all looked to her.

Riley reached out and put a hand on top of Hilda's. Putting down her tissue, Hilda took Riley's hand in hers.

"Hilda," Riley said softly. "I think you're right—your aunt passed the curse onto you. The knife is part of it, but the other part..."

Hilda broke eye contact and looked down as she took a deep breath.

"I know," Hilda said.

"What?" Wahid asked. "What is the revelation that you both just had?"

Hilda looked up at him. "There are three things that were inextricably linked by that ceremony. It's the knife, the demon, and me."

"What are you saying?" Wahid asked.

Hilda didn't respond, but the answer seemed to dawn on Wahid anyway.

CHAPTER TWENTY-THREE

Jessica

Decision

"We can't let her do it," Riley said.

"It's not up to us," Joe said. "This is completely her decision."

"It's not," Riley said, raising her voice. "We have the knife. All we have to do is not give it to her."

"Riley," Laura said. "First of all, we can't predict exactly what's going to happen."

"That's nonsense, we all know exactly what's..."

"Riley," Laura said. She took Riley's hands in her own.

Jessica glanced over at Hilda, who was sitting alone at the table, looking through the window at the pounding rain.

"Imagine being haunted by this for decades," Vivian said.

"I don't have to imagine," Riley said. "I *have* been haunted for decades. That doesn't mean I condone suicide."

"Wait a second," Christopher said. "That's taking things a little too far, don't you think. When I went to Mexico, we didn't call it suicide. When you went off to that house, you knew the risk but nobody called it suicide."

"We're talking about letting her go out into the rain with the knife and taking him on alone," Riley said. "We all know that's suicide."

"I took him on," Jessica said.

"Not in the rain," Riley said. She swiped her arm across her face, brushing away angry tears.

"It's her choice," Billie said.

"She thinks we're forcing her into it," Riley said.

Joe was about to rebut that point, but Jessica put up her hand.

"Riley, how about you go talk to her alone. Tell her what you just told us—you're afraid she's doing this out of a sense of duty and you want her to understand that she doesn't have to do it. Okay? Give her that information and let her reevaluate."

Riley took a deep breath and then let it out with a shudder. "Okay."

Jessica turned to the side to let her by and they watched Riley cross the room.

"She's going to talk her out of it," Joe said.

Jessica shrugged. "If she can talk Hilda out of it, then Hilda wasn't serious in the first place."

Over at the table, the two women were talking so quietly that Jessica couldn't hear a thing. Leaning forward, it seemed like Riley was pleading with Hilda to change her mind. In response, Hilda only shook her head.

"We should be ready either way," Ullman said.

"What are you thinking?" Billie asked.

"The approach up in Oregon seemed to work well," Ullman said.

"What did you do up in Oregon?" Christopher asked.

The information had already been handed out in the packets, but nobody had a chance to read them yet. Everything had happened so quickly with Hilda that the group had only received a quick explanation of the small team's accomplishment.

Jessica listened to Ullman begin to explain and then she moved away from the group, walking down the length of the counter to approach one of the windows. The glass was cold and resonated with the raindrops pelting it. The sky was glowing with purple and gray. The unexpected rain clouds were imperfectly reflecting the lights of the city.

She thought about her life before Joe had showed up at that meeting. That wasn't really living. Day after day, she had been waiting to get to work. This was the work that she was intended to do. It was unfinished business ever since that night her family had been ripped from her. Jessica knew what Hilda's answer would be. Nothing Riley could say was going to sway her.

"Everyone," Hilda said, standing. "I need you know that I'm making this decision for me—not because of some sense of duty to anyone. I understand the risks. I've always understood them, even before blood was drawn because of my actions. From that first moment, I knew that I was taking my life into my hands. Now, I need to finish what I started. Please, bring me the knife."

Everyone looked to Ullman. Only a few of them really knew that Ullman had hidden the knife, but everyone else assumed it. He was a part of the house. It didn't hold any secrets from him.

With a tiny nod, he stepped away from the group. Joe and Billie were quick to join him. The three of them left together.

While Jessica stood at the window, she sensed someone approach to stand next to her.

"I was right about you," Laura said.

"Pardon?"

"When Joe went to go meet you, I told him that you were going to be the catalyst."

"Why?" Jessica asked.

"There was just something about you. The rest of us floundered wildly after we were attacked. There were so many suicide attempts, drug addictions, and prison sentences. Every day, people suffer through violent crimes and random attacks, but the people who meet him are almost always devastated with, I don't know, like PTSD or something. But you just picked up, brushed yourself off, and continued with your life. I was able to track you through college records, job applications, taxes, and whatever. You just kept moving."

"You don't know the whole story," Jessica said.

"I think I do. I mean, I bet I know more of the story than anyone else. Anyway, when I found all that out, I just knew that you were going to be the catalyst. In the course of a few months you've been able to accomplish more than Simon and all his money, and he was working at this for years."

"I haven't done anything," Jessica said.

Laura smiled.

"Some day I'd like to know your story," Jessica said.

Laura's smile faded.

Ullman came back through the doorway from the hall, followed by Billie and Joe. He held the real ammo case out in front of himself. People moved to the side, clearing a path for him. Jessica wasn't surprised when the lights flickered and then went out. In the corner, an emergency light came on, powered by a battery.

Billie lifted a familiar bag to the counter—it was the one that Ullman had packed all of their emergency gear into.

From it, Billie began extracting flashlights and headlamps. She handed them around and the room lit up with various beams. Jessica barely noticed any of that. Her attention was on the ammo case that Ullman set on the table in front of Hilda. Flipping the latches, he had to tug at the lid to break the seal. Hilda's shoulders rose when she took a deep breath.

Billie came over with a raincoat and some lights.

The blade reflected the beam of light up towards the ceiling when Ullman pointed a flashlight into the box.

Hilda put on the raincoat slowly, not taking her eyes off the blade.

With a nervous laugh, Hilda whispered, "I don't know if I can make my legs work. I'll probably pass out before I get outside."

Riley put a hand on her shoulder.

People kept a respectful distance and watched as Hilda took a headlamp and stretched the band over her head.

Before she reached into the box, Hilda paused with both hands on the table, holding herself up as she looked at it.

"I hoped I would never see it again," she whispered, shaking her head.

Riley patted Hilda on the back without saying a word.

After taking a deep breath, Hilda reached in and removed the sealed bag from the box. She turned the knife over in the beam of her headlamp. Eventually, Hilda nodded and straightened up. With both hands, she pressed the bagged knife to her chest and then walked to the door.

"Someone get this?" she asked.

Ullman reached past her, unlocked the door, and swung it inwards. The sound of the falling rain nearly drowned out Hilda as she said, "Don't open this door again until it's over, okay?"

Ullman nodded.

Hilda stepped out into the rain and Ullman shut the door and locked it behind her.

For a moment, Jessica thought that Hilda was just going to stand there, frozen in place.

Then, with a big stride, Hilda stepped out onto the patio.

Rain

They were all practically pressed against the windows, watching. Jessica had to turn off her lamp so it wouldn't reflect off the glass. The others did the same. The power was out, but Ullman flipped the switch for the outside light a few times just to be sure.

Hilda stepped several paces away from the house before she hunched over and opened the bag. Dropping the plastic bag to her side, she held out the knife, letting the rain bathe it as she brushed water from her eyes with her other hand.

Next to Jessica, Billie had both hands pressed flat against the glass. Jessica could hear Billie breathing as she watched.

"She's saying something," Billie said.

Jessica could see Hilda's lips moving, but the rain drowned out any sound that she was making. As she spoke, she raised the blade with both hands, like she was offering it to the sky. In response, lightning flashed. Jessica heard someone gasp, but it wasn't until the next flash of lightning that Jessica saw him. Beyond Hilda, at the edge of darkness, Jessica saw the silhouette of the man.

He took a step towards Hilda and Jessica imagined what he must be saying.

"He just wants to get dry," Billie whispered.

"Maybe she'll remember the incantation," Riley said.

The man lifted a hand and for a moment Jessica thought he was reaching for a blade. Instead, he rolled what must have been soaked tobacco in a piece of paper and lit a weak flame before putting it to his lips. Jessica wondered if Hilda had heard the ring of the lighter over the sound of the rain.

"He's toying with her," Billie whispered.

"She'll be okay," Jessica said.

The cigarette should have been too wet to light, but the orange end flared when the man inhaled. Mingled with the splashing rain, they saw the mist cascade down from his mouth when he exhaled. Jessica had seen the same thing so many times, but it still struck her as remarkable. The impossible was playing out right before their eyes. It never got any less shocking.

Hilda took a tiny step towards him, still holding out the knife like she was offering it to him.

"What's she doing?" Billie whispered. "She could kill him with it."

"Would it work?" Jessica asked. "We tried that. Maybe it stopped him briefly, but it didn't kill him."

Billie frowned and didn't answer.

Jessica could hear her own heartbeat pounding in her ears as she watched. Out in the rain, neither figure moved but the tension still built with every second that passed. Jessica thought that she wasn't going to be able to breathe if the standoff continued.

The man took one last long drag from his cigarette and flicked it to the side. Jessica saw the orange glow extinguish when it hit the patio.

The man stepped forward and reached for the knife with one hand. Putting his other hand on Hilda's shoulder, he pulled her into an embrace. Hilda wrapped her arms around him. Turning her face to the side, she rested her head on his shoulder.

Her headlamp lit up the underside of his chin and then it flickered out.

When the lightning flashed again, the figures were caught in the strobe, a statue of two lovers embracing.

Jessica blinked away the image burned into her eyes.

The wind gusted and the rain became a deafening roar before it faded away. With one more rumble of thunder, the sound of the rain falling was gone. All that was left was the insistent drip of water falling from the edge of the roof and landing in the puddles on the patio.

"She went with him," Riley whispered.

Jessica realized that Riley was right. The patio was empty. The man and Hilda had disappeared.

Ullman turned the key in the lock.

"Wait," Wahid said. "Just wait for a moment."

The keys jingled on the ring when Ullman removed his hand.

Nobody spoke as they looked out into the night. After a few minutes, Jessica realized that she could see the moon and a few bright stars above. Soon after, the patio lights flickered on and she lost sight of everything except the moon.

Ullman unlocked the door and opened it. The air that rushed in felt dry as a bone. It was quickly sucking up all the rain from the patio. Jessica waited by the window as the others stepped out into the night air. She kept waiting for the lights to snap back off and the man to reappear in a sudden burst of rain.

Billie and Dylan moved off to the side and lit cigarettes. Joe and Riley were holding court with a few of the others. Jessica assumed they were giving a first-hand account of what had happened up at the house.

Ullman came back through the door.

"There's no sign of her," he said.

Jessica nodded.

"Does she have friends or family that should be notified? Will anyone miss her?" Jessica asked.

"According to Laura, no. We were the only people she spoke to regularly."

With a sigh, Jessica pushed away from the window and went to join Ullman as he walked outside to join the others. Once she was outside, she wanted to see for herself. Ullman walked with her as she roamed the patio, trying to find any sign that Hilda or the man had met out there. The water was evaporating so fast that she could almost see the puddles shrinking before her eyes.

Billie stubbed out her cigarette and approached Jessica while she looked out at the hills in the distance.

"What did you mean about her being okay?" Billie asked.

"Huh?"

"I said that he was toying with her and you said that she would be okay. You sounded so confident."

"Oh," Jessica said. It took her a few seconds to remember the conversation. "I didn't feel dizzy."

"Dizzy?"

"Whenever death is close, I feel dizzy. I didn't feel dizzy so I knew that Hilda was going to be okay."

"So you don't think she's dead?" Billie asked.

Jessica shrugged. "I don't know. Maybe I'm just wrong about when I get vertigo. Maybe it doesn't have anything to do with death."

Billie thought about that and then went back to Dylan.

Jessica looked up at the sky. Beyond the glow of the lights, it seemed that the clouds were completely gone.

CHAPTER TWENTY-FOUR

Mel

Meeting

Mel sighed.

"With enough perspective, I suppose it's possible to reframe the events, you know? I always feel guilty when I think this way, but I'm going to say it out loud for the first time. Maybe Mom wouldn't have hated what happened."

He took a breath and shut his eyes as emotion moved through him.

"She knew she was dying. It wasn't a surprise or anything like that. All of her doctors were very clear about her prognosis. She was losing herself from the present backwards, does that make sense? What happened five minutes ago was a complete mystery to her, but she had a pretty good grip on five years ago and a wonderful recollection of fifty years before that. She was at the end of her rope and it was fraying from the bottom up."

Mel leaned back in his seat.

"I was driving her crazy. When she was lucid, she was desperately trying to make peace with the idea of mortality, but I kept fighting and fighting, looking for other answers. I remember one time, driving to an appointment, she kept talking about how perfect it would be if she had an accident, like slipped in the shower or something, and just..."

Mel snapped his fingers.

"From that perspective, I suppose... I mean, she died fast and in her sleep. I don't imagine she understood what was going on those last couple of seconds. One of the cops I talked to said that she wouldn't have even felt it. He was no doctor though, so who knows. Even a few seconds of intense pain had to be better than the agony she dealt with every day."

Riley nodded and mumbled something to Mel.

"Yeah," Mel said. "When I try to rationalize things, it makes me guilty. Feels like an excuse to let myself off the hook. But it wasn't my fault, you know? I mean, we all have the same story, right? Random stuff happens. Can't blame ourselves."

"Of course not," Jessica said.

Mel smiled and took a deep breath. "That's my story. Not as harrowing as others. I feel like I've made peace with everything, pretty much. These last few weeks I've been remembering the best times with Mom. She was truly one of the funniest people I've known."

Riley patted his back. A couple of people leaned forward to offer their condolences, even though his story was about something that happened more than a decade before. It seemed appropriate. Mel spoke as if he had come out of the darkness.

"Any questions for Mel?" Joe asked.

Jessica waited until he followed that with, "Any other business tonight?"

She raised her hand.

"As some of you know, this is my last meeting. I was planning on just slipping away, but I thought better of it. I want you all to know how much my time here has meant to me. I'm going back to Oregon. The board has offered me really good rent on the house there, and I'll be working at the Croc 'N Shop until something better comes along."

"It feels like we're just getting to know you," Vivian said. "I hope you'll be back."

"I will," Jessica said. "When the cold and damp gets to me up there, I'll be back. And there are plenty of guest rooms in the house up there. I hope you'll all consider visiting me there as well."

She looked around and saw plenty of smiles in return.

The meeting wound down with talk of when they would be getting back together. Jessica wondered how long the group would continue. She could imagine them each taking one more turn at telling their story, but then what? Would they still need to rehash the past, or would they finally feel empowered to move along?

A couple of people came by to shake her hand or offer a hug.

Joe waited for the others to disperse before he approached. She opened her arms and pulled him into an embrace.

"I can't thank you enough," she said. "You were my first contact. You found me out there in the wilderness and brought me in."

"I'm so glad you came," he said as they broke apart. "I never thought you would, but I'm so glad you did. Thanks for everything."

She nodded.

They talked about plans for a bit. Joe was thinking about spending more time with his nephew's family, although he was reluctant to pick up and move. Jessica wondered how much of that had to do with Vivian. It seemed that the two of them were closer than they liked to admit.

When the conversation was over, Jessica headed for the stairs to pack up her stuff. One of the second floor bedrooms in Simon's house had almost started to feel like home. She had officially moved out of her apartment, so it pretty much was.

After a quiet knock, Billie said, "Hey."

Jessica didn't hesitate. She dropped the shirt she was folding and crossed the room to hug Billie.

"You smell like cigarettes," Jessica said with a smile.

"I know. Dylan and I are going to quit. He's getting us that pill. Next week."

"Good luck with that."

Jessica took a breath and regarded Billie with fresh eyes.

"You look better," Jessica said.

"Better than what?"

"Good. I should have said, you look good."

"Thank you."

"Are you sure you don't want to come up to Oregon with me? Just for a bit."

Billie shook her head. "I'm not ready yet. If our last trip taught me anything, it's that I wasn't ready to leave this place yet. Besides, I'm starting work on Monday. It would be a hell of a commute."

"Work?"

Billie nodded. "Bussing tables at first, then we'll see."

Jessica smiled. "Good for you."

"I'll come up and visit though. Let me get established and then when I can take time off I'll come up for a long weekend or something."

"That's a deal," Jessica said, putting out her hand.

"Are you nervous at all?" Billie asked. "New town? All alone."

Jessica laughed and went back to the bed to finish folding her clothes.

"That's my typical state. I'm always moving to a new place. But this time, I have a distinct advantage. I already know the place and I already have a job."

"If you hate it, come back, okay? You always have a place here," Billie said.

Jessica looked at her a momen't and then nodded.

"I will."

Ike Hamill
December 2021
Topsham, Maine

About *The Rainman*

With some books, the first scene arrives fully-formed. My only job is to not mess things up writing it down. I thought we would learn Jessica's story in that first meeting, but it turned out that the details wouldn't come until later. For me, it always helps to know what happened in the past, but it's almost never useful to guess what will happen in the future. I'm always wrong.

People ask, "Are you Joe in this story? Are you Jessica?" I try to see the world through all of them, of course. I try to make every character the lead character in their own story while capturing the parts of their narrative that intersects this one. But, in truth, I'm Vivian in this book. She's the outsider's outsider. She's the one who feels ashamed of her troubles because they don't measure up. There are no supernatural monsters in my own life —just the regular ones. Death finds us when we have the promise of youth or it can bring cold mercy. This book is a meditation on the inevitable, I guess. It's only senseless to the ones left behind.

Jessica fights the idea of dwelling on the past throughout this book. She is disturbed by the notion that she might still be haunted for another decade or more. In the end, I think she found more resolution in acceptance than anything else.

I hope you enjoyed this book, and will tell a friend about it!

Thanks for reading,
Ike

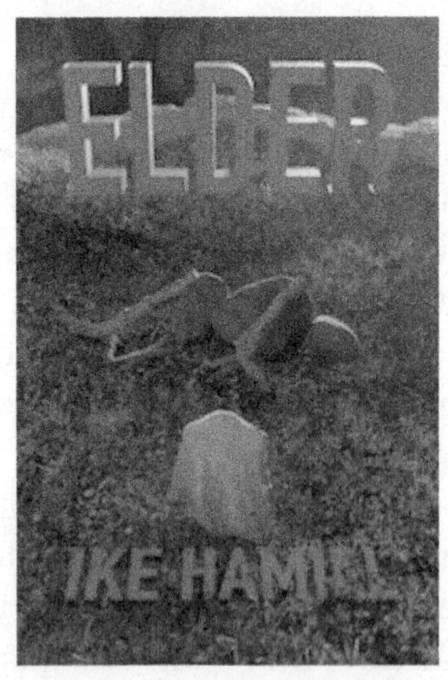

Elder

They said he wouldn't walk again. They couldn't have been more wrong. Then again, the doctors didn't know who they were dealing with. My old man has been up against far worse in his time.

I only wish they had been right.

The Hunting Tree

For thousands of years a supernatural killer has slept in the White Mountains of New Hampshire. An amateur ghost hunter has just woken him up. Now that he stalks the night once more, he's traveling east. Although the monster's actions are pure evil, he may be the only thing that can save humanity from extinction.

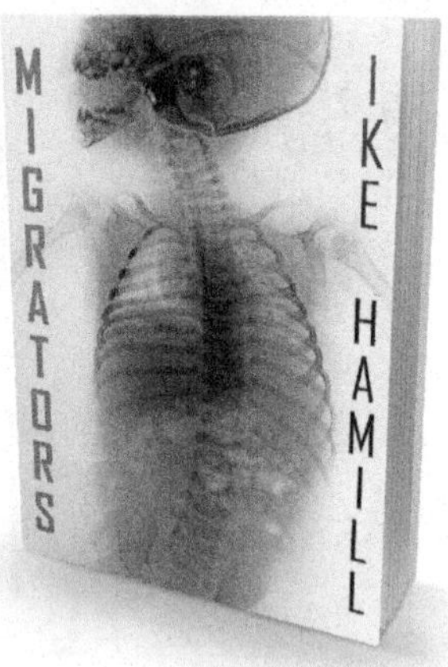

Migrators

Do not speak of them. Your words leave a scent. They will come. Somewhere in the middle of Maine, one of the world's darkest secrets has been called to the surface. Alan and Liz just wanted a better life for themselves and their son. They decided to move to the country to rescue the home of Liz's grandfather, so it would stay in the family. Now, they find themselves directly in the path of a dangerous ritual. No one can help them. Nothing can stop the danger they face. To save themselves and their home, they have to learn the secrets of the MIGRATORS.

Transcription

Thomas has found the biggest story of his career, and he can't believe his luck. He's sitting in the prison cell that at one time housed each of The Big Four, the state's most notorious murderers. There's only one problem: he's beginning to understand what drove them to commit their crimes. He's beginning to feel their madness.

Years later, his son suffers a curse. Every night, he's compelled to transcribe his father's stories. If he misses a single night, he'll do something terrible. It has happened before. James has given up everything to his curse, and it controls every moment of his life. James can only imagine what will happen if one of the stories gets out. In the worst case, people will die.

And the worst case is coming.

Made in United States
North Haven, CT
05 March 2023